Seven Steps to Treason

SEVEN STEPS TO TREASON

MICHAEL HARTLAND

MACMILLAN PUBLISHING COMPANY
New York

Macmillan Publishing Company
866 THIRD AVENUE, NEW YORK, N.Y. 10022

Library of Congress Cataloging in Publication Data

Hartland, Michael.
    Seven steps to treason.

    I. Title. II. Title: 7 steps to treason.
PR6058.A69496S4 1984   823'.914   84-9705

ISBN 0-02-548530-X

10   9   8   7   6   5   4   3   2   1

Printed in the United States of America

For my daughters,
Ruth and Susanna,
neither of whom bears the slightest resemblance
to anyone in this book

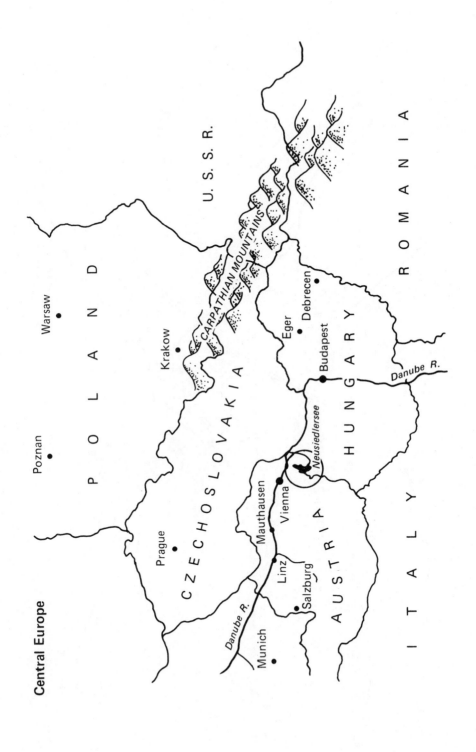

Central Europe

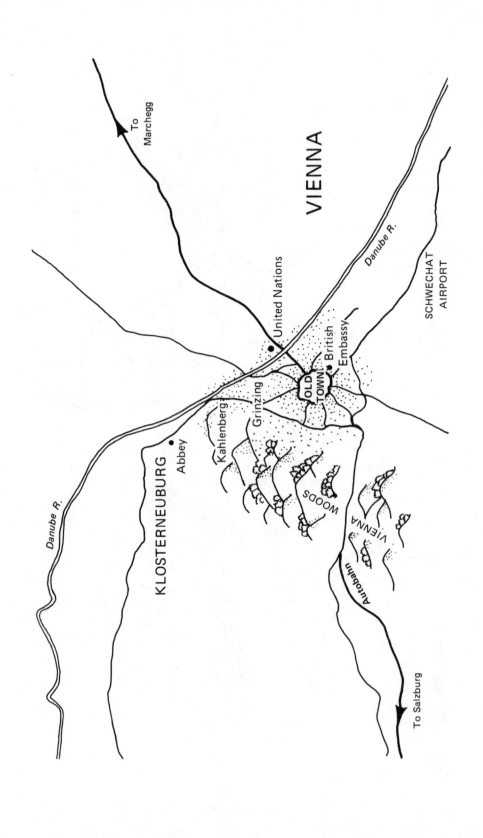

1 Burgenland

SHE LEFT HER BICYCLE in the shade of a pine tree and walked down to the lake, aware that the young man had also stopped. He had been cycling a few hundred yards behind her for a couple of hours now—in fact, he had been in the distance ever since yesterday evening, when they had both stayed at the same *pension* in Podersdorf. He had not spoken to her—and she had not seen him in the morning, when she drank her breakfast coffee on the terrace, alone. But later, cycling along the track through the sand dunes and reeds of the lakeshore, she had realized that he was following—and now he was strolling through the trees toward her, with elaborate casualness. She was not perturbed by this, let alone frightened: this was Austria, peaceful and bathed in September sun. She needed an adventure and, as she pretended to watch the yachts tacking across the blue waters, her nerve ends began to tingle with lazy anticipation.

Now he was there, quite close—a handsome face with dark curly hair, wide smile, a gold medal visible on the nut-brown chest under his open red shirt. She continued to study the lake. The Neusiedlersee stretched away in both directions, its reedy shore desolate but punctuated by the bright colors of tents on campsites. Most of the lake lay in Austria, but away to the south—to her left—it ran across the frontier into Hungary. Beyond that invisible line there were no yachts and no bright colors; black watchtowers stood every half kilometer along the shore.

"It is a beautiful lake." The stranger spoke at last; he had a slightly guttural accent.

She smiled at him, distantly. *"Bitte?"* She would see how long he would take her for an Austrian, with her suntanned skin and flowing fair hair.

It did not work. "I am not intruding?" he asked. "What is your name, please?" He looked at her appraisingly—she was beautiful, a slim girl aged about nineteen or twenty. The gray eyes, set in an oval face, had a certain gravity, full of character, which belied the coltish look of the long brown legs that seemed to go on forever below her frayed denim shorts.

She hesitated. "My name is Sarah—but how did you know I was English?"

"You are too slim for an Austrian—I thought you might be English or Swedish." He laughed in an engaging way, despite the heavy-handed compliment. "You are on holiday?"

"Yes."

"I am called Rudolf—Rudi."

"And are *you* on holiday, Rudi?" This conversation was getting banal.

"No. I work in a bank in Vienna. I have just come down to Neusiedlersee for the day to go bird-watching." He gestured towards the long stretch of empty shore farther south, a wilderness of sand dunes, reeds and pine trees. It was shown on her map as a nature reserve.

She grinned at him—and, with the freckles by her nose, that suddenly made her look more inviting, less Nordic and distant. They strolled a little way along the shore, very correctly, without touching. Sarah Cable, she smiled to herself, you're an ambassador's daughter and you're letting yourself be picked up by an Austrian bank clerk with a lousy line in patter—and you're enjoying it, you slut.

"Do you live in Vienna?"

"Yes," she said. "We've been there about two years. Before that we were in London—and before that Stockholm. I'm very flattered you thought I might be a Swede! I'm going back to London next month—I want to go to university."

He looked a little sad. "I should have liked to go to university. Do you live with your parents?"

"With my father—he's divorced." And he relies on me too much emotionally, she thought, since Lucy died and Mummy pushed off. I should have got a job or started a degree a year ago, not hung about being his bloody housekeeper and going to all those ghastly diplomatic parties. But it was my own fault. He didn't *make* me stay—and look how jealous I felt when he took up with that Jewish slut half his age, only a few years older than *me*.

"I have my own apartment." He said it proudly, as well he might on Austrian wages.

"That must be nice." Her mind was still elsewhere, on her father. And now she was punishing him by taking off on her own for a week. "Touring Burgenland, Daddy," she had said, with deliberate vagueness—he didn't even know where she was. "I want some time to myself, to think things out." But she had done that after only one night. In her heart she was glad that he'd found someone else, even though it might fizzle out in the end. He'd been desperately unhappy with her mother. The divorce had been a relief all around, an end to years of grinding bitterness. She still disliked his new find—Naomi was her horrible name—but the truth was that, now her father was no longer alone, it would be much easier for Sarah to go away and start her own life. And that could only be for the best.

The young man called Rudi was saying something. She smiled at him. "Sorry—I was miles away. What did you say?"

"I said, would you like to come with me to see some of the marsh birds? They are very interesting. You can share my field glasses— and my lunch. I have bread and salami—and some beer." He sounded very Middle European, very correct.

She hesitated. She was not in the habit of going off with complete strangers—and it was such an obvious pickup. But something about him mesmerized her; curiosity and a desire to feel abandoned overcame the sudden surge of caution. She heard herself say, "That would be great—really nice."

The sun was hot on their backs, as she matched his long stride— for they were both tall—and she felt ridiculously happy. Just a night away and she had things back in perspective. Dad deserved a bit of fun at his age, poor old sod. She'd been unreasonable when she flew at him; but she'd still leave him alone in that echoing house in Grinzing for the full week. He deserved that for not telling her about Naomi properly. And serendipity had found her a friend for the afternoon, which looked as if it was going to be fun.

* * *

They cycled farther south and had lunch in the hollow of some sand dunes by the water. Rudi had provided a banquet: french bread, Hungarian salami—her favorite, even if the people who made it had to be kept in by barbed wire—soft Austrian goat cheese, smoked eel from the lake, and bright yellow *Pfefferoni*. It was a little odd to feel that he must have packed it knowing he was going to pick her up—or was it romantic?

They chatted lazily in the sun. He insisted on practicing his labored English—which was convenient because she still found German difficult—and he became much more interesting as his speech became more confident.

They did not watch birds. After lunch and several bottles of Schwechater beer, they swam in the lake: she in the bikini she wore beneath her blue shirt and shorts, he in black swimming trunks. Afterward it seemed natural to hang their bathing suits on a thorn bush to dry, while they lay side by side on a large towel, naked in the sun.

She wriggled in pleasure as he stroked her gently, all the way down from her shoulders, over her narrow buttocks to the tops of her thighs. Turning over, she looked at him through half-closed eyes. He was kneeling and smiling down at her. Her eyes traveled from the dark hair on his chest, irresistibly downward. His penis was not like the others she had seen—and there had not been so many—but brown and straight, like the end of a heavy, tarred rope. Her convent education reasserted itself and she felt herself blushing, then purring in pleasure as he fondled her breasts. She knew that she had quite good breasts.

Lying naked with this virile stranger, drowsy in the heat, she wondered what would happen next. Part of her wanted to make love with him, part of her thought that might spoil the magic. Part of her felt guilty—and a little scared. Without reaching a conclusion, she drifted into his arms, feeling his tongue between her teeth and his hand between her thighs. She rolled on top of him, responding to the kiss, her whole body suddenly coming alive. She closed her eyes, but did not feel him entering and thrusting inside her as she expected.

Instead there was a sudden sharp pain high on her left thigh. Her eyes started open in surprise. "Ouch! I've been bitten by a mosquito." She smiled down at him coyly. "On my bottom." She reached around to rub it, but found she could barely move her arm; and then she felt the terrible numbing pain spreading from her leg.

He pushed her off him roughly and jumped up, his eyes hard and all affection gone. Squirming in the sand, she saw the metal instrument glinting in his hand; and in a surge of horror she knew what had happened. Pushing away her terror, she tried to stand up, to run away—but her legs were leaden and she fell back to the sand, panting from the effort. Oh Christ, but the agony was everywhere and she could no longer move any of her limbs. She opened her mouth to scream, but the stiffness had reached her jawbones and no sound came.

The pain seemed to recede and, in a moment of horrifying lucidity, she remembered that no one knew where she was—and no one, but no one, had seen her with this man. Then the sun suddenly burned with a blinding intensity, her sight blurred, and she lost consciousness.

* * *

The man who had called himself Rudi pulled on his clothes. He put the tiny steel needle gingerly into a metal sheath, careful not to touch its tip, and took the big hypodermic from the saddlebag of his bicycle. Kneeling by the girl's body, he took her arm and carefully injected the liquid into a vein. Now she would sleep for twenty-four hours. Her skin felt cold and clammy, so he was relieved when the other man appeared from the trees with a blanket. It was important that she should not die. They wrapped her body in the blanket and laid her in a patch of shade, working together swiftly, saying little, as if they had done it before. The man who had picked up Sarah waded out into the lake, between banks of reeds, and sank her bicycle beneath the water. Then he waded back and disposed of his own in the same way. A rubber dinghy was carried from the small van, parked on the track a hundred yards away, and the van drove off.

Systematically, everything that showed they had been there was sunk in the lake. Then the two men loaded the unconscious girl into the dinghy, her clothes in a bundle by her feet, and raked over the sand with a piece of driftwood to remove the last traces of what had happened.

They paddled out silently to a mudbank, where they vanished into the high reeds. After beaching the dinghy, they spread themselves out on the dry mud to wait for nightfall. No passing yachtsman could have seen them, but in any case none came near that afternoon. Later there was no moon. No one saw the black rubber shape as it moved slowly down the lake at midnight, paddles pushed deep to avoid splashing, and passed into Hungarian waters.

By morning they would be in Budapest.

2 Vienna

IT WAS TEN-THIRTY AT NIGHT when the inflatable boat reached the Hungarian shore. At about the same time, His Excellency Mr. William Cable sat in the darkness of a box at the Vienna State Opera, balancing his large frame on a small, velvet-backed chair as he peered between the heads of the two Chinese in the front row. Normally Cable enjoyed opera, but this production of *Madama Butterfly* had been lifeless, almost dreary and he stifled a yawn as the curtain fell on the last act.

Slowly the lights went up to reveal the five white and gold tiers of boxes and balconies rising to the glittering crystal of the dome. Below Cable the orchestra seats were full of *bürgerlich* Viennese in evening dress; above, the gallery started to stamp and boo as the conductor appeared onstage with the principal singers. The little party in the box stood up, the two Chinese guests still looking puzzled and out of place in their drab gray uniforms. The French ambassador and his wife led the way out to the grand staircase, marble balustrade and green carpet sweeping down to the foyer.

Cable shook hands with the guests and said good night, through their interpreter. The two Chinese smiled and bowed. God knows why Delacroix had invited him to this evening with Peking's Third Deputy Minister of Heavy Engineering, but no doubt some devilish purpose would emerge later.

Cable excused himself from the inevitable nightcap at the French residence and fled toward a side stairway. As he went, he noticed one of the heavies from the Soviet Embassy staring at him curiously; but the man turned away abruptly before he met Cable's glance, finding a sudden interest in a black marble bust of *Gustav Mahler—Director of the Opera 1897–1901*.

Outside, Fritz was waiting with the car. He opened the door and Cable stretched back in the rear seat. They nosed through the crowds and accelerated down the Ring toward the Schottentor. It had been raining; as they weaved past the clanking red trams, streetlights reflected on the wet pavements beneath the trees at the side of the boulevard. The car was a Ford Minster, appropriate to the rank of a Grade Four ambassador—the real ambassador, accredited to Austria, had a Rolls-Royce. Cable was only the British representative to the United Nations organizations based in Vienna. But he smiled to himself as they sped under the yellow sodium lights toward Grinzing—it was, after all, a lot better than picking up garbage cans. Not a bad berth after a stormy life.

The car stopped outside the large house in Himmelstrasse. He climbed the steps to the front door and Fritz drove off to take the car back to the embassy garage. In the hall, Cable's *Putzfrau* had left some mail and a list of people who had phoned. There were several square white envelopes addressed to "H.E. Mr. William Cable"—invitations. He put them aside in favor of a cheerful postcard from Sarah. It ended "love to Pig Face from Oddjob." He smiled at her use of their childhood nicknames for each other and hoped she was feeling less angry—she had gone off in such a huff. The card was postmarked Eisenstadt, so she must already be in Burgenland. Cable had been divorced for nine years and was used to being alone, but he would miss Sarah while she was away. His face softened as he wondered where she was tonight and what she was doing.

The house was empty and echoed hollow to his footsteps. There was nothing personal of his in the drawing room. The floor was polished parquet, a few oriental rugs scattered between the chintz-covered armchairs provided by the Foreign Office: a place for official entertaining, not a home. He opened the french doors onto the terrace, but the phone rang before he could step outside. It was his First Secretary, Paul Skilbeck. "Sorry to bother you this late, Bill." Skilbeck's tone, ever supercilious, said that he didn't really give a damn. "But I've been called in to the embassy. A telegram came in on my other network . . ." He paused meaningfully. "I think we'd better talk about it tomorrow."

"Okay—I'll be in the office all day." Cable frowned. Skilbeck was an intelligence officer with a diplomatic front job—in reality only half-time on Cable's staff. It was an irritating relationship, for Cable was kept in the dark about most of Skilbeck's other activities, even though he had once been an intelligence officer himself before "going straight" as Skilbeck called it, somewhat patronizingly.

"Yes I know, Bill, but I've got to be over in UNO-city for a UNIDO meeting all day. Couldn't we meet over there? We could have lunch together at the Napoleon."

"Can't do it, Paul. I've got Laszlo Kardos for lunch in town. I'll see you at the embassy about nine, before you go to UNIDO. That do?"

"Very well, Bill—see you tomorrow." Skilbeck sounded annoyed and hung up abruptly. He didn't like it when Cable behaved like his boss. Cable shrugged and poured himself a lager.

In the garden the air was cool after a hot day. The house was on the hills north of Vienna and the terrace looked out across the city, a panorama of silver lights. Immediately below the balustrade the ground fell away down a slope covered in vines, at night just a long expanse of darkness. Away to the left, hidden by trees, there were sounds of laughter from the local *Heurigen:* they would be full of tourists, eating slices of roast pork and knocking back the new wine by the *Viertel.** Someone was playing an accordion.

Cable sat down on a garden bench and stared into the darkness. He wanted Naomi. It had been a lousy day and he wanted to look into those incredibly deep eyes, to unburden himself, to share the funny side of a night at the opera with the two puzzled Chinese. Later her cool body would entwine his as he gave himself to delighting her . . . but not tonight. She had gone away for two days and the little flat in the Third District would be empty.

The silence was broken by a sharp metallic click behind him and Cable turned around abruptly. A man dressed all in black was standing there, almost invisible except for his white face, a large-caliber pistol pointing directly at Cable's chest. Cable started and heard his glass shatter on the ground.

"Keep quiet and don't move," said the intruder quietly. "Otherwise I kill you." Cable's eyes were fixed on the gun. It was a Volkov with a silencer, a killer. It could blow a hole a foot wide

*Quarter (of a liter)

in his body. He sat rigid, keeping his hands still. Two other men emerged from the shadows, also dressed in black, and moved behind him. "Stand up, very slowly, and put your hands on your shoulders."

Cable obeyed, his brain racing to find a way of resisting. No point shouting—the nearest house was too far away. No one could see—the terrace was shielded by a thick belt of trees. Where was the policeman on the gate? . . . Why the hell had he not been there when Fritz dropped Cable off half an hour ago? He cursed inwardly—he should have reacted and phoned the police post in the village right away. Now he was being kidnapped and there was absolutely nothing he could do to stop it. These men wouldn't shoot him if he made a break for it, but they'd stop him violently, smash him up and make sure he didn't get a second chance.

They closed around him and his hands were jerked backwards. He felt the cold steel of handcuffs on his wrists and a blanket was thrown over his head. "Walk," said a voice and he stumbled forward, feeling hands gripping his arms to guide him. His feet were on gravel and he realized that they were taking him to the back gate, into the lane behind the house. Hands pushed his head down and he was kneed roughly into a car, the blanket still muffling his head. He felt shoulders pressing against his on both sides and fell back against the seat as the car accelerated away.

* * *

They drove for about twenty minutes. When they stopped, the blanket was removed and he was hustled out of the car. It was parked on a rough track leading to a quay by fast-flowing water. They were in the shadow of a towering warehouse by the Danube, the darkness broken only by pale yellow light from an open wicket in the high gates across its entrance.

"Walk," said the voice again. Cable stepped awkwardly over the threshold of the wicket, for his wrists were still pinioned behind his back, and stumbled through the gloom between stacks of wooden crates.

The small office was brightly lit, with cheap metal furniture. No one had bothered to cover up the cyrillic script on the wall calendar; the warehouse must belong to a Russian trading company. A youngish man sat on the edge of the desk, swinging his legs. He had a broad Slavic face, with a high, bald forehead, and looked directly at Cable.

"Good evening, Ambassador. You have not been kidnapped, as you may think. You will be free to go quite soon, but first I have a message for you. It reads *"Golitsyn, Hanoi, 1971."* He paused and watched Cable's face suddenly become haggard. "The message comes from a senior official of my government. It continues, that the time has now come when we shall require your cooperation— if, that is, we are not to betray you to your country's security authorities." He gave a half-smile, as if expecting a response.

"Who *are* you? I don't think you said." Cable's anger concealed the dryness of fear in his throat.

The young man's eyes narrowed as he lit a cigarette. He blew the smoke directly into Cable's face. "I am not here for a discussion, Ambassador. You know perfectly well who I am and what I am talking about."

Cable snorted defiantly. "Go to hell."

"Don't be foolish, Ambassador." He sighed. "Do I have to spell it out? Thirteen years ago you betrayed your trust and we have evidence that could end your career, disgrace you—and send you to prison for a very long time."

Cable could feel his heart beating painfully. His facade of anger was in danger of slipping away to reveal his inner panic, but he struggled to keep his voice firm. "Thirteen years ago I betrayed nothing—absolutely nothing—and your people bloody well know it. Now release my hands and take me back to Grinzing! You have no right to keep me here."

The Slav gestured at him impatiently. "Balls, Cable—be your age. Just remember what happened in 1971—to Golitsyn and, the next year, to you. It may be true that you were—as you would no doubt say—'framed,' but—"

"Framed?" shouted Cable hoarsely. *"Framed?* The whole bloody thing was a fabrication!"

"Our evidence is convincing enough, Cable." The young man's tone had taken on a sudden cutting edge. "And you still have plenty of enemies in Whitehall who would be delighted to see it—people in your own bureaucracy who would like to lick your blood . . ." He paused, his eyes mocking. "Terrible, isn't it? Clever and successful people always have enemies, you know—they attract hatred, particularly when, like you, they were not born to rule."

Cable flinched, recognizing an unwelcome truth in what he was hearing. He stopped blustering. "What do you want of me?"

"Now that sounds more sensible—*much* more sensible."

"I said what the hell do you want?" Cable still spoke aggressively, but his fear was becoming evident.

"I cannot tell you yet. In a few days we shall contact you again. If you cooperate, we shall leave you alone for the rest of your life." His eyes bored into Cable's. "If you don't, we shall ruin you."

Cable stalled, horrified to hear himself but anxious only to get out of the warehouse. "And if I do 'cooperate,' what possible guarantee can I have that you won't go on blackmailing me for the rest of my life?" The words were almost inaudible.

"I am authorized to say that we will not. We have saved you up all these years for something really important. When it's over," he made a chopping gesture with his hand, "finish. You have my word as an officer. You have the word of my superior, as an officer. What do you think we are, animals?"

Cable remembered Golitsyn. "Yes," he said quietly. The man launched himself off the desk and aimed a kick at Cable's groin. The pain was sickening and he doubled up, coughing, the steel of the handcuffs cutting into his wrists behind him as he tried to clutch himself.

"Get out!" shouted the Slav. "You will hear from us—and don't try playing silly buggers by going to your security people in the meantime." His face twisted in contempt. "We can ruin you, Cable. Don't bloody well forget it! Now go and fuck your Jewish bitch—and that is something else we have on you. Do they know about her in London?" He spat out a string of Russian obscenities and marched out of the door.

Someone tapped Cable on the shoulder and they hustled him back through the warehouse, into the car, saying nothing. As they drove off, he looked back and saw the black shapes of a tug and a string of barges moored on the river. Had it been daylight, he was sure that they would have been flying the red and gold Soviet flag. Then the blanket was thrown around his head again.

* * *

When they took the blanket off, he saw that the car had stopped at a lonely spot on the Hohenstrasse, high in the forest outside the city and about half a mile from his house. The handcuffs were unlocked swiftly and he was pushed out, sprawling on the sharp flints of the roadside. He stood up rubbing his numb wrists as the car sped off. He was not surprised that it had a Vienna diplomatic license plate.

Cable started to walk stiffly, automatically, down the lane toward Grinzing. His mind was churning, trying to come to grips with the reality of what had just happened. As he passed the pretentious Viennese mansions, each guarded by its high metal fence, and stepped around the expensive BMW and Mercedes cars parked under the trees, the whole thing seemed like a dream, a mad nightmare. But when he reached the house in Himmelstrasse, its front gate was unlocked, swinging in the slight breeze—and there was still no policeman outside.

3 | Budapest and Leningrad

SARAH WOKE with a splitting headache. The sedative was still in her bloodstream, so she did not leap up in panic. Instead she turned painfully onto her side, blinking in the dazzling light, and tried to focus on her surroundings.

Her sight was blurred, but she could see that she was lying on a thin rubber mattress, which was flat on the gray concrete floor. There was no bed—no furniture of any kind. It was a narrow cell, with no window and white-tiled walls. The light came from a dome of thick glass in the ceiling. At one end of the cell was a heavy door painted institutional green; at the other, a bucket.

Pulling the rough blanket around her, for she was still naked, Sarah sat up and cuddled her knees. Her head hurt like hell and her throat was raspingly dry. Her mind went back to the young man by the lake and she wanted to rage at herself for being caught by such an obvious trick, but all she felt was a curious, tense calm. She wanted to cry, but could not.

There was a click and she turned to see an eye staring at her through a judas window set in the door. The controlled calm vanished and she staggered to her feet, lurching to the door and hammering on it with both fists. "Help—where am I? Let me out, whoever you are! I'm British, I have diplomatic status! You have no right to keep me here!" She heard her voice crack "Oh God, *please* let me out, *please!*"

The judas window snapped shut and the door stayed closed. Sarah went on banging hopelessly for several minutes, but there

[14]

was no response. Her eyes brimmed with hot tears of impotence and fear and she sank back to the floor, sobbing quietly.

*   *   *

The view across the river to the island fortress of Peter and Paul was always somehow more than life-size. Major General Nadia Alexandrovna Kirov* stepped out onto the balcony of her northern office and blinked in the sunlight. The Neva flowed by, gray-blue and half a mile wide, churned up by white hydrofoils scurrying downstream to Petroverts and Kronstadt.

Opposite, the spire of the cathedral at the center of the Peter and Paul rose high above its massive bastions and towers. At the foot of the stone walls of the fortress, the river was bordered by a narrow beach crowded with sunbathers. Soon it would be autumn, but today it was still hot and the bright colors of towels and cast-off summer clothes contrasted starkly with the bleak stonework above. The general looked across the river wistfully. She had swum from that beach herself, as a child.

She loved Leningrad, particularly when she escaped there in the summer from the stifling heat of Moscow. Sighing, she put on a pair of sunglasses and opened the file on the metal table. She had just been telephoned from Budapest. The girl had been pulled across the frontier successfully. Now she must consider the father.

Life had not been easy for the general since Brezhnev died. With the elevation of her Chairman, Yuri Andropov, to the leadership, she might have expected to secure her position, maybe even promotion. She was, after all, one of his nine deputy chairmen, albeit the most junior. But the timing had been disastrous. Just when she needed strength for the developing power struggle, there had been a chain of failures. In Britain, they had broken the ring of agents she had nurtured for years at their center for interception of radio communications in Cheltenham. Her key agent, in place for fifteen years, had gone to jail for thirty-five. Two others had been sentenced quietly later, along with another long-term agent at NATO in Brussels. Her access to this priceless source of intelligence—and through it to the similar American National Security

*See *Down Among the Dead Men*, Michael Hartland, 1983.

Agency—had been blocked. The product of twenty years' infiltration had been destroyed.

Then Andropov had died; and for Kirov it had been a struggle to stay in her position, let alone in power. Under the new leader she had been pushed further and further from the center. Now she faced grave danger—and so did the policies for which she stood, for Kirov was no longer motivated solely by personal ambition. When she had been promoted to deputy chairman, she had assumed a veneer of statesmanship that had come to have a certain reality. Too many madmen in both Washington and Moscow were willing to drift too close to open conflict; and that frightened Kirov. Her fists clenched. She needed a success—a *real* success.

Kirov sighed and her eyes strayed back to the vista of the river. She was nearly sixty, but below her well-cut gray hair, she had the face of a handsome woman ten years younger. Away to the right the cruiser *Aurora*, which had shelled the Winter Palace in the Revolution, bobbed at anchor: it was now a museum. To either side of the balcony the embankment was lined with the massive buildings of Peter the Great's city—imperial palaces, the Hermitage, the Admiralty.

Her eyes narrowed as they returned to the file. Fortunately Michaelov wasn't doing too well either. His penetration of Western operations to support anti-Soviet nationalist movements was pitted with failure: Afghanistan, Armenia, the Muslim republics of the south, Czechoslovakia, Poland. These movements had always been irritants. Now they threatened grave danger. The general was going to take in Michaelov's washing; and His Excellency Mr. William Cable, Her Britannic Majesty's Ambassador to the United Nations Organizations in Vienna, was going to help her. Not that he knew it yet, but Cable was going to restore her fortunes.

She picked up another file and started to reread it. It had a red stripe for Secret—and Cable's name on the front. She already knew most of it by heart.

*   *   *

John William Cable had been born forty-nine years before in Portsmouth, a naval port on the south coast of England. His parents had been poor, but more members of the proud middle class than working class. Kirov smiled at the file's quaint deference to these very British distinctions. Ah—his father had been a hospital clerk and they lived in a mean terraced house, that was clearer. Cable was the eldest of three children, but the others were all born after the Second World War. In the war his father had joined the army in 1940 and returned in 1946; during these six years he had been continuously abroad, in North Africa and then the Far East. So up to the age of ten Cable had barely seen his father. He had lived alone with his mother on the wartime pay of a soldier in the ranks, supplemented by her earnings from a munitions factory.

Cable had gone to a grammar school, then taken a degree in languages at London University. Afterward he did his national service in the navy; and suddenly his horizons expanded. His intellectual power was noticed, he was commissioned but spent only a token month at sea. First Lieutenant Cable was moved rapidly into intelligence work and trained as a cryptanalyst, a code breaker, working on other countries' intercepted military and diplomatic radio signals. He was brilliant at it and soon came to the notice of his department head, David Nairn—who was also, as it happened, a world class chess player and writer of a regular chess column in one of the better Sunday newspapers. When Cable's two years' conscription was over, Nairn arranged for him to be recruited into the regular intelligence service, exchanging his uniform for civilian clothes but doing the same job in the same office in Cheltenham.

The early sixties found him on an intercept station in Australia, high in the hills behind Sydney. There was a photograph stuck in the file: a man in his late twenties, medium height, broad shouldered, a very confident, masculine look to his face. He had done well: his reports marked him good on both technical competence and management of his small staff. Respected. A potential leader. Bit of a social conscience—he had done some voluntary work with a group down near Circular Quay, befriending down-and-outs and meths drinkers—and he seemed to make friends easily. Hospitable colleagues invited him home and he became used to the outdoor life of barbecues by swimming pools in backyards and parties on the beach.

Kirov looked at the faded photograph again—a strong, intelligent face with thoughtful eyes. She sighed. What she was going to do might ruin him, but the more she read the file the more she *liked* this man. And God—what a lousy deal his own country had dealt him. Unjustly chucked out of a successful career in their intelligence service, then thirteen years of crummy jobs which belittled his ability, ending with the sop of a tenth-rate ambassadorship in a diplomatic backwater. Kirov was well aware that even a tenth-rate ambassadorship would exceed the aspirations of most normal people—but that was not the point. Cable was no more normal than she was: he had been on the way to the top. He had tasted success and deserved it—then known the bitterness of failure with nowhere else to go, for he had a family to feed and nobody wanted ex-intelligence officers. Nobody except . . . yet he seemed totally loyal. Yes, he must be bitter—but was he bitter enough? That was why she needed the daughter. . . .

Now the file was drawing on reports from agents in Britain and Australia, with snatches from Cable's interrogation ten years later, particularly the sessions under sodium pentathol, the "truth drug," when he would have talked freely with no consciousness or memory of what he was saying. In Australia he met Judith, small, dark, serious, sexy but uncertain of herself. She had found him reassuring, someone to lean on; years later she had given him the Simon and Garfunkel record *Bridge Over Troubled Water* on their anniversary as a memento of those early months. In the boundless confidence of his late twenties he did not heed the occasional distance he felt between them nor the troubled look in her eyes when her face was in repose. Before returning to England, they went for a month's holiday on the white tropical sands of Queensland. Walking hand in hand beneath the palms by moonlight, Judith had clung to him and cried in her happiness.

Sarah was born eight and a half months later, in Cheltenham—a tiny premature baby who was never too strong and became the troubled child of a troubled mother. Then he had been posted to Paris, with a cover job as a first secretary in the embassy. It had been three years in which everything went right, particularly the birth of Lucy. He had half-hoped for a son, but fell in love at once with this beautiful child when he held her, wrapped in a towel, just after her birth. At first Sarah, now three, had been prone to jealousy—but after a few days he heard her call from the bedroom where she was standing by the cot, "Oh, Mummy. Our baby's *smiling*. She's smiling at *me*." Lucy had transformed the small Cable family. Even as a baby, then a toddler, her sunny, equable personality influenced them all. She was a loving and generous child.

In 1969 they went back to London, where Cable bought a suburban house in Teddington. It was convenient for the short train journey to his new office near Waterloo Station, the headquarters of the Secret Intelligence Service, often known as "the Cut" because it was so close to the street market of that name. He had been there only a week or two when he was summoned to the gaunt David Nairn, now director of East and South Asia Division.

Nairn had offered him a special assignment for two years—in Vietnam, where the war was bleeding the country to death as the communist stranglehold on the south increased. "You had it easy in Paris, Bill, and it's time you got ready for wider responsibility—something bigger, here in the Cut or overseas. After all that electronic stuff you ought to run some old-fashioned agents for a bit—and it's time our allies got to know you."

Cable did not want to go. Judith's insecurity was already turning into depression and returning to London had made it worse. Suddenly the comfortable diplomatic apartment, and the lavish allowance to employ domestic help, vanished. Judith had never had to cope with two boisterous children in their own modest—and largely unfurnished—house before. It was also the first time Cable had worked in London; and he was realizing that the service had all the tensions and petty jealousies of any other organization. A lot of people resented Cable's meteoric rise; he had acquired enemies whom he had never met, enemies who hated him for his innate skills and for being picked out by Nairn.

For the first time Cable had tried to get off the escalator and take control of his own life, sensing the dangers. But Nairn expected his staff—most of all those he relied on—to move without question on his real-life chessboard. He had offered Cable to the CIA as a British star-turn to strengthen a weak and demoralized American team—a loan that he expected to be repaid with massive interest in the future. He did not understand family problems. A widower for sixteen years, Nairn's entire life had been given to the service—and it showed. As for Cable's other doubts, Nairn knew best about careers and Cable was needed in Saigon. It was an order and that was the end of it. Kirov had noticed this ruthless streak in Nairn before—and his blind-spot on human factors. He had been wrong to force Cable to go; and the consequences were Nairn's responsibility.

The family stayed behind, for Saigon was dangerous with the

Vietcong already dug in on the outskirts. Cable was given the temporary rank of lieutenant colonel in the Australian Army. He needed a military rank for his own protection if he fell into enemy hands and no British forces were involved in the war, whereas Australia and New Zealand were well committed. In Saigon, Cable did what had been expected of him and rapidly built up a string of informants in the villages around the beleaguered capital, then penetrated the Vietcong cadres, aiming at their high command in Hanoi. He had gotten close to those around General Vo Nguyen Giap himself. Kirov noted his success with professional admiration.

In 1971 Cable's reputation stood high. In London and Washington it was common gossip, in the closed intelligence community, that Bill Cable was a coming man. Perhaps he would make chief— certainly he would make the top.

And then it had all been shattered: a hideous, tragic end. As she read the flat prose again, Kirov wondered who had set Cable up. The report did not say. It had been supplied from GRU records and the first time she saw it she had almost retched. Now she was familiar with it, but it was still horrific, vile. The general shuddered and stared out of the window. Far away, beyond the *Aurora*, was the Finland Station, where Lenin had arrived to begin the October Revolution. Far away in the other direction, outside the city, she had dug trenches in frozen earth with a pickax, under shellfire, in 1942. The three-year siege against the Germans had found her a schoolgirl with a warm family, left her a Party member and alone in the world. Nadia Alexandrovna had lived a hard life, but she retained her puritan Marxism. Under Stalin she had almost lost her life. She had standards—and some things could still sicken her, even if now she found it convenient to build on them.

She read the end of the file again. "Barbarians," she muttered, tossing the papers onto a side table and wiping her fingers with a handkerchief, as if they had been covered in blood.

4 | Vienna

IN THE MORNING the sun was streaming into Cable's bedroom window. He turned away from it, staring at the ceiling. He had slept fitfully, tossing and turning, waking up several times bathed in sweat, and now he showered and dressed slowly, automatically. From the window he could see the onion-topped tower of Grinzing church rising above the trees and, beyond it, the heat haze hovering over the city. Away to the left ran the broad, muddy sweep of the Danube.

About eight-thirty Fritz drove him to the embassy, down the village street of Grinzing, where every other house had a bush of pine twigs hanging outside to advertise its new wine, then along the embankment by the canal. The embassy was a gray stucco building in Reisnerstrasse, close to the center of Vienna in the Third District, a Union Jack hanging limply over the door. It housed three ambassadors: one to Austria, one to the never-ending Vienna negotiations on arms reductions—and Cable. He often felt that having three ambassadors in one capital came close to debasing the currency.

He took the lift to his office on the third floor. He had tried to push the events of last night out of his mind after getting up, but they had crowded in on him again as he sat in the back of the car, idly turning the pages of *Die Presse*. He ought to report what had happened—and do it at once. He could speak to Barron, the ambassador to Austria, who was senior to him in rank; or he could get in touch with Security Department in London. Yet something in him hesitated. He had been trying to forget for thirteen years and he could hardly face it even now, but it *had* to be faced. The truth was that there was a document in Moscow that could ruin him—and some bitter men in London who would like to see it happen. It was not so simple. If he came clean, he would be out of Vienna in twenty-four hours and out of the service in a month; and the young Russian was right, he might even end up in jail. Poor Sarah—no mother, no sister and now a derelict father . . . but to cooperate with them was unthinkable. Or was it? In a mood of black depression, he opened the door of the big office. Seeing Skilbeck sitting there already only made things worse; he had forgotten he had arranged to see him at nine and it was already ten past.

Skilbeck was short and red-haired. To outsiders he exuded a boyish charm that usually made them tell him more than they should, but within the embassy he had a hard, suspicious manner. He was the senior SIS officer in Vienna—the head of station.

"Morning, Bill," he said. "Traffic heavy this morning?"

"Yes, it was a bit. Sorry I'm late."

"Doesn't matter." Skilbeck smiled icily—he had no chauffeur-driven car and came to work by tram. "My UNIDO meeting isn't till half-past ten."

Cable sat down behind the desk. There was a large pile of correspondence and telegrams in the IN tray; he riffled through it wearily. "Well, Paul—what can I do for you?"

Skilbeck looked around to make sure that the door was firmly closed. "I'm afraid you'll have to do without most of my time for a month or so, Bill." He spoke quietly, but as if he were giving an order. "There's a big covert operation coming up. I'm sorry about it, but the instruction comes direct from the head of my service. I have to run this thing from here."

Cable frowned. "The time is no great problem—young Holt will just have to work a bit harder than usual. But why are you telling me, Paul? I generally don't know half of what you're up to."

Skilbeck looked shifty. "This is the big one, Bill; it could make a few waves if anything goes wrong. London instructed me to tell you—I guess they thought you should know." Plainly he disliked having to let Cable in on his secret.

This angered Cable, who exclaimed, "Know? But I don't *know!* All you've told me is that there's 'an operation.' What *kind* of operation, Paul?"

"I don't have authority to say," Skilbeck replied stiffly.

"Aggressive or defensive?"

"I suppose it might be construed as aggression by the other side—I would prefer to see it as defensive."

"And does *Barron* know?" Cable could tell, from Skilbeck's silence, that the more senior ambassador did know. He heard the menacing tone of the young Russian in the warehouse, the words that had been churning in his mind ever since—*In a few days we shall contact you again . . . if you cooperate, we shall leave you alone for the rest of your life. If you don't, we shall ruin you.*

He stood up and walked over to the window, noticing a convoy of large black cars drawing up outside the Russian Embassy, a little way down on the other side of the street. "Look here, Paul." He was feigning controlled anger. "Are you saying that *my* mission—not Barron's—is the control center for some kind of subversive operation directed against the East?"

"More or less—yes."

Cable turned around sharply and fixed the other man with a firm gaze. "And if it goes wrong, there'll be a row? This is a neutral country these days—remember? The poor man's Switzerland. Maybe you'll get kicked out by the Austrians? Maybe *I* will, as head of the mission?"

Skilbeck shifted uncomfortably. "I suppose it's possible, Bill. Of course, we don't envisage anything going wrong."

"Good grief—we've all heard that one before! Now you damn well listen." Cable began to speak with slow emphasis. "I think that, as head of this mission, I must be in on whatever lunacy you're up to. Then I can calculate the risk to wider British interests and be prepared for damage limitation if you fail." God, he thought, how pompous he sounded.

"I can't tell you," snapped Skilbeck. "I've already explained. I don't have authority to do that."

"Then bloody well get it!" roared Cable. "I'm not putting my mission in jeopardy for your lot unless I know exactly what's going on. Is that clear—do you understand me?"

"I will report to Century House." Skilbeck rose stiffly. "If you insist."

"I don't 'insist,' Paul. You're posted here as a first secretary in *my* mission and I'm fucking well *ordering* you to do it." He paused to let both the obscenity and the force of his anger sink in. "I expect an answer in twenty-four hours, unless you want me to send a telegram to your director-general myself. So just go and do it. Do it *now*."

"Very well." Skilbeck strode out, red-faced with anger, closing the door with a bang.

Cable turned back to the window. Now why had he acted like that? It must be details of this operation of Skilbeck's that they wanted from him—so why the hell was he arranging things so that he could hand them over? He had taken the first step toward treachery in the last fifteen minutes. It was terrifying. He ought to retrace it quickly, before it was too late. Instead he just stared blankly at the papers on his desk, their confusion mirroring the turmoil in his mind. The young Russian's voice seemed to echo in his ear—*Golitsyn, Hanoi, 1971*.

He picked up one of his phones, a direct line from the embassy, and dialed the number of the art dealers where Naomi worked. She was not there. "*Nein, mein Herr*," said the whining Yiddish tones of the proprietor. "Fraulein Reichmann is out at a private showing, then she is going to value some pictures for me—at a house down near the Central Cemetery. She is not coming back today."

Cable thanked him, saying that there was no message. He could not talk to Naomi until the evening—but could he talk to *anyone*, even Naomi, about this?

* * *

Naomi had come into Cable's life with a bang, seven months before. It was the day the PLO blew up the Palais Auersperg.

The Israeli ambassador was giving a reception for Moshe Kagan, his deputy foreign minister, who was in Vienna for what were described as "economic discussions." But there had been rumors for some months that the Austrian Chancellor was playing host to secret meetings between PLO and Israeli officials, who were trying to negotiate some kind of accommodation before open war broke out again. The negotiations were complicated by the fact that both the government of Israel and the PLO were divided in themselves. Kagan was a young liberal politician spearheading Israel's peace faction and in a short time he had come to command great international respect. He also seemed able to carry his elderly, but still bitter and warlike, prime minister along with him. The hopes of an increasing number of frightened people in the Middle East were being invested in Moshe Kagan.

The reception was in a large room on the first floor. Beneath the crystal chandeliers, waiters in white jackets pushed their trays of watery gin and Campari through the crush of diplomats. Cable shook hands with Kagan, the guest of honor, at the door and circulated a little. He chatted to his friend Laszlo Kardos, a worldly monsignor who represented the Vatican to the United Nations agencies in Vienna. Kardos had great charm and a sharp wit, tempered by kind, intelligent eyes twinkling above his black beard. "There are a lot of people I don't know," Cable almost shouted to him above the din. "Who are they?"

"Must be the Viennese Jewish community—it's still quite big. Not as big as in 1938 of course."

"No, I suppose not." Cable seized another drink from a passing tray—turning to find Skilbeck at his elbow, staring curiously at a small group in a corner. The center of attention seemed to be a short, stocky man in an elegant light gray suit. He was almost a cartoon caricature of Jewishness, crinkled silver hair swept back from a high forehead, face dominated by a nose shaped like a map of Israel. He was in earnest conversation with the grave figure of Vienna's chief rabbi.

"Who's that you've got your eye on?" asked Cable.

The clamor of the party was deafening, so speech could be relatively private; even so, Skilbeck put his head close and almost whispered, "I *think* it's Aharon Yadin."

"Yadin—who's he?"

"The head of the Mossad." Skilbeck's tone had an uncharacteristic quality of awe, almost reverence. "You must have heard his code name, Melchior?"

"Can't say that I have. The Mossad? You mean he's at their embassy—why haven't I seen him before?"

Skilbeck shook his head, looking even more reverential. "No, Bill. Not the *local* station. He's head of the whole shebang back home, boss of the Israeli intelligence service."

"Good lord—what the hell's he doing here?"

"That's just what *I* was wondering."

Cable moved on, leaving after about half an hour, for he had a dinner engagement with the Pakistani ambassador and wanted to go home first. He was halfway down the grand staircase when the explosion rocked the building. There was a thunderous roar and a blast of hot air rushed after him from the reception room. Plaster rained from the ceiling; the marble balustrade cracked and crashed downward, taking two screaming figures with it.

After a momentary blackout, Cable found himself flat on the stairs, with a girl in a green dress spread-eagled on top of him. For a few seconds there was silence—then from above came more screams and the crackle of burning. He pulled the girl to her feet. She swayed as if dazed, so he picked her up and carried her rapidly down the wrecked staircase and out into the street.

Ambulances and fire engines were beginning to arrive, with policemen in green overcoats linking arms to keep back the crowd. Cable put the girl down and she turned to him with a half-smile. "That was very gallant of you, thank you. Are you all right yourself—your suit looks a bit singed."

She was a little over five feet tall with thick black hair, which kept falling forward. She pushed it back repeatedly with her right hand—he was to come to know it as a characteristic gesture. Her face had once been pretty; now it was a little careworn but still attractive, with candid brown eyes that were suddenly beautiful when she smiled. "Thank you," she said again. "You saved my life."

"No, you'd have got out anyway—but the sooner the better. Look at the place now." Flames were leaping from upstairs windows of the building and already three teams of firemen were high on ladders, playing water down into them. A stream of people was being helped into ambulances.

She was wearing a short, strapless cocktail dress and clutched her shoulders with her bare arms, for it was February, with a bitter wind and snow lying in the streets. "You must be freezing," he said. "Here, have my jacket—we'll never get our overcoats out of there. If I can find my car, I'll take you home." They walked together through the rubble strewn across the road, the girl clutching his coat around her. With the fire engines, the noise, the blanket-covered bodies on the pavement, it reminded Cable of the blitz of Portsmouth when he had been a child.

Cable approached a policeman whose overcoat was heavy with gold braid—he was clearly in charge. "I'm from the British Embassy," he said in German. "Is there anyone British hurt? Is there anything I can do to help—carrying stretchers or something?"

The police captain waved him away. "The injured are all going to the *Allgemeines-Krankenhaus*—check there for your people. Everything is under control—the best help you can give is to go home." Cable hesitated. *"Um Gottes Willen—go!"*

By some miracle they found the Ford Minster a few minutes later. Fritz pushed them into it, along with one of the embassy's third secretaries and his wife; they both looked stunned and Cable told Fritz to take them home first.

*   *   *

She had an apartment in Bayerngasse, only a mile away, and the car was there within half an hour. "Won't you come in for a drink?" she asked.

"Thank you—that's very kind—and may I use your phone? I ought to ring the Pakistani ambassador; I was supposed to be at his house for dinner."

The apartment was on the fourth floor and there was no lift; they passed the usual wall of mailboxes in the hall and climbed the ill-lit stairs. Inside, her place was small but welcoming and comfortable. The living room had space for three modern easy chairs, a couch, lots of bright cushions, and a wall of shelves overflowing with books.

He declined coffee and she poured two beers from the fridge in the tiny kitchen. She turned on a transistor radio and they caught the end of a news flash about the bombing. Eight people had been killed, said the announcer ". . . *including the deputy foreign minister of Israel, Mr. Moshe Kagan, who died of his injuries in the Allgemeines-Krankenhaus at seven-thirty this evening.*" The program switched back at once to a cheering crowd at the Austria-Scotland football match being relayed from Glasgow.

The girl turned away and Cable saw that there were tears in her eyes. He put his arm around her shoulders. "Come and sit down—you're suffering from shock, you know."

She shook her head. "No—I don't think so. I'm from Israel and I've been almost blown up before—I'm used to it. I'm just terribly sad about Kagan. Our country's in an awful mess and he was a kind of savior."

"I suppose that's why someone took the trouble to plant that bomb. Who do you think it was?"

"Oh—the PLO. One faction or another."

They talked on for over an hour. Her name was Naomi Reich-mann and she was a *sabra*, an Israeli born in Israel, though her parents had come from Hungary after the Second World War. Her mother was dead and her father lived in Tel Aviv. She worked for an art dealer in the First District and had strong views on Middle East politics. "It can't go on like this, you know—we just *have* to find a way of giving the Palestinians something of their own. A country can't stay at war forever."

Cable found her entrancing. She sat in one of the armchairs with the green dress hiding her legs, which were tucked under her. But he could see the soft curves of her body through the thin material and knew that she would be beautiful naked. Then he remem-bered that Fritz was still sitting outside in the car; and British am-bassadors were not supposed to lay single girls they barely knew, least of all Israelis.

She solved the problem for him. "Your driver is still waiting, you know," she said with a smile. "Thank you for looking after me. I'd like to have offered you something more than a can of Budweiser. If I asked you and your wife to dinner one evening, would you come? It's not very grand—not quite what you're used to."

"I don't have a wife, I'm divorced—but I'd love to come, if you ask me."

She looked taken aback, then replied hesitantly, "How about next Sunday then? Eight o'clock?" and kissed him chastely on the cheek. "Good night, Ambassador."

*   *   *

Cable was wary of getting involved. She was an attractive woman, a delightful companion, but any ambassador caught up with a girl half his age had to reckon with the possibility of her being an agent for a hostile power. Yet he couldn't bring himself to ask Skilbeck to check her out—it seemed too distasteful. For two months he met Naomi every week or so and they went to concerts, or to art exhibitions outside Vienna. Sometimes they went out to dinner, usually in restaurants deep in the country where they would not encounter the diplomatic community.

By May they were increasingly relaxed in each other's com-pany. Cable felt liberated after the years of loneliness since his divorce; and Naomi seemed to need him in return, but their meetings were still chaste and discreet. Cable was surprised that such a lively and independent girl was willing to put up with it, but he began to realize that his initial concern had been unnecessary. Naomi was quite evidently no more than what she seemed—a nice Jewish girl spending a few years working in Central Europe, where her parents had once lived. She did not ask him political questions; in fact she expressed little interest in politics outside the Middle East, on which her views were passionate.

One evening he was looking for Fritz after a dinner at the Intercontinentale when he almost bumped into Delacroix, arm in arm on the pavement with a stunning Viennese girl, laughing and chattering away in German. Cable was embarrassed and hid in the shadows, as they crossed the road and let themselves into an apartment block. Minutes later, two windows on an upper floor were lit up; the girl could be seen in the left-hand one, stooping— evidently to turn a bed down—before she drew the curtains. Then the other light went out. When Fritz arrived, Cable settled into the back seat thoughtfully. If Delacroix could do it so openly . . . why the hell was he being so careful? He was a single man. There was no rule to prevent him having a girl friend if he wanted—he was missing out and so was Naomi.

* * *

The previous weekend they had driven into the mountains of the Salzkammergut, staying in separate rooms at a *pension* by the lake in Hallstatt. The next, Naomi suggested a contrast and they drove out into the flat plain east of Vienna, the beginning of the Hungarian *puszta*. This was not the Austria of the tourists—just a belt of workaday farmland ending at the frontier, punctuated by dusty villages and the rocking beams of pumping engines over wells.

They had lunch at a *Gasthaus* in Marchegg, a sleepy little town clustered round the twin symbols of provincial Austria: the volunteer fire station and the *Konsum* general store. After trout and a liter of white wine, Cable drove down a narrow street leading off the square, up a slope to the top of the embankment holding back the wide river which forms the border.

The Morawa was flowing by fast, gray waters edged by waterlogged beds of reeds. Naomi turned and looked back at the little town of single-story houses with steep roofs, walls washed pink or dark Habsburg yellow. In the fields an old man in baggy peasant clothes was hoeing a field of onions, mopping his brow in the sun. She took Cable's arm. "It's eerie, Bill. So quiet, such a pretty town, so unspoiled—and only a few hundred yards from the other side, from the other half of the world."

There was nothing to show it was the frontier except a rusty sign on the Austrian side—*Achtung! Staatsgrenze!*—and a black steel watchtower on the Czech bank of the river. There was no sign of life on the other side—even the watchtower looked empty. Beyond the river, Czechoslovakia consisted of marshes broken up by patches of blue-gray water, then parched yellow grasslands, with misty hills in the distance.

"God—it looks desolate," she whispered. "Don't they have *people* over there?"

"Must be a closed border zone—probably five or ten kilometers deep. What's the memorial? Refugees?" There was a pillar of stone, surmounted by an eagle, a few yards away.

Naomi peered at the inscription. "No." She giggled. "It's a monument to the hundred and twenty-fifth anniversary of the Austrian customs service, 1830 to 1955. Good grief—aren't the Austrians a nation of bureaucrats? Is there anywhere else in the world where they'd put up a monument to their *tax collectors?*"

"Don't be irreverent, my girl," laughed Cable, slapping her firmly on the bottom.

"Brute!" She ran ahead along the towpath, wrinkling her nose and grinning at him wickedly over her shoulder.

They walked a long way beside the river before driving farther north into a range of hills. The evening found them in a pretty village called Michelstetten, parking outside the *Gasthaus* in the square. After dinner, Cable asked the proprietor if they could stay the night.

*   *   *

The room was typically Austrian—spotlessly clean and full of heavy country furniture. There was a dormer window with cheerful red and white check curtains and, on the walls, a stag's head and a picture of the Sacred Heart. The bed was huge and wooden, covered by a mountainous white comforter.

Naomi kissed him briefly and began to undress as if they had been sleeping together for years. She had been wearing a powder-blue summer dress, which made her look feminine and fragile. Naked, she was beautiful, but her body reminded Cable more of a girl-soldier. It was lithe, athletic—a practical kind of body, her skin tanned a golden brown all over, with just a trace of paler flesh to each side of the black triangle of her pubic hair, slim arms and legs showing the slight swell of powerful muscles. She was standing by the window, and when she turned with her back to him, reaching up to close a gap in the curtains, the buttocks below her narrow waist were firm and round, almost boyish.

Cable smiled wryly at his own pale skin and slight paunch; but his self-consciousness was banished when she threw her arms around his neck, small breasts pressed hard against his chest. There was the fragrance of a musky perfume and he could not stop caressing the fine texture of her skin. She drew him onto the bed, looking up at him gravely, then with a tentative smile as she wrapped her legs around him; and they made love, at first tenderly and then with great vigor. He felt her back arch and her body shudder through a series of climaxes as she clutched him to her with closed eyes. Yet he also felt a curious distance between them, despite their closeness earlier in the day. There was something unfulfilled in their love-making; and afterwards, when she lay beside him stroking his face, he sensed that she was crying.

5 | Budapest

THE CELL was suffocatingly hot, but Sarah still woke up shivering. She did not know how long she had been locked up. At intervals a hatch in the door opened and a small metal tray was pushed in—it always contained a plastic mug of water, black bread, and a piece of sausage. At longer intervals the light in the ceiling was dimmed and she slept. She suspected that the light was dimmed more frequently than every twenty-four hours and that she was being deliberately confused about the passage of time; but there was no window so she had no way of checking.

Occasionally she broke down and wept, but mostly she was surprised how calm she felt. As she lay on the gray foam mattress, she passed the time by trying to remember poetry or do calculations in her head. Sometimes she thought about her father and her own life—or just stared blankly at the ceiling.

After what seemed like two days, she was getting used to the routine, to the boredom and the slow passage of time. Her calm was shattered when suddenly, without warning, the door opened. She heard a rattling of metal outside the cell and looked up, expecting another tray of food. Instead, the door swung inward and two burly women entered, both dressed in blue uniforms. One had a sergeant's chevrons on her sleeve. Sarah shrank back in panic; at last something was going to happen and, whatever it was, she was terrified.

The women closed the door and, unsmiling, handed her a bundle of clothes. They stood back and it was clear that she was meant to get dressed. She was embarrassed at being watched by the two women guards, and her inner fear made her movements shaky as she put on white bra and pants and a blue cotton dress that was curiously demure in design. It had long sleeves and a high neck, with a white lace ruff—and it fit quite well. The sergeant held up a small mirror and handed Sarah a brush; she stroked her fair hair a few times, noticing in the mirror that she looked quite presentable, despite feeling that she badly needed a bath.

She was marched down a corridor and into an office, which had high windows overlooking a courtyard. It was a pleasant room with a table covered by an old-fashioned embroidered cloth on which stood a vase of flowers, a pot of coffee, and a plate of small chocolate cakes. They made Sarah sit down at the table and an elderly white-haired man sat down opposite her, his eyes twinkling kindly. Suddenly a flash bulb popped and she turned toward it instinctively as it flashed again.

Then she realized that someone had just engineered a photograph of her in a pretty dress in what looked like someone's drawing room, when she had just spent two days naked in a prison cell—they hadn't even bothered to give her shoes, the bastards, knowing that her bare feet would be hidden by the tablecloth. Bewildered, she shrank back in the chair and felt hot tears of impotence and fear rising. "Where am I?" Her voice was a hoarse whisper. "I don't understand what's going on. For God's sake—what are you trying to do to me?"

The white-haired man smiled gently. "First give me your name, please."

"Sarah—Sarah Cable."

"And your address?"

"I live at Himmelstrasse 49, Grinzing, in the Nineteenth District of Vienna." She wished she could stop weeping.

"And your father is the British ambassador to the United Nations in Vienna, Sir William Cable?"

"*Mr.* William Cable—yes he is."

The elderly man smiled again. "Thank you." He pushed a typewritten sheet and a pen toward her. "Now perhaps you would just sign this piece of paper—and then maybe you would like some coffee?"

She blinked at the paper, a white smudge through her tears, and felt her hands shaking. "What are you asking me to sign?"

The white-haired man shook his head sadly. "The paper is in

English," he said. "You may read it. It is a statement about your illegal entry into this country, an apology for the heroin you were carrying—and for your attempt to sell it to students here in Budapest."

Sarah was still trembling, but suddenly her fear gave way to a surge of anger. "You bastards," she breathed. "So I'm in Budapest, am I? Illegal entry? I was bloody well *kidnapped*. Heroin? What a filthy thing to suggest."

"Sign it!" he shouted.

It was the wrong thing for him to do—she bridled and ripped the paper in two, astonished at her own fury. "I'm not signing anything and you have no right to keep me here!" Her courage faltered as she sensed the two large women moving in behind her. "I demand to see someone from the British Embassy—at once."

"You will see no one until that paper is signed. You are *helpless*, child—no one knows where you are. We can do whatever we like with you." Her arms were gripped roughly and a cold eel of fear turned in her stomach. Suddenly she was too terrified to speak.

"Sign it—or we shall have to make you." He spoke softly, but his voice was full of menace. "There is nothing to be gained by trying to show how brave you are, Miss Cable. I do advise you to save yourself unpleasantness. If I recall correctly you are only nineteen and have no experience of life. These two women are much stronger than you and not so young and pretty—they would *enjoy* exercising a little violence on a girl with a body like yours."

"Go to hell." She forced the words out through dry lips.

She was wrenched backwards and pulled through the door, screaming, "Stop it, you bitches! Let me go!" She struggled violently, but the two women were too powerful for her. She was dragged helpless down a flight of stairs, her heels banging on every concrete step with a sickening stab of pain.

They threw her to the floor outside a metal door and stood back, looking down at her with arms folded. Sarah struggled awkwardly to her feet and faced them with a defiant expression, her body aching all over. The sergeant's mouth twisted into a grotesque smile. They seized her again and she felt the dress ripped and her other clothes being torn off. Then she was naked and one of the women was holding her as the other opened the door. Her arms were twisted behind her at an excruciating angle and she bent forward sharply, trying to escape the pain; she felt a heavy blow on her back and shot forward into a darkened cell.

As she landed, the floor seemed to scorch her arms and legs and she recoiled upward, to crack her head on a ceiling barely four feet high. The door clanged shut, leaving her in total darkness. Gingerly, she knelt down again; when her knees came into contact with the floor she realized that it was made of steel, icy-cold and painful to touch—that was why it had seemed to burn. She winced and her breath drew in sharply. Inching over to the wall in the dark, she found that it, too, was made of steel.

In a few minutes she was shivering and could feel her body becoming rapidly colder. It was terrifying. Surely you could die in a place like this? She could not find any position that was not agonizing. The least painful was to crouch, resting on her knees and elbows, keeping the rest of her body off the floor, although she did not think she could stay like that for long. She clenched her teeth in an effort to stop them chattering. Something in her said that she must not break down, or she would be lost, but then the dull ache of cramp began to grow in her arms and legs and her elbows gave way. She collapsed on the floor, sobbing helplessly and whimpering with pain.

* * *

After Skilbeck's angry departure, Cable spent most of the day in his office at the embassy. It was a large room, overlooking the Reisnerstrasse, furnished with a mahogany desk and six green leather armchairs arranged around a coffee table. The furniture was heavy and ambassadorial; it would have been quite an impressive office, if it had not all been so old and tatty.

Usually Cable found it a pleasant place to work, especially when sun was pouring in, as today, through the high windows with their dark blue curtains. Its pretentiousness amused him, for he was only a counselor with the personal title of ambassador. But today the room felt like a prison cell, as he shuffled papers automatically, snapped at his secretary, and stared at telegrams with sightless eyes. Why the devil was he holding back from reporting last night? It had been an outrage—anyone else would have gone straight to the police. He stood at the window, watching the pairs of policemen patrolling this street of embassies. Their green uniforms were shapeless, consciously eschewing the country's heel-clicking Nazi past, but their backs were straight and their Schmeisser machine pistols were all carried at the same angle of well-trained readiness.

The truth was that he was *afraid* to report it. Ever since his capture in Vietnam and the hatchet job done on him by Stuart, there had been a question mark against Cable's name. It was unjustified, but it was there—and there was no escaping the fact. If he reported this odd incident, he knew that somehow it would be turned against him. Old enemies would bring up old questions and it would be a short step to reopening the court of inquiry. It had taken him nearly thirteen years to rehabilitate himself—to get back to a half-respectability so fragile that it could be destroyed overnight. It would not matter that he had never been disloyal; after Vietnam he had lied to them to save his reputation and his career—and somebody in Moscow could prove it. The bastards had him over a barrel.

Every hour that passed made it more difficult, for a report of his kidnap should have been made last night, as soon as he was released. It was going to look very odd when he made it hours, a day, two days late. And then there had been the row with Skilbeck, which was bound to be remembered, demanding information that he didn't need to know—information that would help an enemy. Two steps toward treason; and they had been terrifyingly easy to take.

The day was broken up by lunch with Laszlo Kardos. Cable's car took him into the First District, the old town, a warren of cobbled streets clustered around the spire of the cathedral. Kardos had booked a table at the Salut, a small French restaurant. His host was already there, at a scrubbed wooden table with a red- and white-checked cloth, in a corner under the beamed ceiling. With his merry eyes and full black beard, Kardos looked like the *patron* of a bistro in provincial France, not a Jesuit representing the Vatican diplomatic service.

The two men had met at a reception during Cable's first month in Vienna, striking up an instant rapport. Perhaps it had been because they both had pasts in which they had been more tested than they were now, and closer to the heart of things. Vienna, by comparison, was a diplomatic backwater; Austria is a small country and the United Nations enclave in its capital markedly less important than UN headquarters in New York.

Cable liked Kardos, although the priest always made him feel somewhat inadequate. He was Hungarian, a concentration camp survivor, who had been ordained in the Stalinist occupation just after the war. He had worked in a slum area of Budapest until arrested and tortured by the AVO, who had kept him in jail under harsh conditions for five years. His life had been saved by the 1956 uprising, when Father Kardos had been released by his jailers so that he might plead for their lives. It made no difference; most of them were dangling from lampposts outside the prison, some still writhing slowly to death, when Kardos was borne away by the mob. Two days later he had stumbled across the frontier at Andau in the stream of refugees into Austria, an emaciated thirty-year-old in a patched cassock, only hours ahead of the Russian tanks.

And here he was nearly thirty years later: a worldly priest who had become a pillar of the Vatican diplomatic service, a monsignor who had served in Rome, Washington, and Brazil before returning to Europe ten years ago. He beamed at Cable and poured him a glass of red wine. "A Bordeaux, my friend, light and fruity—it would go well with the *entrecôt bordelaise.*"

They chatted on over a rich lunch chosen by Kardos, but Cable was preoccupied and ate little. He listened politely as Kardos emphasized the Vatican's concern for the subject peoples of Eastern Europe. "Although I am accredited to the UN, Bill, you must all realize that much of my work is devoted to improving conditions in the Soviet satellites. I would not be here otherwise; I would sooner be a parish priest than a diplomat."

Cable almost choked. "Are you *sure*, Laszlo? There can't be too many Viennese clergy who lunch at the Salut."

Kardos boomed with laughter, making heads turn in the restaurant. "In a parish I shouldn't *need* the Salut so much. There would be other compensations. But to business, my friend—I am not spending Peter's pence on you for nothing."

"You never do, Laszlo—what can I do for your mysterious masters in the Vatican?"

"They are concerned, as you know, about the proliferation of nuclear weapons in the world."

"You have always made that very clear, but supposedly only the five great powers have them."

"What about Pakistan, Bill?"

"Pakistan?"

"We read in the newspapers that other states than the original five are developing these weapons—and that Pakistan is actually on the verge of exploding its first atomic device. Is that true?"

"I don't know any more than you see in the papers."

"Come now, Bill—I don't believe you. You are your country's ambassador and I am not asking out of idle curiosity. If the Holy See is to use its influence effectively, we need to be well informed —as well informed as you and the United States or the Soviet Union."

Cable chewed a piece of steak, distracted by his own thoughts but trying to concentrate.

"The Vatican lacks an intelligence service," continued Kardos. "But I cannot believe that the combined resources of yourselves and the United States—not to mention Australia, Canada, and New Zealand—have not given you a very accurate idea of exactly what point Pakistan has reached. Are they halfway there, nearly there— or could they actually explode something?"

"I'm just our man at the UN, Laszlo—no one tells me that kind of thing."

"I doubt that, Bill—but let us not quarrel about it. We would simply like to know as much as you and your allies are prepared to tell us. No more, no less."

"Have you thought of asking the Pakistani ambassador?" Cable smiled mischievously. "Or Chima, that shifty nuclear attaché of his—the one the Americans call Chima the Bomb?"

"I am *serious*, Bill. Would you be kind enough to consult London and see what can be revealed?"

"Certainly I will—but I'm not sure you're going to be told much. This is strategic information."

Kardos shrugged. "We shall see. At least you can assure your masters that the Vatican is not going to war with Pakistan—our intentions are strictly honorable." He gave a deep, rumbling chuckle. "We have even signed the Non-Proliferation Treaty!"

Cable smiled bleakly, but said nothing.

"So that is my message, Bill. Now—what about you?" He studied Cable with concerned eyes. "You don't look your usual robust self, my friend, if I may say so." Cable sipped his wine nervously, coming close to confiding his problem to Kardos, for he had a desperate need to share it—and he often felt he could trust the priest more than his own colleagues in the British Embassy. But he held back, making small talk instead until it seemed decent to excuse himself, soon after two-thirty. He was driven back to the embassy, reflecting that, much as he usually enjoyed Kardos' company, his message could have been conveyed in a short phone call and Cable wondered why he had been wined and dined so extravagantly.

He decided to leave the office early, to get a few hours to himself before that evening's dinner with the Japanese, to make a firm decision on what he should do. He was putting papers into his briefcase at four o'clock when Skilbeck came in. He spoke abruptly. "Could we have a word downstairs, Bill?" "Downstairs" meant a small, stuffy room two floors below that was the property of the intelligence staff. It had no windows, double-padded doors, and was guaranteed bug-free. They sat down on the two upright chairs by the metal table and Cable heard a security guard closing the outer door.

"I did what you asked, Bill." Skilbeck's face was opaque. He sounded neither annoyed nor apologetic. "The DG agrees that you should be indoctrinated for my operation."

Cable nodded. "I see."

"Well—it's what you wanted isn't it? You'll be joining a very select group here in Vienna—there's only Barron, myself, a CIA representative, and one other, apart from the field agents."

Cable nodded again, saying nothing.

"I can't tell you any more now—to be honest I'm waiting for some of the details myself—but can you be free all day tomorrow?"

"All day? Yes, I could be."

"Okay, then take the day off. We have a planning meeting and you can come to it—then the others will know about your involvement and you'll be fully up to date. The meeting's not here—it's in Salzburg, that's why you'll need the whole day."

"Salzburg? Why? What time?"

"Two in the afternoon. We chose Salzburg to be well away from Vienna. No other reason."

"And whereabouts?"

"A safe house in Nonberggasse—number thirteen—I'll tell you how to find it. You realize you can't go in your official car."

"Yes. May I use my own?"

"It has WD.25—British Embassy—diplomatic plates doesn't it?"

"Yes, of course."

"No, you can't. Hire a car or go by train. Try and look like a tourist."

* * *

Back in Grinzing, Cable changed into some old trousers and a sports shirt and went for a walk in the woods on the Kahlenberg, high above the village. His shoes crunched on pine needles as he followed a steep path, shaded by trees from the sun, which was already low in the sky. His thoughts were still confused. Now he was going to Skilbeck's meeting and, despite agonizing all day, he hadn't yet reported on last night. A third step in the wrong direction. In his heart he knew that he ought to come clean now and risk the consequences, but perhaps he could play it low key. No dramatic phone calls—he could just write a report and send it to the Security Department in London. That would avoid the awkwardness of talking to Barron and would help to fudge the question of his delay. So why the devil was he delaying? He shied away from the question.

He came to a break in the woods and looked down at Grinzing, nestling around its onion-towered church at the foot of the vineyards. Beyond lay the city, the spires of St. Stephens and the *Votivkirche* marking the old town, dwarfed by high modern buildings rising on the outskirts. In the silence of the forest, he again heard that menacing Slavic voice: . . . . *if you cooperate, we shall leave you alone for the rest of your life. If you don't, we shall ruin you. . . . Golitsyn, Hanoi, 1971.*

6 | Vietnam—1970

CABLE'S VILLA in Saigon was a low white building, French colonial in style. It stood in a tree-lined avenue and behind the house was a wide, shady veranda looking down into a lush green garden. The illusion of suburban tranquility was disturbed only by the high chain-link fence, topped with barbed wire, which surrounded the villa—and the sounds of artillery and explosions forever in the distance.

He arrived in June, when it was intensely hot and humid. It felt strange to be parted so suddenly from Judith and the children. He missed them all—the two girls, he noted sadly, more than their mother—but settled down to his single life remarkably quickly. Two Annamite girls looked after the villa, tiny birdlike creatures with delicate olive features above their white tunics. They kept the place spotless, produced food and iced drinks, did the laundry, anticipating his every need. He felt that if he had taken one of them to bed, she would have satisfied him with the same unemotional oriental efficiency. The Australian Embassy paid the bills and Cable was driven to work in an air-conditioned Chevrolet, as befitted a temporary lieutenant colonel. Apart from the constant danger, it was not an uncomfortable life.

The office building he used was a concrete slab on the edge of the embassy quarter. It had no nameplate by the door and everyone knew it belonged to the CIA. Cable's room had veneered mahogany furniture; next door was his Vietnamese assistant, Tho Hang. Tho was tough and wiry, intelligent, with very grave eyes. He had been a South Vietnamese army officer, the garrison commander in a small border town taken by the North Vietnamese People's Army three years before. His four children had died in the shelling and his captors had made him watch his young wife kneel to be beheaded before marching him off for interrogation. A few days later, the column had been ambushed by South Vietnamese troops. Tho had been released and flown south. Because he spoke English, they made him an intelligence officer. Unlike most Vietnamese, Tho rarely smiled.

Now he and Cable were walking, slowly and economically in the heat, through a slum area of Saigon. Tenements rose high on either side of the alley, crisscrossed by lines of washing high above the heads of the jostling crowd. Little groups of Vietnamese sat chattering in doorways, an old woman squatted in rags begging, there was a foul stench from thick brown water running down the open drains.

The crowded alley decanted the two men into a wide French boulevard and they sat down outside a cafe, shaded by a red umbrella. Cable wanted to talk—and he was certain that his office was bugged, probably by the South Vietnamese and the Americans, as well as by the Vietcong. Speech outside the cafe was well masked by the roar of traffic and the occasional burst of automatic fire from a bombed site farther down the boulevard. God knows who was shooting at whom; if it was more than a hundred yards away you ignored it.

The Vietnamese sipped his *pastis* and waited, studying the broad-shouldered European. Cable had an honest square face, handsome in a rough kind of way, blue eyes firm and confident. Tho Hang liked, even admired, him. Cable paid the waiter and leaned back, his white shirt showing sweat stains on the chest. "We're not doing well, Sam, not well at all."

Tho had been nicknamed Sam by his previous, American, boss; he seemed flattered rather than insulted, so Cable continued the practice. "There was Phan Van Tien," Tho offered. "He got close to Hanoi's high command."

"And they shot him. He lasted only seven weeks."

Tho nodded silently. It was true. For six months he and Cable had worked with only one objective: to penetrate the military high command in Hanoi. There was a desperate shortage of good intelligence on what the twin enemies, the Vietcong and the People's Army of North Vietnam, were planning. In his heart Cable knew that the war was lost. The Americans were betraying their trust and would abandon Vietnam, but the South Vietnamese Army was still fighting. Were the communists out for a quick kill or slow strangulation? The answer could make a lot of difference, both to the military and politically.

"Boss," Tho began slowly. "I not think we doin' it right. We try get our agents into defense work, as cadres close to Giap. We ain't got so many agents anyway—and they don't have *time* for get accepted before they gotta produce. By time our boys get trusted, this bloody war be finished."

"So what should I do instead?"

"I not know, boss. If I did, maybe I get that big Yankee desk and you get my tin table." They both laughed and Cable called for more drinks.

On the way back to the office, they passed a street of shops that the Vietcong had just destroyed with a rocket. In the last few weeks the war had finally moved into the city. The rubble was still smoking and littered with bodies, bloody white bundles from which broken limbs stuck out at grotesque angles, some crushed by balks of timber. The paving was scattered with splintered glass, squashed mangoes, and the scorched carcasses of chickens, where market stalls had been blasted away. The noise of screaming sirens was deafening, as sweating Vietnamese ran from ambulances with stretchers, looking for the living.

An elderly man struggled to his feet, carrying a small girl in his arms and weeping. Her legs had been blown away above the knee: two tiny stumps of burned and lacerated flesh and bone, spurting scarlet arterial blood down the old man's white trousers.

* * *

Just inside the door of the concrete building, Cable was stopped by a U.S. Marine guard who saluted him casually. "Colonel Cable, sir. There's a gook in for interrogation downstairs. Major Maxton said maybe you wanna see him."

The Vietcong boy was very young, perhaps seventeen. He had been stripped naked and his bony limbs made him look even younger. There were bruises and lacerations all over his body— he had been brought in from the delta by a South Vietnamese unit, who had beaten him up badly. The slant eyes stared out from his close-cropped skull in undisguised terror.

It was punishingly hot in the cellar and the stench was appalling. The Marine guards were sweating profusely and the prisoner stank of urine and fear. Cable lit a cigarette to mask the smell. "What's this got to do with me?" he rapped at the American major, a Negro with rimless glasses.

"This guy's a courier, Colonel. Came all the way down the Ho Chi Minh Trail with orders for those bastards out in the paddies. He was in Hanoi two weeks ago, says there's some new advisers working with Giap. Europeans."

"Russians?"

The major shrugged. "Guess so. Could be of interest to you."

"It's interesting, yes—though I don't see how it can be much help. I'll get Tho Hang to interrogate him."

The major grunted, pouring out some iced water from a green bottle. The boy's eyes pleaded with them; he had been kept without food and drink, in the intense heat, for twenty-four hours. The major spoke to him gently in Vietnamese. The boy nodded vigorously and started to cry. The major pushed him a glass half full with water and turned to Cable. "Get Tho down, then—the kid's ready to talk."

* * *

Cable turned Tho's report over in his mind for several days before the idea occurred to him. He sent a ciphered telegram to London. A week later he met David Nairn in Singapore.

* * *

Nairn was still running the East and South Asia Division. He greeted Cable affably, the row before his posting to Saigon clearly forgotten. They were back on their old Cheltenham wavelength—a curious reserved closeness. However close you were to Nairn he always seemed distant, although Cable long sensed that behind the cold exterior there was a kind heart—years ahead, he was to discover just how kind. Nairn's hair was iron-gray and his face gaunt, weather-beaten skin stretched tight over angular bones, the gauntness intensified by bushy black eyebrows jutting out over deep eye sockets. Cable thought he looked tired and ill.

They had lunched at a European club, then walked across a park to the High Commission, keeping to the shade under the trees—although Singapore was cooler than the oven heat of Vietnam.

Nairn was direct as soon as they entered the office. "I was interested in your telegram, Bill. Been thinking about it—I might just have an asset for you."

"What sort of asset? Is he expendable? Most of mine get shot after six weeks."

"Not expendable at all." Nairn shot Cable a hard glance. "You'd have to take great care of him. He's so valuable that I'm not sure we should even *risk* him on a war that was lost years ago. . . ." The soft Scotch voice trailed away.

"Tell me, David."

"You've tried bloody hard to penetrate the high command in Hanoi—and you've done no better than your CIA predecessor. Not to put too fine a point on it, Bill, the operation has been a failure."

Cable nodded agreement. "Yes, it has—I'm sorry."

"Nobody blames you—you've tried. But I think the answer may lie in these new Soviet advisers. The problem, all along, has been to recruit Vietnamese agents who could get into the inner councils. The time factor makes it impossibly difficult—they grow their cadres slowly, from children, so anyone who actually makes it to the top is likely to be loyal, or flushed out long before. But I followed up your lead and you're right—there are a handful of Russians working on the final plan in Hanoi now, with Giap and his most trusted advisers. If we could get one of *them*, we'd have instant access. Coupled with intercepts, we'd be laughing."

"And how do we get someone like that? Who are they, these Russians? Top army officers? Lifetime KGB men? You got another Penkovsky, who can get miraculously drafted to Hanoi?"

Nairn walked over to the window, studying the Chinese crowd milling down the street toward the harbor, and lit his pipe. "I have a man in Hanoi, Bill. I've had him twelve years in Moscow. I wasn't going to use him in Vietnam . . . but I could." He turned around and fixed Cable with that same penetrating stare. "I'd prefer not to. Can you make it with your Viet sources in, say, another six months? I reckon this war has another two years to go. Tactical intelligence we get anyway—it's the final strategy that matters now. But it's not *our* war, Bill. You're a temporary Aussie, remember—and it's not even their war, really. The Yanks got themselves into this bloody mess."

"I can't answer that. Maybe I'll get a breakthrough—but there's no sign of it. It's damned unlikely. Will your bloke still be there in six months?"

Nairn shook his head. "I shouldn't think so. Look—I'll give you a few days. I'll risk it if you honestly believe it's *necessary*. It has to be your decision."

* * *

They met in Singapore again, a week later, and Nairn required Cable to sign a special indoctrination memo, which was locked immediately into a safe. "Every word is Top Secret from this moment, Bill—U.K. eyes and ears only."

And so Cable became the temporary controller of Colonel Igor Golitsyn of the GRU, Russian military intelligence. Golitsyn had volunteered his services to SIS in Berlin in 1958 by dropping a note into a British diplomat's car. His first offering had been the cover names of 370 Soviet "illegals" in the West—and he had continued to be invaluable ever since. He had been sent to Hanoi three months before, in his capacity as a senior intelligence officer, with a brief to advise Moscow on the supply of arms and equipment for the campaign to end the war. He was already a confidant of General Giap and his colleagues—and, once activated, he provided Cable with a stream of gold.

For nearly a year Cable settled into an easy routine. Every day he received decoded intercepts from Little Sai Wan in Hong Kong. Every week or so they were supplemented by short-wave radio messages from Golitsyn, occasionally by copies of documents brought south by trusted fishermen. Cable was absorbed into the CIA hierarchy in Saigon. His product was invaluable, and his stock was high.

They gave Golitsyn the code name Popeye.

7 | Tokyo

IT COULD NOT last forever. For ten months Cable worked seven days a week with Tho Hang, analyzing Golitsyn's product and comparing it with other sources, mostly radio intercepts and information from minor agents. Cable had the chess player's mind common to most successful spy masters. As he penetrated the nerve centers of the enemy in Hanoi, he came to ignore the din of fighting in the suburbs of Saigon and the stench of bodies ripped open on the streets. His letters to the family also became less frequent: he was totally absorbed in mastering the plans of the enemy.

And then, without warning, Golitsyn pushed the panic button. A message came at the end of one of his radio transmissions: deciphered, it read SILENT BUDDHA 71. It meant that Golitsyn wanted a face-to-face meeting on the seventeenth of the month—and that he was able to travel to Japan for it. Cable was relieved that, even if Golitsyn was in trouble, at least he was still free to move about. There were twelve prearranged rendezvous and times for panic meetings—one in Hanoi itself. But there was little likelihood of a Western intelligence officer making that one, just as it might prove difficult for Golitsyn to get past the ban on Russian officials entering Hong Kong or Singapore. Japan was the nearest neutral ground.

* * *

Cable took an American military flight to Taiwan, then Cathay Pacific to Haneda airport outside Tokyo. He stayed overnight in the Fairmont, a small comfortable hotel by the moat of the imperial palace and close to the British Embassy.

The meeting place had been chosen carefully: out of the city, but a spot frequented by Western tourists, so that two Europeans would not attract much attention. Cable plunged through the rush-hour crowds at Tokyo central station, past the barrier manned by gray-uniformed ticket collectors clicking their punches incessantly like a plague of crickets, and took the express to Kamakura. Stepping from the humid platform into the icy air-conditioning of a first-class Green Car, he settled back in the red plush seat for the hour's journey.

The little resort was eerily quiet after Tokyo. Cable left the station and walked down to the sea, pausing from time to time under the trees to check that he was not being tailed—but the street was always empty. He turned right along the front, past the groups of young men playing handball on the beach and the separate groups of Japanese girls in bikinis lazing in the spring sun. The Pacific rollers broke in flurries of foam on the sand.

The shrine of the Daibutsu, the Great Buddha, was in a leafy garden a little way back from the sea. Cable walked below the flowing oriental roof of the gateway, down an avenue of cherry trees heavy with pink and white blossom. The Buddha sat in the lotus position on a stone plinth at the end—a great greenish-bronze figure some forty feet high, staring down at him through half-closed eyes.

He recognized Golitsyn from the photographs he had seen—a tall, thin man in a blue tropical suit. He was sitting on a bench, in the shadow of some dark green Japanese pines. Cable sat down beside him, quietly reciting a sutra:

"The light pervades
All the world . . ."

The Russian turned to him:

"And all who see it
Will be saved by the Buddha."

Cable smiled. "Good to meet you, after all this time, Popeye. I am Peter. Were you followed here?" He spoke in Russian. Golitsyn looked startled. "Good God, I hope not. I'm a dead man if I was." He had a thin, wary face and there was fear in the eyes behind his rimless spectacles.

[48]

"I think we're safe enough here." Cable was disturbed that his most valuable asset had such a terrified look about him. "You've done well, Igor, very well. Your material is invaluable and London is very pleased with you." He meant to sound reassuring, but knew that the words sounded trite.

"Good." The Russian looked away from Cable, suddenly distant. "Peter—if that is what I am to call you—I have never asked for a crash meeting like this before. I am taking a grave risk by coming here—you understand that?"

"Of course. We know you must have a problem."

"Yes, I do. I have a very serious 'problem' as you call it, so serious I should perhaps not return to Hanoi."

Cable looked puzzled. "What's gone wrong—surely you're not under suspicion?"

"It is possible. I think my access to papers may have been restricted—and that is not the only sign."

"Is this something sudden? You've never had anything like this before, in all the twelve years you've been helping us?"

"No—I have often felt anxious, of course, but there has never been any reason to believe that I was suspected. Now I feel something."

"Won't you increase any suspicion there might be by coming here?"

Golitsyn shook his head. "No, I had legitimate business at our embassy in Tokyo—that is why I chose it. I had to meet my GRU general." For the first time he smiled, wryly. "Like many of the *nachalstvo*, the 'fat cats,' he prefers the comforts of Tokyo to the hard life in Hanoi."

"Why were you meeting him?"

"That is the other reason for my concern—he says there is a possibility of my being ordered back to Moscow. But why withdraw me *now*, when the war is coming to a climax and the Soviet liaison team is so important in Hanoi, to ensure military supplies for the army and the Vietcong? I don't like it. I don't like it at all."

Cable asked more questions and they talked on in the shade of the trees, awkwardly—like a pair of ex-lovers meeting by chance or a divorced couple arguing about maintenance. He could not make up his mind whether Golitsyn's fears were genuine or whether his nerve had cracked under the stress of living a double life for twelve years. It was vital to draw the right conclusion. If Golitsyn was about to be blown, he should be offered sanctuary in the West. On the other hand, that would destroy him as a source—and he was a well-established top agent. It was Cable's job to keep him in place for every last week that he safely could. Eventually he said, "You have a family in Moscow, don't you, Igor?"

"Yes. There is Yelena and two children. If I stay here, what will those bastards do to them?"

"Do you *want* to stay here, not go back to Hanoi?"

Golitsyn looked furtively over his shoulder, at the empty avenue of cherry blossoms. Suddenly his calm was gone and his voice rose almost to a scream. "Of course I don't want to go back—my nerves are in tatters and every minute I fear arrest! But I am worried, desperately worried, about my family." He turned on Cable, his eyes vulnerable and pleading. "You bastards have taken twelve years of my life. I cannot stand any more and I think someone is onto me. For God's sake, you owe me my life back! Can't you get us out? Get us *all* out?"

Cable wondered what Nairn would have done. "Slow down, Igor," he said soothingly. "It's barely half an hour since I knew you had this trouble. Does your wife know. . . ?" He paused awkwardly.

"That I'm a *traitor?*" Golitsyn spat the word. "No, she does not. If she knew, her fear might give us both away. We are both secret Christians, but that is all."

"Can you communicate with her? Securely?"

"We write letters—I expect they are opened. Phone calls are difficult—and probably tapped. I might just get a letter carried back by a comrade and delivered personally. But he might just hand it over to GRU security. . . ."

"Yes, I see. In that case I think it would be better for my people to contact her in Moscow . . . we can find a way of doing so. It is spring and she could take the children to a Black Sea resort like Sochi. Possibly we could lift them off from there by boat. I'd have to get approval from London, of course."

"Possibly?" Golitsyn's tone was bitter, full of anger. "*Possibly?* It had better be more than possibly—and to hell with London's approval! I met Nairn once in Helsinki—he said he was called Maxwell, but I knew it was Nairn—and he said 'when the day comes, Igor, just ask and we'll get you all out.' Well—the day has come. So you bloody well keep the bargain—get us out, get us *all* out!"

Cable put his hand on the other man's shoulder. "Don't shout, Igor—you'll attract attention. I hear you. Now let's just be calm and practical—what about *you*. Can you still leave Hanoi easily? This time you have been summoned to Tokyo—how difficult would it be without an official reason?"

Golitsyn's anger seemed to subside and suddenly he sounded despairing again. "For me—at the moment I am free to come and go as I please. If they arrest me . . ." He shrugged. "I would still be happy if Yelena and the children were safe."

"But you *can* still just go to the airport and get a scheduled flight out?"

"At the moment—yes. There are not many 'scheduled flights' from Hanoi but I think I could still get a local flight to Vientiane or Bangkok quite easily."

"And how safe are you to go back?"

"How the hell do *I* know? I'll take the risk to get my family out. I suppose they may be watching me, without a firm conclusion that I am an agent—in that case I should be free enough for some weeks." He shrugged again.

"Right." Cable stood up decisively, walking to the gate of the shrine with Golitsyn beside him. "Go back and stick it out for another two weeks. Leave the family to us. We'll tell you by radio which day to leave and we'll lift your family out simultaneously. Until then just carry on as usual."

"You can deliver that?"

"I have the authority—yes."

"And we'll have a home in England or America? An income? Protection?"

"You know you will. We promised that right at the beginning."

The Russian's eyes looked moist as they shook hands. "Thank you," he said to the man who could save him or leave him to die. "I don't know your real name—just 'Peter.' "

"That is enough. You can trust us."

Cable watched the Russian board the green tram back to the station, his angular height standing out among the short Japanese. He hoped he would have as much courage, if ever he needed it.

* * *

Cable took a Pan American flight back to Taipei, where he went to the U.S. Air Force office to ask for transport back to Saigon.

The major in charge examined his identity papers. "Okay, Colonel Cable, we godda Galaxy goin' down wid a few other guys in half an hour."

The ungainly transport aircraft took off late in the evening, with six American officers, a New Zealand journalist, and Cable huddled on mailbags and crates of tank spares in its hold. After a time most of them dozed, for there was insufficient light to read and it was too noisy to talk. Cable did not sleep for a long time, his mind going over and over his encounter with Golitsyn. Had he done the right thing in sending him back to Hanoi? Only time would tell. In the end he, too, began to feel drowsy and closed his eyes.

He woke up with a start as the plane rocked sharply. The deck tilted again as the Galaxy banked and Cable had to cling to a girder at the side of the hold to avoid sliding downward. His eyes adjusted to the dim blue light. At the front one of the flying crew was squatting on the ladder from the flight deck, being berated by the New Zealander, who was wedged against a pile of crates strapped to the floor, swaying from side to side as the plane rolled.

"What do you mean—Gulf of Tonkin?" the New Zealander was shouting. "What the hell are we doing over the bloody *Gulf of Tonkin?* You must be hundreds of miles off course. Goddammit, we're in North Vietnamese airspace—and unarmed!"

The crewman shrugged, spreading the arms of his quilted flying suit, and said something inaudible. "Cameras?" roared the New Zealander. "What the hell do you mean, cameras? D'you mean those motherfuckers in the CIA got their infrared junk strapped under this crate? This is a spy trip and no one fuckin' told me? Jesus H. Christ!"

Cable and an American pulled themselves over to the ladder. "What's going on?" asked Cable calmly.

The airman was young, barely twenty, and had a crew cut. "We're being attacked by North Vietnamese fighters, sir. The captain is taking evasive action." He scrambled back up the ladder before he could be asked anything else. At that moment the aircraft was rocked by an explosion somewhere near its tail. The lights went out, but the plane banked again and began to climb. The roar of the engines became deafening, but even so Cable could hear the clatter of tracer shots outside. He clung to a girder, feet wedged against a crate, as the plane yawed up and down sickeningly. It was terrifying, being confined in the dark, knowing that the battle outside might destroy them at any moment.

There was another explosion. An arc of red-hot splinters lit up the cabin for a few seconds, revealing the white faces of the others, full of terror. Shards of torn metal whistled past Cable's head. Another explosion. A scream of agony. The acrid smell of burning and the hold was full of choking smoke. The deck slanted downward abruptly, and Cable could feel the damaged aircraft gathering speed as it descended. He tensed for the impact of another explosion, his eyes smarting in the smoke, which was forcing its way down his throat painfully. A man was groaning somewhere nearby.

The engines had stopped and the noise of the wind outside rose to a scream; Cable was pressed backward by the force of the descent and prayed that he would pass out before the crash. Then he felt as if his body was being ripped apart as the stricken aircraft suddenly slowed and pulled out of its dive. By some miracle the pilot had regained control. Two minutes later there was a sickening impact, then another, and the shriek of rending metal as the plane bounced on soft ground.

Someone managed to open a door at the side of the hold and Cable leaped out with the others, landing with a splash in shallow water. He ran from the wreckage looking back to see that the Galaxy had plowed into a paddy field, its tail crackling with yellow flames. As the fire spread forward, the heat was fierce on his face and the glow lit up the small group of Europeans huddled together on a bank in the paddy.

There were no other aircraft to be seen in the vast dome of black sky overhead, but the grinding of gears and two yellow headlights, dim under blackout shields, showed that a truck was approaching them down a track. A large man in a flying suit spoke. "Seems we lost that dumb Polack, Jablonski, and the New Zealander in there." He jerked a thumb at the aircraft, now crackling in a wall of orange fire. "Now that's the army coming. So just give yourselves up nice and easy. No heroics. Name, rank, and number. Be polite, but they ain't entitled to more than that. I'm the captain and I'll do the talking, if any of them speaks English. Just take it easy and wait for Uncle Sam to get us out. All rightey?"

The truck stopped and a file of soldiers climbed out, wearing bamboo helmets and carrying rifles with fixed bayonets. Two carried old-fashioned oil lamps, but the paddy was still illuminated by the blazing aircraft. Cable stepped forward to be made a prisoner of North Vietnam.

8 | Hanoi

THE CAMP was a collection of wooden huts, thatched with palm leaves and surrounded by a double wire fence and watchtowers. The dozen prisoners were lined up before a table where a young woman in the high-necked gray tunic of a cadre sat in the open air, a black umbrella on a pole shielding her from the blazing sun. When it was Cable's turn she looked up at him with implacable hostility, slanted eyes unwavering under the peak of her forage cap, and held out her hand.

"Your identity documents." She had a sharp high-pitched voice and spoke English with the stilted precision of one who has learned it from books. Cable pulled the damp wad of papers from his shirt pocket and handed it to her. He had left his civilian jacket in the burning aircraft, fearing that if he appeared in civilian clothes he might be shot out of hand as a spy; his white shirt and light brown trousers had the look of a uniform.

The woman recorded his name, rank, and service number on a list. "Cable?" she queried. "That is an Australian name? You are a lieutenant colonel in the Australian Army—yes?"

"That's right."

She wrote something in Vietnamese script by his name and pointed at a hut door, through which all the previous prisoners had vanished. "Go there."

"May I have my papers back?"

"No."

Cable shrugged and walked into the hut, followed by two soldiers carrying AK-47 assault rifles in a threatening manner. An elderly man in a white apron was standing by a low stool. He gestured and Cable realized that he was supposed to sit down. He did so, his taut muscles reminding him that the stool had been made for people at least a foot shorter, and felt the man cutting off his hair with blunt scissors that pulled painfully at his scalp. He kept his face impassive, but flinched when the barber lathered his head with tepid water and began to shave it with a scratchy cutthroat razor. Cable heard the guards leave, presumably to fetch the next prisoner, and the old man began to speak in French, as he wiped the razor on his apron and stood back to inspect his work. "I used to do this for the Sûreté commandant when the French were still here, you know—always the head, sometimes also the neck for those condemned to the guillotine. Nothing changes." He chuckled quietly, gesturing Cable to leave by another door.

* * *

Cable never saw the men he had landed with again. For two days he was locked in a narrow cell and given no food except a few grains of rice, which he ate with his hands, and a cup of dirty water. On the third day, two impassive guards took him from the cell into a yard, where about thirty other prisoners were already standing in a line, handcuffed together in pairs. A long chain was shackled to the steel links of each set of handcuffs, so every pair of men was tied to the couple in front. They wore the rags of United States Air Force and Navy uniforms and their ankles had been bolted into leg irons; most of them were gaunt, emaciated, their skins showing the chalky pallor of long imprisonment.

Cable was handcuffed to the last prisoner and felt irons being clamped around his ankles. He tried to smile at the man he was now chained to, a small fellow of about thirty with horn-rimmed spectacles. "Where do you think we're going?"

"I hate to think, buddy, I hate to think." He spoke in a flat, hopeless tone. "If it ain't Noo Yoik, I ain't interested."

"What's your name?"

"Chuck." He did not ask for Cable's name in return.

"I'm Bill."

"Yeah? Hope you're having a good time, Bill."

An old Czech Tatra truck was driven into the yard, its sides showing rust through the yellow and brown camouflage paint, and the file of men climbed up into it, awkwardly because they were so hobbled with chains. The guards urged them on with fixed bayonets, sometimes drawing blood and seeming to enjoy it. The prisoners squatted on the floor of the open truck and it set off through the gates, down a road of beaten earth, a plume of dust rising behind it. The road ran through paddy fields and Cable looked curiously at the figures of women in black pajamas, working knee deep in water and bent double to tend the rice shoots. Their heads were shielded from the sun by wide straw hats and he wished that his had been too, for it was oppressively hot and he could already feel the crown of his shaven head beginning to burn. The air was suffocating—so sultry that sweat was coursing down his body, making his shirt and trousers wringing wet. They passed a village of thatched huts on stilts, and several water buffalo drawing plows across paddies that had not yet been planted. Except for the red-brown hills in the distance, it looked very much like the south.

He guessed that the other prisoners were the crew of bombers that had been shot down—the Americans had been bombing Hanoi and Haiphong heavily in recent months. The men did not seem to know each other—probably they had been chosen for that reason, to keep their solidarity to a minimum—and they chatted desultorily as the truck bumped along. They fell silent when they came to the outskirts of a town, shrinking from the hostile gaze of passers-by, each man alone with his fear.

Soon the narrow cobbled streets were jammed with a noisy throng of people: peasants hurrying home from market with empty produce carts, anxious to get back to their huts before the blazing heat at midday, soldiers on bicycles, tiny Vietnamese schoolchildren in straw hats, porters pushing through the crowds with baskets of chickens or vegetables hanging from bamboo poles, which cut into their shoulders. The truck passed a stretch of water surrounding two islands on which there were temples. "Do you think that's the Lake of the Restored Sword?" Cable shouted, above the din of the crowds and traffic, to the man to whom he was handcuffed. "If so, this must be Hanoi."

"Yeah, I guess it's Hanoi." He sounded uninterested, almost catatonic in his terror.

Then they were passing through an area ravaged by bombing: acres of rubble and the charred remains of wooden buildings. Rough shanties of oil drums and canvas had been erected among the ruins, close to the circular mouths of one-man air-raid shelters, concrete barrels sunk into the ground along the sides of what had once been busy streets. There was an overpowering smell of sewage and putrefaction, as if there were still decaying corpses buried under the rubble.

They stopped in a modern street lined by a large, silent crowd. At intervals, stands of bamboo scaffolding had been erected. Soldiers with fixed bayonets prodded each pair of prisoners out of the truck until they were lined up behind it, the chain shackled to a ring in the tailgate. The truck started to move forward slowly, with the file of prisoners shuffling behind it. Cable could feel the waves of hatred from the crowd and the silence was eerie.

Suddenly a piece of concrete was hurled at the first pair of prisoners and struck one of them on the head. The man stumbled, blood oozing from his scalp, and fell—to be dragged along the cobbles by the chain attached to the truck. It was like a signal. Cadres with megaphones started to scream slogans, in stilted American phrases, and the crowd chanted them in imitation. "Pigs! Murderers! Hang the imperialist murderers!" The chant rose to a wild, intoxicating roar of hate, a mob baying for blood. "Hang the killers of our women and children! Make them bow their heads in shame!"

More missiles were hurled at the file of prisoners—bricks, garbage, broken bottles. Several more fell and the soldiers ran beside them, jabbing them with bayonets as they were dragged along with the flints of the road flaying the skin from their bodies.

Cable felt something soft strike his face and realized from the smell that it was human excrement; then something hard and sharp hit his temple with such force that he collapsed to his knees, blinded by blood. As he struggled back to his feet, deafened by the howling of the mob, a guard struck him viciously in the stomach with his rifle butt and he bent double, coughing. "Kowtow, Yankee," screamed the crowd. "Kowtow, you butcher of children! Hang your head in shame!" As Cable tried to straighten up, a bayonet jabbed between his shoulders and he felt it cut into his flesh, so that he remained bent double with blood trickling over his shoulders until the bayonet was twisted out, which made him cry out in pain.

When nearly all the airmen had been brought to the ground, the howling rose to a crescendo and the mob closed in—kicking, stamping, gouging, and tearing at them. Cable was horrified to see women and young children among them, spitting and scratching at him as his shirt was ripped away; then he fell and his body jerked and twisted convulsively as a dozen feet smashed into his stomach and groin, which exploded into searing agony.

Eventually the crowd fell silent and began to disperse, as if someone had given an order. Cable lay on the ground bleeding and panting, seeing for the first time the stand on which European television crews were packing up their cameras. The prisoners all lay or crouched in the dust, no one speaking, each man shattered and solitary in his pain and humiliation. Cable knelt up and reached over to the young airman called Chuck, to whom he was still handcuffed. The man was doubled up, sobbing. As Cable touched him he flinched and screamed with pain. He turned over and Cable recoiled at the sight of his face. The horn-rimmed spectacles had been smashed and the sharp pieces of lenses ground into his eyes, which were now sightless, bloody sockets.

9 Hanoi

"So sorry," said the cadre, his voice high and thin. "You are an Australian soldier, not an American pilot—it was an error that you were included." Cable nodded, knowing that it had been no error.

After being beaten up in the street, he had been taken away, separately from the others, to the old French Sûreté jail in the heart of Hanoi. There he had been thrown into an underground cellar, still manacled and in leg irons, and left without medical attention or food. A bowl of water was on the floor, so that he could drink from it like an animal. He stayed there in the dark, nauseated by the smell of his own filth, for what seemed like two or three days. Some of the time he was mercifully unconscious, waking to a body racked with bruises and cramp.

Then it all changed. The cell door opened and he emerged blinking in the light. He was half-carried to an upstairs interrogation room, where the cadre was waiting for him, immaculate in his high-necked gray tunic. His face was round and youthful, almost effeminate, although his hair was gray and he moved like a man of fifty or sixty. He gazed at Cable for some time with a look of implacable stillness, then smiled. "My name is Tran Van Thieu. Would you like a shower and something to eat?"

Now it was a week later and they walked in the garden of a temple several hours drive from Hanoi, lush with palm, banyan, and orange flame trees. The temple was surrounded by a moat, crossed by spindly wooden bridges, and had a curving Chinese roof of green pantiles supported by red-lacquered pillars.

Thieu picked a green papaya and offered it to Cable. His interrogation so far had been gentle, but he was becoming more pressing. Much of the day they sat on the veranda of the government guesthouse in the grounds of the temple, just the two of them, the guards with their khaki uniforms, green forage caps, and AK-47s discreetly in the distance. Thieu spoke good, if somewhat sibilant, English. He said that he had once been a student at the London School of Economics while working in the kitchens of the Strand Palace Hotel.

"Colonel Cable." He picked a papaya for himself and bit into it delicately. "You really must cooperate a little more. This war is bleeding Vietnam to death and the sooner it is concluded the better. Through an unfortunate error you have experienced the feelings of our people as the barbaric Nixon and Kissinger send B-52s to rain bombs on our women and children . . . to bomb a country with almost no aircraft to defend itself."

"I cannot help you. I am a prisoner of war—you have no right to ask me."

Thieu smiled again. "Please, Colonel Cable—may I call you Bill? We have walked in this pleasant garden for several days now. You are an officer of the British intelligence service, masquerading as an Australian colonel. Under the rules of war you could be executed." He spread his hands wide in a graceful gesture. "But let us not talk of such things. You have caused us great problems and I think you owe me something for rescuing you from that stinking cellar."

"I am a prisoner of war—I should not have been in that stinking cellar in the first place."

They had stopped, standing to watch two long-necked cormorants diving to fish in the waters of the moat. Normally Thieu followed the conventions of Vietnamese politeness and did not stare directly into Cable's face, but suddenly he met his eyes and snarled viciously, *"Which Russian is the traitor?"*

"I don't understand your question."

"Yes you do." After the glimpse of the suppressed violence behind Thieu's oriental stillness, he was calm again. "For God's sake stop playing with me. We have a delegation of twenty Soviet officials and military officers in Hanoi to assist our high command. One of them is *your* man. His code name is Popeye—we know it. Which one is it?"

"I don't know of any Soviet agent in Hanoi. Sorry—I don't think you understand how humble my duties were in Saigon."

"Then you don't deny that such an agent exists?"

"I didn't say that—I don't know, one way or the other."

"For the thousandth time, Cable—what was the purpose of your journey to Tokyo?"

"Official consultations about the war—I can't tell you more, but it was nothing important."

Thieu's normally impassive face showed more than a hint of irritation and Cable noticed a pulse twitching just above one of his almond eyes. "You are being foolish," he snapped, leading the way across a wooden bridge into the door of the temple, which was guarded by two stone lions.

Cable followed him inside, stopped in horror—then struggled to show no emotion. The temple was an empty shell, containing nothing except a chair in one corner. A man was slumped on the chair, held by two guards. His body was shrouded by a white smock and his face was unrecognizable, a puffy mass of blood and bruises, but Cable knew that it was Golitsyn. His gray hair had turned white and there was a look of naked terror in the eyes that stared out through slits in the swollen face: he had been appallingly tortured, but still had enough control to show no sign of recognition.

"I believe you are old friends?" Thieu spoke almost inaudibly.

Cable swallowed, suddenly feeling unsteady on his feet. "Who is this man? Why did you bring him here?"

"You *know* who he is. We *know* that you know. Stop lying."

"If you know so much, why keep asking me?" Cable fought to keep his eyes from the destroyed creature in the corner, the man of courage whose body and mind had been torn apart by electricity and pincers and head screws and God knows what else while he, Cable, had walked in this green garden. But, if he denied all knowledge, there was a thin chance that he might yet leave sufficient doubt . . .

"Stop lying!" For the second time Thieu raised his voice. "I merely require your confirmation—he has already confessed." But Cable sensed that this was untrue.

"I do not know this man." Cable turned to leave the temple, but two guards with AK-47s barred the door.

Tran Van Thieu faced Cable with contemptuous eyes. "You will save your Russian traitor nothing, Cable. We know everything and, when our Soviet friends are satisfied that the full extent of his treachery is clear, we shall dispose of him in a traditional Vietnamese manner."

"I said I do not know this man."

"He is Colonel Igor Golitsyn!" screamed Thieu. "And you are his controller! Confess it and then we can talk in a civilized fashion about what is to be done. You—I promise—will be freed and sent back to Saigon very quickly."

Cable resisted the hint to negotiate about Golitsyn's fate; clinging to his training on resistance to interrogation, he remained impassive and silent.

"Very well—take them both away!" Cable was seized by the two guards and frog-marched outside. His last glimpse of Golitsyn was of a lacerated body as the smock fell aside while he was being lifted onto a stretcher by his guards. He would see him only once again.

*   *   *

Golitsyn was carried to the guesthouse and laid on the floor of a bedroom, guarded by two soldiers. In the course of the afternoon a large Russian limousine arrived carrying two Europeans who conferred for some time with Thieu. At about five o'clock they shook hands and left, with the ambivalent air of priests of the Inquisition handing a heretic over to the secular arm. As their car bumped down the red-dirt road, one of them opened his briefcase and drew out a bottle of vodka.

The temple stood on an island in a small lake, surrounded by a walled garden. The guesthouse was a building with a curling Chinese roof of red tiles, the eaves ending in a snarling ceramic dragon at each corner; once it had housed Buddhist monks. Behind the temple, part of the garden was laid out very formally, with trimmed shrubs and gravel paths in the shape of the Chinese character for eternity. Here there was a plain building which had not been used for many years. It was square, with gray stone walls, a gold roof, and, unusual for Vietnam, a chimney. Inside it was a single bare chamber surrounding a large rectangular block covered in white tiles with bronze doors at one end, a few feet above the floor. It was a Buddhist cremation oven.

As the evening progressed, the sun sank low behind the distant outline of the Annamite Cordillera, its jagged peaks thrusting high into a darkening purple sky. The air was still hot and the guards were sweating as they loaded wood and charcoal into the furnace. When they lit the fire it crackled into fierce orange flames and they shrank back from the intense heat.

Four soldiers carried Golitsyn from the guesthouse, still wearing the bloodstained smock and tied with ropes to his stretcher. The stretcher-bearers paused at the door of the crematorium, then advanced slowly at a nod from Thieu. Golitsyn's eyes started in terror and he began to scream when he saw the open bronze doors and the fire blazing in the furnace.

Cable stared in horror from his place in the corner, the weight of his body pulling on the ropes which bound him to a similar stretcher, propped against the wall. An hour before, he had been taken from his room, stripped naked, and beaten with rifle butts for thirty minutes. Then they had dressed him in a loose white smock, tied him to the stretcher, and carried him into the heat of the crematorium.

He wanted to shout something to Golitsyn, to show that he was not totally alone as he died, but one of the guards struck him viciously on the face the moment he opened his lips. Cable closed his eyes in pain. When he opened them the roar and crackle of the flames filled the small building, weird yellow light dancing on the walls. Golitsyn's whimpering rose to a piercing shriek of agony as his legs were pushed slowly into the red-hot charcoal, his body bucking violently against the ropes that bound it to the stretcher. When his hair caught afire he gave a long, hideous cry, the inhuman laughter of a madman, as the air was forced from his tormented lungs and the bronze doors were closed behind him.

The stench of burning flesh filled the chamber and Cable felt hands seizing the handles of his stretcher. He saw Thieu's face looking down at him with a bland smile. "And now, Cable, it is your turn."

*　*　*

In England the tall, gaunt man in a dark suit walked slowly from Teddington Station in the mild spring evening. When he came to Langham Road he strolled under the lime trees until he came to a house that needed painting and rang the doorbell. The woman who answered it was in her thirties and had an Australian accent. Her eyes were opaque with tiredness and her manner offhand. "Yes— what do you want? I'm just putting my children to bed."

"You must be Mrs. Cable?"

"Yes—what of it?"

"I'm David Nairn—from Bill's office."

"Oh God—what's happened?"

"May I come in?"

They sat in the untidy kitchen, drinking mugs of instant coffee, while the two small girls squabbled around their feet. "I'm sorry the place is such a mess," said Judith aggressively. "I can't cope on my own. What did you say—Bill's been captured? I thought he worked in an office. He's not a bloody soldier." She did not sound unduly interested and Nairn wondered whether even news of Cable's death would have penetrated her depression. She half-listened as he told her what had happened, explaining that the Foreign Office would ask for more information from Hanoi, but that her husband might stay a prisoner until the end of the war. Every few minutes she screamed at the children. "Lucy! Sarah! For God's sake stop fighting. If you can't share the bloody dolls' house I'll give it away!"

After half an hour Nairn left, leaving his home and office phone numbers and asking if he could return in a few days to see what else he might do to help. Judith shook her head. "I shouldn't bother—I'll still get paid every month won't I?"

"Of course—and if the allotment isn't enough we'll increase it or help out some other way. We want to do everything we can for you while Bill's a prisoner of war."

"I'll manage. I've had to ever since he went away. Christ—what sort of husband would go away and leave us in this dump? I don't think he gives me and the girls a second thought. He only lives for his bloody job, not for us, and I hate it." She burst into tears as she opened the front door for him.

*   *   *

Cable stared at the furnace in disbelief as they carried him toward it, his mouth clamped in a rigid line. Every muscle in his body tensed as the heat played on his legs and he could feel the soles of his feet blistering. He closed his eyes.

But then the heat lessened and he heard shouting above him. With a desperate surge of hope he opened his eyes and looked around. The bronze doors had been closed and Thieu was leaning over him. At first Cable could not make out the words, his mind a whirlpool of terror and confusion. Slowly, incredulously, he began to realize that the agony he expected was not there, that he was still alive and could hear Thieu's mocking questions. "Do you want to save yourself, Cable? Or do you want to burn?"

Cable answered with his eyes, his lips moving but making no sound.

Thieu smiled in victory. "There is a price."

*   *   *

Back in the guesthouse it was soon done. Cable sat at the red lacquered table, still wearing the white smock, which showed dirty bloodstains from his beating, and read the two typed sheets. They were in English: a simple statement naming Golitsyn as a British agent, with details of his recruitment and of services he had rendered. It even said that Golitsyn's wife was not involved and asked for her not to be maltreated.

"What happens if I sign this?"

"We don't burn you." Thieu gave a contemptuous smile. "I thought that was clear."

"But how can I trust you? Suppose I sign it and you just . . ." Cable's hands were shaking as he held the sheets of paper.

"What use would you be to us dead? I have talked with a high cadre from Moscow and you have nothing to fear. Just sign it. You will be taken back to Hanoi and then to a camp for a little road building in the sun—but you will be released in less than a year, to resume your life in the West and your highly successful career in your intelligence service."

"And . . . ?"

"And one day we or our Soviet friends will require your cooperation."

"Supposing I don't cooperate?"

Thieu's face worked viciously. "Then they will see that you are denounced as the traitor who betrayed Golitsyn to save your own skin! Your people have just lost a most valuable agent, Cable, but they have no reason to suspect you. So long as you keep quiet about today, you will be safe enough. Only if they are ever given that statement will there be trouble—and then you will be finished." He smiled again—his changes of mood would have been alarming even if Cable had still not been in a state of confused terror. "You will have to see that it remains a secret, won't you?"

Cable picked up the pen hesitantly, then put it down again. "The oven is still alight," hissed Thieu.

Shortly after he had signed the statement Cable was pushed into the back seat of a rusty Voiga car—all the vehicles in the north seemed to be at least twenty years old—and driven off, sitting between two guards holding assault rifles. The car drove north along the coast road, passing empty beaches of dazzling white sand fringed with coconut palms. Sampans and batwinged Chinese junks floated lazily on the azure sea. Cable stared out of the open car window, clinging to the passing beauty for his sanity, knowing that in a few hours he would be back to the cruel realities of hunger, pain, and fear. At that moment he hated himself.

10 London

CABLE LEFT HANOI nearly a year later, in an American military aircraft sent to bring back a batch of sick and wounded GI prisoners who were being released after negotiations by the Red Cross. The flight was timed for midnight so that it would not be witnessed by North Vietnamese troops and civilians, the airfield in darkness, except for hissing yellow flares immediately around the aircraft. The weak light showed a grim procession of men on crutches or carried on stretchers into the cabin. Their clothes were the rags of combat dress and most had a distant, shell-shocked look—eyes opaque, unable to admit the pain, deprivation, and degradation they had suffered.

Hardly anyone spoke on the flight to Taiwan. The aircrew handed out cigarettes and chocolate, which made some of the ex-prisoners vomit after their months or years on a thin diet of rice.

There was no hero's welcome for Cable. At Chiang Kai Shek Airport, Taipei, he was separated from the others. A man he didn't know, who said his name was Ryder and that he represented the service, met him and led him through a side entrance guarded by hard-faced Chinese Nationalist police to a suite of rooms in the terminal building. He showed Cable into a room where some Western clothes were laid out on a couch; a shower room was visible through a communicating door. "Hope the gear fits, squire. I'll leave you to rest for a few hours. We fly out to London at ten tonight."

Cable felt exhausted after the march to the airfield and the uncomfortable flight. "You know, Ryder, I'd sooner leave it twenty-four hours—I think I need to adjust a bit before I face the family. Would you rebook me, please, and find us a hotel for the night?"

"Can't do that, squire. My orders are to escort you straight back to London."

Cable bridled. "What's the bloody hurry? I've been locked up in that stinking camp for ten months—one more night's not going to make any difference."

Ryder shrugged. "Maybe they want to give you a medical check—or a medal." His tone was ironic, almost insolent, and he walked out before Cable could respond, banging the door behind him.

Cable stood nonplussed for a moment. Who the hell did this Ryder think he was? On his rapid rise through the service, Cable had never been status conscious, but suddenly he felt threatened, anxious to establish with this oaf that he was dealing with an assistant director of the department, a temporary lieutenant colonel who had just survived ten months of hell at the hands of an enemy—somebody who bloody well *mattered*. He strode to the door, but to his fury found it locked from the outside. Then he saw himself in the full-length mirror on the wall, a shrunken figure, hollow-cheeked, eyes sunk in his close-cropped skull. His thin, bony ankles stuck out below coarse prison trousers, his feet still in wooden sandals soled with strips of old rubber tire. He sat down heavily on the bed, trembling and feeling close to tears.

* * *

They landed at Heathrow at seven in the morning, after a weary fifteen-hour flight, and were met by two silent men who drove them to a safe house near Box Hill. Cable was too tired to protest and lay down on the bed in the room he was shown to, falling asleep at once with the thought that he would phone Judith and go home to Teddington later in the day.

When he awoke he had a shower and dressed in clean clothes from the wardrobe, except for the same ill-fitting blue suit from Taipei. There was a pleasant formal garden outside the window. The door opened, with no knock, and Ryder entered. Cable felt a flash of irritation—how the devil did this prat know he was awake? Was he under some kind of surveillance? The time had come to assert himself. "Ah, there you are, Ryder. Perhaps you'd get me a car. I want to phone my wife and go home now."

"You can't." Ryder's tone was unapologetic, indeed openly insolent. "Stuart's here to see you."

Cable looked puzzled. "Stuart? Why? What's my coming home got to do with him?"

"He's been head of personnel for nearly a year."

"Good lord, has he—I didn't know." Cable disliked Clive Stuart. He was a little runt of a man, who had joined the service just after Cable, scraping in with some difficulty despite a public school background—which contrasted uncomfortably with Cable's easy brilliance and working-class origins. Once Cable had thought they were friends and about seven years before he had used his closeness to Nairn to protect Stuart when a messy divorce and depression requiring psychiatric treatment had threatened his career. About a year later Nairn had taken Cable out to the Spanish Patriot, a pub near the office. "Be careful, Bill, that man's a shit. He used you when it suited him—but now he sees you as his main rival for the top and never misses a chance to stab you in the back. He wants the top much more than you, *much* more—and he'll ruin you to get it."

Cable studied a rose bush in the garden. So while he'd been a prisoner, Stuart had gotten himself promoted. Why the hell should he let that bastard see him like this—with his prison haircut and cheap suit on a shrunken body? Should he just walk out? No, he would prefer to give Stuart an earful for the lousy treatment he'd been given since reaching Taiwan. "Okay," he snapped at Ryder. "Take me to Stuart. I can give him half an hour before leaving."

Ryder gave a crooked smile. "This way, squire." He led the way down a corridor and opened a paneled door.

Cable strode through the door purposefully and stopped in his tracks. It was a large room, a library, furnished with a long oak table. Stuart's small frame sat behind the table, with two men on each side of him. The table had a very formal look, with carafes of water and piles of blue crested paper; there was a single chair on Cable's side of it.

Stuart looked up, unsmiling. "Hello, Bill. This is a court of inquiry, set up to examine your conduct while seconded to the Australian Army in South Vietnam, and then as a prisoner of war in the Socialist Republic of North Vietnam. Please sit down."

Cable gripped the back of the chair in front of him and remained standing, wanting to sound aggressive, but conscious only of shock—and of his hunger and exhaustion. "Court of inquiry? What the hell do you mean? I've just got back after ten months as a prisoner of war. I'm ill and worn out and I'm going home to see my family. I don't have to answer to you for anything—I'll call on the chief in a day or two." He turned around sharply, only to find that the door had been locked.

He turned back furiously. "What are you bloody well playing at? I've been getting this kind of crap ever since I arrived in Taiwan—and I've had enough of it. Open this bloody door and find somebody else to play with!"

"I said sit down, Bill." Stuart sounded pained but firm. He was acting his part to perfection—he'd already put Cable hopelessly in the wrong. "We all want to *help* you, Bill, but a report has to be made. The chief doesn't want to see you—he has commissioned *me* to conduct an inquiry, in particular into the arrest and execution of Igor Golitsyn, one of our most valuable agents for many years. We just want to get at the truth, Bill." He smiled with all the sincerity of a hungry crocodile.

Cable sat down slowly on the straight-back chair, shaking with anger. "This whole procedure is disgraceful," he rasped, his throat dry. "If I'm supposed to have something to answer for, I should have been given proper notice of it. You can't just launch into an inquiry like this. I'm entitled to be accompanied by an advisor and I object to you personally as chairman."

"Did you *need* notice, Bill?" sneered Stuart. "Do you *need* an advisor—an advocate? A lawyer perhaps? What do you have to hide? If you really insist, you can remain in custody"—he paused meaningfully—"while we find someone to hold your hand."

Cable said nothing. He knew that Stuart was confusing him into acquiescence; every second he stayed would make it harder for him to walk out, but he was too weary to resist. "On my left," Stuart was saying with self-conscious formality, "are representatives of the Security Service and the Ministry of Defense. On my right a representative of the Foreign and Commonwealth Office and John Leslie of our own service."

"Don't the others have names, then?"

"There is no need for you to know them."

"Why not? What have *you* got to hide?"

Stuart suddenly banged his fist on the table. "This is an official court of inquiry, Cable"—it was no longer "Bill"—"kindly treat it with respect. Now shut up and listen while Leslie presents the case against you. Don't interrupt—you can ask questions later."

Cable thought how much he would like to punch in Stuart's little rat face. He said nothing as the nightmare continued, with Leslie—whom he recalled as a crony of Stuart's—shuffling papers and starting to speak. Cable listened, appalled, at the tirade of twisted fact and falsehood directed against him:

incompetence in a key post . . . gross errors of judgment . . . questionable expenses . . . hazarding a key agent who had risked his life for years in our service . . . betrayal of that agent when captured yourself . . . how else was Golitsyn's conduct proved . . . how else do you come to be released at the suggestion of the enemy? . . . we did not ask for you to be given special soft treatment, early release . . .

Leslie made it sound as if nearly a year of dysentery, which reduced you from 168 pounds to 112 and destroyed your confidence as a human being, was some kind of privilege. "And *why* have you been sent back so soon, Cable?" His voice rose in contempt. "Another George Blake, perhaps? He was in communist hands somewhat longer, but that was twenty years ago. No doubt techniques for conversion have improved. What is your secret brief from your new friends, eh? Blake got forty-two years—remember?" He paused, menacingly. "If you come clean, we might be able to avoid criminal charges."

Cable stood up. "I've had enough, Stuart," he said quietly. "I'm not sitting here to be insulted, to have my loyalty questioned by this shit after what I've been through while you've all been safe at home."

"Very well, Cable." Stuart spoke in a pained, superior tone. "You do not help yourself by insulting the court, but I am prepared to adjourn the inquiry until nine tomorrow morning." He pressed a button on the desk and two heavily built men came in. "You will be brought back here then."

Cable walked out between the two guards. He knew he was powerless to resist.

* * *

The ritual continued throughout the next day, with Leslie slowly tracing the events of the past two years, implying at every turn that Cable was at best suspect—at worst a traitor. Several times Cable demanded the use of a telephone and an interview with the director-general. Each time, Stuart refused abruptly. Despite a night's sleep, Cable was still exhausted and found it difficult to concentrate. His attention wandered constantly.

On the long flight back from Taiwan, he had concluded that the best thing would be to be open about signing Thieu's statement—and to explain why. Surely no one could blame him; and if he'd confessed it, no one could blackmail him either. But faced with an inquiry that was obviously hostile and out to destroy him, his resolution faltered.

"Did you see Golitsyn after your capture?" demanded his interrogator.

"Yes."

"Where?"

"At a disused Buddhist temple outside Hanoi."

"At a *temple?*"

Cable shrugged. "It was being used by their security people—Golitsyn was being held there. He'd been badly tortured and they confronted me with him."

"Had he confessed?"

"I don't think so."

"Why don't you *think* so?"

"Because Thieu was pressing me so hard to admit that Golitsyn was our man."

"Which you did, didn't you?"

"I did nothing of the sort!" shouted Cable angrily. "I thought there was a slim chance of saving him if I insisted he was unknown to me. I never admitted he was our agent—I never admitted *I* was either."

"You're quite sure you didn't confess him as our man? Perhaps from the best of motives—to save him from further torture, perhaps? That would be understandable—even humane. No one would blame you—we just want to get at the truth."

Jesus Christ, thought Cable, they must think he was naïve. He leaned forward and spoke very slowly, fighting against a wave of tiredness, "I did not—repeat *not*—admit that he was our agent."

"So you kept quiet and let them torture him?"

"He had been tortured already, before I even knew he had been arrested. He wasn't tortured after they confronted me with him."

At this point Stuart joined in. "May I clarify something?" Leslie put his papers down and Cable faced his enemy, meeting his gaze steadily. Stuart had a small, thin face with swarthy skin and black hair that gave him an almost Latin appearance. "So Golitsyn was tortured." He paused pointedly. "Were *you* ever tortured, Bill?"

The question was put in a gentle tone, but the eyes focused on him had a sneer of triumph in them. Cable could not speak. The question was loaded and demanded a positive answer. *Yes,* he wanted to shout. *I was beaten up by a mob in the street who blinded the man I was chained to by gouging glass into his eyes. I was smashed up with rifle butts until I couldn't stand and then they made me watch Golitsyn burn. If you don't call that torture, you should try it. I've known more pain and fear this last year than you'll know in your entire bloody life.* But some deep, inexorable pride intervened. He could not bring himself to admit the humiliations he had experienced to this little runt, so that he could probe and gloat over them. Cable knew it was irrational—worse, it was madness—even before he opened his mouth, but he heard the words come out, flat and definite. "No— I wasn't tortured."

Stuart looked disappointed. "Were you ever drugged?"

"No." Cable hesitated, then seized on the opportunity, a possible let-out for the future. "At least I don't think so."

"You don't *think* so?" The question was laced with suspicion and contempt. "What do you mean?"

"I wasn't tortured, but several times I was beaten up—to unconsciousness. I might have been given pentathol or something similar and questioned when I came to—I would have no recollection of that."

Stuart gave a snort of disbelief. "For God's sake—just give me a straight answer. Are you saying that you did not admit that Golitsyn was our agent? At any time? In speech or in writing?"

"Yes—I am saying that." Vaguely Cable knew that he had been driven into a fatal lie, but he was too confused and exhausted to care.

"Never?"

"No—never."

* * *

In the evening, Cable was locked into his bedroom and brought a meal on a tray. He heard the sound of cars crunching on the gravel and driving away, guessing that Stuart and his stooges were leaving for the night.

After about an hour, he had decided what to do. The window

was, as he expected, screwed shut from the outside; but the panes of glass were large. The room was on the upper story of the house, but the window gave on to the sloping tiled roof of some kind of extension. Cable gathered the blankets from the bed, rubbed soap from the wash basin all over the lower window pane, and pressed the blankets hard against it. He rapped hard with his shoe all around the edge of the glass. Some of it shattered on the tiles outside— with a noise that sounded, in his tense state of mind, like the clang of a burglar alarm—but most clung to the fibers of the blankets. He drew the blankets and glass back, dropped them to the floor, and scrambled through the empty frame, feeling a sharp cut and warm blood trickling down his calf.

Slithering down the tiles, he felt himself falling in space, then landing on the soft earth of a flower bed.

He sprinted across the lawn, oblivious to the pain in his leg. There was no sound of pursuit—the house behind him was largely in darkness. He came to a high wall and could see in the moonlight that it was too high to climb and topped with barbed wire. Cursing quietly, he walked swiftly along the path inside the wall until he came to an equally high wooden gate, beside which was a small hut with a light burning inside. Before Cable could decide what to do, a figure sprang from the hut holding a revolver and shouting, "Hey—stop! How the bloody hell did *you* get out!"

Cable launched his emaciated 112 pounds at the man, sensing that it was Ryder, and put all his strength into a neck punch with his balled fist. There was a sharp cry and Ryder slithered to the ground. Cable stepped back, panting from the exertion—and realizing that if the blow had failed he would not have the strength to repeat it.

His luck was in—there was a large iron key in the gate, which swung open silently on well-oiled hinges. Cable stepped outside, turning to lock the gate behind him, and tossed the key into a hedge. He was in a village street, which ran down toward the lights of a busy road, the Dorking bypass.

There were still no sounds of pursuit as he arrived at the main road, turning north toward Leatherhead and trying to thumb a lift as he walked. After five minutes a truck drew up and the driver stuck his head out. "Where yer goin', mate?" he bellowed above the roar of traffic.

"London."

"Okay—take yer t' Kingston. 'Op in." Cable scrambled up into the big cab, full of blue tobacco smoke and the din of Radio 1. He was dozing when the driver shook him awake half an hour later. They were at the gates of a timber yard near Kingston bridge. Cable waved good night to the driver and staggered across the bridge, wondering how to complete his escape with no money. He hailed the yellow light of a passing taxi and got into the back before the driver could turn funny about the fare. "Hartington Road, Chiswick," he said firmly.

* * *

The taxi waited outside the riverside block of flats, its meter clattering noisily, as Cable climbed the concrete stairs to the door he was looking for and pressed the bell. After a long interval the door was opened by a gaunt middle-aged man in a shabby green cardigan; he stared over his gold-rimmed, half-moon spectacles in astonishment.

"Good God, Bill Cable. What on earth are *you* doing here? I thought you were still resting up in Taiwan. You're bleeding—have you been in a fight?"

Cable looked down at his torn trouser leg and the stain of dark blood. "Can I come in?" he said to David Nairn.

11 | London

AFTER NAIRN'S INTERVENTION, the court of inquiry continued, but the atmosphere was changed. Stuart was carpeted by the director general for going behind Nairn's back—for Nairn was still the operational director for Southeast Asia—and for confining Cable like a prisoner at Box Hill. Nairn sat in on the inquiry, as the chief's personal representative.

It was no surprise when a report was produced exonerating Cable. It noted his own insistence that he had resisted interrogation while a prisoner-of-war, although he could not know what had transpired when he had been given drugs. It noted the leaks from Eastern bloc embassies, suggesting that Cable had betrayed Golitsyn—Stuart had seized on these with glee. But if Cable had been turned, insisted Nairn, why leak the knowledge to his own organization—surely he would be of more use in the future if he were still in a position of trust?

But if mud is thrown, a little always sticks, however unjustly. There would always be a question mark against Cable's name, for he had been subject to interrogation by an enemy; and he was blown as an intelligence officer. He could not stay in the service, and within a month of his return he was summoned by the chief to be told just that. They sat, awkwardly, in armchairs in a corner of the director general's office on the top floor at the Cut, furnished with rosewood antiques and looking out across the river to the Houses of Parliament. Sir Ian Walker was a Scot, like Nairn, and noted for his terseness. "I'm sorry about this, Bill," he said, looking out of the window, not at Cable's face. "But you'll have to go."

"You've had nearly sixteen years from me, Ian—it's the only profession I know."

"Aye, well—not quite, Bill. I'm arranging for you to transfer to the regular diplomatic service, you know that life well enough. I'm afraid you'll lose your promotion to AD—they'll take you in as a first secretary—but you're only thirty-eight. You can make a new career there if you've a mind to."

Cable's face was rigid. "When does all this happen?"

"You leave here today and go on leave for a month—give you time to sort yourself out. Report to FCO personnel department on the first of March—I expect your first posting will be in London."

Cable nodded; it seemed impossible that a way of life he had followed for so many years would be over in a few hours.

"Oh—and, Bill . . ."

"Yes, Chief?"

"The Australians recommended you for the Military Cross for what you did—before and after your capture—in Vietnam. You ought to know that—but I had to turn it down, of course."

Cable was stunned. "Why 'of course'? . . . I don't understand."

"I'm sure you will, Bill, if you think about it later. You've been quite lucky, you know. Now have a good break—and good luck in your new job." He stood up and shook hands formally, with none of the old camaraderie he had shown when Cable had been a valued adviser, a man on the up escalator.

Cable walked to the lift slowly, suddenly sick and shattered to realize that he was no longer trusted—that Walker suspected him. He had not been given a job and an office since the inquiry, so there was nowhere to go but home. He took the train from Waterloo to Teddington.

* * *

At the house in Langham Road, the two girls eyed him with suspicion. In two years they had half-forgotten him and had learned from their mother to blame his absence for the turmoil and unhappiness of their home. Sarah was now seven, slim and athletic, and Lucy, five—a chubby little girl with a huge smile and the same warm nature he remembered from Paris. They both looked remarkably beautiful to him as they bounced around in pajamas.

Judith was sitting in the kitchen eating slices of bread thickly spread with morello cherry jam, which dripped crimson down her chin; although the central heating was full on, a fan heater poured out heat near her thin ankles. She always went for warmth and food when depressed. The sink was full of greasy dishes; and dirty plates and saucepans covered every flat surface.

Cable had been wondering how to break the news of his sacking to her; now, as he looked into her lifeless eyes, he knew that there was no point in even mentioning it. He felt a sense of tearing inner regret at the wreckage of their marriage—and knew that despite Judith's negative outlook and recurring depression, both of which had always been there, it was mostly his own fault. She could not cope with a husband whose job took up so much time and nervous energy—let alone one foolish enough to go away for two whole years. She was so switched off that she could hardly cope with just being alive, let alone with any kind of responsibility. He had always known it and had been mad to think it would somehow come right in the end.

He put his arm around her shoulders. "They're changing my job, Jude—I'm going to stay in London now."

"There's nothing to eat," she said. "You can go to the Chinese takeout if you want something. I don't much care."

He tried again, sweat running down his chest from the heat in the stifling room. "Jude—I'm trying to say something. I'm not going away anymore."

She shook his arm away, spreading another slice of jam. "It's too bloody late for that—why don't you just piss off again?" She started to weep, with loud, snorting sobs that racked her whole body.

Sarah put her head around the kitchen door. "Get out!" screamed Judith. "Can't you see I'm talking to Daddy?"

"Sorry, Mummy." The child bit back a tear and looked at Cable, eyes frightened under her fringe of fair hair. "Daddy," she said hesitantly. "Will you read us a story?"

*   *   *

It was too late, as Judith had said, but they stuck it out for nearly a year. There was no longer any love between them; Cable's feelings for her fluctuated between compassion and anger. The bitterness that had become part of her soul was always near to the surface, an insuperable barrier between them. If he had not been so troubled about the effect on the children, Cable would have walked out and taken them with him. Instead he tried to make up for

Judith's systematic neglect. He dressed the girls and gave them their breakfast before he left home in the morning; he tried to arrive home in time to bathe them and put them to bed. They had always been precious to him. Now when he looked at the pair of them sleeping he felt a love that was almost painful.

Cable commuted by train to a humdrum desk job in the Foreign and Commonwealth Office. There was nothing special about the February day when he reached home about six-thirty. Usually the children were looking out for him and flung open the front door; but this time the house was in darkness. While he fumbled for his key, a woman neighbor appeared, followed by Sarah, who had clearly been crying. The child ran to him and threw her arms around his waist. "Oh, Daddy. Our Lucy's been hurt. She ran in front of a car and they took her away in an ambulance."

"That's right, Bill," said the neighbor. "Judith's gone with her—they're at the West Mid., in Isleworth. I'm awfully sorry."

* * *

Cable drove to the West Middlesex Hospital in sheer panic, praying aloud to a God he did not believe in. "Don't let her die. For Christ's sake, don't let her die."

She looked very small—a tiny figure on a high bed in the intensive care unit. Her eyes were closed and her face looked tranquil and beautiful, but her head was covered by a white gauze dressing. One tiny plump wrist was pulled away from her body, attached to an intravenous drip. Judith was standing by the bed and Cable took her in his arms. She met his eyes reproachfully. "I couldn't bloody cope. It's not *my* fault."

"What happened, darling?"

"She ran into the road." Judith answered dully. "I told her not to, so she bloody well did."

There was a Pakistani doctor and several nurses clustered around the bed. The doctor pulled Cable to one side. "You are the father?"

"Yes."

"My name is Dr. Ibrahim. I'm sorry—but your daughter's condition is not good. The X rays show that she has serious head injuries—I need your permission for a surgeon to carry out an operation to relieve pressure on certain parts of her brain."

"Of course."

"Then please sign this." He thrust a form and a ballpoint at Cable.

Lucy was wheeled away on a trolley and Cable waited with Judith in a small white room. Three hours passed, during which they found little to say to each other. Eventually the doctor came back. "Would you like to see your daughter?"

Cable stood up. "How is she now?"

The doctor's soft brown eyes looked grave. "She is still unconscious and having difficulty in breathing, so we have put her on life support. We shall know the prognosis better after twenty-four hours. I have done what I can."

Lucy's face still looked tranquil and beautiful, but her tiny body, now in a small white smock, was dwarfed by the mass of cylinders, rubber tubes, and boxes with dials standing on chromium trolleys round her bed. Every few seconds a nurse applied an oxygen mask to her mouth and nose. Her arm was again linked to a drip.

"Can one of us stay here?" asked Cable.

"Of course," said a nurse. "You can sleep here if you like, there's a room with a bed next door."

Judith stayed first. "She's my daughter too, you know," she said accusingly, making Cable realize how much she had resented him taking over looking after the children, even though he had done it to relieve her—just as she had resented him going away to Saigon. Fundamentally she hated his failure to cure her depression and make her happy; she hated him for her own inadequacy. Whatever he did, she would be bitter.

A week passed very slowly and Lucy did not wake up. "I am somewhat concerned about her failure to regain consciousness," said the doctor called Ibrahim. "But there is no great cause for alarm yet. There is no evidence of permanent brain damage—this long period of unconsciousness may be nature's way of healing her."

It was the seventh day after the accident when Cable arrived at the hospital to relieve Judith, around five in the afternoon. She met him at the door of the room where Lucy was, her face a mask of exhaustion. "She's dead, Bill," she said quietly.

"Oh God—no."

"She died half an hour ago." Their eyes met, for the first time in months without rancor or bitterness, in sudden, shared sorrow. "Come with me and see her." She took his hand shakily.

The tiny body was lying on the bed, still and beautiful in its white smock. Lucy looked as though she was sleeping, deeply and peacefully; her eyes were closed but her mouth was smiling. Cable felt his eyes fill with warm tears and a terrible, heartbreaking grief welling up inside. Judith clung to him and they both wept.

* * *

Judith walked out, without saying why or where she was going, a month later. She wrote to him from Sydney after six weeks, asking for a divorce. Cable felt a sad relief. He explained to Sarah as best he could, early one Sunday morning, so that they would have the day to get used to it. "Mummy's not going to come back," he said, hoping that he would not break down. "She's gone to live in another country, a long way away." He put his arms around the child.

Sarah, now eight, looked solemn. "And Lucy won't be coming back either, will she?"

"No, darling. Our Lucy's dead. She died in the hospital, you remember." For a moment he almost choked as he remembered the undertaker cradling the small white coffin in his arms at the graveside, as he held Judith sobbing in her grief.

"Yes, it was very sad and I cried a lot. I loved Lucy, Dad—not just because she was my little sister—she was very *kind*."

"We all loved her—so did Mummy. Mummy still loves us all, Sarah. It's just that she wants to live somewhere else now."

"Yes, Dad." She stood on tiptoe and kissed him. "Don't worry—we'll manage. Don't cry, Dad, I'll look after you."

12 | Salzburg

THE MORNING AFTER his lunch with Laszlo Kardos, Cable rose early. By eight o'clock he was striding down the village street in Grinzing. He took a taxi from the rank by the tram terminus and an hour later he was in a train speeding along the Danube Valley toward Salzburg. Vienna was a drab place, decidedly East European, apart from its picturesque center; but whenever Cable escaped from the city he was overwhelmed by what a beautiful country Austria was. Outside the train window, pretty white villages were dotted in the lush green fields. Every other hill seemed to be topped by the pointed turrets of a castle or the many-windowed rectangle of a monastery. Soon they were in the mountains, snowcapped crags plunging down into lakes that were a sparkling blue where the sun caught them, but black and cold where they were in shadow.

* * *

Salzburg nestles in a curve of the river Salzach, dominated by a long spur of dolomite: a sheer wall of rock towering four hundred feet above the clustered houses of the old town like a protective arm. On its highest point stand the stone ramparts of the Hohensalzburg, the massive fortress built by the prince-archbishops between the eleventh and fifteenth centuries.

Cable followed Skilbeck's instructions and took the funicular rail car up to the castle, paying eleven schillings for a single ticket. At the top he had time to kill and wandered aimlessly through the tourists on the terrace overlooking the city. Cannon on heavy oak carriages pointed downward through the battlements. By one, a

[83]

young American soldier was taking a photograph of his wife holding a baby, who was sick just as he clicked the shutter. "Aw, gee, Keith," she wailed in a Deep South accent. "That's definitely wad I need—a *photograph*. You god any Kleenex?"

Cable drank a cold beer, the city spread out below him. It clustered around the green copper dome of the cathedral: like an Italian Renaissance town, a higgledy-piggledy muddle of pink and white buildings, broken up by red-tiled roofs and the spires of minor churches. Yellow trolley buses moved slowly along by the curve of the river. Above the sound of traffic he could hear the clip-clop of horses' hoofs from *fiacres* carrying tourists through the Domplatz, where a large checker-board was marked out on the paving for open-air chess, and the strains of an organ playing in St. Peter's Church just below the battlements. The irony brought a half-smile to his eyes. Aw gee, this is definitely what I need: sitting around in a castle with a lot of bloody tourists when I should be in London talking to Security Department before the Special Branch come for me with a pair of handcuffs. . . . His eyes closed as if in pain.

* * *

The meeting was in Nonberggasse, a track that wound down the hill behind the fortress, on the side away from the city. At first it ran through trees, then there were houses, perched on the slope overlooking the plain which ran to the high peaks of the Obersalzberg. Number thirteen was a gray stone building with a steep alpine roof—there were no windows to the lane. Cable knocked at the door, which Skilbeck opened at once, leading him into a sunny courtyard. Two men, obviously soldiers despite their jeans and T-shirts, were on guard with Armalite rifles.

"Not bad for a safe house," said Cable gruffly, to emphasize that he had a right to be there, whatever his colleagues might think.

Skilbeck was not bearing grudges. He gave a distant smile. "One of the best views in Austria. I'm going to apply to be custodian when I retire."

"You mean somebody actually lives here?"

"Sure—how else do you think we keep it secure? He's an Austrian who fought in the commandos all through the last war—I mean *our* commandos. His wife's from Yorkshire. They've been here since 1947, since the occupation."

They sat around a dining table in a back room and the Yorkshire wife served coffee before disappearing to leave the door firmly closed. Apart from the Britons, there was an American, introduced as Al Nosenzo, who had CIA written all over his button-down shirt, and a handsome Pole with flowing gray hair and a heavy moustache. "I am Tadeusz Rozinski," he said with a smile.

Skilbeck rapped the table in a businesslike manner. "Good afternoon, gentlemen. First may I introduce my ambassador, Mr. Cable, who is joining our group as from today? Then, before we get into detail, I must stress that the governments of the United States and Great Britain are not the promoters of this venture, but we stand ready to help in whatever ways we can." He turned to the mustachioed Pole. "It's really your show, Mr. Rozinski. I think you'd better tell us about it."

The Pole had a deep, impressive voice. "Thank you for meeting with me, my friends. As some of you know already, I was one of the early elected leaders of our free trade union in Poland, Solidarity. Once I was a professor of political economy, but after falling foul of the Party, when Solidarity was launched, I was to be found working in a tractor plant near Krakow." A glint of amusement showed in his eyes. "And it is likely that my labors as a fitter were more productive by far than anything I achieved as a Marxist economist." They all laughed politely.

"I was harassed by the authorities and arrested twice, but never imprisoned. When martial law was imposed, my comrades believed that I was one of those who might well be shot if taken away by the army—I was much less of a public person than the national leaders like Lech Walesa—so I went underground. I left Poland illegally—with my family, thank God—two years ago." He paused dramatically. "And now the time has come to return."

Cable looked up. "You mean you are going back to join the underground as some kind of Western agent?"

"Oh no, Mr. Ambassador," boomed Rozinski. "I am going back as a Pole and I am not going alone. We are going back to fight."

Cable did a mental double-take, remembering the tragic streams of refugees fleeing from Russian tanks after the Hungarian uprising and the Prague Spring. "To fight?" he queried.

"Exactly—and, unlike the wretched Hungarians and Czechs, Poland is going to win."

* * *

After the meeting Cable accepted Skilbeck's offer of a lift back to Vienna and they walked down the steep track together. Skilbeck's Lancia was parked in a space cut into the hillside at the bottom, where mountain violets and patches of moss grew in fissures in the rock. Cable noticed that the CD plates had been removed from the car—and it had a false registration number.

They were roaring down the autobahn, past the blue waters of the Mondsee, before Cable spoke. "Is this thing straight up, Paul?"

"What do you mean?" Skilbeck sounded brusque, as if put out by the question.

"I mean, is the whole thing serious? Is Rozinski really going to be dropped into Poland with less than thirty men, to start some sort of uprising? If so, I think it's crazy—you're all living in the 1930s."

"Of course it's bloody serious. Look, Bill—" Skilbeck's tone became a friendly growl, which Cable knew from experience meant that he was about to lie or become patronizing. "You wanted to know what's going on—now you do. For God's sake don't start questioning the whole frigging setup. Other people have been working for more than a year to get it right."

Cable flushed with anger. "All I'm trying to do is decide whether it's as lunatic as it sounds. So *is* it going to happen the way Rozinski said? I find the whole idea of dropping armed men behind the Iron Curtain preposterous—and bloody dangerous if it went wrong."

"Dangerous? For whom?"

"For us—the West."

The car swept past a truck, with Bulgarian plates, pulling a heavy trailer, and Skilbeck studied the road in silence for a time. "Yes," he said, grudgingly, "I suppose it could be. But you must understand, Bill, that Rozinski and his friends would be doing this *anyway*. They left Poland with the express intention of going back with arms to start unrest, if Solidarity couldn't make progress peacefully. Now, of course, Solidarity's outlawed and most of its leaders are in jail. The whole country's at boiling point—martial law didn't work. Food is desperately short, hospitals are closed for lack of drugs and because so many doctors and nurses have skipped the country—a lot of people want to hit back. Rozinski wants to take in enough arms to trigger a full-scale uprising—like '56 in Hungary."

"That's exactly what bugs me. Are you old enough to *remember* the Hungarian uprising? It was a tragedy. In the end the Russian tanks ran all over them. Just as they did in Czechoslovakia when there was a chance of the government becoming half civilized."

"So what? We didn't *make* the Hungarians revolt—they just did. We aren't *sending* Rozinski back. He'd go anyway, even if he could muster only one friend and two clapped-out Lee-Enfields. All we and the Americans are doing is giving him some decent equipment and communications—to give him half a chance. Look, Bill"—he began to speak slowly and precisely, as if talking to an idiot child—"it's nothing new. Ever since the 1917 revolution the Soviets have been a threat to us, an enemy. And Russia has always had a problem with subject states—and difficult regions within the Soviet Union itself."

"Like the Muslim republics in the south, Kazakhstan or whereever?"

"I suppose so—but I was thinking more of the Ukraine, where we've supported nationalist movements aiming at revolt ever since the last war. Maybe before it, for all I know."

"But that's comic opera stuff. Those Ukrainian nationalists are going nowhere except the Gulag. Good God, it's like all those crazy infiltrations into Albania in the '40s, hundreds of volunteers dropped by parachute, supposed to bring down Hoxha—all betrayed by Philby and shot."

"The satellites are different," said Skilbeck severely. "The Russians have a real problem there—and the biggest is in Poland, what with the Church an' all. Pretty much the whole population—even most of the army—wants to chuck out the Russians and hang the quislings."

"You mean you think there can be a successful uprising, that the army—*the army that imposed martial law*—will turn and fight the Russians? It would be pathetic—like the Polish cavalry charging the German tanks in '39."

"Maybe, Bill, maybe. But look—if your enemy has a problem that diverts him from going after you, you try to make it worse for him, not better. So we will help anyone—Poles, Afghans, Ukrainians, even bloody Martians—to upset the Russians. Maybe Rozinski will get a real counterrevolution going—he's as well placed as Lenin was in 1917, for God's sake. Maybe he'll end up in front of a firing squad. Just get one thing clear, Bill." His voice rose

[*87*]

above the engine. "Either way it's good business for London and Washington. I don't give a bugger whether he succeeds or fails. I just get him in efficiently and see that he makes a bit of mayhem. Okay?"

Cable stretched back in the leather seat. "Does he know we're using him like this—poor bastard? Do you think he has any chance at all?"

"Since you ask—yes, I fucking well do." Skilbeck's voice had a sudden cutting edge. "It's slim, bloody slim—but there's never been a place nearer to real revolt than Poland is today. It could catch fire. I really believe it could—so do London and Washington."

"I doubt it."

"Well, it's what they say." Skilbeck's tone was suddenly sober. "Anyway we'll help him, with the Americans, to put up a good show."

"And when does all this happen—when does Rozinski's private army go in? And how?"

"You don't need to know that, Bill—not yet anyway."

Cable knew that was only too true. He looked out of the window; they were passing Melk, the dark yellow walls of its Baroque monastery perched on a bluff over the Danube. He wanted to scream "Don't!" as he heard his voice, the voice of a stranger, saying, almost casually, "I think I do, Paul. Perhaps you'd get clearance to tell me." He had taken the fourth step.

Skilbeck took his eyes from the road for a moment and gave Cable a curious glance. Then he shrugged. "Okay."

13 | Budapest

SARAH WAS UNCONSCIOUS when they opened the cell. Two women guards pulled her out, her skin icy and clammy, and carried her to an interrogation room. They shook her until her eyes opened, then wrapped her in a blanket and brought in the same middle-aged official with white hair. This time he made no attempt to be avuncular and spoke curtly. "Here is your statement. Sign it." He thrust the paper and a pen at her across the table.

"No." She felt terrified inside, but struggled to conceal it.

"Do you want to go back—to go back to *freeze*—in that steel room?"

"I'm not signing anything to say I'm a drug pusher. It's not *true*. I insist on seeing the consul from the British Embassy."

"You will see *no one* until you sign that paper."

"My father is an ambassador." Now she was weeping. "I'm not signing anything that you can use to put pressure on him."

"You would be wise to sign it, Miss Cable." He banged the table threateningly. "There will be serious consequences if you do not."

"You have no right to keep me here." She bit back the tears furiously, her hands trembling.

"Sign it!"

"No—I just said *no!*" Her voice rose to a scream. "You can stuff your 'confession'—do you want me to tell you where?"

His face worked and he seemed about to strike her. Sarah was petrified with fear, but sensed that she was, in a way, hitting back—his failure to intimidate her was something for which he would be held to account. Then he stood up, abruptly. "Very well." He spat the words at her and left the room. She was taken aback and felt almost elated in her relief; she had expected to be browbeaten for hours, perhaps physically beaten or put back in the freezing cell. Then one of the guards tapped her on the shoulder and she felt sick inside as she wondered what could happen next.

The woman thrust a bundle of clothes at her and Sarah put them on: no pretty dress this time, just a black jacket and trousers of a thin, coarse material that scratched her skin. She was irritated that the two women stood staring at her as she dropped the blanket and dressed, but she tried to ignore them and pulled on the rough clothes swiftly. The shoes in the bundle were her own, brought from the Neusiedlersee.

When she was dressed the female guards took her down in a lift to an underground garage, where a prison van was waiting. One of the women smiled at her; she may have been trying to be friendly but a steel tooth gave her an ugly, sinister appearance. "You are going on a long journey," she said in carefully prepared English.

Sarah looked at the van—it was painted black and she guessed that it was what the Russians called a *tshorni voron*, or black raven. And if it was a "long" journey she must be going farther east. She recoiled as she was handed over to two guards with Asiatic features who smelled of garlic, but allowed herself to be pushed into the van and then into a narrow steel cell off its central corridor. She sat perched on the metal seat as the doors were clanged shut. The engine started and she felt the van driving up a ramp. She sat staring at the steel door, her face rigid; but then she was only nineteen, vulnerable and terrified. Her head dropped and she began to weep.

*　*　*

In Vienna, Cable was cheered to find a second postcard from Sarah in his mailbox. It was a picture of yachts tacking across the Neusiedlersee and she had posted it three days before.

At the embassy Skilbeck took him into the small secure room and opened a file. "I can tell you a bit more now, Bill. No notes of course—but you know all about that from the past."

"Yes, I do." Cable tried to sound casual, as if he wasn't particularly interested.

"The operation is code-named PIRANHA. Rozinski wanted to call it Sobieski—"

"Good grief," muttered Cable.

"After Jan Sobieski, King of Poland." Skilbeck smirked. "Who—as of course you know"—he smirked again—"liberated Vienna from the Turkish siege in 1683. Rozinski was rather taken by the idea of men from Vienna liberating Poland three hundred years later."

"This whole bloody thing is comic opera."

"That, Bill, is a matter of opinion—and your opinion is not the official one." He paused abruptly. "Well—what else would you like to know?"

"Whatever you care to tell me. For example, how exactly is this man Rozinski involved?"

"Rozinski is a former leader of Solidarity, just as he said. He's one of those who always favored a more violent approach and he escaped when martial law was imposed. He's been in Paris ever since then, planning to return and collecting a like-minded group around him."

"How big is this group?"

"Twenty-eight, some of them regular soldiers who've defected over the last year or two."

"And how, for God's sake, does Rozinski expect to get an uprising going with only *twenty-eight* men?"

"He doesn't, Bill. He has four resources. First, money—they've collected a lot, mostly from the Polish community in America. Second, arms—they've already smuggled huge caches of submachine guns, grenades, bazookas, and the like into Poland. They're well hidden—and they could arm a thousand or two. Maybe more. Third, his men here, who will spread out in small groups, like missionaries, to start violent uprisings on a prearranged plan."

"And the fourth?"

"Sheer guts—and the fact that it's Poland. A Catholic country where they all hate the Russians. Held down by an army of questionable loyalty to the government and that shit Jaruzelski. The place is tinder-dry, ripe for a bit of aggravation."

Cable sighed. "And just what is all this sudden violence supposed to achieve? You really think Rozinski can drive the Red Army back into Russia, set up a new democratic government in Warsaw?"

"No, Bill, I'd say that was a trifle optimistic. I told you in the car yesterday—he creates mayhem and the world is reminded what a collection of bastards they are in Moscow. That's a sufficient result. Maybe there *will* be some longer-term effect. Maybe they'll actually *get* a popular rising going. I don't know."

"And what do we do to help even if they *do* get a rising going?"

"We?"

"The West—the Americans, us, NATO, the European Community, and Britain."

"No one's told *me*, old chap—I'm just a cog in the machine. Maybe they'll tell *you* now that you're included—you're an ambassador after all." He gave a small, ironic smile.

"You know bloody well we won't lift a finger to help. Succeed or fail, Rozinski and Co. are all goners."

Skilbeck nodded with false gravity. "Could be, Bill. Could be."

"And what's *Kardos* up to? His name was mentioned. How does he fit in?"

"He's only on the fringe, really. As I understand it, quite a lot of priests in Poland are mixed up with Solidarity. Not the Church hierarchy as such—at least, not so far as I know—but individual clergy who also hate the Russians. They're providing safe houses for Rozinski's men to hide in. Some of them have radio sets for communications—and I think coded messages have gone through the Vatican equivalent of the diplomatic bag."

"And Kardos?"

"He's the link man here for the clergy in Poland, that's all. He's not involved in the planning. We wouldn't ask him to a meeting like yesterday's and he doesn't know any of the key details. He just helps with communications."

"Does the Vatican know?"

"I think not, although sometimes I'm not so sure."

"He's not Polish—why should he be messing about with all this stuff? If the Vatican finds out, he'll spend the rest of his life cleaning out monastic latrines."

"As I say, Bill, I'm not sure there isn't some official Church involvement—no one's told me. And our Laszlo is fiercely anticommunist—he was locked up and tortured in the '50s before he escaped from Hungary, you know. I can see *exactly* why he's doing it."

"Possibly. Where are Rozinski's men now? When do they go in?"

"I don't know when they go in and, even when I do, I can't tell you without special clearance."

"Which you've asked for?"

"As a matter of fact, yes I have." Skilbeck's eyes were showing anger and his jaw was tightening.

"And Rozinski's men?"

"I don't bloody well know. I think they're scattered about in remote places outside Vienna, in ones and twos. They were together training at a disused army camp in France up to two weeks ago. Now I think they keep on the move to avoid attracting attention. Rozinski can be reached through one of the canons at Klosterneuburg, the abbey just north of the city."

"Where do you normally meet Rozinski?"

"At the abbey, at Klosterneuburg. I believe he often stays there, with one or two of the others. It's a big rambling place with a high wall, mostly closed to the public, so it's really rather suitable. Anyway, Bill, I've told you all you need to know—*more* than you need to know—so let's leave it there, shall we?"

Cable stood up stiffly and tapped on the closed door so that the security guards would let them out. "That was most helpful." Skilbeck looked at him curiously, as if about to say something, then shook his head and went out silently.

* * *

The black Zil swept across Red Square, its tires drumming on the cobbles. Major General Kirov huddled in the corner of the leather seat in the back, for it was a cold autumn day and the car had not warmed up on the short journey from Dzerzhinsky Square. Outside, the sky was blue and the air crisp, sunlight playing on the clustered red and gold domes of St. Basil's Cathedral and the usual queue snaking toward the ugly porphyry and granite block of Lenin's tomb. A pair of newlyweds, the girl still in her long white dress, were taking the traditional walk among the fir trees by the Kremlin walls, photographed by a group of relatives.

As the car passed the Place of the Skull, the round stone platform once used for Tsarist executions, Kirov turned back to her papers. She did not notice the gray-uniformed militiamen presenting arms as she passed through the Spassky Gate and seemed lost in thought until the car jerked to a stop outside the Council of Ministers building, a red flag floating from the low dome at its center.

The general walked across the yellow gravel and through the glass doors, where her identity papers were examined by a Kremlin guard; even a high-ranking KGB officer could not pass here without a security check. She took the lift to the third floor and walked, looking pensive, down a high corridor hung with crystal chandeliers. The meeting would be difficult and there would be no one to support her—as so often she would be alone in her corner.

She was the last to arrive. The foreign minister was at the head of the table, his gray face unsmiling above the neat gray suit and dark tie. Kirov often wondered whether he had set out, early in life, to achieve the ultimate in self-effacing grayness; he had certainly succeeded. Michaelov sat on one side of the table with two men from the Foreign Ministry. On the other side was Malinovsky, surrounded by military aides, his marshal's tunic covered in gold epaulettes and medal ribbons. He was a great bear of a man, head bald above his broad Slavic face and his breath usually smelled of expensive Cuban cigars. It infuriated Kirov that he always turned up in full uniform, trying to make her look—in her neat blue tweed suit—like a housewife at her village soviet.

The military aides were ushered out into the corridor by the secretary, a fussy young man from Gromyko's ministry, and the foreign minister tapped the table. "The forty-eighth meeting of Foreign Affairs Committee G is now in session."

As for every meeting in this building, the proceedings were being recorded on tape in the technicians' room at the end of the corridor, following a procedure that went back to the time of Stalin. The technician on duty that morning was a handsome man in his thirties. Ten years before Anatoly Grechko had been allowed to attend a conference for electronic engineers in San Francisco, a special privilege for a loyal Party member in a position of trust. The homosexuality he had concealed in his own country had led to his being picked up in a downtown bar; to a night of pleasure and freedom he had never known before; and later to an interview at his hotel with two hard men from the FBI who had shown him a series of frighteningly explicit photographs of himself and his temporary friend. He had been so shaken that it had never occurred to him not to return to Moscow at the end of the conference, to his apartment, his well-paid job, and his few real friends.

Last night the girl from the American Embassy had given him a list of requirements for that week. One had been "Anything involving Major General N. A. Kirov," so, as the meeting down the corridor droned on, a second spool of tape turned on a machine beside the one making the official record. Late in the day he would put it into his pocket and drop it into a garbage bin in the basement; he was not required to risk carrying it past the Kremlin guards. He did not know how the Americans collected their tapes from the garbage, but somehow they always did.

* * *

That night Cable lay beside Naomi's sleeping form listening to her regular breathing and unable to sleep as he went over it all again and again. He had passed another evening of indecision and drunk too much brandy after dinner. He knew perfectly well that by concealing the Soviet approach he was laying himself wide open. He had let three days slip by, doing nothing to protect himself because he could not face a resurrection of the accusations of 1972, the misery of living surrounded by unspoken mistrust and suspicion.

To this day he could not explain his lie to the court of inquiry. He had done nothing shameful in Vietnam—on the contrary, he had behaved with great courage—so why the hell had he let the runtish Stuart confuse him into lying about it? But it was too late now; Golitsyn had died and he *had* lied about it. If he confessed that he was being blackmailed, all of thirteen years later, the conclusion would be obvious. Doing the "right" thing would just lead to disgrace—not to mention a trial under the Official Secrets Act that could send him to prison. He could take it—but Sarah didn't deserve that, poor kid. He shied away from the knowledge that he was systematically finding out more and more about Skilbeck's lunatic operation, subconsciously preparing for betrayal. . . . If there were seven steps to treason, he had already taken five of them. He fell into a fitful sleep.

14 | Vienna

NEXT MORNING was sunny and Cable woke to find the room bathed in bright light. Naomi was standing by the window naked. Suddenly she raised her hands, which had been resting on the hard mounds of her buttocks, and touched her toes vigorously six times—then stood erect, swaying from left to right and running her fingers down her hips and legs to the knee. He burst out laughing. "What on *earth* are you doing?"

She turned around, blushing, and laughed too. "Some exercises they taught me in the army years ago. I don't do them often—only when I feel particularly unfit." She reached for his dressing gown and put it on. "But I can't with you watching—it's obscene! I'll get some coffee instead; and then I'm taking you out for the day, Bill. Something's getting you down and you need a break."

"I can't take a day off just like that, love."

"It's Saturday, Bill. Had you forgotten? The embassy's closed for the weekend."

He shook his head wryly, running his fingers through his graying hair. "As a matter of fact, yes—I had."

* * *

They set off in his car, the green Volvo he had bought tax-free as a diplomat a year before, but Naomi drove. She ignored his bad-tempered silence as he sat beside her, staring moodily at the passing countryside. He felt edgy and would have preferred to be alone with his problems, but gradually he relaxed as she drove up the Danube. Within an hour the car was following the course of the river, on the floor of the V-shaped valley known as the Wachau. Green hills rose steeply to each side; the lower slopes covered in vineyards, thrusting up to peaks on which churches and castles perched precariously. The valley was not merely beautiful—it had an unreal, fairy-tale quality.

They stopped at Durnstein, where Naomi made him climb up the steep path, sweating in the sun, to the ruins of the castle where Richard the Lionheart had once been imprisoned. Then they drove on, higher up the Danube, to a small town where they stopped at an inn overlooking the river. Cable was still too preoccupied to feel hungry, so they lunched on mushrooms fried in bread-crumbs—and a *Viertel* of Kremser white wine each.

He gazed at a tug pulling three long barges—laden low in the water—slowly upstream, struggling against the fast current. Naomi spoke from time to time, pointedly ignoring the fact that he had been grumpy and silent all morning. They were sitting outside in the sun and she was wearing jeans with a short-sleeved check shirt, her bare forearms resting on the table, sun-burned and showing the hint of firm muscle. He reflected that it was not just her body that was strong. Even when she played the fragile girl, staring up at him with her secret smile as they made love, part of the intense masculine power he felt was induced by her; and at times like this, when he was down, her inner strength was transmitted to him like a blood transfusion.

She took out a map and spread it on the table. "What would you like to do now, Bill? Shall we go farther up the valley?" She looked puzzled. "Though I'm not quite sure where we've gotten to."

"I'll find out." Cable beckoned to the innkeeper and asked in German where they were.

"You are in Mauthausen, *mein Herr*."

Naomi started, as the man went back to polishing glasses behind the bar. "*Mauthausen*," she whispered. "Oh, Bill, I've always meant to come here—my father was in the concentration camp."

"Poor bastard—you never told me that. The camp's still here of course—it's been preserved as a kind of monument. Do you want to go and see it?"

She hesitated. "I'm not sure it's a very good day for it . . . perhaps another time?"

"Nonsense. If it would mean something to you, I'd like to share it."

They asked directions from the innkeeper, who seemed less than happy to be asked about the town's most infamous connection; but he told them to take a side road to the top of a plateau above the Danube. "Follow the signs, *mein Herr*, to the Konzentrazionslager—they say 'KZ Mauthausen.' " He gave a grimace. "You will recognize it easily enough—there is nothing else up there."

*   *   *

The first sight of the camp was a shock. The car climbed for what seemed miles on a twisting road through shadowy forest, for the sun had gone in. Suddenly they breasted the top of the hill—to be transfixed by the massive stone walls and black watchtowers of the camp. It was a bleak spot, a high plateau looking down into the quarry where the prisoners had once worked. The wind howled across it, making the air much colder than in the valley, where the waters of the Danube glinted silver far in the distance.

They drove right into the old SS garage yard, in the lee of the high stone wall—more like a traditional prison than a camp—topped by five strands of barbed wire still strung on electrical insulators. The garage doors were painted lime green and there was an empty swimming pool. "That must have been for the SS guards," said Naomi. "Wonder if they had to heat the water? They used to spray the prisoners with fire hoses, you know, then make them stand naked in the snow, in the middle of winter." She shivered.

They walked up the rock steps to the main gate and she gripped his hand tightly as they passed through it, the pointed roofs of its twin watchtowers black against a gray sky. Cable paid the required twenty schillings to the custodian, who was sheltering from the cold in a room at the side of the gate.

Inside they faced the barren expanse of the parade ground. On the right were buildings of brick and concrete—the administration block, the camp jail, the gas chambers, and the crematorium. On the left stood the rows of wooden huts, each one surprisingly long, painted in a faded green limestone wash. Their roofs were covered with torn tar paper, and ventilators stuck up from them like chimneys.

There seemed to be no other visitors and they walked through the camp alone, saying little; oppressed by the atmosphere of cruel squalor. In one hut the rough wooden bunks had been pre-served—narrow plank beds which had been shared by six pris-oners or more as the camp filled up—along with tin mugs and bare deal tables. The gas chambers were half underground, small and tiled white like a shower bath. Next door the red-brick cremation ovens waited, ash still visible through their rusty cast-iron doors, steel stretchers for the insertion of corpses lying in front of them. The walls of the crematorium were covered in memorial plaques—written in a dozen or more languages from Serbo-Croatian and Russian to Hebrew and English, reflecting the sad diversity of the thousands who had come to Mauthausen to die. Someone had placed fresh flowers in a vase on the concrete floor. To one side was a dissecting room with a stone table, slightly tilted, with a central drain slit emptying into a hole at its foot.

"For the extraction of their gold teeth," muttered Cable. Naomi shuddered.

They went on to the jail, where Naomi paused at cell number nine, its tiny window, above head height, banging in the wind from the plateau outside. "Daddy was in this cell—he told me," she said without emotion. "He was due to be executed—but he was saved by the chaos at the end of the war."

"Lucky fellow." Cable put his arm around her shoulders. "But I can't imagine what it was really like, you know. We can only *see* it—which is nasty enough—but it's just a shell, without life. Then there would have been the stench of the drains, the hunger and dysentery, the casual blows and floggings, the pain, the screams."

She squeezed his hand. "Oh God—don't. I'm Jewish. *I've* been brought up to know what it was like—it was sheer living hell. Poor, poor Daddy. Poor all of them."

It was not, however, the ruins that moved them most. In the remains of the camp hospital there was a little museum housing the mementos of suffering and the statistics of death, so huge as to be beyond comprehension. Naomi paused a long time before a graphic photograph of a line of prisoners with shaven heads, dressed in rags, toiling up the long, steep "Staircase of Death" from the quarry, each carrying a large block of granite in a wooden back carrier strapped to his wasted shoulders. Then she clutched Cable as they saw a little collection of ragged prisoners' clothes, thin blue-and white-striped pajamas offering no protection from the cold, and sad worn-out shoes and sandals with paper-thin soles. Somehow these spoke more powerfully of the piteous condition of the prisoners than the whips and instruments of torture they had just passed.

"Oh Bill," she whispered, tears suddenly on her cheeks. "People like Daddy had to slave in that quarry wearing *those*. It's too cruel, too awful. I can't bear to look anymore. Let's go—for God's sake, let's go home."

*   *   *

Cable dozed in the car and, when they got back to Vienna, woke to find Naomi driving past the house in Himmelstrasse. "Where are we going?" he yawned. "To the flat?"

"No—to my favorite *Heurigen*, Schubel-Auer, down in Nussdorf. I want to forget about that bloody camp."

Schubel-Auer was entered through an arched gateway leading into a cobbled yard. The building was stone, centuries old, and they found a table in a corner of one of the barrel-vaulted rooms with white-washed walls that honeycombed it. Cable ordered a liter of *alt*—open wine a year old—and fetched a simple meal of salt bread and roast pork from the food counter.

He poured her some red wine and a glass of mineral water. "You never told me your father was in Mauthausen before—how did it happen?"

She hesitated, as if reluctant to talk about it. "Oh, he came from an Austro-Hungarian Jewish family—I suppose more Austrian than Hungarian with a name like Reichmann—and they had a business with offices in both Vienna and Budapest. It was some sort of textile company—all I know is that he hated it." She hesitated again. "When Hitler annexed Austria in 1938, Daddy was working in Budapest and all the rest of his family were in Vienna—they were rounded up and sent to Treblinka, where they were gassed. Daddy was safe enough in Budapest, because Hungary was allied to Nazi Germany and the Hungarian Jews were left free. But he thought this would change—and in any case he was against the Nazis and the Hungarian fascists, the Arrow Cross. So he took to the hills and joined the partisans. Even in Hungary there was some resistance, you see."

Cable lit his pipe as she continued. Her reluctance to talk had now vanished. "He was in a guerrilla group that carried out sabotage for the Allies—until he was captured in 1944. By then the

Jews in Hungary were being persecuted just like the Jews in the rest of Nazi Europe—and Eichmann himself was in Budapest organizing massive deportations to Auschwitz. But it was also then that a few people woke up and tried to save Hungary's Jews—not just by hiding one or two, but by negotiating with the Nazis, who were in pretty bad shape themselves by 1944. There were leading Zionists like Joel Brand—and, of course, the Swedish diplomat, Raoul Wallenberg. The first deal was done when about two thousand of the Jews who'd been rounded up for Auschwitz were allowed to go to Switzerland, in exchange for a huge ransom collected from the Jewish community in Budapest itself—gold, jewels, and foreign currency. Of course two thousand wasn't many—half a million Hungarian Jews still went to Auschwitz and the other camps and were gassed.

"But then bigger deals were organized, with the help of the Jewish Agency in Switzerland. Eighteen thousand Jews for ten thousand trucks for the Waffen SS on the eastern front, plus tons of tea and coffee, millions of tins of soup. Funny to have your life so precisely valued—how many tins of soup would you give for me I wonder?" She gave a brittle laugh and gulped some wine. "The Jews in the internment camps were allowed to choose those who were to go free. Daddy says it was awful. People all *knew* Auschwitz was a death camp by then, that no one ever came back. So parents were weeping as they offered to stay so that their children could line up to go free—saying good-bye in squalor and in a hurry. No time to notice the tragedy, the courage they were showing. Daddy was chosen—a rabbi nominated him, saying that the Jewish race would need strong young men after the war—and six trainloads of Jews went west to Austria. An SS man switched the points so that one of the six trains went to Auschwitz anyway—a sick Nazi joke."

She gave a bleak little smile—"I don't know if Brand and Wallenberg got any of the cans of soup back. But Daddy was on one of the trains that *did* get to Austria—where they were put into work camps. It was no picnic, believe me—he was made to work eighteen hours a day in an underground factory, making shells—but at least they weren't gassed. Then he quarreled with one of the others—Jews are a quarrelsome lot, you know—and the other man betrayed him, told the SS guards Daddy's real name and that he was a partisan. It was a silly, ironic end after surviving so much.

Daddy was hoicked off to Mauthausen to be hanged, but no one got around to it in the chaos as Germany collapsed that winter and he escaped to be back in Budapest by the time the Red Army arrived early in 1945."

"He *escaped?* That can't have been so easy."

"I suppose not; but I think the *Kapos*—prisoners in charge of other prisoners—were pretty much running the camp by then and it wasn't so difficult to get out."

"I always thought the *Kapos* in concentration camps were communists rather than Jews."

"Were they?" She shrugged. "I don't know." For a few minutes she had hardly drawn breath, as if lost in the pride—or, in some curious way, the liberation—of sharing her father's story. Suddenly she had clammed up again. It was Cable who broke the awkward silence. "And when did he go to Israel?"

"Straight after that—in 1945."

"And your mother?"

"They met in Israel. She was Hungarian, but they didn't meet until they were both in Haifa. Mummy died a few years ago—I think I told you."

"Yes—I'm sorry."

Naomi sighed. "I've gotten used to it."

"What does your father do now?"

"Daddy . . . ?" She broke off. "Oh look, Bill, I didn't really mean to tell you all this . . . let's go home."

Cable knew that he had heard all that he was going to. He wondered why she was being evasive and looked at her questioningly. She bit her lip, clearly reading his thoughts. "I'm *not* being evasive, Bill, I'm just fed up with talking about it. Daddy was a soldier in the Israeli Army, that's all, until he retired last year. He lives in Tel Aviv. We aren't very close anymore."

* * *

The house in Himmelstrasse was cold and she pushed Cable toward the stairs. "Go and put the fire on upstairs, darling—I promised to ring Dr. Sollinger at the gallery before he goes to bed."

A few minutes later she entered the bedroom looking annoyed. "Damn," she said. "I'll have to work tomorrow even though it's Sunday. I'm sorry." She pulled off her jeans and threw them angrily into a corner, but her face softened when Cable took her in his arms. "That was a day I shall never forget," she whispered. "Hold me tight, Bill . . ." For a moment her eyes looked moist. ". . . you're a very *reassuring* kind of man, you know." Her face nuzzled his shoulder and, for the first time when they had been near to making love, he felt no reserve between them. Something had changed. He had become accustomed to her strong body, to the discovery of the delightful, unexpected womanliness she concealed; but now they clutched each other with an intense closeness and dependence, a simplicity they had never known before. The threats and agonies of his other life seemed far away.

On the bed she moved against him naturally, easily, as his hands moved slowly downwards and his fingers began to explore gently between her thighs. She sighed and lifted her face to him, eyes sparkling but half-closed, kissing him hungrily, her tongue flashing into his throat. Her body started to move in harmony with his, eyes suddenly open and radiant as he entered her.

Afterwards she lay on top of him naked, her skin golden in the glow from the electric fire. "Oh, Bill, I've wanted so much to feel *safe* when you make love to me." She smiled down at him wryly. "Not much of a *femme fatale*, am I? But I don't care—feeling safe is enough." She kissed him tenderly on the brow. "I need you so much, darling . . . and it was so important tonight. . . ."

* * *

In the morning Cable woke to hear the bell of Grinzing church tolling for Sunday morning. The bed was empty and he sat up, puzzled. Then he saw a note propped up by the bedside lamp: *Didn't wake you—you looked so contented. Will ring when I get back. Love you. N.*

He drew the curtains and was about to run a shower when the phone rang. It was a man's voice, one he did not recognize. "May I speak with His Excellency?"

Cable was puzzled by the quaint formality. "Yes—this is the ambassador speaking."

"Ah, good. My name is Gordon—I think you are expecting a call from me?"

"Am I? Are you sure you have the right number?"

"Oh yes, Ambassador, I have the right number." The voice paused mockingly. "*Golitsyn—Hanoi—1971.* Do you know where the Strombad is, by the Danube in Kritzendorf?"

Cable had gone white. "Yes. I think so."

"Be there at six tomorrow morning. Without fail." There was a click followed by the dial tone. Cable stood looking stupidly at the receiver. This was it, the summons he had hoped would never come—the sixth step, the last before he would be in too deep ever to get out. But he would meet them. Of course he would meet them, he had no choice—but then he *must* go to Security; he could not vacillate any longer. Or could he? He turned on the water, feeling fearful and depressed.

* * *

Five days before, in a red-brick office block on the outskirts of Cheltenham, a young intelligence officer had been sifting through the computer print-outs of his overnight intercepts. In the eight hours for which he was responsible, hundreds of diplomatic and military signals had been intercepted in Europe alone, by the radio and satellite stations in Scotland and the West Country, by the army in Germany and RAF Nimrods in the air. Only those that contained key words he had fed into the computer had been printed out.

He paused at a flimsy piece of A4 paper. A numerical reference told him it was a signal picked up by a Nimrod patrolling in the Baltic. It appeared to be a Soviet diplomatic telegram from Vienna to Moscow, printed out because it contained the code PIRANHA *en clair* in Russian among its headings, along with its classification, time of dispatch, and addressee—who was a department head in the KGB. The body of the telegram was in a difficult numerical code that had been only partially deciphered by the computer.

He was troubled by this telegram, for it was the first indication that the opposition knew about the operation called PIRANHA, whatever that might be—all he knew was that it existed, was classified Top Secret, and was connected with Vienna. Worse, if he tried to fill in the gaps where the code had not yet been broken, it seemed to imply that the information came from a source in the British Embassy itself. Or perhaps that it could be *checked* with a source in the embassy? He tried several ways of fitting Russian characters to the numbers, scribbling in pencil on a squared pad.

Eventually he passed the copy paper to his section head, who marked it for action by the Foreign Office security department, with copies for information to the Cut. Later that day the double envelope containing it, sealed and stamped TOP SECRET, was loaded with boxes containing thousands of others into a large van, painted dark green and carrying no markings to show it belonged to the government, which set out on the hundred-mile journey to London.

In a few days, inquiries would start in Vienna. If there was a traitor they would soon find him.

*   *   *

Cable spent Sunday alone, halfheartedly drafting the report he might make after the assignation in Kritzendorf. He sensed that the danger in delaying any longer could be fatal; but his mood changed from hour to hour. Sometimes he felt determined to come clean; then his fears of the outcome crowded in again and he vacillated, calculating the odds. Could he give them what they wanted and still get away with it? Could he live with himself afterward?

Early in the evening he began to wonder what had happened to Naomi and rang her flat, but there was no reply. There was still no reply an hour later. What had she said—*I have to do something for the gallery . . . ?* He knew that old Dr. Sollinger who ran the little art shop lived in an apartment above it. Perhaps he would answer if Cable telephoned; perhaps Naomi was there with him, hanging pictures for an exhibition?

Eventually, he dialed the gallery's number. He recognized the thin, elderly voice that answered. "Manfred Sollinger speaking."

"*Gruss Gott, Herrn Doktor.* Is Fraulein Reichmann there? If so, may I speak to her?"

"*Ach nein, mein Herr.* Today it is Sunday and the gallery is closed. Fraulein Reichmann is not here—she will be at work on Tuesday morning."

"But I thought she was working with you today?"

"*Ach nein, mein Herr.* Fraulein Reichmann has a few days off for a little holiday. I do not know where she is. *Auf Wiedersehen, mein Herr.*"

Once again Cable found himself listening to the dial tone and staring stupidly at a telephone receiver. He put it down slowly and walked to the window, his footsteps echoing eerily in the empty house; as he looked out into the dark garden he began to feel horrible inside. Now why on earth should *Naomi* lie to him?

15 Vienna

IT WAS STILL DARK when Cable left the house in Himmelstrasse at five-thirty on Monday morning. He did not want to be seen by the policeman on the front gate, so he had parked the Volvo in the lane behind the house the previous evening. He crept out of the kitchen door and through the back gate, stepping only on the grass to avoid crunching the gravel. He felt like a criminal and started to hate himself again.

He had oiled the lock on the car door so that it opened silently. Inside, the warmth of his breath misted up the windshield, for it was bitterly cold; he wiped it away with the back of his glove and let off the hand brake so that the car rolled forward slowly, down the lane through the empty vineyards. He used only his dim lights. When he felt out of earshot of the policeman guarding his house, he started the engine and switched on the headlights.

He drove north, through the shadowy forest and up the hair-pins of the road over the Kahlenberg, feeling nervous and tense inside. At the top of the hill he passed the high television antenna, outlined against a gray dawn sky, and started the steep descent to Klosterneuburg. The twin spires and domes of the monastery were visible in the half-light, standing out above the black cluster of its buildings. Perhaps Rozinski was sleeping there, thought Cable, waiting in ignorance—waiting to be betrayed.

He drove through the narrow cobbled streets of the town, huddled below the walls of the abbey, and took the road north to Kritzendorf. It was parallel to the Danube, but the river was about a mile away to his right and hidden by trees. He had never been there before, although he knew that the area between road and river was a huge, flat wasteland of forest and marsh, broken up by narrow tracks leading to wooden holiday chalets. In the summer it was alive with Viennese enjoying themselves, when they could avoid the mosquitoes; now it would be deserted.

After a few miles he was in Kritzendorf, passing a farmer driving two cows with tinkling bells along the empty village street. Just after the station he turned right, bumping across a level crossing. The car went over a wooden bridge, its tires drumming hollow on the planks, and through a gateway below a peeling sign saying STROMBAD. At the end of the track, two wooden towers flanked an archway leading to the shore. There was a cluster of desolate kiosks and cafes, windows shuttered and paint peeling off. In summer it might be quite pleasant—now it looked like the entrance to Mauthausen.

Cable got out of the car. The wind moaned through bare trees, the car park was empty, and it was unpleasantly cold. Nothing relieved the bleak grayness of dawn—gray trees, gray buildings, gray sky—except the red AUSTRIA TABAK sign on one of the kiosks and the occasional white trunk of a silver birch. He walked through the arch; he wasn't the first to think of it as a prison camp—someone had sprayed *Arbeit macht Frei* on the wood of one of the towers. Beyond a muddy beach, black waters flowed past swiftly; on the far bank was a cement works, half hidden by mist. There was no sign of life. He walked up and down past rows of grim, black-tarred changing cubicles, stamping his feet to keep warm. After ten minutes he began to feel a surge of hope: perhaps no one would turn up. He had taken the perilous sixth step in coming—but the final reckoning would be put off.

Then the tension returned inside him as he heard a car engine approaching and the sudden silence when it was switched off. A few minutes later the figure of a man appeared under the wooden arch. Cable's stomach lurched, for the figure appeared to have no face, but then he realized that a stocking mask hid the features between a dark felt hat and a black overcoat. The man beckoned. "Get back in your car and follow." He had a thick Slavic accent. Now there was a second car in the parking lot—an anonymous Mercedes that did not have diplomatic number plates.

Cable started his engine and the man climbed in beside him. One hand was slipped inside his overcoat, as if holding a pistol.

Cable followed the Mercedes. The two cars did not return to the main road, but drove for twenty minutes along a maze of tracks through the marshy woods. No one could have followed them without being seen and heard. Eventually, in another clearing by the river, they came to a wooden chalet standing alone. A light was burning in the window.

Four men from the Mercedes spread out around the chalet. The man accompanying Cable motioned him to go up the steps to the door, which was about ten feet above the ground, for the summer house was built on wooden pilings against flooding from the Danube. Inside, it was furnished with a few wicker chairs and smelled of damp. The man in the stocking mask drew a heavy pistol from his pocket and stood inside the door as a guard.

Cable recognized the figure silhouetted against the pale rectangle of the window overlooking the river. It was the young Russian with the domed forehead and Mongol eyes—the man who had threatened him in the warehouse six nights ago, but who now smiled in a friendly way. "Good morning, Ambassador. You will know me as Gordon. Please sit down. I am sorry this country has such a lousy climate—would you care for a little schnapps to warm you?" He held out a silver hip flask.

Cable shook his head abruptly. "No I wouldn't. What the hell do you want of me this time?" He sat down on the edge of one of the wicker chairs.

The man who said his name was Gordon sat down opposite and extracted a cigarette from a cardboard package. He tapped it on the back of his hand, lit it, and exhaled a ring of blue smoke luxuriantly. "One of the few benefits of my job"—he smiled—"is that I can buy Virginia cigarettes."

"For God's sake," snapped Cable. "I haven't come here at this hour—and under these conditions—for a social chat. Just tell me what you want—I haven't got much time. If I'm not back within an hour, my absence from the house will be noticed."

"Please don't get angry, Bill—may I call you Bill? I hope we are going to be friends. I think we have enough time—your car calls for you at eight-thirty, if I recall correctly?"

Cable shrugged. "Usually." It was unsettling to feel that they knew his movements so well.

"Good. As I say—please don't get angry. It was your own people who sent you to Vietnam back in 1971. It was *your own* people who accused you of treachery when you got back—most un-friendly of them. I didn't know such things could happen in England's green and pleasant land." He raised his eyebrows iron-ically; it made him look like Lenin. "You cannot blame *us* for these things, my friend—nor for making a little use of them. Now to business, Bill. We know that there is an operation code-named PIRANHA, aimed at a socialist country in membership of the War-saw Pact. Please tell me all that you know about it."

Cable hesitated. "I have heard the name, I think, but I have no knowledge of it—I'm afraid I can't help you." The Russian lit an-other cigarette. "Bill." He spoke slowly and patiently. "I am not a complete bloody idiot. You are an *ambassador* and this operation is based in your embassy."

"So what?" snapped Cable. "If you know so much, you will know that our intelligence service and our diplomatic service are quite separate, with separate chains of command. It is perfectly possible for intelligence officers, who also work as diplomats in the em-bassy, to be engaged in something without their ambassador knowing."

Gordon sighed. "I hope you are not trying to deceive me, Bill. I can just about believe what you say, but I am also sure that, whatever you do not know today, you can—in your position—find out by tomorrow, or even sooner."

"Perhaps." Cable spoke guardedly. "It may not be so easy."

"No, Bill, not perhaps—*certainly*. You can do it perfectly eas-ily." He paused, exhaling blue tobacco smoke, then went on briskly, "So I will give you forty-eight hours to discover everything there is to know about operation PIRANHA. I shall also give you a little camera and some film so that you can photograph any useful doc-uments. Do this for us, my friend, and we shall not resurrect your past—you do understand?"

"For God's sake—do you expect me to trust you? How do I know you won't be asking me for information for the next twenty years?"

"I told you before—you can trust us, Bill. We are men of honor. Give us what is required and we shall leave you in peace for the rest of your life."

"And supposing I cannot discover what you want?"

"*Cannot*, Bill? But I am sure you can. If you *will not*, that is a different kettle of fish." His Mongol eyes flashed menacingly. "You're a family man, aren't you, Cable?"

"I asked a question, damn you! Supposing I cannot do what you ask in forty-eight hours? It may not be enough time."

"If I believed that you are trying, I might—I repeat, *might*—give you another day or two to deliver." Cable met his eyes challengingly, saying nothing. "But *if* I believe that you are not fulfilling your side of the bargain, I shall see that tapes of our conversations and other material go to the British security authorities. That—coupled with the unfinished business of Golitsyn and the statement you signed in Hanoi—will ruin you, Bill. You will be publicly disgraced, no pension, no way of getting any kind of other work—and very likely you will go to jail. In fact," he mused, "I am *sure* that you would be tried and imprisoned. You are basically an upstart. Not an old Etonian. Not an officer in the Guards. Not even from Oxford or Cambridge. You are from the wrong social class to be allowed to get away with it."

Cable pretended to be shaken by the threat and dropped his eyes. "Very well. On the clear understanding that you will never come back to me, I will try to find out what you want."

"Good—I felt sure that you would be sensible, Bill. We shall meet here at six in the morning on Wednesday, unless I notify you otherwise. If you wish to make contact with me, ring this number." He scribbled a telephone number in pencil on an empty cigarette package and tossed it to Cable. "Ask for Gordon."

"Is that all?"

"I think so, Bill, I think so." He paused reflectively. "Of course, Bill, *some* men in your position—not you, of course, but *some* men—might try to double-cross us. To go to their authorities, report this conversation, and then try to fool me by giving me phony information. *You* wouldn't do that, Bill, now would you?"

Cable's throat was suddenly dry. "No, of course not. I have made a bargain."

"I'm so glad, Bill." The Russian's tone was barely audible, almost a hiss. "I'm so glad." He drew a photograph from his pocket and handed it to Cable. It was a picture of Sarah, looking startled, sitting at a table with a vase of flowers and a dish of cakes. An elderly man sat opposite her, smiling in an avuncular way.

Cable felt the color drain from his face. "What's this?" He could hardly speak. "Where was it taken? Where did you get it? *What the hell's going on?*"

"Don't you know? I thought you might recognize her." The

Russian's eyes mocked him. "After all—she *is* your daughter." An icy fist of fear began to clench in Cable's stomach. "She was arrested a few days ago, after entering Hungary illegally. She was carrying a large consignment of heroin to sell—I believe you call it happy dust in the West—which is, of course, against the law. She will be tried in the usual way."

"Don't be ridiculous! Sarah's on holiday in Burgenland. She would never cross the frontier illegally—and she wouldn't know an ounce of heroin even if she saw one. What kind of frame-up is this? What are you trying to tell me, for God's sake?"

"Your daughter is in our hands, Ambassador. We shall notify your embassy in Budapest of her arrest on Wednesday, after you have produced what we want. If you have been cooperative we shall—when we have verified your information—be ready to release her quietly and that will be the end of the matter." The Russian paused for effect, lighting another cigarette. "If you are not cooperative, she will not be released."

Cable's face was suddenly drawn and haggard. "What are you saying—what will you do to Sarah, you bastards?"

"If she goes to trial, the penalty for drug peddling is death—I think by hanging, in Hungary." He shook his head sadly. "But of course the pretty daughter of a distinguished foreigner, an *ambassador* no less, might be reprieved and sent for a long spell in a labor camp, so she would never go to trial. I am to inform you, Ambassador, that if you do as I ask, your daughter will be returned unharmed, with little or no publicity. If you do *not* cooperate, she will be found hanged in her cell, her suicide a confession of her guilt."

Central Intelligence Agency   Copy No. 5 of 6 copies
Langley, Va.

TR/W/ 8—A973/JC

Source: Regular and Reliable

EXTRACT FROM DAMAGED TAPE RECORDING OF A MEETING
HELD RECENTLY AT THE COUNCIL OF MINISTERS'
BUILDING, MOSCOW

Note: The chairman's introductory remarks indicate
that this was the 48th session of Foreign Affairs
Committee G, which reports direct to the Politburo.
Personal names are not used in the discussion but
references to participants by rank or post, and
voice prints, suggest that those taking part were:
the Minister of Foreign Affairs (A. Gromyko — in
the chair), Marshal Y. Malinovsky (Third Deputy
Minister of Defense), Maj. Gen. N.A. Kirov and Col.
I. Michaelov (Committee for State Security), and
two others unidentified. The exact date of the
meeting is unknown. Original Russian text available
on request. Tape badly damaged before entering
Agency custody.

———————————

CHAIRMAN: The forty—eighth meeting of Foreign
    Affairs Committee G is now in session. May we
    first look at the minutes of our last . . .

— interference on tape
for 3 minutes, 8 seconds — #

UNIDENTIFIED: . . . this change will be circulated
    in writing.

CHAIRMAN: May we now turn to item 3, the question
    of Plan Alexander as proposed by the Minister
    of Defense?

MALINOVSKY: Better take the alternatives Cyrus and
    Darius, too.

KIROV: I have no objection to that.

CHAIRMAN: Very well. Will you introduce the paper,
    Marshal?

MALINOVSKY: Thank you. As you know, comrades, even
    after five years we are still having
    difficulties in restoring normal conditions in

Afghanistan. The main problem is that the
Muslim guerrillas who threaten the authorities
in Kabul find a safe haven in the refugee camps
in mountainous northern Pakistan, which are in
fact their operational bases . . .

— interference —

. . . we have made representations to the
Pakistani Government, but they are basically
hostile to us. We need to go into Pakistan with
sufficient force to destroy those camps. Plan
Alexander is designed, given a suitable
political opportunity, to do this. The force
envisaged consists of two tank divisions
and . . .

KIROV: I don't wish to interrupt the Marshal's
introduction, Comrade Chairman, but he seems
about to go into military detail.

MALINOVSKY: Yes—of course I am.

KIROV: In that case may I first express my grave
and fundamental reservations about the whole
scheme?

CHAIRMAN: Please do, General.

KIROV: To destroy a few refugee camps is a
tactical objective which may well be
justified . . .

MALINOVSKY:(interrupting) Of course it's
[expletive] justified. These Muslim guerrilla
swine have to be stopped—our boys are having a
bad time. Get captured and you get flayed alive
or your [obscene Russian expression for
genitals] cut off. We can't go on like this—we
could end up with a mutiny.

KIROV: I well understand that, but it is not so
simple. The military have been proposing these
short, sharp moves against Pakistan or Iran—
because they adjoin Afghanistan—for some years
now. The argument is that one can ignore wider
strategic considerations—and that the United
States would keep out of it. If the country we
had entered resisted strongly, to the point of
a minor war, we could suppress them and achieve
the objective of centuries—a warm water port on
the Indian Ocean.

CHAIRMAN: That is not what Plan Alexander says. It
is envisaged only in Darius.

KIROV: My objection is that Alexander is ludicrously unrealistic. We cannot risk territorial aggression. The United States would resist, in support of Pakistan, however much we tried to limit our . . .

- interference -

. . . idiotic cowboy warmonger in the White House . . .

- interference -#

. . . impossibly dangerous venture.

MALINOVSKY: I disagree—it is absurd . . .

- the next 10 minutes, 8 seconds of tape are damaged and unintelligible. In this interval the topic appears to have changed to Operation Sobieski -

UNIDENTIFIED: . . . to sum up, Comrade Chairman, Operation Piranha is an aggressive operation of a paramilitary nature, sponsored by the United States, Great Britain——and, we believe, with a degree of Vatican blessing. Men and weapons are to be infiltrated into a socialist country to foment counterrevolution. Their numbers are probably not large——although the quantity of weaponry may well be. We are working to identify the precise target and date.

CHAIRMAN: What is your estimate of the target, General?

KIROV: Poland is the most likely, because of the present state of unrest there——and the Church involvement suggests Poland. But the obvious target is not necessarily the right one. It could be Czechoslovakia or Hungary or Romania. I discount Bulgaria and the German Democratic Republic.

MALINOVSKY: And when?

KIROV: We should know in a few days. As you will see from my report, my long-standing agent in Vienna, code-named Plato, is unable to discover these details but we have activated a new source——over whom we have a powerful hold——in the British Embassy.

CHAIRMAN: This is the source code-named Socrates?

KIROV: Yes. Socrates is in fact a senior
     British . . .

— interference for
4 minutes, 36 seconds — #

MALINOVSKY: . . . for once I agree with our
     glamorous general [laughter]. This double
     blackmail of Socrates will give him powerful
     reasons to cooperate--you say Plato will know if
     your Socrates tries to deceive us?

KIROV: I expect to have all the facts I need in a
     few days--and to confirm from my second agent
     that Socrates is telling us the truth. If he is
     not fully cooperative, I have the means to
     force his hand . . .

— interference —

     . . . vulnerable, the daughter . . .

— interference for
6 minutes, 3 seconds — #

CHAIRMAN: . . . we seem agreed then. We permit the
     infiltration of these bandits, then crush them
     on arrival with maximum publicity?

MALINOVSKY: It won't need the Red Army--the local
     militia can do it . . .

— the remainder of the tape
(approx. 9 minutes) is too
damaged to be intelligible — #

SECRET

Copy No: 1 of 4 copies

<u>To</u>:   Director General

<u>From</u>:   C H Stuart
        Hd/External Liaison

SUSPECTED BREACH OF SECURITY AT
UK PERMANENT MISSION TO UNITED NATIONS, VIENNA

1.   In 1972 I chaired a court of inquiry into the conduct of
Mr J W Cable, now HM Ambassador to the United Nations Organizations
in Vienna. Report filed in your office.

2.   Please see the attached transcript from Langley, which has been
drawn to my attention. I suggest that Cable may well be the
unidentified source "Socrates" referred to therein. While
conceding that there is no evidence that he had been approached
at the time of this meeting (which is of recent but uncertain
date), I propose an urgent investigation. I am ready to go to
Vienna to question/warn Cable myself and would be grateful for
instructions.

3.   A recent intercept ref: JV/4u/29-1326/VV is also relevant.

C H STUART

Copies to: Hd/Security Dept — FCO
            Registry

SECRET

16 | Vienna

CABLE ARRIVED AT THE EMBASSY soon after nine on Monday morning and shut himself in his office, alone. "No visitors, Jill," he said to his gray-haired secretary. "No phone calls, unless it's the Foreign Secretary in person." He smiled slightly, glad that he could still play the relaxed ambassador, despite his inner turmoil. "And he doesn't know we exist."

"I expect he does." She laughed. "It could be worse—we might be in Ulan Bator. I'll get you some coffee."

He sat at the handsome mahogany desk, a drafting block and a pad of squared paper on its leather top in front of him. There must be no more vacillating. If he was to save Sarah, the only way was by turning to London. It was a risk—he couldn't trust them—but he could trust the unknown faces in Moscow even less. Just *do* it, he snapped at himself—and do it *now*.

Now that he had made a decision, the words came easily and the finished report sounded convincing. He shortened it—that was legitimate if it was going by telegram—which left the exact sequence and dates of his contacts with Gordon conveniently vague. He stressed that Sarah's life was threatened and that the Russian had asked for a second contact that Wednesday, in only two days' time. He asked for immediate instructions on how to react. When it was finished he took a one-time pad and enciphered the report himself, marking it SECRET: PERSONAL FOR HEAD OF SECURITY DEPT. FROM CABLE, VIENNA.

When the sheet of letters and figures was complete, he asked Jill to summon Squires, the chief cipher clerk. He appeared a few minutes later. Like Jill, he was one of the old guard, a grave man of about fifty, who looked like a skilled craftsman—an electrician or a cabinetmaker perhaps. "What can I do for you, sir?" He did not sit down until invited to do so.

"I've ciphered this telegram myself, Geoff—it's on a delicate security matter. Could you send it yourself, please—I don't want to start any unnecessary rumors."

"Of course, sir. No one else will see it but me and I'll bring the copies back to you myself for retention." He had the eyes of a man of total trustworthiness. Cable knew it was unnecessary to tell him to keep his trap shut. He would—it was an unwritten part of his job description.

"What about the other end?"

"I have a mate in main registry in London, sir. If you agree I'll ask him to pick it up and take it straight to the addressee. I can ring him now and it'll be there within the hour."

"That's fine—yes, do that. Thank you."

"Sir."

"There's one other thing, Geoff. I want it repeated to Sir David Nairn personally. He's the deputy director general of—"

"Yes, I know of Sir David, sir," said Squires quickly. "That's no problem—I'll repeat it to him at Century House and make sure they have the code reference. Anything else sir?"

"No thank you, Geoff. And I know I can rely on your discretion."

"Of course, sir."

*   *   *

Cable half-expected a response that afternoon. But there was silence and at three he called for the car and Fritz drove him to a meeting at UNO City. The traffic was heavy and, when they reached the Danube, the big Ford inched across the Reichsbrucke in a slow procession of cars.

The United Nations complex stood on the left at the other side of the bridge. Although often called "UNO City," it was in fact just a group of six concrete towers, all of different height, joined together by a squat cylindrical building which provided the main meeting halls. It housed the Vienna office of the UN and three autonomous UN agencies. He was going to a meeting of the agency for relief of Palestinian refugees, which had been bombed out of

Beirut. The whole place was a hideous, concrete monument to a lost ideal. It contained four thousand officials: a mad mixture of idealistic Swedes and Dutchmen, shady men from the developing countries of Latin America and Africa, often mysteriously related to the president of the day and running crooked deals on the side, men and women with a higher loyalty to the intelligence services of the Soviet Union or the United States, and countless nubile secretaries hoping to be laid by a large tax-free salary.

The car growled up the ramp into the car park below the plaza in front of the building and Cable took the escalator up into the central rotunda. Walking across the wide empty space, he nodded to the German ambassador, who was evidently going to the same meeting, and waved to the burly figure of Laszlo Kardos at the newspaper stand.

Five minutes later he sat down with thirty others in a room overlooking the lake behind the building. A blue UN flag stood propped in the corner. The ambassador from Pakistan raised a point of order and all eyes glazed simultaneously. He always spoke for at least an hour. Cable opened a file and stared sightlessly at his papers, thinking only of Sarah.

*　*　*

After the meeting he went back to the embassy. The secretaries had gone home and the outer office was empty, but Jill always left any new telegrams or messages on his desk. There was a note under a weight on the blotter: an invitation to dinner from the Swedish ambassador. Nothing else. Nothing from London.

For a few minutes Cable sat there, fingers drumming on the wood, looking at the telephone. Eventually he shrugged and stood up—there was nothing to do but wait. Fritz drove him home to Grinzing. In the car he tried to read the English newspapers that had come in on the one o'clock flight from London. It seemed callous—but more agonized worrying would do nothing to help Sarah now. It was more important that he should be in a fit state to make London get her out. Whatever might be dredged up from the past, he had not betrayed Rozinski and PIRANHA and he had not betrayed his trust as Her Majesty's ambassador. He had a right to be in this expensive bulletproof car—and a right to demand their help. That was all he had to fall back on now.

The dark blue Minster turned off the main street of Grinzing and up the narrow hill into Himmelstrasse. As they rounded the corner, Cable's knuckles tensed on the copy of *The Economist* he was skimming. There was no policeman outside the house. He leaned forward, whispering urgently through the open glass panel. "Drive on, Fritz. Don't stop! Something is wrong."

The driver responded unquestioningly, although his face—if Cable could have seen it—looked astonished and frightened. He gathered speed again and went some two hundred yards farther up the street until Cable's house was hidden by the trees. Cable ordered him to park and the two of them got out. "Come with me, please, Fritz. I think there may be a burglar in the house."

"Would you like me to call the police, sir?"

"Yes—tell them to be quick."

"There is a telephone kiosk down the road." The driver fled toward it with relief.

Cable walked down an alley between two large villas, then along the lane at the rear of the houses. Rows of vines, twisted branches about four feet high, ran down the hill on his right, toward the city, where lights were coming on in the dusk. At the back of his own house a car he had never seen was parked—a rusty brown Skoda. He made a note of its registration number.

Cable took the handle of the gate in the wall, which should have been locked. It was open. He turned the handle cautiously and stepped into the garden, which was almost in darkness. There was a faint light behind a ground-floor window of the house.

He crept along the terrace, peering through the glass, but could see nothing inside. Just outside the kitchen door he tripped over something soft and fell hard on the paving stones. In the dim light from the doorway he saw that it was a body wearing the green overcoat of a policeman. Cable turned it over gingerly and recoiled as the head lolled sideways—there was a gaping knife wound in the neck, from which dark blood was still oozing to soak into the fibers of the man's coat. The face was colorless, dead eyes wide open and looking surprised.

Cable stood up slowly. He would go no farther until more police arrived. He waited in the shadows for about five minutes, until there was the wail of a siren coming up the hill. He heard car doors slamming and the clatter of steel-shod boots running at the front of the house, followed by hammering on the door.

There was a crash somewhere inside and the light thud of footsteps. He shrank back into the darkness of a tree as two shadows shot from the kitchen door and ran across the lawn to the back gate. There was the whir of a starter and the sound of the Skoda driving off at high speed.

Cable entered the house, turning on the lights in the kitchen. Boots were stamping from room to room upstairs, and two police, with machine pistols at the ready, were already in the drawing room. They covered him with their guns and one challenged him in German, "Stand still and raise your hands!"

"I'm the ambassador—I called for you. This is my house."

The pistols stayed on him. "Stand still! If you are the ambassador, produce your *Legitimationskarte!*"

Cable pulled the small red identity card from his wallet and the policeman seized it. "I saw two men run out of the back," said Cable sharply. "They escaped in a brown Skoda with a Salzburg number plate. Shouldn't you get after them?"

One of the police returned the identity card and the other started to gabble into a two-way radio, pausing to turn to Cable. "Do you have the car number?"

"Yes. S 706.315."

The man went on speaking into the crackling mouthpiece and Cable left the room. In his study next door, every drawer of the desk had been taken out and emptied on the floor. The cupboard was open; pictures had been taken down and thrown aside in the search for a wall safe. The carpet was rolled back and the underfloor safe had been opened, its steel flap twisted as if an explosive had been used. Perhaps that was the noise which had attracted the policeman from the front gate.

In the rest of the house drawers had been emptied and cupboards flung open, particularly in Sarah's bedroom. There were papers and clothes everywhere. The house had been ransacked, but methodically, and nothing seemed to have been taken. Cable returned to the drawing room, where a more senior policeman had arrived: his green uniform was well cut and he had red tabs and gold stars on his collar. "Mr. Ambassador." He stood up, bowing slightly, his cap under his arm. "Please accept the regrets of the Republic of Austria for this outrage. Perhaps I could, however, take down one or two details?"

Cable shook his head. "I am grateful to you for coming—but I doubt whether you can do much unless you find the two men who broke in."

"We are trying, of course."

"In the meantime this building is British territory and before we do anything more I must telephone a colleague at my embassy. We may prefer you to do nothing—the motive of these men was not theft. It must have been political."

"But, Mr. Ambassador—one of my officers, assigned to guard you, has been *murdered*."

"I regret that very much, but I must ask you to take his body away as soon as possible—by the back gate. Please wait here while I telephone."

* * *

Two hours later Cable was climbing the concrete stairs to the flat in Bayerngasse. The police had left his house and two security guards from the embassy had arrived to check whether any documents were missing and to stay the night. Cable had excused himself and driven off in the Volvo. He parked a little way from the apartment block, in the shadow of the trees along the edge of the Stadtpark. He had found some papers related to the Geneva arms negotiations tossed on the floor of his study—the lack of any headings and a deceptively low classification had probably made the intruders overlook them. Since the only safe in the house was blown open and the embassy guards were not cleared to handle them, he had pushed the papers into a document case and taken them with him. He still had them tucked under his arm as he reached the fourth floor.

Naomi flung her arms around his neck as she opened the door. "Oh, Bill, how lovely to see you! I only got back half an hour ago—I was just going to phone."

He squeezed her and looked stern. "Where the devil have you been?"

She stepped back sharply. "I can go away for a day if I want—you don't *own* me, you know!"

"Of course not—but I thought you were just going to the gallery to work on Sunday."

"No—I didn't say that. I had a job to do for old Sollinger, but it was valuing a house full of stuff near Linz."

"Why did you have to do it on Sunday?"

"It was furniture and pictures belonging to someone who had died—a lawyer wanted a valuation in a hurry before putting them up for sale. Sollinger couldn't spare me in the week so I went up and did it on Sunday." She shrugged irritably.

"It didn't take you twenty-four hours to get back from Linz—it's only a hundred miles."

She went white, then suddenly raised her arm and slapped his face. "What *is* this—the bloody Inquisition? Don't you believe me? It's no business of yours whether I took three hours or three days to get back—getting screwed by the entire Austrian Army on the way!" She stamped her foot. "But, if you want to know, I didn't get screwed by anybody—I just stayed the night in a *pension*, because I finished very late, and came back this morning. It took all day because the car broke down—the petrol pump—and it took hours for the OAMTC to come and repair it. That's all." She started to cry. "I'm sorry I hit you—but does my going away for a day matter so much, for God's sake?"

The previous night he had wanted to rationalize his suspicions, but now he sensed that she was lying. He had come to confide in her, but suddenly he was cautious. "I needed you," he said. "I've been feeling a bit battered these last two days—Sarah's been kidnapped."

"What? Are you serious?" Then she saw from the look in his eyes that he was. "Oh Bill—my poor darling. What's happened?"

"Sarah's been kidnapped by someone—the KGB I suppose—and locked up in Hungary. I only learned this morning and now they're trying to blackmail me to spy for them, in return for her release."

"God—how *awful*."

"And tonight they ransacked my house and cut the throat of the policeman guarding it."

She put her arms round him. "And I went away just when you needed me. Oh Bill—I'm so sorry." He felt her tears warm on his neck and looked down at her face, now swollen and ugly with crying, wondering whether she was acting.

She sat him down in one of the modern Swedish armchairs, fetched a bottle of red wine with two glasses, and knelt on the carpet by his feet. Quietly he sipped the wine and told her of the events of the past week, although some instinctive mental gate clicked shut and stopped him mentioning Golitsyn or Vietnam; nor did he mention Rozinski, although he hinted that what he was being asked to betray was an operation to foment trouble in one of the Soviet satellites. In the warmth of the little room, it was like making a confession—he had nobody else to confide in—and he felt better for it. Naomi had stopped crying, but her concern shone through the shock in her face.

"I'm desperately worried about Sarah," he said. "They're threatening to kill her. She must be utterly terrified—she's only nineteen."

She stroked his face gently. "Yes—I know how much you love her. But for God's sake, Bill, you're an *ambassador*—what's your government doing about it?"

The little mental gate clicked shut again and Cable said nothing about his report to London. It wasn't a conscious decision to deceive her; after sixteen years as an intelligence officer he was working on automatic pilot. "I haven't told them—what could they do that would be any use?" He took another sip of wine. "Perhaps I should just do what these other bastards want and hope to God they keep their side of the bargain and release Sarah." He paused, watching for her reaction.

At first she did not respond, but sat silently staring into her wine for a few minutes, her face serious in the yellow light from the table lamp. "It's not the right thing to do, but you've done your bit for your country in the past, Bill—you've done it for years. Now Sarah should come first." She spoke without emotion, neither approving nor disapproving. "Would it work? Could you get away with it?"

* * *

He left her at midnight, half-asleep on the sofa, letting himself out of the apartment quietly. He had reached the Stadtpark when he realized that he had left the small document case in her apartment. Cursing, he hurried back and sprinted up the stairs. He rang the bell by her door in two short bursts, so as not to wake her too sharply. There was no response. He rang again, long and continuously, then began to hammer on the door. There was still no answer.

One of the other doors on the landing opened and a heavily made-up girl, with blonde hair so lacquered that it looked like a helmet, peered out. She was wearing a long *peignoir*, which slipped aside to show that she was naked underneath. "She must be out," she said, raising one knee suggestively like a nightclub dancer. "Can I help?"

"No," muttered Cable, turning away in disgust and glaring at the locked door with frustration. He hurried back down the stairs. At the street door he paused and considered looking for a telephone box to ring Naomi and wake her up, but he was feeling leaden with tiredness and turned away towards the Stadtpark.

The man in the Volkswagen Beetle at the curbside checked the time and made a note by the yellow light from his pocket torch: *Cable left for a second time at 00.25 hours.* The seat beside him was empty; his companion had tailed the girl when she left on foot just before Cable came back. He yawned, wondering how long she would be away and where she had gone. Bugger it—he should have knocked off at midnight. Still, there was a job to be done and they hadn't picked up the girl until she got back, on the train from Budapest, at seven that evening.

17 | Vienna

FOR THE FIRST TIME in a week, Cable felt able to look the security guards straight in the eye when he arrived at the embassy on Tuesday morning. A metallic "Morning, sir" crackled through a microphone from behind their bulletproof glass screen in the entrance hall.

Upstairs, his office seemed less like a prison. His secretary had laid out the morning post and telegrams for him on his desk. He sorted through it quickly—all routine stuff, nothing in response to the report he had ciphered yesterday. That was odd; it couldn't be every day that an ambassador—even only a grade-four ambassador—reported that his daughter had been kidnapped and he was being blackmailed by the KGB. Of course the report wouldn't have reached Security Department until yesterday afternoon, but he had stressed that he needed urgent guidance before meeting the Russian again on Wednesday—and it was now Tuesday.

He walked to the door and asked his secretary to put a phone call in to the head of Security Department at the Foreign Office in London. A few minutes later his telephone buzzed. He picked it up. "Yes?"

"The head of department isn't there, but I have a Mr. Fisher on the line."

"Okay—I'll speak to him instead."

After a series of clicks he heard a supercilious voice: "Fisher—Security. What can I do for you?"

"It's Cable here, from the Permanent Mission to the UN in Vienna. I sent an urgent report yesterday and thought there might be a reply this morning. Do you know the matter I'm talking about?"

There was a pause. "You're Cable, are you? Yes—I know the case." He said the word *case* with a hint of distaste.

"Well—what the devil's happening about it?"

"I can't discuss it on an open line, Cable. But I think someone's coming out in a day or two—not from here, but one of our friends from south of the river. They'll notify you."

"But dammit—it can't wait *two days!*"

"You aren't the only case on just now, you know." The supercilious voice emphasized the word *case* again. "Just get on with the job in hand, old boy, and wait to be contacted. You've done your bit." The line went dead.

Cable fiddled with the paper knife on his blotter, picking it up like a dagger. There was something ominous behind that man's evasiveness. He stabbed the knife savagely into the leather desk top and reached for the other phone, which bypassed the switchboard, dialing the number of the Cut in London. When the operator answered, "Century House," Cable asked for Nairn.

A pleasant woman's voice came on the line: "Sir David Nairn's office."

"Is Sir David there please? It's Bill Cable, ambassador to the UN in Vienna, here."

"Oh yes, Mr. Cable. No—I'm afraid Sir David is away. Since he became deputy director general he does seem to travel rather a lot."

"When will he be back?"

"In three days' time—may I ask him to ring you then?"

"Where is he?"

The woman hesitated. "You know I shouldn't really tell you that, Mr. Cable. Actually he's between Hong Kong and Singapore and I'm afraid there's *no* way you can get in touch with him. But I saw that you sent him a copy of a ciphered report yesterday and I've repeated that to him in Singapore."

"Good—thank you. Well, perhaps you would just ask Sir David to get in touch with me in Vienna as soon as possible?"

"Of course, Mr. Cable."

"Thank you." He hung up and walked over to the window. The Soviet Embassy, down the street, stood massive and silent as ever; there were no cars outside today, just the Austrian police guards in their long green overcoats, cradling their machine pistols. Nairn's absence and the lack of response from London was unsettling—and he was painfully worried about Sarah. He had suffered alone for a week. Now he had done the right thing, come clean—and he was *still* alone, damn them all. Worse, there was this nagging doubt that he could no longer trust Naomi.

His secretary came in. "You haven't forgotten the IAEA board meeting, have you?" He had—today was the first day of a four-day session of the governing board of the International Atomic Energy Agency, one of the UN bodies for which he was responsible.

"Thanks, Jill—what's the scene, then?"

"Lunch at the restaurant in UNO City with the European Community delegation leaders, for coordination. The board starts at three. You ought to leave at twelve-thirty."

"Who's the host at the European lunch?"

"Madame Vandenbemdem, the Belgian ambassador."

"Can't I send apologies?"

"No—I don't think so. Someone from the UK has to go and Mr. Skilbeck isn't available."

"Delacroix never damn well turns up."

Jill gave a knowing smile and adjusted her neat row of imitation pearls. "Well—we all know they do things differently in France. I'll order the car for twelve-thirty?"

Cable nodded. It was well known that one of Delacroix's girl friends had an apartment near the United Nations enclave, from which he would emerge looking relaxed and chirpy five minutes before any important meeting. "Okay," said Cable. "I'll go over at twelve-thirty."

*   *   *

The afternoon was ghastly. The boardroom was large and without windows, with ice-cold air conditioning. The thirty-four members, each representing a different country, sat at a huge horseshoe table, their aides clustered behind them, facing the chairman, who sat below a white plastic emblem of an atom surrounded by a garland of olive leaves. The lights were bright and the room was carpeted in a hideous orange.

The chairman was a senior official from the Japanese Foreign Office who led them through the dreary agenda in cut-glass English—busily interpreted by the staff, in glass booths above, into Russian, French, and Spanish. Every chair in the room had an earphone and a dial to choose between English or one of the other three languages. Cable was required to deliver the British point of view on each item, generally by reading a typewritten brief prepared in London. The rest of the time he was supposed to follow the discussion closely, in case a further statement was needed. With two thirds of his mind on Sarah, he found it impossible to concentrate. Thank God the UK governor's chair would be taken by an undersecretary from London for the rest of the week.

The meeting broke up at six and Cable drifted around the room. Kardos sat in a corner where he had been listening, for the Holy See was not a member of the board. "Any news on Pakistan, Bill?" His eyes crinkled into a smile above the black beard. "You look tired, my friend—do you have time for a drink downstairs?"

Cable was about to say "Yes" when a UN clerk pulled at his sleeve. She was pretty, Austrian—wearing a traditional dirndl with an embroidered pinafore. "I'm sorry to interrupt, Mr. Ambassador, but your secretary telephones and asks to speak with you urgently."

"Is she on the phone now?"

"Yes—in cabin three just outside the door."

Cable nodded to Kardos. "Sorry, Laszlo—would you excuse me for a minute?" He hurried into the lobby and picked up the receiver. "Yes—Jill?"

"Mr. Cable? I thought I should ring you. I've had an urgent telegram from London, which I don't understand. Shall I read it to you? It's not classified."

"Yes, please." Cable suddenly felt anxious.

"It's addressed to you, from FCO London. It says, 'Have received your ADLON 84271 of 17 September. Investigator from Defense Department arrives 20 September. Kindly render every assistance.' "

"That's all?"

"Yes—that's all. I don't think I've seen this 84271 telegram."

"No. I ciphered it myself." Cable bit his lip to retain control. "Okay, thanks. I'll see you in the morning." He put the phone down and stood in the box feeling sweat coursing down his face. He wiped his forehead with a handkerchief; his hands were trembling. Defense Department was a common euphemism for the intelligence service—but there was something wrong with the message, just as there had been something wrong that morning when he spoke to the runt called Fisher in Security Department. He'd asked for help—not for an "investigator." He sensed that he was under attack again—all his worst fears were being realized.

He strode to the rotunda and down the escalator to the diplomatic car park. It was crowded with large black cars, but Fritz was waiting at the curb with the Ford Minster. "To the embassy, sir?"

"No. Take me home to Grinzing, please."

* * *

Back at the house Cable sent his car away and poured himself a large whiskey. He rang Naomi's flat, but there was no answer, so he rang the art gallery. The proprietor said that she had gone home. Irritably, he pulled on his heavy green loden overcoat and left the house.

He strode down into the village, feeling angry and depressed, his shoulders hunched against the cold wind. The main street of Grinzing was dark, lit by pools of yellow light from the street-lamps—and empty. The tourist season was over and it was too early in the evening for the Viennese to come out to the *Heurigen*.

He turned into a *Heuriger* he had not visited before. It was a single room off the street with a bare wooden floor and tables and chairs painted dark green. There was a counter of cold food at the end and two girls in dirndls to serve the wine. Apart from a couple in a corner—American, from their accents—the place was empty.

Cable sat down in the opposite corner, close to the old-fashioned beehive stove, covered in blue tiles and reaching to the ceiling. It was alight and gave out steady heat like a modern radiator. One of the waitresses approached and he ordered a *Viertel* of red wine, which she brought in a small glass tankard. He gulped it down and ordered another, which he drank more slowly. He thought vaguely that he should get something to eat or dilute the wine with mineral water, but his anger and depression made him lethargic. Every time he thought of Sarah, locked up and terrified, he wanted to kill the young Russian who called himself Gordon; and then the threat to her if Cable double-crossed them crowded in on him and he wanted to weep. Now he *had* double-crossed them—by sending a written report to London. God—a *written* report. If they had good sources in the Foreign Office they might even get to see it. He needed the help of his own people badly—and he wasn't getting it.

After the fourth *Viertel* he began to feel anesthetized and his sight was blurred. He ordered a fifth, ignoring the fact that he had already drunk over a liter, and downed it savagely, leaving a hundred-schilling note on the table and staggering out into the street, watched curiously by the two American tourists.

There was a sound of running and he felt a tug at his sleeve. It was the waitress, her cheeks flushed. He pulled away angrily. *"Ja—was ist los?"*

"You forgot your overcoat, *mein Herr,*" she said timidly, helping him on with the loden. "And your change."

"That's okay—thank you." Cable waved the money away.

"Thank you, *mein Herr.*" She bobbed a slight curtsy.

The cold air outside sobered him up to the point where he realized how erratically he was walking. He turned up the dark hill, out of the village street, and into Himmelstrasse, stopping to lean against a garden wall. A shadowy figure approached and took his arm. "This way home, my friend, not far to go." Cable recoiled at the unknown, Slavic voice, but strong hands gripped him and guided him toward his own gate.

"Ambassador," whispered the voice, urgently. "Can you hear me?"

Cable recoiled again. "Yes—who the devil are you?" He started to hiccup noisily.

"You go to the IAEA board at ten tomorrow? Yes? But Barker from London comes to take your place as leader?"

"Yes." They had reached the gate.

"Then slip out at eleven o'clock. Take the lift to the twenty-seventh floor of the UN building, tower A. Go to the emergency stairs and walk up two flights—to the roof. Gordon will see you there."

The figure slipped away and Cable staggered up the steps to his front door, fumbling for a key. He was not too drunk to be horrified that Gordon had him under such close surveillance. Instead he pulled himself upstairs and switched on the light in his bedroom, still hiccuping. Naomi sat up in bed, her hands raised to shield her eyes from the sudden glare. "Hello, Bill, where *have* you been? You look smashed—are you?" The document case he had left in her apartment lay on the bedside table.

"I kind of thought you might be here," he muttered. A man outside to watch him in the evening, a girl inside to keep tabs on him all night. . . . He pushed the thought away, leaning down to kiss her naked shoulders.

18 | Vienna

THE IAEA BOARD meeting resumed at ten on Wednesday morning. The thirty-four delegation leaders normally stayed in their places around the horseshoe table throughout the meeting, but their aides were constantly in and out of the crowded boardroom—and there were at least a hundred people clustered on chairs behind the delegation leaders or against the walls, clutching papers and trying to look busy—so Cable was able to slip away without difficulty shortly before eleven.

The huge modern building had been built by the Austrian government and given to the United Nations free, as a gesture of the country's new democratic, neutral respectability after the Nazi period. When it was designed the UN was a hopeful, expanding organization—a situation that had since changed. Whole corridors of the building were dusty and unoccupied; Cable met no one as he walked to the lift. On the twenty-seventh floor he hurried down the curving corridor. A door opened and the pockmarked features of Hernandez, the Argentinian legal adviser, looked out. "Oh, Bill." Surely he was not expecting him? "Do you have a minute? I need your support for the renewal of my contract."

Cable brushed him aside. "Not now, Larry. I'm tied up with board business—shouldn't you be down there too?"

He hurried on, vanishing through the door to the emergency stairs, which slammed shut behind him. He ran up the two flights and emerged, panting, through a steel door onto the roof.

The cold wind cut into him like a scalpel, for he wore no topcoat over his lightweight suit. He was twenty-eight floors up and the view across the city, to the hills where patches of snow could be seen on the upper slopes, was magnificent. But the fierce gusts made it hard to stand. Gordon waved at him from the shelter of the small square building housing the lift motors: he was wearing a sensibly long overcoat and a fur hat.

The two men huddled in the lee of the concrete wall. The straight line of the Danube looked comparatively narrow from this height, cars and trucks streaming across the long bridge like black ants. Gordon gave a half-smile. "I think we are unlikely to be disturbed up here—we must not stay too long or you will freeze to death." He paused. "Well—what can you tell me?"

Cable hesitated, feeling a surge of irritation. His own people had had two days in which to tell him what to say—but no one had bothered. He would just have to play it by ear as best he could. "PIRANHA is an operation to infiltrate an armed group into one of your satellite states," he mouthed slowly, almost shouting against the wind. "They are to start unrest—I suppose an uprising against the government. I haven't been able to discover much more."

The young Russian's eyes penetrated him. "Is it Poland?"

Cable's mind saw Sarah's face, young and full of terror, as she had run to him after Lucy's accident. Damn the Foreign Office, he thought. Damn Century House. "Yes."

"Good, Bill. I really think you are trying to help us, which for the girl's sake is just as well. Now there are some vital facts missing: How many men? Where are they now? How will they be transported in? Date? Time? How will they be armed? Finally— and most important—will they take bulk supplies of weapons and explosives to arm dissidents and saboteurs already in Poland?"

"I don't know any of that. I don't have the detailed plan—just a broad outline."

Gordon's eyes narrowed. "But you can find out, Bill—you can *find out*, can't you?" He clutched his fur hat in a sudden gust.

"I'll try—I want Sarah back."

"Can you do it in twenty-four hours?" Cable noticed that the threatening attitude of the dawn meeting at Kritzendorf had gone; the young Russian was coming to trust him.

"I'll try—could we meet late tomorrow afternoon?"

"Yes—on the Kahlenberg. I'll be in the woods near the car park outside the Krapfenwald swimming bath. It's closed at this time of year, so there'll be nobody else around. At twelve minutes to six."

Never on the hour or the half-hour, thought the retired professional in Cable. Always make it look casual. Aloud he said: "I'll be there."

"Good—and, Bill, you still have the little camera I gave you?"

"Yes."

"Then photograph all the papers you can, okay?" Gordon punched him playfully on the shoulder. "Not that we don't trust you or anything, but I need hard evidence, okay?" He turned, hurried across to the door near the parapet, and vanished.

Cable trotted after him, seizing the handle of the orange door to open it. It remained closed, bolted from inside. For a moment he panicked—if he had been locked out he could die in the cold. Then he realized the obvious precaution. Gordon did not want to be followed—he would have left another door open for Cable. He battled his way round the high wall of the parapet, leaning forward into the wind, until he found another metal door. Stepping through it, the sudden warmth and quiet made him realize just how cold and deafening it had been outside.

* * *

After lunch with the British delegation to the IAEA meeting, Cable was driven back to the embassy in Reisnerstrasse. He called Jill into his office. She sat down efficiently, knees together and pencil poised, not a hair out of place, two years older than he and the salt of the earth. "I want a Flash telegram to London, repeat to Singapore for Sir D. Nairn."

"Flash?" she queried. It was the highest priority there was—reserved for world crises and declarations of war.

"Yes, Flash. Classification Secret. Re my ADLON 84271 of 17 September, an investigator is not needed but will be assisted if sent. However I need urgent instructions, repeat urgent instructions, on my response to hostile agent by 14.00 hrs 20 September latest. Cable."

"Is that all?" She had kind gray eyes in a worn face. "Is there something wrong?"

"Nothing I can tell you about, Jill. Just type it and get it off, please."

She had barely left the room when there was a tap on the door and Skilbeck's red head appeared. "May I come in, Bill?"

"Sure—come and sit down." He waved him to a chair by the desk.

Skilbeck sat down awkwardly. "We had Barron down in a great tizzy while you were over at UNO City. I think perhaps you should go and see him." He looked embarrassed. "It's about a demarche from the Hungarian Embassy—to do with your daughter."

"What about her?"

"They say she's been arrested in Budapest—for smuggling heroin."

Cable leaned back, suddenly feeling in command of the situation. "Sarah's been *kidnapped*," he said quietly. "And two nights ago someone from the Soviet Embassy tried to blackmail me—offering her safe return if I worked for them. I refused."

Skilbeck looked puzzled. "Did you *tell* anyone this, Bill? I do think you ought to go and talk to Barron, you know." His tone was suspicious.

"Tell Barron's office he's welcome to pop down and see me anytime," said Cable icily. "For your own information, Paul, I sent a full ciphered report to FCO Security Department—and to your outfit—on Monday. But for God's sake keep it to yourself—no one else needs to be involved, not at present anyway."

Skilbeck looked angry. "But if someone's trying to blackmail you, you ought to have told me. What about PIRANHA? It's a desperately sensitive operation and you're in the middle of it—but it's my bloody responsibility, not yours!"

"This all happened only two days ago," snapped Cable. "And nothing is jeopardizing PIRANHA. Someone has kidnapped my daughter on behalf of Moscow Center and is trying to blackmail me. I've made a report and asked for urgent instructions from London—I hope something will arrive by tomorrow at the latest and no doubt the question of PIRANHA will be covered." He shuffled the papers on his desk impatiently. "All we can do now is keep calm and wait." He looked up curtly. "That seems to be it—okay?"

"But, Bill—it's not as simple as that!" Whatever else Skilbeck was about to say was lost as the door from the outer office opened without warning and a small man with thin gray hair and a red face marched in, clutching a newspaper. It was Barron, the ambassador to Austria.

"Cable!" he exploded, throwing the newspaper onto the desk. "What the *hell* is going on?" The paper was the tabloid *Kurier* and its front page was filled with the photograph Cable had seen at Kritzendorf: Sarah with the elderly interrogator in Budapest. The headline was crude: BRITISH AMBASSADOR'S DAUGHTER ON HEROIN CHARGE.

Cable leaned back, looking a great deal more relaxed than he felt. "I'm sorry I couldn't tell you before. Sarah's been kidnapped and taken to Budapest—the KGB are trying to blackmail me for her release. I've made a full report to London and I'm waiting for something to happen."

"But what's all this about her smuggling heroin, for heaven's sake! It makes it look like the bloody girl is *my* daughter."

Cable stood up abruptly. "My daughter has been *kidnapped*, Barron. The drugs story is all hogwash—a way of threatening us with a show trial and a nasty sentence. She was kidnapped from Burgenland, near the frontier. I've made the necessary report and I'm waiting for instructions. She's my *daughter*, Barron. How the devil do you think *I* feel about it!"

"You mean she *wasn't* in Hungary? She wasn't smuggling heroin?" Skilbeck eyed him suspiciously. "You're saying it's a *frame-up?*"

"Of course it's a bloody frame-up and I'm expecting London to move heaven and earth to get her out."

"I suppose they will. Anyway, it looks as if she's being pretty well treated." Skilbeck gestured at the newspaper picture, looking at Cable curiously. "And I don't see how anyone can *blackmail* you if it's all over the papers."

"I'm damn sure the story wasn't given to the *Kurier* by the Russians or the Hungarians. That's a leak from here—from someone in *your* mission." He stabbed a finger at Barron's well-cut waistcoat. "Yes it *does* make it hard for them to blackmail me—and just for the record, they weren't having much luck anyway."

"No—no, of course not." Barron looked apologetic. "We'd better draft something to give the papers, Cable—a denial, I suppose. Perhaps you and I could do it together?" He pulled out a gold-nibbed fountain pen and glared at Skilbeck over his half-moon spectacles. The younger man took the hint and left.

Barron sat down at the long table and pulled a sheet of blue paper toward him. "Very well." Barron started to write in a fussy italic script. "I suppose we should clear this with London and get it out for the morning editions."

* * *

It was gone nine when Cable got back to Himmelstrasse. He was not surprised that Naomi was not there. The unspoken suspicion between them had been growing and they had parted coolly in the morning. He made himself some cheese on toast in the kitchen, studiously avoiding any alcohol, and went to bed.

He was woken at six-thirty by a persistent ringing. At first he thought it was the phone, but when he reached out in the dark to pick it up he realized that the noise came from downstairs. Someone was at the front door. He pulled on his dressing gown but could not find his slippers; he hurried down to the hall, the bell still ringing insistently, his bare feet cold on the tiled floor. When he opened the door three figures were standing in the darkness. The light from the hall fell on the face of the small one who had been pressing the bell. The face broke into a supercilious smile. "Hello, Bill."

"Stuart." Cable took a step backward. "What the hell do you think you're doing here? Do you know what the bloody time is?"

"Get dressed, Bill. You are to come with us." Stuart stepped into the house. His small body was wrapped in a tight double-breasted black overcoat and his smooth, olive face had hardly aged in thirteen years. The two men who followed him in were both neatly dressed, but heavily built with hard faces. One closed the door firmly.

"I'm not going anywhere," exclaimed Cable through dry lips. "I'm an ambassador with a job to do. Just get out of my house!"

"I'm here on behalf of Foreign Office Security Department, Bill. We are going to a safe house in Salzburg where we can talk without interruption. Your office will be informed when the embassy opens at nine o'clock."

Cable's anger overcame the horror he had felt when he opened the door. "Get out!" he roared. "Get out before I kick you out—and take your repulsive friends with you. Who the devil do you think you are? I'm surprised that even a shit like you has the balls to behave like this!"

"We are acting on orders from a high level, Bill." Stuart's upper-class accent was as precise as ever.

Cable made to pick up the phone but one of the heavies pushed him away from it. "You 'eard what the man said," he growled. "Go and put some clothes on."

"That's right," said Stuart, pulling a blue envelope from his inside pocket. "Here is the official request from Security Department asking you to accompany us. You can read it if you want." He nodded and one of the others produced a pair of handcuffs. "Now—are you going to cooperate or do these fellows have to make you?"

Cable hesitated.

"Oh for God's sake," shouted Stuart. "Stop pissing around. If you want it the hard way, we'll pinion you and frog-march you out to the car just as you are—it's at the back, no one's bloody well going to see."

Cable knew that he had no choice. With a glance of contempt he turned to the stairs, followed closely by the others. An hour later he was in the back of a Ford Granada, wedged between Stuart's two acolytes, as it turned onto the autobahn towards Salzburg. It was like being kidnapped by the Russians all over again.

19 | Moscow and Vienna

SARAH WAS BECOMING A CONNOISSEUR of prison cells. She was certain that this one was near Moscow, for the van that had brought her from the airfield had a small, barred window. Through it she had glimpsed a hideous old-fashioned skyscraper, standing on a ridge above a river—it reminded her of a photograph she had once seen of the university building on the Lenin Hills.

No one had spoken to her when the van stopped in a yard; two guards had hustled her down a corridor and into the cell. It had a narrow metal cot, wooden table and chair—and a window, high in the wall, through which she could see the sky. She was stiff, after being shackled for much of the journey, and stretched her arms and legs in relief. The long periods of solitude had forced Sarah in upon herself. She rarely wept now and had discovered more inner strength than she expected. Even so she wished that she had more to pull out of her mind for entertainment—poetry, music, mathematics, jokes, anything. To fill the void she had turned back to familiar childhood hymns.

She sat down and slowly began to recall every word of *For all the saints, who from their labours rest*, which was a good long one and should occupy at least twenty minutes. She was humming the tune quietly to herself when the cell door opened. A youngish man in a civilian suit came in. "I am Bykov." He spoke in English. "From the Committee for State Security. Are you being well treated?"

Sarah stared at him silently. She always felt a surge of fear when they talked to her. "So far—better than I was in Hungary."

"Good. I expect you would like to write to your father, so I have brought you some paper and a pen."

Sarah was astonished. "I have asked to write a letter before and been refused—why now? Will you censor what I write?" She eyed him suspiciously.

"You should not have been refused and of course I shall read it—you are a prisoner, what do you expect?—but do not let that inhibit you. You want to go home, don't you? You want to avoid being tried for drug offenses? Our penalties for crimes of that sort are very harsh."

"Of course I want to go home—and I haven't committed any drug offenses."

"That is, alas, what I would expect you to say, but I have read the evidence." He smiled slightly. "However, I am here to be helpful. I suggest you write to your father stressing your desire to return home as soon as possible. It may do some good and we shall see that such a letter is delivered to him."

Sarah sat down at the small table where he had placed several sheets of coarse paper and a ballpoint. "Where are we?" She picked up the pen. "Moscow?"

He smiled again. "It does not matter where we are—just put the date. I will come back later." He rapped on the cell door and was let out.

Sarah stared at the blank paper. At last they had let something slip—if they wanted her to write to her father, at least he must have been told what had happened to her. In the long days since her capture, she had nursed a hollow fear that he would not know—would just think she had vanished, with no idea where to look for her until—unless—she was put on trial. She felt perceptibly more confident: if he and the authorities in the West knew where she was, then surely they would be harassing the Soviet embassies in Vienna and London to get her released?

She wanted, desperately, to write to her father now that the pen was in her hand. After so much silence and solitude it would be almost like talking to him again. But what was she to say? *Dear Daddy—I've been kidnapped and locked up, first in Budapest, now in Moscow. Please get me out.* No—she couldn't see her little censor passing that. For the thousandth time she asked herself *why* they had kidnapped her? Why her—Sarah Cable? If it was to put pressure on her father, why had they chosen him? Why not a proper ambassador—to somewhere that really mattered like Bonn or Washington?

Poor Daddy—he must be going frantic. He wouldn't show it; he never did. He looked so tough and dependable, no one would realize how desperate he was inside. He was the sort of man everybody relied upon—or hated because they were jealous of his ability and the respect he could command. He must have been quite something when he was young: when she was a child, before whatever it was went wrong in Vietnam, before Lucy died and Mummy left him.

Her thoughts were interrupted as the door opened again and a woman in blue beckoned her into the corridor, saying something in Russian that Sarah could not understand. They walked without speaking down a flight of stairs and into a small yard. The guard gestured vaguely and Sarah realized that she was being given an opportunity to exercise. She started to walk briskly around inside the high wall, fearing to run.

There was a long flower bed at the far end, where a figure was hoeing the soil, watched by another guard. The prisoner was an old man, very tall, wearing the same kind of coarse black clothes as Sarah. He looked up as she approached: he had a haggard, thin face with wild eyes and a shock of white hair. He cackled and the guard struck him with a truncheon; instinctively Sarah knew that he was insane.

The guard shouted at her in Russian and gestured at her to keep away. She walked on slowly and, when she glanced back, the old man had gone and she was alone in the yard. It was the first time she had seen another prisoner and, remembering his white hair and stooped shoulders, she felt that he had been there a very long time— a very long time indeed. The thought appalled her and she shuddered; could she end up like that? It was all very well being sentimental about Daddy—but suppose he just couldn't get her out? Suddenly she felt close to tears again and a black cloud of depression settled on her as she continued her walk around the wall.

* * *

Cable puffed up the steep gradient of Nonberggasse, below the massive towers of the castle outlined against a pale blue autumn sky. Stuart was beside him, the two gorillas behind. They climbed in strained silence, the sheer rock face to their left, stone houses perched over the drop on their right.

Stuart rang the bell and the solid oak door of number thirteen opened silently. A man in jeans and a parka was waiting in the yard, armed with a Browning machine pistol. "Which one of you is Cable?"

"I am."

"Identification?" Cable and Stuart both produced their British passports.

"Is Mr. Leslie here yet?" snapped Stuart.

The man with the Browning ignored him. "Wait here." He went into the house, leaving the four of them standing in the cold yard. It was five minutes before he returned. "Okay, Cable—go through into the dining room. Sir David wishes to see you alone first." Stuart made to follow, but the Browning barred his way. "You wait, chummie. Sir David will call you in later."

"I don't understand," cried Stuart. "*Who* will call me in? What the devil's going on? I'm supposed to be in charge of this."

"Not anymore, sir." The man stressed the "sir" so heavily that it was almost an insult. "There's been a change of plan. Mr. Leslie couldn't make it—Sir David Nairn came instead."

Stuart's face went black with fury. Something had happened to outmaneuver him since he had left Heathrow at six yesterday evening: something he did not understand. "I must see Nairn at once," he spluttered.

"No—you wait in the drawing room, sir—inside on the left. As for you two," he waved the Browning at the two gorillas. "You field support?" They nodded. "Okay—I'm Wilson. You're under my command now. Piss off and find a pub in the town—don't come back till five this afternoon."

Cable walked across the dark corridor into the room with the big window looking out at the white peaks of the Obersalzberg; he felt light-headed with a crazy mixture of confusion and relief. The familiar figure of Nairn was sitting at the dining table, hunched in a wooden chair with a high carved back. Cable was shocked at his appearance: Nairn had always been gaunt, but now his face had the color and texture of parchment—he looked like a man who was gravely ill. He did not stand up, but waved Cable to a chair. "My God," he said without preliminaries, "what a bloody fuck-up." He still retained a slight Scots accent.

Cable sat down. "You can say that again. I can't stand much more—what the hell's supposed to be going on?"

Nairn gave a distant smile. "You don't sound very pleased to see me, Bill."

"Of course I'm bloody pleased to see you, even though it's taken you thirteen years. But my daughter's been kidnapped and I'm being blackmailed—I can't get any sense out of Security Department and I had Stuart on my doorstep with two thugs at six-thirty this morning, acting like I was under arrest. Now I find you here. *I've had enough*, David. I repeat—what the hell's going on?"

"Can *you* tell *me*, Bill?" Nairn fixed him with the luminous deep-set eyes that had first penetrated him at Cheltenham thirty years before.

"Oh, for God's sake," snapped Cable. "Stop playing games."

Nairn shrugged. "I'd better make it clear that I'm here first and foremost to save Skilbeck's Operation PIRANHA, for which I'm ultimately responsible in London. I got various reports—and your telegram to Security Department—copied to me in Singapore. It all seemed the most God-awful mess, so I broke my journey back to London here. Anyway"—he smiled distantly—"I always did like a night in Salzburg—there's a nice little *pension* down there." He gestured through the window to the jumble of houses clustered at the foot of the hill. "Run by a couple called Struber and well within the subsistence allowance." Nairn was well known for an ingrained sense of thrift going back to his Quaker childhood in Paisley.

"You didn't come just for a night in Salzburg," said Cable quietly.

"No." The same distant smile.

"Well—what the blazes is Stuart up to? Is he still out to destroy me, after all this time? For Christ's sake—he must be out of his skull."

"Ah, yes—Stuart. When I arrived here last night I discovered that he'd been tipped off by someone in FCO Security Department as soon as your report arrived. He went to Walker and volunteered to come out and bury you." Nairn raised his eyebrows and the Scots accent became more pronounced. "That's what he came for—and he'd taken a devil of a lot of trouble to keep it from me. He didn't know I was responsible for PIRANHA. You've been bloody lucky, Bill—if this Polish thing wasn't mine, I shouldn't be here at all."

The coincidence did not ring entirely true, but Cable did not question it. "However it happened, I'm bloody glad to see you. I've been going crazy with worry and Stuart was the last straw—this is the first time I've felt half optimistic for nearly a week."

"Ay—it must have been a lonely few days for you." There was little warmth in Nairn's tone as he went on sharply, "There's one other thing to get clear."

"Yes."

"This really is the last time I can pull your chestnuts out of the fire, Bill. I'm only doing it because I sent you to Vietnam in the first place and I still feel responsible for what happened there. I know it wasn't your fault, nor do I like seeing a shit like Stuart trying to screw a good man; but it's the second time around and there can't be a third. I haven't got that much pull—and I shan't be at Century House forever."

"No, David—I understand that. It would help if you just got rid of Stuart: the man's a psychopath."

"For some purposes we *need* psychopaths . . ." Nairn opened a file briskly. "So let's get back to Skilbeck's Polish operation. I know the background—now what *exactly* have you told this fellow who calls himself Gordon, so far?"

Cable answered in two or three clipped sentences.

"You confirmed it was Poland, did you?"

"Yes— but I think they already knew."

"Probably they did." Nairn glanced at a telegram that was clipped in the file. Cable could see that it was classified Top Secret, followed by a symbol he did not recognize. "And you're meeting this Gordon just before six today—with him expecting all the details?"

"Yes—how the hell do you know?"

"An intercept."

Of course, thought Cable; but it was still unnerving. He wondered how much else Nairn knew. He felt the other man's eyes on him, as if they were reading his mind. "I think Gordon is a KGB major called Yuri Avramov—and if he is, he's not easy to fool." Nairn pushed a typewritten sheet across the table. "So here are the details of PIRANHA for you to give him this evening. Study them carefully."

Cable started. "You want me to hand this over—just like that?"

"No. You take a photograph of it with the camera he gave you—he *has* given you a camera, hasn't he? They usually do."

"Yes, he has." Cable glanced down the sheet. "Is this all *true*—

a landing by helicopter on moorland near Poznan in six days' time? Twenty men? Near this village with an unpronounceable name? Is the list of arms caches authentic?"

"Bill." Nairn's voice was suddenly harsh. "It doesn't *matter* whether it's true or not. You just memorize it and tell our friend Gordon. There's a whole bundle of papers here for you to photograph to back it up. And there'll be some leaks in London and a few telegrams for them to intercept, all pointing in the same direction. *Make* yourself believe it—then he'll believe you."

Cable ran his fingers through his hair, the relief he had felt at finding Nairn in Salzburg evaporating fast. "But for Christ's sake, David—they've got *Sarah!* If I lie to them, they'll know within days and they'll *kill* her. He's told me quite plainly—and I believe him. I don't trust them very far—but on that I *do* believe him."

"She's under arrest and it's in the papers, Bill. The worst they can do is try her and send her to jail—and I don't believe they will."

"He said they'd fake her suicide—she'd be hanged in her cell." Cable's eyes were pleading. "I believe him, David. They'll kill her if they think I'm deceiving them."

Nairn looked as if he was hearing something that, for a change, he did not know already—but he recovered quickly. "I suppose they might . . . but we have to start from where we are. They're blackmailing you, Bill, and they wouldn't be doing it if they hadn't misjudged you. You've got a muddy reputation and they think you'll crack—but you haven't and you won't." He paused reflectively. "So I want you to hand this stuff over—and do your best to make them believe it."

"Do I have any choice?"

Nairn shrugged. "I can't make you do it. You could just tell them you've been blocked from all access to the details of PIRANHA— which will be true, because from now on you'll be told nothing. I don't suppose they'd believe you, which would make Sarah's situation even worse." He banged the table with his fist. "But you're a brave bastard behind that bloody awful kicked-in exterior, Bill. You've still got *guts*, man. You'll do what I'm asking because it's the right thing to do—if it doesn't sound too high flown, because it's your bloody duty to do it."

Cable wondered whether he was hearing correctly. "And what about Sarah?" he asked quietly.

"We'll do everything humanly possible to get her out safely."

"Does that really mean anything? Don't try to deceive me, David."

Nairn met his gaze, but he looked uncomfortable. "I can't guarantee we'll succeed, Bill."

"What will you do?"

"Our ambassador in Budapest is delivering a note today, denying the drugs charge and saying she was kidnapped—protesting strongly and demanding her immediate return."

"Then you do *believe* she was kidnapped?"

"Of course I do." He grimaced. "Not everyone does. There are a few buggers about who'd *love* to think your daughter peddles heroin—but the note's going to the foreign minister in Budapest anyway."

"Thanks."

"Then we'll make loud diplomatic noises in Moscow as well—and at the United Nations in New York. If Gordon believes you and we make enough diplomatic fuss in the next few days, we might just get Sarah back before the date in that spoof note I've given you."

"And if you don't?"

Nairn avoided meeting his eyes. "I think I've primed the FCO to do everything that's possible, Bill—and I'm going back to London tonight. I promise you I'll follow it up." He stood up abruptly. "Of course there's an element of risk. Sarah is in their hands and in the final analysis we're helpless; she's in danger every minute until she's physically back over the frontier. We just have to hope."

Cable stared out of the window at the cold mountains. The truth was that he might never see Sarah alive again—and both he and Nairn knew it. "It's not so easy just to hope, David." The room felt very still. "She's all I have left in the world. You've never had any children—you can't know what it's like."

Nairn put an arm around his shoulders. "No—I suppose I can't. But you'll go through with it, Bill, won't you? You'll feed that stuff to Gordon tonight?"

"Yes. I'll do it."

"I knew you would." Nairn paused thoughtfully. "I knew I could rely on you—I never doubted your loyalty."

Cable looked up, puzzled at this curious choice of phrase. Nairn's face was expressionless. "That's why there's one other thing I'd like to clear up, Bill."

"Yes?"

"I hear the GRU may have a signed statement fingering Golitsyn, supposedly made by you in Hanoi back in 1971. Blackmail material."

Cable felt as if he had been kicked in the stomach and sat rigid for a few moments, transfixed. When he looked up, Nairn's luminous eyes were boring into him. "Well—Bill? Am I right in thinking this document's a fabrication—if it exists at all?" He paused meaningfully. "It's not *true* is it?"

Instinctively Cable sensed that he was being tested—that Nairn *knew*. God knows how, but he knew. "Yes, it's true." His voice sounded hollow and far away. This was the end, but nothing mattered except that they should get Sarah out. "It's not true that I betrayed Golitsyn—I gave nothing away at all despite . . . despite everything they did to me . . . ."

"Yes," said Nairn softly. "Go on . . . ."

"But they made me watch Golitsyn burn—it was horrible. He suffered terribly and it seemed to take forever. Then they told me it was my turn—unless I signed that phony statement. It wasn't just that I was afraid—I was exhausted and confused . . . I'd been ill for days with dysentery . . . they'd beaten me up a few times and my brain didn't seem to work properly anymore . . . it was a reflex . . . I signed it."

"Oh, Bill, you bloody, bloody *fool*. Why the devil did you keep quiet about it when you got back?"

"Because I was thrown by the court of inquiry—I was still worn out and muddled. Maybe I was too angry and proud to admit what I'd gone through to Stuart; I honestly don't know quite how it happened. I shouldn't have been there, for Christ's sake—I should have been in hospital. The whole thing was set up to screw me."

"Ay—but I was there at the end."

"It was too late by then."

The luminous eyes bored through him again. "My God—I can see how it happened, Bill, but it doesn't make it any easier now. I believe you—but others won't if it comes out. You understand that, don't you?"

20 Vienna

CABLE FLEW BACK to Vienna on an internal Austrian Airlines flight and took a taxi from the airport to Grinzing. It took him twenty minutes to photograph the documents in his study; he deliberately made some shots out of focus to give the impression of a nervous man in a hurry.

He left the house at half-past five, with the film in the pocket of his long green loden. There was a bitter wind in the streets and, for the first time that autumn, he put on his fur hat. It was made of silver-gray Siberian fox fur and seemed suitable for the occasion.

He walked down the hill into the village street of Grinzing, pausing in the darkness of a doorway to check whether he was being followed. There was no sign of movement in the shadows, but he was certain they were there. No doubt Nairn was having him watched as well, he thought wryly—perhaps the British and Soviet tails would share their hip flasks of schnapps when they bumped into each other in the bushes.

The thought amused him and he walked on with a lighter step, past the front of a *Heuriger*, two spotlights shining on the pine bush over the door, the sound of a violin and singing coming from behind the curtained windows.

He climbed up the hill at the other side of the street: big comfortable *bürgerlich* houses, behind high wire fences, soon giving way to the darkness of the vineyards. The lane was lit by modern lamps on concrete posts, casting pools of bright white light. Sometimes he could see the twisted shapes of the vines clearly, as they rose up the slope away from the road.

It was a steep climb and he was soon out of breath. The effort of keeping going helped him suppress his emotions, but he could not push away the unpleasant knowledge that what he was about to do might lead to Sarah's death. And what then? He could never live with himself if that happened: he saw her face before him, the strong-willed young woman giving way to the frightened, trusting child whose sister had just been knocked down by a car. He shrugged in the dark. There would always be a few sleeping pills to mix with whiskey, or the Smith and Wesson revolver he kept in the glove compartment of the Volvo—perhaps they were a doomed family and that was how it had to be.

As he breasted the hill and approached the darkened buildings of the swimming pool, he was tempted to turn around and go back to the house. There was still time not to go through with it. The film was in his pocket, but he hadn't deceived them by handing it over. If he didn't turn up they'd be confused, perhaps leave Sarah alone until the diplomats could get her out. . . . He brushed the thought aside and carried on walking.

The pool buildings were a solid black shape, the shield of the city council outlined against the sky at the center of the portico, surrounded by trees which swayed in the wind. There was a little moonlight and, looking back down the lane, he could see the lights of Vienna and—beyond the band of darkness which marked the waters of the Danube—of the UN complex on the road to the frontier.

The car park was empty and Cable waited in the shadow of a bus shelter, used only in the summer, feeling cold despite his fur hat and thick overcoat. Moments later a car drew up—an English Jaguar. It was a nice touch. Inside, the blue light from the dashboard caught the familiar high cheekbones of the young Russian. The window was lowered and a hand beckoned. Cable opened the car door and got into the passenger seat. The back of the car was empty.

Gordon made no attempt to drive off, remaining parked in the shadow of the trees; the engine was still running and the heater blasted out hot air. "Well?" he asked curtly.

Cable handed over the film. "It's all in there." He was surprised how firm his voice was; it didn't sound as if he were lying. "There is a group of men—not more than twenty—which will be taken into Poland by helicopter in six days' time, the twenty-seventh of

September. They'll land at two in the morning, near a village out-side Poznan. The name's in the documents—I'm afraid I can't pronounce it."

The little Slavic eyes bored into Cable's. "That's good work, Bill. What else?"

"Several big arms dumps have already been established. There's a list on the film, with location and contents. The group dropped in on the twenty-seventh will be armed with Armalite automatic rifles. Also grenades and a couple of bazookas."

"Do you know their targets after Poznan?"

"I think Gdansk and Warsaw."

"Good, Bill." The young Russian sucked in his breath. "Really good. It's all in the documents, you say—was it difficult to get them?"

"No—but it was damned difficult to photograph them."

"But I'm sure—with your training—you managed it?"

"Yes—now what about your side of the bargain. What about Sarah?"

"All in good time, Bill. I hear there's already been some diplo-matic pressure for her release and I'll see what I can do to speed things up. If the material you've just given me is authentic—as I'm sure it is—you have my solemn word, as an officer of the Soviet intelligence service, that she will be released unharmed. Of course, it may not be until after this landing at Poznan . . . you do un-derstand?"

"I want her back before then," said Cable roughly. "I've done what you wanted, turned traitor, betrayed my own people. Sar-ah's *innocent* and she's only nineteen. She's been held for ten days or more already and I can imagine what your jails are like—I bloody well want her back *now*." He was almost shouting.

"As I said, Bill, I'll see what can be done." Gordon's friendly tone could soon give way to a menacing sharpness. "Now, two more things—where will you be at midnight tonight?"

"At my home, of course."

The narrow eyes smiled. "Forgive me for asking—you are sometimes elsewhere, I believe. If I need any clarifications or any of the prints haven't come out, I'll ring you then. Do you think your phone is tapped?"

"Not by my own people—God knows about the Austrians or others."

"Good. Secondly, Bill, I have a personal message for you from a very high-ranking officer of my service. If the information you have brought is genuine we are grateful—and we do not forget our friends. Nor should you feel too badly about it—you may, in fact, be helping us to preserve this uneasy peace."

Cable laughed contemptuously. "For God's sake, don't give me that kind of crap. I've done what you wanted—I'll look after my own conscience. Just don't come back to me again—*ever*. Is that quite clear?"

"I said we would not, Bill—that is part of the deal. Now, I'm sorry I cannot give you a lift, but I think you'd better walk back the way you came for the sake of security."

Cable stepped back into the cold and the Jaguar shot off, up the hill to the Hohenstrasse. Within ten seconds its red taillights had vanished and he was quite alone.

* * *

Nairn took Austrian Airlines flight OS225 to Zurich, then a British Airways connection to London. He landed at Heathrow at ten to eight in the evening. It was raining hard and his driver held an umbrella over him as he dashed across the pavement from the terminal and into the back of the black Rover. "Thanks, Len," he muttered, breathing heavily as a rivulet of rainwater ran slowly down his forehead. "Acton first, then I'd like to go home for an hour. I'm afraid it's going to be a busy night."

"That's okay, sir. I told the wife not to expect me till morning. Be quite like old times—been a bit quiet since you became deputy to the chief."

"Quiet? Yes, I suppose it has a bit."

They drove fast through streets shining wet under the street-lamps, weaving through the heavy traffic. Nairn had the reading light on and was peering at some papers, oblivious to the steady whir of the windshield wipers and the noise of the rain drumming on the roof. After twenty minutes the car stopped outside a high wooden gate which opened silently. Len drove into a covered yard and Nairn got out. He climbed a flight of wooden steps slowly, as if he were very short of breath, and entered a long upper room. A plaque on the wall proclaimed it as the headquarters of a territorial army regiment and some faded photographs of groups of soldiers hung on the walls.

Six men were sitting around a long table covered with green baize. All were in civilian clothes, but four had that sharp, well-pressed look that said they had to be military officers. The four made to stand up as Nairn came in, but he motioned them hurriedly to stay seated and took a chair at the table himself. "Good evening, gentlemen."

One of the military types replied, "Good evening, Sir David. Some of us only got up from Hereford a couple of hours ago—but we are ready for you."

"You have a scheme, Colonel Thorne?"

"We have a scheme, sir."

"Okay—expound."

* * *

It took Cable twenty minutes to walk back to the house from Krapfenwald. He was astonished to find Skilbeck waiting for him in the drawing room. "Hope you don't mind me letting myself in, Bill—I've pinched some of your gin, too."

"Help yourself—I didn't know you had a key. Do you make a habit of breaking into your colleagues' houses?"

Skilbeck gave a crooked smile, ignoring the jibe. "No—of course not. I just thought you might want someone here when you got back—it must have been a hellish experience."

Cable poured himself a beer from the drinks cupboard. "There *are* people I'd have been glad to see, Paul—but I'm not sure that you're among them."

"Okay, Bill. I don't want to intrude if you'd rather be on your own—I just wanted to be available. I *do* understand a bit how much Sarah must mean to you. That's none of my business, of course," he added hastily. "But what you've just done took some guts. Forgive me for being impertinent enough to mention it."

Cable almost laughed. He had never seen Skilbeck looking awkward before. "It had better bloody well work," he said gruffly. "I don't want company—I just want my daughter back. Okay?"

"Sure, Bill, sure—I understand." Skilbeck placed his empty glass on the coffee table. Cable did not offer him another drink and he stood up, looking awkward again. "I had thought you might like to get away from things—go out to a *Heuriger*, have a few *Viertels?*"

Cable downed his beer expressionlessly. "Okay—why not?" It was true—a few hours enforced absence from the real world might be therapeutic. "But not a *Heuriger*—I'm sick of fat pork and fizzy wine. It was nice of you to come up tonight, Paul—I'll take you out to dinner somewhere decent. What about your wife?"

"She's not here, Bill—she's gone to see her mother in Birmingham for a week."

"Pity—anyway I'll take you to the Gasthaus Winter."

They drove south along the Danube, to the neat little restaurant at the confluence of the river and the Danube canal. It was past midnight when they emerged, after some excellent salmon and far too much wine. Cable dozed in the car as Skilbeck drove his Lancia somewhat erratically back to Grinzing.

* * *

Two hours later Nairn's Rover drew up outside Bentley Priory on the outskirts of London. An RAF sergeant opened the car door. "They rang from the gate to say you were coming up, sir. Would you come this way please?"

The stooped figure in its shabby suit loped after the serviceman in his crisp uniform, revolver butt sticking out of the holster on his white webbing belt, through the guarded door and down concrete steps into an underground bunker.

The small control room was occupied by only five people: three officers and two girl NCOs wearing headphones. An illuminated map of Central Europe was displayed on a screen and they all sat in a row behind a console of switches and flashing lights. A red line was zigzagging across the map from Vienna, across Czechoslovakia and into Poland, drawn automatically by a hidden computer.

One of the officers looked up. "Good morning, sir. There was really no need for you to come—but you can see how they're getting on. The plane has made a fast zigzag flight low across Czechoslovakia. No sign of detection whatsoever."

"Thank you, Wing Commander. How far are they from the drop zone?"

"They'll be parachuted down in about ten minutes, sir. Here, south of Crakow." He stood up and pointed at the map with a ruler.

"How far is that from Poznan, as a matter of interest?"

"Poznan, sir? A hell of a long way—about two hundred and fifty miles."

Nairn nodded. "Whose is the plane?"

"A civilian freighter, sir, Greek registered—they'll claim to be off course if anything goes wrong."

"And what happens after the drop?"

"Complete radio silence and the plane takes a straight course southwest back to Austria."

They sat in silence for a few minutes. Nairn leant back and watched the red line inching across the map. He felt bad about Cable, particularly the need for total security, which had led him to ask Skilbeck to take him off out for the evening—although that had been for Cable's protection as much as anything, in case it all went wrong.

The red line stopped growing and one of the girls looked up as her headphones crackled. "They've dropped safely," she said. "The radio's gone dead."

"That's how it should be." The wing commander turned to Nairn. "That's it, sir—it seems to have worked. Your Poles are in." He stood up briskly. "Now is there anything else we can do for you? I believe you have an executive jet flying back to Vienna at five this morning. Can we take you to Northolt, sir?"

"I have my own car, thank you," said Nairn thoughtfully. Yes—the Poles were in, nearly a week ahead of the date Cable had given to the Russian. Poor Cable. Poor Sarah. It had been a hard decision to take and his face was grim as he mounted the concrete steps, still accompanied by the armed sergeant.

* * *

A thousand miles to the east, the old Dakota banked over the dark countryside, its engines droning in the silence of the night sky. The last Pole tensed in the open rear door, feeling the slipstream whipping at his face. The green light went on and he launched himself into space with a feeling of exultation. There was a steadying jerk as the black silk opened above him. His right hand held the parachute harness and his M-16 was strapped across his shoulders. Like several of the others he was wearing a rosary round his neck and he fingered the tiny crucifix at its center, his lips forming the words of the Hail Mary, as he floated downward into Poland.

21 | Vienna

Next morning Fritz came for Cable with the Ford Minster as usual, at eight-thirty. Cable descended the steps outside his front door, carrying his black security briefcase, suffering from a hangover. "I'm not going straight to the embassy today," he said. "Take me to the abbey at Klosterneuburg first, please."

"To Klosterneuburg, sir?" Fritz sounded puzzled.

"Yes. I want to see the church." He paused, fumbling. "We may use it for an international service—to do with the UN." The lie sounded transparent—and it was unnecessary. Why bother to explain?

"You know it is a *Catholic* abbey, sir?"

"Yes, of course I do," snapped Cable irritably. "Just drive me there, will you? I must be back in the embassy by ten o'clock."

* * *

The car bumped over the cobbled streets of the little town clustered around the abbey, past dark, narrow shops that had been there for centuries, with traditional iron signs hanging outside—a key for a locksmith, a row of bottles for a vintner—mixed up with modern buildings filling gaps left by the war and the Russian occupation. Fritz parked in the tree-lined Rathausplatz and Cable walked alone through the abbey gates.

He had not been there before. The monastic church was a plain Gothic building with twin spires over its west front. The east end was joined to the curving Baroque facade of the residential part of the abbey: four rows of windows set in walls washed a deep

Habsburg yellow, capped by a roof of red-brown tiles. Two green copper domes in the shape of crowns were visible behind the line of the roof atop the disused imperial apartments. Fifty years before, black-habited Benedictines would have been scurrying across the yard; now it was empty.

Inside, the church was a riot of Baroque color, if somewhat dusty. Marble columns thrust up to the gold leaf and vivid paintings on the barrel ceiling; between the pillars, chandeliers lit high frescoes of the Stations of the Cross. The chancel steps led to a choir lined by carved misericords, culminating in the sanctuary lamp and a richly gilded altarpiece.

Cable wanted to pray. He wanted desperately to pray, to the same God for whose help he had wept when Lucy lay dying. He knelt in a side pew, trying to communicate in his despair to something greater than himself. But in a surge of bitterness he remembered the tiny white coffin he had buried in Teddington cemetery, the mad, desperate look in Judith's eyes, the cremation ovens in Mauthausen, the torn and twisted body of Golitsyn. He stood up abruptly, knowing in his heart that he should not have come. He would find no comfort there, or anywhere else, unless he could find it in himself.

Walking back down the church, on a reflex he paused before the statue of Our Lady, pressed a ten-schilling coin into the box, and lit a votive candle. *If you're there,* he thought, *for pity's sake DO something—give me Sarah back. She's all I've got left. She isn't a wreck like me and she's got her whole life in front of her—don't let those bastards kill her.* The statue stared back at him opaquely and he noticed that the paint on her blue robe was peeling off in places. As he left the church an elderly woman in a black head scarf was coming in. She dipped her finger in the stoup of holy water and crossed herself devoutly before tottering over to a confessional in the corner.

Outside, Cable felt the wind cold on his face again; his features were harrowed but rigid. In the center of the yard was the town's 1914–18 war memorial—a stone cross surrounded by a balustrade in which black iron characters spelled out the German text of *Greater love hath no man than this, that a man lay down his life for his friends.* Reality, he thought bitterly, was not always so simple. They could have his crummy life—and welcome—if it would buy Sarah's freedom. That was a sacrifice he could make almost without thought, but it was not open to him. He felt another wave of impotent anger and cursed. It would be a far greater sacrifice, crushing and unbearable, if he had to live with the knowledge of her death. He pulled himself together at the gate of the abbey, trying to walk briskly toward the dark blue car waiting for him. Fritz got out and held the rear door open.

"To the embassy, sir?"

"*Jawohl*, Fritz. The embassy, please."

* * *

David Nairn had returned to Austria in the early hours of the morning, arriving in an RAF executive jet at a military airfield under cover of darkness. After a few hours' sleep at Skilbeck's flat, he had entered the embassy by a back door; and now he sat in Skilbeck's small office, listening to the younger man intently. His voice showed none of the irritation and distaste he was feeling.

"I'm sorry, Sir David," Skilbeck spoke almost petulantly. "But I really *must* tell somebody. The fact is that Bill Cable has this very close friendship with an Israeli girl called Naomi Reichmann."

"You mean she's his mistress?"

"Yes—I suppose so."

"Then say so, man. Don't pussyfoot." Nairn spoke irritably. "Well—go on!"

"A few weeks ago I learned that Fraulein Reichmann was making suspicious visits to an address in the Second District—which is a pretty seedy area, not exactly on her circuit as an art dealer and an ambassador's girl friend."

"What do you mean 'learned'? Do you mean you had your own ambassador under surveillance?"

Skilbeck colored. "No, of course not. Not exactly. Somebody I employ saw Cable leave the girl's flat late one night—about one in the morning. He *wasn't* there to watch them, honestly, Sir David—he was keeping an eye on Makarov."

"Yes—I know the file."

"Well, shortly after—just past one in the morning—this girl comes out, gets into her car, and drives off. The second man on my team follows her, thinking there may be some link with the Makarov business. She goes down to the Second, stays about half an hour at this scruffy apartment block near the Prater, occupied by a known Soviet informer, and comes back. After that I'm afraid . . . well,

I *did* put them under intermittent surveillance." He looked defensive, then burst out, "Well—what the hell else could I do?"

"Nothing—you were quite right." The quiet Scots voice still had an undertone of disgust. "And what were the results?"

"Nothing definite. The Reichmann woman has been behaving suspiciously—that's all. Every day or two she makes a curious trip somewhere, often late at night, as if she's keeping a rendezvous to make a report, or using dead-letter boxes."

"But you haven't observed who she meets—or found a dead-letter box and checked it?"

"No, we haven't."

"So either you're wrong"—Nairn spoke sharply—"or, if you're right, she and her friends are highly professional. . . ." There was a long silence, broken when Nairn rapped out, "Well—which is it? What do you conclude? *You* asked for this discussion, Paul."

"Look," Skilbeck snapped back, "I don't like this any more than you do. Bill's my boss, for Christ's sake—I've got a lot of respect for him as a diplomat. But the Russians are trying to *blackmail* him. This girl he's picked up with—or did she pick up *him*—is acting funny. It's too much of a coincidence. Strikes me the conclusion is bloody obvious."

"She's their agent?"

"Yes."

Nairn swore quietly and lit his pipe, appearing to go into a trance. "Short," he muttered, as if reading from a file stored in his memory. "Tending to plumpness, with a snub nose and that effervescent zest for life—with its hint of great sexuality—common in mid-European Jewish girls . . ."

"Sounds quite like her—what are you quoting from?"

"It's not *her*, Paul. Don't you know it—? It's a contemporary description of Litzi Friedmann, the girl who picked up Philby in this very city in 1933. He married her, you know, and took her back to England—she was twenty-three and had been recruited to the Party years before by Peter Gabor, who'd escaped from the Horthy regime in Budapest. He became head of the Hungarian secret police in 1945—they called him 'the Beria of Hungary,' a really nasty piece of work." Nairn sighed deeply. "God this bloody place gets me down—it's a filthy no-man's-land between East and West, peopled by crooks. You can't trust *anybody*—anything can happen. Invaders come and go—Turks, Nazis, Russians—but they just go on sitting in those bloody cafes out there, plotting and stabbing each other in the back. A whole city of spies and conspiracy. Terrifying." He refilled his pipe savagely. "So you could be right about Cable's girl, Paul. I hate it, but I'm afraid you could."

"What happened to her—to Litzi Friedmann?" asked Skilbeck curiously.

"Litzi? Oh, she left Philby after a few years and came back to Vienna. Gabor recruited Philby too, of course, but that was all fifty years ago. They've recruited a hell of a lot more since then . . . Litzi Friedmann was still alive and well when I last heard anything. Lives in some style in East Berlin—still a respected Party member with some kind of official job. Probably got the Order of Lenin by now."

There was another long silence. Eventually Skilbeck said, "So what do we do?"

"God only knows. I'm glad you told me all this, Paul—I just wish I'd known before. Do you think Bill suspects anything?"

"No, I don't."

"I'll talk to him, put him on his guard. You keep an eye on her and let me know the result. Okay?"

"But is it wise to talk to Cable?"

"Why shouldn't it be?"

"Well—if he's in it too . . ." Skilbeck paused awkwardly. "I mean, I heard there was some fuss out in Vietnam a long time back—damn it, Sir David, she might be Cable's courier to a Soviet controller!"

Nairn's eyes flashed anger, then had a troubled look. "I know— I've taken account of that possibility. Why the hell do you think you were out on the town with him last night? I didn't have any other bloody choice." He lit his pipe, thinking of the transcript of the distorted tape he had read in Singapore . . . of the two sources in Vienna. Cable could be the one in the embassy—the girl could be the other. It seemed to fit, even though he wished to God it didn't . . .

Cable arrived at the embassy some fifteen minutes later. As he left the lift on the third floor, he inserted his magnetic card into the lock of the inner door and stepped through as it clicked open. He was met by Jill with an anxious smile. "Sir David's come back, Mr. Cable. He's waiting in your office."

* * *

Half a mile away, Naomi Reichmann was feeling angry and frustrated. She had telephoned Cable several times the previous evening, getting no reply, and eventually driven up to Himmelstrasse about ten o'clock. The house had been in darkness and she had waited outside for an hour before returning to her apartment in the Third District, puzzled. Today she had telephoned him at the embassy six times. On each occasion the phone had been answered by that bloody secretary with a plum in her mouth, who assured her that "the ambassador is in a meeting and cannot be disturbed. I will say that you telephoned."

Naomi knew that she was being fobbed off. Yet he'd been in such a state only two nights ago, had needed her so much . . . it didn't make sense . . . unless something had gone badly wrong. Could he have been got at by one of his security people? Despite all the precautions, could they have discovered her trip to Budapest? As the day grew on, she became more and more troubled. Soon after five, she pulled on her leather boots, buttoned her coat up to the chin against the cold, and set out across the Ring to Reisnerstrasse.

22 | Vienna

AN HOUR BEFORE, Cable had been seated at his desk in the embassy, initialing some routine telegrams to show that he had read them. It had been a depressing day, an anticlimax as he waited for something to happen after yesterday's tension. Silence about the Poles. Silence about Sarah. Stuart's ignominious departure to possible dismissal in London had been a relief, but then there had been the miserable fifteen-minute chat with Nairn about Naomi, which told him what he knew already, but did not want to hear . . . all in all, a day best forgotten.

There was a tap on the door and he looked up as Nairn came in, followed by Skilbeck. Both were silent and gray faced. He looked at them questioningly. In the end it was Nairn who spoke. "It's a fuck-up, Bill," he said very quietly. "We heard a few minutes ago—a total disaster."

Cable stood up abruptly. "What do you mean?" The fear in his voice was unmistakable.

"The Poles. They were parachuted in last night. It was a secret operation—very few people knew—and I was going to tell you later on today. But we've just heard that they failed. They were surrounded as they landed—by the army or the fighting wing of the PZPR. They were *waiting* for them, Bill—they *knew* they were coming."

Cable shrank back, feeling unsteady on his feet. "Christ, no—not that. How did it happen?"

"They surrounded them with searchlights, a big force, machine guns, armored cars. Called on them to surrender. The Poles refused—they fought, God help them, and resisted for an hour or so. They were all killed—all except one, who was wounded and managed to hide in a ditch. It was the middle of the night and there was no moon, so he was somehow able to stay hidden when the army left with the bodies of the others."

"The one who survived crawled to the house of a priest," added Skilbeck. "The priest fetched someone connected with underground Solidarity, who got a message to Warsaw by radio. In Warsaw someone else phoned a number of Western embassies. They didn't know it was our show, of course—they just thought we should know what was going on."

"You're quite sure about all this?" Cable sank into one of the old leather armchairs.

"Yes, we've checked back through the Warsaw station. There's been no public announcement in Poland—nothing at all—but there are plenty of rumors flying around. And the plane didn't come back—they must have shot it down."

"The whole thing was a trap," said Skilbeck flatly.

Cable looked at them with wide, pleading eyes. "But if they *knew*, why kidnap *Sarah*, why blackmail *me?* It's mad, insane—I don't understand."

"They were checking on someone else, though God knows who." Nairn paused as Cable glared at him accusingly. "I'm very sorry, Bill."

"Sorry? *Sorry?*" Cable's voice was almost a scream of pain. He was still staring at Nairn, eyes blazing with fear and fury. "Christ, David—do you know what you've done? They'll kill Sarah!" He felt tears on his cheek and covered his face with his hands. "You *deceived* me . . . you *bastard.*"

He heard Nairn speaking in the distance, felt an arm around his shoulders. Then the door closed quietly, and he realized that he was alone.

* * *

Cable stayed immobile in the armchair for more than an hour. After a time he stopped weeping. The room grew dark but he did not turn on the lights. At five-thirty there was a tap on the door and Jill came in. She switched on the old green-shaded desk lamp and cleared his OUT tray, as if it were perfectly normal to find one's ambassador sitting alone in the dark like a zombie. She paused by his chair. "I'm very sorry about Sarah," she said hesitantly. "All the girls are, but I'm sure they'll get her out all right. Will you be okay now—is there anything else I can do?"

"No thanks, Jill—I'm going home. You should too. Good night."

"Good night, Mr. Cable."

Cable rang the garage to ask Fritz to bring his car to the front door and pulled on his overcoat. He had no idea what had happened to Nairn and Skilbeck—and he didn't much care. He walked slowly out of the office and took the lift to the ground floor, where he acknowledged the security guards' "Good nights" like a sleepwalker.

The car was waiting by the pavement in the light of a street lamp and Fritz held the rear door open. Cable was about to get into it when he heard running feet and a tug at his sleeve. "Hey— where the devil do you think you're going?" He turned around: it was Naomi, eyes looking up at him angry and accusing below her head scarf.

"I can't stop and talk now," he snapped, turning back to the car, aware that Fritz was looking away with embarrassment.

She seized his arm again. "Yes, you bloody well can! Good grief, Bill—I've been trying to get in touch with you for two days—I've been going *frantic*. Stop behaving like a bastard! What the devil's wrong?" Her voice had risen to a shriek.

Cable grasped her by the shoulders and shook her. "Shut up!" He raised his hand threateningly. "Shut up or I'll smack your face. I've had enough today—without this kind of crap outside my own embassy!" He pushed her sprawling into the car. "Take us to the Cafe Landtmann, Fritz."

They were at the big cafe on the Ring in five minutes. Cable pushed Naomi roughly out of the car and told Fritz to wait outside. He strode through the double winter doors, Naomi stumbling behind him, and took a table in a corner. The place was empty—barren rows of marble-topped tables waiting under their curling brass lamps, for the evening rush—except for two old men playing chess and a woman in a white fur hat reading one of the newspapers provided by the management.

A waiter in a dinner jacket approached and Cable ordered two coffees, then turned to Naomi brusquely. "Well—what do you want?"

She had taken off her head scarf and was pushing the thick black hair back from her eyes with that characteristic nervous gesture of her right hand. She still looked furious. "What the hell do you mean—*what do I want?* I thought we were lovers—we've been virtually living together for months! You're in terrible trouble and I want to *help*—then I find you're suddenly trying to avoid me, your secretary lying to me. Why, Bill—*why?*"

"Do you still have a key to the house in Himmelstrasse?"

"Yes."

He held out his hand. "Then I want it back. Now." The waiter brought two cups of coffee, each on a small oval tray with a tiny jug of milk and a glass of water. Naomi's lower lip started to tremble. "But why, Bill—*why?* I *love* you—it's not my fault you're in this mess—for God's sake let me try to help."

"It's too late for that," he snarled. "I'm sorry—*I* thought we were lovers, too. I was wrong."

She started to weep. "But *why*, Bill? Is it this operation you told me about—and the blackmail? Have your people warned you off me? Do they think I'm some sort of spy—is *that* it?"

"Well—you are, aren't you?"

She reeled back as if he had struck her, her face a mask of shock. "My *God*, Bill. Of course not—how could you possibly believe such a thing?"

"Oh for Christ's sake stop play-acting! I was in love—I thought *you* were too. I didn't think you were doing it because someone on the Moscow ring road had told you to. Now fuck off. Tell your bosses I've rumbled you—I don't want to hear any more—just get out of my life, will you?"

Her face stared at him: red and blotchy from tears, eyes full of pain. "Was I so little to you, Bill—just a bit of arse to screw? To be kicked out as soon as some bloody security man gives you a nod and a wink? Oh God—you made me so happy, and now— you *bastard!*" Her shoulders heaved as she sobbed. The waiter had discreetly left the room.

She stood up, her fingers trembling as she knotted the head scarf under her chin and tried to bite back the tears. "You bloody fool, Bill—I'm the only real friend you've got, but you're too stupid to see it."

She fumbled in her handbag, pulling out a brass key; she threw it savagely onto the tiled floor. "There—keep the bloody thing!" she screamed. "I hope it cares for you as much as I did."

She turned abruptly, knocking her chair to the floor with a crash, ran to the door, and was gone.

23 | Vienna

IT WAS ALMOST ten o'clock that evening and the windows of the embassy in Reisnerstrasse were in darkness. At the entrance, the flag had been taken in for the night and black steel gates locked across the glass doors. Two policemen patrolled the silent street outside. Only two pale lights could be seen—one from the window of the security guards' control room by the doorway, the other from a thick glass grating in the pavement nearby.

Below the grating was the basement—used as a staff club, with a bar and snooker table, faded advertisements for Guinness pinned to distempered walls that had been stained brown by years of tobacco smoke. It was deserted, except for Nairn and Skilbeck as they leant on the bar. Skilbeck poured out two Worthington White Labels and turned on the old-fashioned television. "Sorry we had to come down here—I think this is the only set in the building."

The older man held up his glass of amber liquid to the brass lamp over the bar, which highlighted the furrows in his gaunt face. "Don't fret, Paul—this suits me fine." The black and white television picture flickered as the time signal for ten o'clock gave way to an announcer reading the news. Nairn groaned as soon as he heard Poland mentioned. The picture switched to newsreel film— the bodies of the Poles laid out ignominiously in a Krakow square, to be photographed along with their piled-up American carbines and grenades. . . . *the Polish authorities have issued a bitter denunciation of the Western governments that sponsored last night's futile attempt to infiltrate a group of heavily armed partisans to start unrest in southern*

Poland . . . "Christ," muttered Nairn. "It's even worse than I expected."

The picture changed to General Jaruzelski, face hard behind his tinted spectacles, declaiming in vicious but incomprehensible Polish to a press conference; then to scenes of street fighting—police with plastic visors on their helmets, staves and shields, spraying rioters with water cannon. There was the sound of automatic firing in the distance, as the picture switched back to the announcer. *Despite a heavy security clampdown it is becoming clear that the liquidation of the partisan group, all of whom were shot soon after landing by parachute, has led to protests by leaders of the outlawed Solidarity organization and violent demonstrations in many cities all over Poland . . .*

"At least they don't seem to have found the one who got away," Nairn commented drily. "What was his name—Gierek?"

"Jozef Gierek. No—I've had a radio message that he's safe and in hiding near the Czech border. The Solidarity underground hope to smuggle him out and back to Vienna in a few days."

"Keep him under wraps if he gets back—he might come in handy if the PZPR don't know he exists."

"Separate from the others?"

"The others?"

"Rozinski and the other twelve Poles who are still here. They were going in two waves, remember? The second lot were to parachute in tonight—that's been cancelled, obviously."

"Of course—I'd forgotten. Where are they now?"

"Since yesterday they've all been hidden in the abbey at Klosterneuburg. They were only supposed to stay one night, but I don't fancy the idea of them on the loose again—shall I see if Kardos can arrange for them to stay at Klosterneuburg for the time being? He's got all that red braid on his cassock—he ought to be able to pull rank with the abbot or the chief fairy or somebody."

Nairn gave a thin smile. "Yes—do that, Paul. And what about Cable?"

"He's gone home—I suppose he's on his own, brooding in that bloody great house in Grinzing. Is there any chance of us getting his daughter out alive?"

"Not much, but that's *my* problem, laddie. I'm more concerned about *him*. He's under a terrible strain—he can't be in any fit state to represent the Queen just at the moment." There was the same thin, ironic smile. "How is he managing to survive?"

"I don't think he *is* surviving, Sir David," said Skilbeck brusquely. "He's in a bloody awful mess and someone ought to get him out of Vienna before he does something daft."

Nairn nodded sagely. Had Skilbeck known it, nearly every encounter he had with Nairn made it less likely that he would ever rise to the top of his chosen profession (unless he chose to defect). Nairn had long since written him off as woefully lacking in the necessary degree of common humanity, but one would not have guessed it from his gentle: "One shouldn't push people down the line too quickly, Paul—Cable's been through hell before and survived."

"Well, don't hold me responsible for him, that's all. I've got enough problems without my ambassador going out of his mind. Look—if it's too difficult to get him home to England, why not the embassy house in the lakes, on Attersee? It's just a wooden place for weekends in the summer—but he could go there for a week or two with a couple of the security guards. It would get him out of the way."

"Do you really think that's necessary?"

"Yes I damn well do. He needs some quiet and seclusion—and protection from our nasty Soviet friends. But *you'd* have to speak to him, Sir David. I couldn't get him to go—I'm supposed to be his subordinate. He'd just tell me to go to hell."

"Okay, Paul—I'll ring him this evening and go out to Grinzing for a chat first thing in the morning. Maybe you're right—I'll see what I can do."

"Thanks. I'll arrange a car from the pool for you."

"If you would. Now, do you still have that new intercept?"

Skilbeck's hand went to his inside pocket. "Yes, but don't you think we should go back upstairs?" He gestured at the dark shadows around the empty room. "We ought to be discussing this and handling these papers behind locked doors if the security handbook means anything."

Nairn had switched on the spotlight over the club dartboard and was tossing darts into it, aiming for double twenty. "Lousy arrows," he grumbled. "You're right, Paul, but I'd sooner stay here if you don't mind—I feel like another White Label. No one can hear us. The whole building is empty except for the guards and one cipher clerk in registry."

"With respect, sir, this room might be bugged."

"Ay, but it's a damned sight more likely that your office is." There was a sudden flash of irritation and a dart thudded violently into the board. "You're an intelligence officer—this is just the bloody bar. Anyway, the whole thing is blown wide open." Nairn nodded toward the television set, where the film of the dead Poles was being shown again. In close-up their bodies looked curiously bloodstained and mangled. "Good grief, do you think they've driven a tank over them? Switch the bloody thing off."

Skilbeck did so, then handed him two sheets of paper covered in computerized print. Nairn sat down in an armchair, put on his half-moon spectacles, and studied the intercept closely. "What does our reference mean?" He pointed to a group of letters and figures at the top below the SECRET—U.K. EYES ONLY heading.

Skilbeck looked over Nairn's shoulder. "It's another one picked up by the Nimrods in the Baltic. Maybe their Vienna-Moscow radio traffic goes via East Germany."

"Through the Disgusting Democratic Republic? Maybe. Pity there are so many gaps—must have been a new code . . . they call Cable Socrates, don't they?"

"Yes."

"And their other agent—their *real* agent—is known as Plato. I suppose their list of classical code names has come round again. Maclean was Homer back in '46, wasn't he?"

"I don't know."

"You *should* know, Paul, if you'll forgive me for saying so. In this business the answer always lies deep in the past—nearly always, anyway. So who the hell is Plato?"

"I think it has to be Fraulein Reichmann."

"Cable's athletic girl friend?" Nairn nodded gloomily. "Unlucky bastard, isn't he?"

"*Is* he?" Skilbeck sounded impatient. "You could say that any ambassador stupid enough to pick up an Israeli girl friend of uncertain background in this God-awful city is just *asking* for trouble."

"I suppose you could, Paul, I suppose you could . . . trouble is, he was in *love* with her. Like his ex-wife, whom you were lucky enough never to meet."

"Why—what was she like?"

"Poison. Absolute poison—I reckon they can see poor Bill coming. . . . Do you still have Reichmann under surveillance?"

"Yes. She had a row with Cable in the Cafe Landtmann about six o'clock and then buggered off home. She's at her apartment now—perhaps she'll lead us somewhere tomorrow."

"Not if she's Moscow trained, she won't. She'll just vanish into thin air." He handed the flimsy intercept back to Skilbeck. "Did you speak to Simon Wiesenthal for me?"

"Yes—he gave me the names of three Jews who were active in the resistance in Budapest at the end of the war, all living in Vienna now. But why on earth do you want them?"

"Naomi Reichmann claims to be from Israel. She also told Cable that her father was active in the Jewish resistance in Budapest during the war. Is it all true? God knows—but if it is, I want to find out more about this father. It may take us somewhere useful, or tell us more about her. And if it's *not* true, then who the hell is she, this sex kitten who's been laying your boss for more than six months? Who *is* she, Paul?"

"I only wish I knew," snapped Skilbeck stiffly. "Do you mean we should have run a check on the girl before?"

Nairn nodded wearily. "Yes—I'm afraid we should."

"But how the hell *could* we? Not long ago you were bullying me for putting her and Cable under surveillance." Skilbeck's voice rose angrily. "Now you're trying to say I did it too *late?*"

"No, of course not—you did everything correctly. Doing things too late is the penalty of being a democracy—if you were in a Soviet embassy you'd have had Cable tailed everywhere as a matter of routine and we'd have put the girl under the microscope months ago." He raised his hand as Skilbeck colored and opened his mouth again. "I know, I know. We're decent, civilized people who don't act that way. We *trust* people, respect their privacy. We're nice guys—and nice guys generally lose."

"If I'd had my way, we'd have put the girl *and* Cable under the microscope a hell of a long time ago. But I suppose this collection of Jewish war heroes might be a start." Skilbeck sounded sarcastic and grudging. "When do you want to see them?"

"Could you arrange for me to keep the car after I've seen Cable in the morning? I'd like to visit their homes on spec after that— no fuss, no prior notice. They'll probably be there if they're elderly and retired."

"I suppose so—but they're all about eighty and Wiesenthal thought one of them might have died the other day. Do you want me to come with you?"

"No—they're more likely to speak freely to a man by himself, particularly another old one." Nairn smiled wryly. "What I'd like you to do is ring the Cousins at the American Embassy—will there by anyone there at this hour?"

"Yes—they run a twenty-four-hour operation."

"Then see what they can produce on a Hungarian Jew called Reichmann, sixty-plus, who was probably in the Israeli Army. Go round there and follow it up first thing in the morning, so we get our answer tomorrow."

"But there must be *dozens* of Reichmanns who've been in the Israeli Army!" objected Skilbeck. "It's a very common Austro-German name."

"I think he may have been a professional soldier and served for twenty or thirty years. In that case I should think he might have made some quite senior rank—that should narrow things down a bit."

* * *

Early next morning, Nairn faced Cable in his study looking out over Himmelstrasse. He had arrived soon after eight, expecting to find Cable barely out of bed and in a state of abject depression. Instead he was up, shaved, and dressed in a gray tweed suit. He appeared to be reading official papers while drinking a cup of coffee in the kitchen, but ushered Nairn upstairs to the book-lined room with his desk and comfortable leather armchairs.

"You going out?" Nairn could not conceal his astonishment. "After that ghastly week I thought you might need a rest. After all, it's Saturday."

"No, I'm not going out. Is there any news about Sarah?"

"No—I'm sorry."

Cable shook his head. "I wasn't expecting anything yet. I thought I might go in to the embassy for an hour or two, to be on hand in case anything comes in."

Nairn looked puzzled. Cable had changed. He had an unnatural stillness about him. His face was pale and tired, but there was a curious strength in his eyes, mixed with a deep, troubled sadness. He looked like a man who has died and come out on the other side.

"Don't you think you should go away for a few days, Bill?" Nairn asked gently. "You've taken a dreadful battering. I'm desperately sorry about Sarah, about Naomi, about everything—but be realistic. You must be absolutely worn out."

"Go away? Where?"

"London, perhaps . . . or Skilbeck said something about an embassy house on Attersee."

"Don't be ridiculous! An empty house by a bleak lake, all shut up for winter? Now that really *would* get me down. Get one thing clear, David—I'm not about to crack up."

"I hope not, Bill—but you must be pretty close to it. Anyone would be."

"No. Of course I'm desperately worried about Sarah; and I'm hurt about Naomi, but I've had all night alone in this mausoleum to think about it. . . . I went to the abbey at Klosterneuburg the other day, you know. I had some idea of praying—of course it was hopeless . . . just made me realize that we all survive or go under alone."

Cable did not mention that at three that morning, unable to sleep, he had left the house and walked through the dark village, up into the blackness of the forest on the Kahlenberg. He had gone on walking for two hours, through the moonlit trees, their silence broken only by the occasional snuffling of wild boar or rabbits. He had set out in a mood of total depression and despair, then stepped back in angry disgust from his self-pity. As he wrestled with his fears he had discovered a grim stoicism, a shaft of steel, deep inside himself. It offered no soft comfort, but by the time he looked down into the shadowy valley of the Danube he had confronted himself and his situation with the reality of a harsh bleakness he had never known before; and in that cold reality, warmed only by the love he felt for Sarah and still, despite her betrayal, for Naomi, Cable had discovered an intense determination to survive.

Now he turned to Nairn, who was lighting his pipe which had gone out yet again. "I don't want to *hide*, David. If I'm going to get through this, I've got to *do* something, something practical—to help sort out the whole bloody mess."

"You're not the best one to do that, Bill."

"No, I suppose not—but there must be something I can do. You say Naomi was an agent who deceived me. I don't want to believe that—it's humiliating for any man. But if she *was*, then surely I should be helping you find out who she was working for, what the point of it all was?"

"Are you really up to that, Bill?" As so often, Nairn had wandered away to look out of the window, his back turned to the person he was speaking to. At the front gate there were two policemen carrying machine pistols—the guard had been increased since the raid on the house five nights before.

There was a silence. Eventually Cable said: "If I'm not up to it, I might as well be dead already. If I sit around brooding any longer I'll go crazy, David—I'd sooner go down fighting."

Nairn turned round. "You know, I really believe you *would*. I wasn't wrong all those years ago in Cheltenham, was I . . ."

Cable shrugged. "I can't get Sarah out by worrying. I'd go over into Hungary if I didn't know they'd arrest me within five minutes . . . but you must have some kind of plan in mind, David. I was an intelligence officer once—for Christ's sake give me something to do!"

"You're supposed to be a bit suspect, Bill. I'm supposed to persuade you to take a rest. I wouldn't want to take a risk and get let down . . ."

"There's no danger of that."

Nairn seemed to make a decision. He suddenly became brisk. "No—I don't think there is. And perhaps there *is* something you can do, Bill, something for which you're the best person."

*   *   *

Two hours later, Skilbeck was sitting in a bare room at the American Embassy, watched by an impassive Marine guard in full uniform. He was sifting through file traces that were coming in by telecopier from Langley. Each was checked by Al Nosenzo in the next office before being handed over to make sure that it was sanitized for access by the alien British.

The phone rang and the Marine picked it up. "Yeah?" He listened. "It's for you, buddy."

Skilbeck took the handset. "Skilbeck speaking." The earpiece crackled and he listened with a frown. "Thanks." He hung up and returned to the table, suppressing his fury. Now he had heard it all. Naomi had not appeared from her apartment that morning. After a few hours one of his team rang at the door, posing as an inspector from the City Council, looking for a gas leak. There had been no answer, but after a few minutes the caretaker had appeared and let him in with a pass key. The apartment was empty, a window to the fire escape swinging in the wind. Nairn had been right. Some time last night the girl had vanished—vanished into thin air.

*   *   *

Nairn took a taxi to the airport at midday. He no longer wanted his movements known to the embassy, so he had dismissed the car after leaving Cable's house. Now he needed to be in London, to ensure that Moscow Center was convinced that PIRANHA was off. If he could do that, there might be just a slim chance of saving Cable's daughter if she was still alive. He sighed. He was not optimistic—but nothing was ever easy.

24 | Moscow and Vienna

THE NEXT MORNING things started to happen. A flurry of telegrams passed between London and the embassy in Vienna about
the final cancellation of Operation PIRANHA. The codes used in them
were difficult—but ones which the Soviet intercept service was
believed to have cracked. A meeting of the Joint Intelligence Committee was held to assess the damage done by the failed drop near
Crakow—and to confirm the wisdom of ensuring that there was
no second try. The minutes, classified SECRET, were routed through
a Home Office registry where one of the clerks was known to be
passing copies of papers to the Czech Embassy.

At eleven-thirty, local time, a dark blue Ford Cortina turned out
of the courtyard of the British Embassy in Moscow, joining the
stream of traffic on the embankment on the opposite side of the
river from the high brown walls of the Kremlin. Some twenty
minutes later the car drew up outside the Ministry of Foreign Affairs and a young woman, a first secretary, walked up the steps to
the glass doors. She paused under the chandeliers of the entrance
hall and showed her identity card to the uniformed guard.

She was kept waiting for half an hour, then shown to the office
of an official in the United Kingdom section. They shook hands
politely and the British diplomat unlocked her black briefcase, its
flap embossed with a crown and EIIR in gilt, and drew out an
envelope. "It is about the case of Miss Cable," she said. "My authorities have a proposal to make."

The man behind the desk spread his arms. "But that is a matter
within the jurisdiction of the government of Hungary, as I told

you yesterday, Miss Probyn, and the young lady is held on criminal charges. It is all most unfortunate, but the Soviet Union cannot possibly interfere in the affairs of another sovereign state."

"No? I thought there were just a few precedents for that." She smiled slightly. "But I am not instructed to discuss substance. My government insists that Miss Cable was kidnapped from Austria and has done nothing wrong. We believe that she is now in the Soviet Union. There is no legitimate action that can be taken against her so let us be frank with each other—you are holding her as a hostage."

The Russian studied her impassively; he was not interested in the buildup, only in the proposal, if there was one. "You have a suggestion to make?"

"Possibly, Mr. Kouprianov. My authorities wish to see Miss Cable released promptly—she is the daughter of one of our ambassadors, as you know. If your side is willing, my government would be ready to discuss Miss Cable's exchange for a Soviet citizen held in British custody."

"I see—any particular Soviet citizen?"

"It would be up to you to make a proposal."

This time it was the Russian official who smiled ironically. "We are such a law-abiding people, I don't know of any suitable Soviet citizens myself. . . . I *do* know that the cases of certain British nationals serving long sentences for alleged espionage on our behalf have been raised before . . ."

"I am not here to negotiate, but to find a basis on which my ambassador might talk to your minister. With some urgency, I may add."

"Yes—of course, Miss Probyn. If you will wait, I should like to consult the head of my section. Would you mind accompanying me to the waiting room?"

"Not at all, Mr. Kouprianov."

* * *

Before nine that morning Cable had picked his way along the concrete walkway on the fifth floor of a block of workers' apartments in the Second District. It was not far from the Prater and the huge Ferris wheel loomed above the roofs of neighboring buildings, its red cars swaying in the cold wind. He was still breathing heavily from the long climb, for there was no lift. In his long green loden and fur hat he looked like one of the occupants of the flats, who stared at him curiously from behind net curtains as he passed their windows.

He had told Skilbeck and Jill that he was taking a few days' leave and did not want to be disturbed. Skilbeck had suggested the house on Attersee, but Cable had brushed the idea aside and the suggestion had not been pressed. Skilbeck and Jill both seemed relieved just to get him out of the office; he was still at breaking point because of Sarah, edgy—and deeply wounded by Naomi. But somehow, overnight, he had also slipped back into his former persona as an intelligence officer. On automatic pilot again, he felt curiously professional and dispassionate, despite the fears and tensions deep in his mind.

The apartments were small and their front doors opened straight onto the walkway, which was open to the wind and the light rain that was falling; at its other side were rusty steel railings and a sheer drop to the yard. Between the apartments were wooden doors which, from the smell, evidently concealed shared—and not very efficient—outside toilets. The whole place would have been condemned years ago, thought Cable, but the destitute had to live somewhere; and in Austria there were always people below the poverty line. Every few years since the war there had been a wave of refugees, some bringing nothing except the clothes they stood up in—from Hungary in '56, from Czechoslovakia, now from Poland. At first they lived in camps run by the government and did whatever work they could get to accumulate some cash. Most moved on—to America, Australia, or West Germany. A few always got left behind.

He rang the bell by the door he was seeking; there was no answer, but he could hear sounds of movement inside. Probably the bell didn't work. He rapped on the frosted glass with a coin and, after a few minutes, a wizened old lady opened the door. She looked up at him with apprehensive eyes.

"*Gruss Gott*. Are you Frau Etelka Abels?" he asked in German.

"Yes—what of it?" She sounded grudging and suspicious.

"May I come in and talk to you? I think you may be able to help me trace an old friend of mine who was in Budapest at the end of the war."

"You from the police?" She still sounded grudging and suspicious, but he was already in the narrow hallway. Once inside, he could see that the decaying apartment was as clean and comfortable as her failing strength and eyesight could make it.

"No—I'm English. You can see my passport if you like."

She shrugged. "You can lie in a passport as well as with your tongue. You say you're English? We wanted to go to England, but we never made it—we got left behind here. If you're English, what were you doing in Budapest? It was the Russians who came, not the English, more's the pity. . . ." Her eyes flashed; once she had shared the spark of vitality—and the beauty—so often to be found in Jewish women from Central Europe. But now she must have been eighty and was starting to ramble on like someone who had not spoken to another human being for a long time.

"The Russians," she said again. "They were barbarians—looting and raping, burning the synagogue. They let us leave in '46. We had to pay them all the money we had for the visa, but we thought 'In Vienna we can work and make more money, make a new life.' My husband was a skilled watchmaker—he still had all of his own tools, inherited from his father. Then at the frontier the train was stopped and the NKVD came aboard. They took everything from everybody. 'The new people's republic cannot let you steal commodities that are in short supply,' they said and laughed at us. 'It is bad enough that you can steal your own labor.' They took Ferenc's tools—all of them. They took our overcoats, even though it was winter, all the spare clothes we had packed, my watch and my wedding ring—even our shoes."

Cable knew that to sympathize would only bring forth more; and he had little time. "Is your husband here?" he said sharply, thinking that this was the moment when sod's law would apply. Her husband would be long dead.

But she flung open the door of the living room. "Oh yes—he's here," she said contemptuously. An old man sat in an armchair, wearing the black hat, beard, and long white hair of a Hassidic Jew. "*He's* here—that's why I am too. He gave up after they took his tools, you know. He said it was like losing his hands." She snorted. "If he had more spine we wouldn't still be in this God-forsaken city, living in a *Scheisshaus* like this, I can tell you."

Cable held out his hand and the old man shook it without getting up. "Herr Abels," he said. "My name is Freeman. I wonder if we could talk a little about Budapest in 1945? I think you might be able to help me trace an old friend."

The old man looked at him with blank eyes, showing no interest. "That was a long time ago." His voice was as hollow as his stare. "What was this 'friend' of yours called?"

"Reichmann."

"That is not a Hungarian name—he must have been an Austrian." He gave a slight shrug. "Anyway, it means nothing to me—there were thousands of people coming and going in Budapest then."

"I understand from Simon Wiesenthal that you were a member of the Jewish Council."

"So Wiesenthal sent you, did he?" The old man seemed to come alive for a moment. "Yes—I was on the Council."

"Then you may have come across Reichmann—I believe he was active in the Resistance."

"In the Resistance? There were not so many in the Resistance—most of us went meekly to Auschwitz." He suddenly started in his chair. "Of course—Reichmann!" The old man's lip curled. "You don't mean *Gideon* Reichmann—the one who worked with Wallenberg?"

"Yes—I think that may be him."

"Well—that man might be a friend of yours, *mein Herr*, but—I can tell you—no friend of mine. I offered him a good price for one of those passports to Sweden they were giving away—thousands of pengöes—but he refused me. *Refused* me, while the trains were still leaving for Auschwitz every day! Said there were limited numbers, you had to have Swedish connections . . ." His voice trailed away.

"Yes," Cable encouraged. "I think that is the man—what *else* can you tell me?"

"Tell you—about that turd? Oh, I can tell you a lot, believe me. But he *refused* me—and look at us now. Do you understand? Despite Reichmann's treachery we survived the war, but did she tell you what happened to us then? How the Russians took everything?" He turned on his wife with an expression of contempt. "They even took her panties—the ones she was wearing—because they were silk. Did she tell you that?"

The old woman left the room hurriedly and Cable settled down to listen to this man whose life had stopped nearly forty years ago. "Where were you living before the Russians came?" he asked gently, switching on the miniature recorder in his jacket pocket, its tiny microphone hidden in his lapel.

*   *   *

Later in the day Cable made a similar call to an address in Grinzing—but this time to a luxurious modern house—then a third to an apartment in a tree-lined street in the Eighteenth District— but there his quarry was out. Finally he called on a retired bank manager who lived in a little house by a lake, in the shadow of the United Nations building on the other side of the Danube. The bank manager had been a prisoner in Mauthausen, surviving until the American liberation in 1945. At that stage of his life he had been a card-carrying member of the communist party.

When he left the bank manager's house, Cable felt both physically and emotionally exhausted. He walked along the gravel path by the bleak lake, his shoulders hunched against the cold wind from the east. He glanced over his shoulder from time to time, but as far as he could tell he had not been followed all day. He had left Himmelstrasse by the back gate, under cover of darkness that morning.

He stopped at a telephone kiosk and made a call to Austrian Airlines, making a reservation for the following day. Then he walked to the Alte Donau U-bahn station to start his journey home. The towers of the United Nations complex loomed up a few hundred yards away, outlined in the dark by the lights in the offices. He smiled to himself—he no longer felt like an ambassador. He was an intelligence officer again, following a warm trail.

25 | London and Tel Aviv

NAIRN'S OFFICE was on the same floor as the director general's, but it did not look north to the Houses of Parliament. The view, when there was one, was over the streets and factories of South London, sometimes with the green of the North Downs far in the distance. Today the Downs—and most of South London—were hidden by a gray haze.

He had not spent a full day in the office for some weeks and settled down at the not-very antique desk, lighting a pipe and riffling through his IN tray. The bombshell lay in his folder of that day's telegrams—a single pink sheet from his head of station in Moscow. The Soviet foreign minister had considered the embassy's proposal and rejected it. There was no one in British custody, including British citizens jailed for espionage, for whom the Soviet Union was willing to exchange Miss S. Cable. That was all—a flat rejection—with no indication of what they would do with her.

He leaned back, cursing quietly to himself. He had expected them to procrastinate, but in the end to seize the opportunity to get back a professional agent in exchange for a terrified teen-ager. What the hell were they playing at? Could they be so keen to punish Cable for trying to deceive them? They'd had the lives of thirteen Poles with more courage than sense—must the bastards have Sarah's as a blood sacrifice too?

Frowning, he picked up his red scrambler telephone.

* * *

At four-thirty that afternoon Cable stood in the arrivals hall at Ben-Gurion Airport, Tel Aviv. He joined a queue shuffling past the immigration desk, feeling unpleasantly conspicuous as he showed his own passport, which identified him as a member of HM Diplomatic Service. As the passport was stamped and handed back to him, he noted one of the two officials at the desk typing something into a computer terminal. The Mossad would know of his arrival quite soon.

He took a taxi to the hotel recommended by Nairn—Maxim's on Hayarkon Street. It turned out to be a comfortable little place overlooking the sea. The proprietor was an Armenian Jew who greeted Cable warmly. "Any friend of Sir Nairn is a friend of mine—vat a pleasure to meet you." He bowed as he reached for Cable's small suitcase. "I got a nice room at the front. Ten percent reduction if you pay in U.S. dollars."

He had not intended to reveal his connection with Nairn, but Nairn had insisted. "The more people who know you're my representative the better, Bill; Maxim is discreet—he'll tell only the Mossad, which may help to reassure them that you really are who you say you are, not some Moscow-trained impostor. It could save precious time."

Cable changed into a casual shirt and trousers, for it was sunny and very hot, then called another taxi. The driver took the road south, along the sea front, high concrete hotels and blocks of flats on their left, the azure Mediterranean breaking on white sandy beaches to their right. After a time he took the road climbing up into the hills toward Jerusalem, branching off into a steep lane shaded by olive trees.

The taxi stopped by a high white wall, at a spot looking down over the city and the still blue expanse of the sea. Cable got out. "Please wait," he said to the driver, walking over to a wooden gate set in the wall. Two television cameras on metal brackets covered the area outside the gate, which was locked, but there was a bell push and the grille of an entry phone beside it. He pressed the bell. A distorted voice came out of the entry phone, speaking unintelligibly in Hebrew.

Cable pressed the button again. "British Embassy," he said. "Visitor for the general."

After a few minutes Cable sensed that he was being observed through a peep hole, as well as by the television cameras; then the gate slowly opened. A well-built man in his sixties faced him. His head was completely bald and he wore nothing but a thin undershirt, blue shorts, and sandals. His body had been burned a dark brown by the sun. He carried a revolver and a pruning hook. "Yes," he said sharply. "What do you want?"

"Lieutenant General Reichmann?" queried Cable.

"Yes—who the devil are you?"

"My name is Cable—I am a British diplomat. May I come in?"

"And I am Mickey Mouse. If you're from the British Embassy show me your passport—and your Israeli identity card."

Cable handed over his passport and the other man examined it closely, page by page. "I don't have a local identity card," said Cable. "I've come from Vienna to see you."

The older man looked puzzled. "I'm rather busy pruning my lemon trees at the moment . . ." His tone was suspicious. "I'll give you five minutes."

Cable followed him into a garden that was shaded by lines of lemon and orange trees; he could see a small white villa a little farther up the hill. The general locked the gate in the wall behind them and led the way to a bench by a pool in which goldfish darted among the lilies. He sat down, motioning Cable to sit beside him and fixing him with penetrating eyes. "Well—what do you want?"

"General Reichmann—does my name mean anything to you?"

"Possibly—possibly not. You have four minutes left."

"General—I am the British ambassador to the United Nations in Vienna. I am also here as the personal representative of the deputy head of our intelligence service. We need your help, in a matter of interest to both our countries."

The other man shrugged. "Then you have come to the wrong place, Mr. . . ." He made a show of consulting the dark blue passport, which was still in his hand. "Mr. *Cable*. I am just a retired army officer. If you're interested in intelligence matters you should send your ambassador in Jerusalem to see Aharon Yadin, the director general of the Mossad. Why come to me?" He stood up and held out his hand. "Shalom."

Cable remained seated. "I came to *you*, General, because we know that you were, in fact, a senior officer of the Mossad for many years before your retirement. We also believe that your daughter, Naomi—whom I knew well myself in Vienna—is a Soviet agent. If we were to reveal this it would—to say the least—embarrass you and your government. It is a very serious matter."

Reichmann's face darkened with anger. "Don't try to threaten me, sir! Your country has, if I may say so, a significantly worse record than Israel in the number of your top officials suborned, bought, or bedded by the KGB. In any case, what you say is arrant nonsense. My daughter is a dutiful Israeli citizen, who happens to be working abroad for a time."

"Do you know where your daughter is at present?"

"Of course, she is in Vienna—where you say you have come from."

"No, General—your daughter is not in Vienna. She has vanished. We do not know where she has gone—nor, apparently, do you. We believe that she is a Soviet agent who has fled to escape detection."

Reichmann looked puzzled and angry, but he did not repeat his request that Cable should leave. He sat down again, as if suddenly resigned to the fact that he could not get rid of him so easily.

"Furthermore," said Cable, his voice rising, "a child of mine has been kidnapped by the Soviet intelligence service, is held somewhere in Eastern Europe and threatened with death unless certain strategic secrets are released. I believe your daughter to be implicated in this matter and we shall have no hesitation in making that known if you are not prepared to help us." He paused. This was where it could all go wrong; and if he blew it the stake could be as high as Sarah's life.

The old man leaped up furiously. "How dare you, sir! Be careful! Men have died for less than trying to blackmail a lieutenant general of the Israeli Army in his own home." He turned to the villa, shouting, "Reuven—*Reuven!*"

A young man in jeans appeared, carrying a Uzi machine pistol: very lithe and fit, evidently a bodyguard. "Keep an eye on this fellow," snapped Reichmann, hurrying into the house. He was gone about twenty minutes. Cable sat in silence, watched by the bodyguard, whose Uzi was trained directly on him. He imagined the old man as he feverishly telephoned one Vienna number after another, only to find that Naomi had, indeed, gone. He felt a twinge of pity.

When the general came back he looked preoccupied. He did not refer to Naomi, but addressed Cable curtly. "So what the hell do you want?"

"For a start you might tell me about Istvan Gyor."

The other man's face remained rigid but he started slightly. "Who is Istvan Gyor?"

"I have just flown from Vienna in the hope that *you* could answer that question. I understand he was with you in Budapest in 1945, when the Red Army arrived."

There was a long silence before the general spoke. "I see you have done some homework, Cable. Damn you. Where are you staying?"

"Maxim's hotel on Hayarkon Street."

"Very well. I must speak to Aharon Yadin. No doubt he will wish to check you out—and woe betide you if you are an impostor, sir! You will hear nothing for at least twenty-four hours—and I may have nothing to tell you, even then. I promise nothing. Please leave me now—I will contact you within two days."

They did not shake hands at the gate, where Reichmann gazed into Cable's eyes with an expression of distaste. "I don't like this, Cable—and I don't think I like you much either. You say you were a friend of my daughter's in Vienna?"

"Yes—I was."

"And now you come to me like this. My God—have you no decency?"

"I too have a daughter, who is in prison and threatened with death—and I believe Naomi is partly responsible. Don't talk to me about decency."

"Get out."

"Shalom, General. Try to make it less than two days."

Cable got back into the taxi, which was still waiting, and it bumped off down the track toward the Jerusalem highway. He hadn't blown it—but he was a long way from winning the old man's trust and confidence. He would need to do better next time—much better. As the taxi descended and the vivid blue of the sea vanished behind an olive grove, he lit a cigarette, conscious that his hands were shaking.

* * *

In Moscow the two guards pushed Sarah through the narrow doorway into the prison office and took up a position behind her as she stood before the desk. An official she had never seen sat at it. "You are Sarah Cable?" He spoke good English.

"Yes."

"It has been decided that you will return to Hungary in a day or two. There you will be held in prison, to await trial on charges of entering that country illegally, smuggling a proscribed drug—that is heroin—across the frontier and offering it for sale to Hungarian students." He paused meaningfully. "You should be aware that the latter two charges carry the death penalty. Now please sign this." He pushed a paper and a ballpoint across the desk toward her.

Sarah's hand was trembling as she picked up the pen. "What is this paper?"

"You can read it—it is in both Russian and English. It is simply an acknowledgment that you have been well treated here and have been informed of your return to Hungarian jurisdiction."

Sarah leaned forward and scribbled a shaky signature.

26 Tel Aviv

CABLE SPENT TWO NIGHTS in the comfortable little hotel on the front at Tel Aviv. He knew that nothing would happen for at least a day, but the waiting was difficult. The first morning he walked over a mile along the empty beach, until the skyscraper hotels fell away and he came to a desolate stretch of sand between the sea and the ruins of a mosque. The desolation matched his own mood and he kicked a pebble angrily into the water. Damn them all. Skilbeck had told him they were still optimistic about getting Sarah out, but he was beginning to feel in his bones that she was already dead. And Naomi . . . he could not *believe* that she had shared his life, given herself to him, purely as an intelligence source. Her betrayal was a wound that could not heal.

He knew that he had to shake off this mood of bitter self-pity. The second day, to occupy the time, he took the bus up to Jerusalem and spent some hours wandering around the narrow alleys of the Old City. Late in the afternoon he left by the Lion Gate and walked down into the Vale of Kidron, then up the steep gravelled paths of the Mount of Olives.

Halfway up he began to feel that he was nearly fifty and paused to rest, breathing heavily and leaning on the stone wall holding back the overgrown garden of the Russian church of St. Mary Magdalene. He was glad of the sharp shadow cast by an olive tree to protect him from the fierce sun. The clustered, onion-topped domes of the church rose above him, a riot of green and gold, a strange piece of Muscovite architecture set down on the dry Palestinian hillside; it had been built by the Tsar not thirty years before the Revolution. He started to go inside, but the gate was chained shut and its paint was flaking off, as if it were not often opened.

He climbed higher up the hill, turning back to look at the old city, clustered on the other side of the valley, dominated by the gold cupola of the Dome of the Rock on the stone platform which had once supported the Temple. A mosque on one side of the valley, a Russian church on the other—he reflected on the irony that the most Jewish thing he could see was the man observing him discreetly from the shade of a tree about a hundred yards farther up the path. The Mossad surveillance team was not far away.

At that moment he thought of Naomi again—and remembered the day he had spent listening to the elderly Hungarian Jews in Vienna. Gradually, it was all becoming clear.

* * *

Late in the afternoon he called at the British Consulate-General and found the local resident in his office. He had become thinner and seedier in more than ten years, with a veined drinker's nose, but Cable recognized him at once; he should have guessed when Nairn mentioned the name.

"Good afternoon, Ryder," he said. "I'm Cable—I think Nairn has spoken to you about my visit here."

"*Good afternoon*, squire." Ryder sounded friendly; perhaps he had forgotten their last meeting, when Cable had left him unconscious at Box Hill with a dislocated shoulder. "Long time no see. Yes—Nairn says I'm to give you every assistance. I gather you're not one of our mob anymore but an ambassador or something?"

"I'm the ambassador to the UN in Vienna."

Ryder raised his eyebrows. "Coo—a real bit of class. We *are* honored. Would you like a snifter?" He gestured to a bottle of Teacher's whiskey standing open on a side table.

"No thanks."

"Suit yourself. Don't mind if I do, do you?" He poured himself a half tumbler, his hands shaking. If he wasn't an alcoholic already, thought Cable, he soon would be. "Just let me know what you want. Our humble resources are all at your disposal." He gave a mock bow. "I don't want to know what you're doing . . ."

"I wasn't going to tell you."

"No. Ours not to reason why, ours just to try and stay dry." He took a gulp of whiskey with a grin.

"I'll try not to upset any of the locals while I'm on your patch."

"Oh yes—do that." Ryder did not sound unduly concerned. "Everything's pretty fragile round here." He handed Cable a sealed envelope. "Two telegrams for you—we deciphered them, I hope that was all right?"

Cable opened the envelope. Both messages were from Nairn: no news about either Sarah or Naomi. "No reply necessary," he said. "I'll keep in touch."

* * *

Next morning he was leaning on the sea wall outside the hotel, watching the waves breaking in flurries of white foam on the sand, the white skyscraper hotels of Tel Aviv stretching away to his left and right. He turned his head as a gray car drew up quietly behind him. General Reichmann beckoned from the driver's seat and Cable got in beside him. Neither of them said anything until the car had left Hayarkon Street and was driving south by the sea toward Jaffa.

"I have consulted Melchior," said the old man gruffly. "Reluctantly he has given me permission to talk to you, within certain limits."

"I think that would be to our mutual advantage."

"That's a matter of opinion. It seems to be a case of us giving and you listening—so there will be some conditions."

"Of course—what are they?"

"Were you my daughter's lover?" asked the old man abruptly.

"That is rather a personal matter, General."

Cable studied Reichmann's profile as he steered the car through the traffic by the sea. He had a strong face, but there was something vulnerable about his bearing today—and he was gripping the steering wheel so hard that his knuckles showed white in his sunburned hands. Eventually he said, "Your allegation that my daughter is a Soviet agent is complete nonsense, you know." But there was a note of doubt—even of fear—in his tone. Cable said nothing and Reichmann glanced at him sharply before his eyes returned to the road. "It does, however, seem that Naomi has vanished—and I am very worried about her." It was clear that he hated admitting it. "We must find her—that is why I asked if you were her lover. She has mentioned you, though not by name. I take it you want to find Naomi as well—you were with her up to a few days ago. Will you help me?"

"Yes—if you will help us." *He'll be shaken*, Nairn had said, *desperate to find her. Tell him we'll cooperate, send a gunboat, anything, if he'll help us pin down this bloody man Gyor. If she's gone to her spiritual home in Moscow it won't help him anyway. If she's just gone to Golders Green for the weekend, it will—and in that case we'd like to get our hands on her anyway.*

"Very well," said Reichmann gruffly. "General Yadin has already made an official request for cooperation to Sir Ian Walker. Telegrams were exchanged yesterday—but I wished to have your personal commitment. If *you* want to find Naomi, I believe we shall do it."

Poor old bugger, thought Cable. He was living in a world of fantasy, shutting out the truth—he would be shattered in the end. He imagined the pain he would have felt if Sarah had betrayed him, as this proud old man had been betrayed, and felt a wave of compassion as the car stopped in a steep street near the harbor in Jaffa. The two men left it and walked down an alley of stone steps, until the general produced a latchkey and let them through a heavy oak door into a courtyard. Beyond was the door of an old Arab house. Inside, the general conducted Cable through to a room with a balcony shaded from the sun by a red blind, looking down onto the port and the Mediterranean. A pot of coffee and three cups were waiting for them. Reichmann closed sliding glass doors to shut out the noise of the harbor, where a freighter was being loaded with wooden crates, and a youngish man appeared. The general introduced him: "This is Nathan Weitz, he is here to represent the head of the Mossad." They all sat down and Reichmann turned to Cable. "Well, Mr. Cable," he said curtly. "*You* came to see *us*. What do you already know?"

Cable sipped the strong, aromatic coffee. "I know, General, that you were a senior officer of the Mossad for many years, before you retired last year. I believe that an operation in which my service is involved has somehow crossed with one of yours, directed against a common enemy, in Vienna."

"And how do you know that?"

"My examination of some recent events led me to that conclusion."

The general's face still showed the strain Cable had seen in the car, but now he roared with forced laughter. "Not giving much away are you, Cable? But I think it is true that both our countries have been harmed by a common enemy in Vienna and it might be wise for us to cooperate. On condition that we also cooperate in the other matter of which we spoke?"

"Of course, that is understood."

"And you will be bound, *strictly* bound, by the undertakings Sir Ian Walker gave to General Yadin yesterday?"

"Of course. I was informed of their telephone conversation and their exchange of telegrams by my embassy last night."

"Very well. You may not take notes and Mr. Weitz would like to check that you have no recording equipment on you, if you would just stand up for a minute or two." Cable stood silently while the third man frisked him expertly. Weitz nodded silently to the general and Cable sat down again. Reichmann poured more coffee and stared down at the freighters loading in the harbor for some time, as if wondering where to begin.

*　*　*

"In 1944 I was twenty-five years old, living rough in the northeast of Hungary—in the foothills of the Carpathian mountains, with a group of partisans. My family were Austro-Hungarians; I was born in Hungary with an Austrian name. They ran a trading business in Vienna and Budapest. All the family but me were in Vienna when the *Anschluss* happened in 1938. They were not allowed to travel out of Austria—out of Greater Germany—after that; and I stayed in Budapest. All my family in Vienna were deported to Treblinka and gassed early in the war. I joined the partisans in 1941." He shrugged. "There didn't seem much else to do, even though the Jews of Hungary were left free because the government was allied with Nazi Germany.

"There were eight of us in my partisan group, four Jews, two Budapest intellectuals, two communists—also pretty long-haired types. A heterogeneous bunch—what held us together was hatred of the Nazis and of our own fascists, the "Arrow Cross," and the fascist government under Horthy. We lived in mountain caves, feeding on what we could hunt or what the peasants would give us. A British officer made contact with us early that year, traveling in disguise through Yugoslavia. After that we were dropped some arms and supplies by parachute—and we had a short-wave radio. Messages came through in simple codes, often phrases used in the BBC news from London. They gave us targets—sometimes in Hungary, sometimes in Poland—and we destroyed them, or tried to. It was similar to partisan action in Yugoslavia—or the Resistance in France."

"Who was the leader of the group?"

"As a matter of fact, *I* was." The general laughed again. "You know what they say—a Hungarian Jew is the only person in the world who will go into a revolving door behind you and come out in front. But it was understood that the second-in-command—who would take over if I was captured or killed—was one of the communists.

"He called himself Gyor Istvan—you would say Istvan Gyor—as with many communists, it was a pseudonym. To this day I don't know his real name. I know now—I didn't know it then—that he had been recruited by Peter Gabor early in the war, when Istvan was just a teen-ager. Gabor, as you know, was a Stalinist hardliner who came out of hiding after the war to become head of the Hungarian secret police.

"Istvan Gyor was impressive—highly intelligent, a fine guerrilla tactician, very brave in combat. One sensed his Marxist commitment, I suppose—but perhaps that is hindsight talking. He had heavy Magyar moustaches that made him look older than his twenty years. He could charm chickens off the peasant farmers—and the pants off their daughters. He was one hell of a fellow.

"In April 1944 we received a radio message that a massive German ammunition convoy was going through to the eastern front, where the Russians were advancing steadily, cutting the German Army to pieces. We were to link up with another partisan group to ambush it. A few days later I was to have a secret meeting with the leader of the other group. We arranged to meet in a safe house— a room over a cafe in a village north of the town of Eger.

"When I arrived, the other leader was not there. The cafe was empty. Then I got a message by runner—there was no phone—to get the hell out of it. I did. Being a partisan is a constant struggle to stay alive—you don't hang about in the face of danger. I was about a mile out of the village—climbing through woodland, up the side of the valley—when the Arrow Cross arrived. I had been betrayed.

"I could see it all, hidden as I was in the forest far above. They came sweeping down the road on the floor of the valley—a dozen roaring motorcycles with sidecars, a camouflage-painted troop carrier and a staff car. About fifty of them, surrounding the little village like a company of black ants. I stood there horrified as the usual round-up took place. The men left in the village were mostly old, and they were soon lined up in the only street; the women and children were herded into the church. I don't know whether the villagers were asked to produce me in exchange for their lives—I was too far away to hear. If they were, no one told the storm troopers where I had gone, for they made no attempt to follow me.

"I could see the Arrow Cross down there, in their green uniforms and black helmets, ransacking the cottages. They marched the old men down to the river and shot them, throwing the bodies into the stream. It was my own countrymen doing this, remember, not the Germans—Hungary was an ally, not occupied. Afterward they mounted machine guns on their truck, near the door of the church; three soldiers went around the building splashing petrol from jerry cans onto its wooden walls. There was a silence—and then I heard the noise of crackling timber and frightful animal screams, borne to me up the hillside on the wind. Orange flames leapt around the church where they had set light to it, and a column of black smoke started to rise.

"Women clutching children and babies started to appear at the door; others were climbing out of the windows. They machine-gunned them down—no one escaped. When the blazing roof of the church had fallen in, the fascists set fire to the rest of the village and drove away.

"My first thought was to go back to my camp, but some instinct warned me against it. I had an uneasy feeling that there might be a trap for me there too. Instead I went down into Eger—I could pass as a peasant in my rough clothes and I had non-Jewish papers provided by our controllers in Italy. While I was hiding there, the gendarmerie brought in five of my comrades and shot them, tied to stakes in front of the railway station. Istvan was not among them.

"After that I fled, making for Budapest, where I thought I might be able to hide until the end of the war. It was a disastrous mistake. Because Hungary was the ally of Nazi Germany, her Jewish population had been spared mass extermination until 1944, but I arrived in Budapest just as Eichmann was starting to round up the Jews for deportation to the gas chambers in Auschwitz. I went underground with other Jewish partisans—I suppose we were the first 'urban guerrillas.' We lived in cellars and traveled through the sewers, doing what we could to save our fellow Jews. Every day the SS rounded up Jews and put them into internment camps— and every day long trains of cattle trucks left for Auschwitz.

"But there was a difference in Hungary. This all happened after the Normandy landings—the Nazis had lost the war, although the fighting would go on for another year—and the Americans and some neutral countries had it on their consciences that they had done too little to save the millions of Jews Hitler had already exterminated. The Swiss and Swedish legations in Budapest were issuing passports to Jews—to make them into Swiss or Swedish citizens. You were supposed to have some connection with Switzerland or Sweden, but that was pretty theoretical. If you had one of those passports the Germans would respect it. You weren't deported— you could stay free. You didn't even have to wear the yellow star on your clothes. It wasn't just that the Germans are so legal-minded and bureaucratic—a lot of them were glad of an excuse to go easy, because they could see a noose for themselves at the end of the war otherwise.

"I started to print Swedish passports—thousands of them—on an old-fashioned press and gave them away. Sometimes they worked, sometimes they didn't. Then I was asked to meet a man from the Swedish legation in a back room at Gerbaud's coffee house—off Veresmarty Square. I thought he would be angry— but in fact he encouraged me. He was Raoul Wallenberg, who had just arrived in Budapest from Sweden. He had the title of first secretary at the legation, but his real job was to save as many Jews as he could. He had the backing of his own government—and huge sums of money provided by the Americans. He was only thirty-one, tall and handsome—with black hair, not blond as one expected in a Swede. And he asked me to join him.

"I accepted at once and that day I was given a passport to make me a Swede—and began one of the craziest periods of my life. Wallenberg was unbelievable. He worked night and day with a staff of riffraff like myself and a few real Swedes. We issued thousands of them—printed in Budapest but genuine *Swedish* passports. The queue outside the legation on the hill in Buda every morning was miles long. Then we acquired other buildings and registered them as legation premises, flying the Swedish flag. Thousands of Jews crammed into them for protection; the conditions were indescribable, filthy and squalid, but at least we were all alive.

"Wallenberg didn't just stamp passports either. He bullied and threatened the SS to respect them. I went with him once to the railway sidings, where they were loading a train to Auschwitz. He squared up to an SS major and demanded the release of those under Swedish protection, while I ran down the lines scattering hundreds of passports! It worked, too.

"Of course, the Germans were furious but they couldn't do too much because there was still a Hungarian government of sorts—and *they* wanted to keep their necks after the war, too. But the round-ups continued and those without neutral passports *were* deported to Auschwitz—nearly half a million Hungarian Jews were gassed there, ten times more than Wallenberg and the others—the Swiss and the Red Cross—were able to save. And both the SS and the Arrow Cross hated Wallenberg and his helpers. They marked us out, to get us.

"One day in October 1944 I was off my guard for a few hours— I walked between two of the 'Swedish' houses, on the street in daylight, not by the sewer, and I was picked up by a group of Arrow Cross thugs. They took me to their headquarters on Andrassy Street. I protested and showed my passport—but they knew who I was. They tore it up, jeering 'Swedish? . . . But you are circumcised—whoever heard of a *circumcised* Swede?' I was beaten with hose pipes and tortured with electricity—not because they wanted information, just for the hell of it. I thought they would shoot me—every day they were shooting hundreds of Jews on the Corso and tossing them into the Danube—but after a day or two I was sent to a transit camp to wait for a transport to Auschwitz.

"All the time I thought, *Raoul will find me—he will come with his big diplomatic car and rescue me.* But he did not come. I found out later that he searched for me, but the SS and the Arrow Cross wanted their revenge and denied that I was in custody."

"But you *were* saved, weren't you?" interrupted Cable. "By one of the barter deals worked out with the Germans by Joel Brand?"

"Yes—I see that you have done some more homework. I was traded for some cans of American soup and a secondhand truck.

There were other deals going on to save Hungary's Jews, as well as the passport business. The Arrow Cross should have shot me at once—after I was in the transit camp they forgot about me. Even so, I was incredibly lucky. I had resigned myself to death in Auschwitz, but instead I was sent to Vienna—three thousand, one hundred and fifty of us on a train—seventy in each of forty-five cattle trucks—it was all very precisely calculated. I worked in a shell factory near Linz—then I was betrayed again. I fell out with one of my fellow Jews who kept pinching my ration of black bread. We were all half-starved and starvation brings out the worst in people. He told the SS that I was really Gideon Reichmann, a partisan leader and one of the evil Wallenberg's helpers. Inside a day I was in Mauthausen. I was tried in about two minutes—as long as it took the *Untersturmführer* to write out my name and sentence—death by public hanging.

"Then I was locked in the camp jail and *forgotten* again! It was November of 1944. The Germans knew that they were facing the most terrible defeat. The *Kapos*—the prisoners in charge of other prisoners—were left to run the camp. They were a brutal lot and most of them were commies."

"Were they brutal to you—a Jew?"

The general smiled bleakly. "Oh no, my friend—it was the *Kapos* who let me out. After about a month a *Kapo* came, unlocked my cell, and took me to the gate. The SS had lost interest—most of them were trying to escape themselves. You could get away with anything by then. But in fact there was an official order for my release. Wallenberg—that incredible man—had made the Germans find me and insisted they treat me as a neutral Swede. It had been a tremendous row and he'd seen Eichmann himself—but he'd succeeded, with a little communist help. The *Kapo* also mentioned Gyor's name and told me I was expected back in Budapest. I was given civilian clothes to replace my prison uniform—and money. I traveled back by train, in a passenger coach. It made a nice change. It took over two weeks to make the journey—it should have been only a few hours, but the Germans were still sending men—or rather Hitler Youth children—east, to be massacred by the Red Army, which was advancing through Hungary. The railways had been taken over by the army. Everything was in chaos.

"In Budapest I was welcomed back by Raoul, who was ecstatic that the Russians were outside the city. You could see the flashes of their guns lighting up the sky all night. I also found Istvan Gyor, living underground, waiting for the Russians to arrive. He said they were planning the reconstruction of Hungary after the war and asked me to join the Communist Party. I said I couldn't join him because I was not a communist—and anyway I planned to go to Palestine.

"I was living in a cellar in Pest, under the ruins of a building that had been bombed, with another Jew. Two days later I returned to find him dead—shot in the head while he slept. I moved out quickly, shifting from place to place, but still helping Wallenberg. Despite living mostly in the sewers, one Friday evening I got together with some other hidden Jews for a kind of simple *shabbat*, around a wooden box in a cellar. We had some candles and a bottle of wine, God knows where we got them. Suddenly I forgot the others there and could think only of Istvan. Like a flash of lightning, I realized that there was a pattern to Istvan's actions. He was not just a communist—he was high in the secret hierarchy and had always been acting under orders from the Comintern—clearing the ground, preparing for the takeover after the war.

"I realized that people like me—non-communist partisans who knew how to fight—were dangers to the imposition of a communist government. So were Wallenberg and his helpers. It was a terrifying, awesome moment of truth. Istvan was not my friend and comrade—he had betrayed me in cold blood to the Germans. He had betrayed our comrades who had been executed at Eger. He had acted on someone's orders to try to recruit me—and when he failed they had decided to shoot me, but they had killed the wrong man.

"The Red Army arrived in January 1945, advancing into Budapest street by street. There was fierce fighting—and the Russians behaved brutally, raping, looting, burning buildings indiscriminately. Communists like Gyor and Gabor came out from the ruins—the Russians had already set up a provisional government at Debrecen, a hundred miles to the east. I feared for Wallenberg, for I knew people like Gyor and Gabor would denounce him—they couldn't understand that he was just trying to help. They knew he had American money and they would see him as an American agent. He had been making plans to use American aid in rebuilding Hungary—the last thing the communists wanted.

"Raoul had saved my life and I warned him that he was in danger. He took no notice and went off to Debrecen to ask the Russians for food for the ghetto. He was arrested and never seen again. He was in Soviet jails at least until the late sixties. He may still be alive—some believe he died about fifteen years ago—I don't know. Alive or dead, I can never forget him. He saved my life twice—and thousands of others. It wasn't his war. He didn't need to be there—he was a kind of saint.

"I could never forget Istvan either—particularly when I learned that he had been with the NKVD squad that arrested Raoul and his driver in January 1945. They never got anywhere near Debrecen, of course. They were stopped by the NKVD just outside Budapest—the bastards slashed the car tires, emptied the money and valuables he had hidden in the petrol tank, and took them away in an armored car.

"For me it was all over. I got out, hitching by rail and army truck to Trieste, where I joined up with a Haganah group taking a tramp steamer to Haifa. I went to Palestine and there I fought the British until Israel was established. The rest of my career you know. As I say—I never forgot Istvan. I have to admit to a certain admiration for his iron commitment, but he had betrayed me and everything dear to me, he had tried to kill me, after fighting with me in the hills. He had betrayed Raoul. I feared what he represented—and I hated him, with a cold, smoldering hate. One day, I thought, I will kill that man.

"I didn't hear of him again for over thirty years."

27 | Tel Aviv

As CABLE SAT LISTENING to the old man, he was transported back into the past and lost track of time. But had he known it, time was running out, for that morning Sarah had been wakened early in her cell at the prison near Moscow. The cell door was open and a bluecap was standing there, with two armed guards behind him. He spoke in English, haltingly. "Get dressed, prisoner. It is time for your move back to Budapest." He spat on the floor. "You will find that drug peddlers are not welcome in Eastern Europe."

Sarah stood up, clutching the coarse gray blanket about her, and fixed him with blue eyes that had grown harder in the last fortnight, wanting to say something cutting. He looked away and she realized that her glance of contempt had been enough. She turned to pull on her clothes, pointedly ignoring the three men who watched her. She was used to it by now.

The bluecap spoke again: "Turn around and put your hands behind you." Sarah did as she was told and felt handcuffs snapped around her wrists. She followed the man into the corridor, the two guards walking behind her. She was troubled by the way they avoided looking at her face, and the little procession had a worrying formality, as if she were already on the way to the gallows. A little eel of fear began to turn in her stomach, but her face remained impassive as they turned at the end of the corridor and began to descend a flight of stone steps.

* * *

The three men sat in silence, looking down into the harbor at Jaffa. The white freighter had now raised the flag of Israel and was moving slowly past the red lighthouse at the end of the pier, heading out to sea.

"At this point," said General Reichmann, "I must make it clear that what more I shall tell you is solely—*solely*—for your information. Istvan Gyor is still alive and the Mossad has plans for him. I must have your word that you will take no action against him yourselves."

"We thought this might arise," replied Cable. "I have authority to say that we will do nothing for one month from today."

The two Israelis looked at each other and Weitz nodded, speaking for the first time. "That will be long enough."

"Good." The general put his head outside the door and spoke to somebody in an undertone, then returned and sat down. "All through the 1970s the security of Israel has been getting weaker. The Palestinian movement has grown in strength and credibility—and receives more world sympathy now than once it did. Personally I have always been appalled by the behavior of the rich Arab oil states—who have never lifted a finger to help their brothers in the refugee camps, preferring to keep them in a pitiful state as a political weapon." He shrugged. "But Israel's record is not without stains either. In any case, some of us in Israel believe that we must make a serious effort to find an accommodation with the PLO if our country is to survive—we cannot go on in a state of war forever.

"The chancellors of Austria have helped us very much by bringing Israeli and Palestinian representatives together—secretly in Vienna—for several years now. We owe a lot to the mediation of Bruno Kreisky—and then of Chancellor Strohmayer. At last we seemed to be getting somewhere—but then things always, somehow, went wrong. A delicate point would be reached—and suddenly the PLO would commit an outrage. The war party here would respond by bombing refugee camps in the Lebanon—and whatever had been achieved would be lost. One step forward—two steps back.

"Of course, there are important people in both the government of this country—and in the PLO—who do not *want* to compromise. The ground for conflict is always fertile. But there was more to it than that. Somehow our secret talks in Vienna were being betrayed. Everything—or nearly everything—about them was known to Moscow—and from Moscow a carefully controlled flow went to the PLO, through the Soviet Embassy in Damascus. No wonder the hard-line groups within the PLO—the Popular Front for the Liberation of Palestine," he spoke the words with distaste, "Black September, and so on—could always mount an atrocity or two at the right time to wreck any compromise between the sane elements in Israel and the PLO.

"It happened to my own family, you know. I had a son, Joseph, who lived with his wife and two children on a *kibbutz* in Galilee. My wife went to visit them one weekend—a weekend when a PLO group chose to ambush a bus with machine-gun fire and grenades. Thirty people were killed—Joseph and his family, and my wife, Esther, among them."

"I'm very sorry," said Cable quietly.

"Thank you—so was I. It made me even more concerned to find the leak in Vienna. We mounted a big operation. It became clear that it was not agents of the KGB or GRU, or those in the pay of other Eastern European or hostile Arab states. So who the hell was it? It had to be someone close to the heart of things—someone the Austrian Chancellor would *trust*. A high-ranking Austrian or a diplomat, perhaps, who might also be trusted by visiting Israelis and Palestinians—at least enough for a little gossip.

"We produced a list of seven—one of them was you, as it happens, so I should confess that I *did* know who you were the moment I saw you in my lemon grove yesterday."

"Me? How extraordinary—why?"

"You had contacts that interested us, with some of the Austrian government. You used to go duck shooting with Kurt Jahn, the junior foreign minister. We also knew of suspicions that had attached to you after you were in Vietnam—that you had been bought by the GRU." Reichmann smiled. "But don't worry—you were easily eliminated, otherwise you would not be sitting here in a Mossad safe house now. In fact, gradually *all* our suspects were eliminated from our list. I went to Vienna myself several times to supervise the operation—even Melchior went once, with Moshe Kagan. The PLO tried to kill them both with a bomb. In Kagan's case they succeeded.

"The Mossad has a running list—the Q list—of people we feel

may present a danger to Israel, whose whereabouts are unknown and whom we should like to trace. That doesn't mean we necessarily do anything when we trace them—we just feel more secure if we *know* where they are and what they are doing. I put Istvan Gyor on this list many years ago and a dossier was circulated to all posts, with his history to 1945 and some drawings of what he might look like twenty years later.

"There were a few false sightings—one in Brazil, one in Canada—then nothing for years. It was Melchior himself who found him—by a sheer fluke. At the reception attended by Moshe Kagan and Melchior, in Vienna nearly a year ago, Melchior was blown flat and stunned by the explosion. He came to after a few minutes and looked around the wreckage of the ballroom at the Palais Auersperg. There were injured people everywhere, but he noticed one man getting up from behind a pillar that had sheltered him from the explosion. That was all, but it was a moment of great tension and the man's face stayed with Melchior. He spent a day resting at our ambassador's house, for he was somewhat unsteady after the attack, and this face kept coming back to him. In the end he realized why. Although there had been this terrible explosion and the building was on fire—that man *had not looked surprised.* And then he recalled a similarity between the face—smoothed and made young by being covered in cement dust—and a drawing on a file. Melchior does have, I should say, a most phenomenal memory for points of detail. He checked the Q files at our embassy and that evening he phoned me in Tel Aviv. 'Gideon,' he said. 'I think I have found your Hungarian friend.'

"Of course, that was just the first glimmer of light—we had much checking back to do and I cannot tell you the details. But a month or so ago we were sure that we had found Istvan Gyor and that he was the source of the leaks to Moscow. Gyor, Mr. Cable, is a long-term mole—he has been in the West under a new identity for nearly thirty years. He is controlled from Moscow—and he is very, very good."

"Who is he?" Cable's question cut through the stillness of the room.

The general smiled bleakly. "All in good time—first there is the question of one of our agents, whom you suggest is a traitor working for the KGB . . ."

"One of *your* agents—I don't understand."

"You don't understand?" The general laughed. "You mean I have actually put my finger on something that the arrogant chess-playing Nairn doesn't know already? There is hope for the Mossad yet." He stood up and walked to the doorway onto the balcony, turning back to Weitz. "Would you leave us alone now, please, Nathan?"

Reichmann stood looking down into the harbor as Weitz left the room, then sat down again. "I thought you knew Naomi pretty well, Mr. Cable—did you never ask yourself what the hell the daughter of an Israeli general was doing working in a crummy art shop in the middle of Vienna?"

Cable started in his seat as the last pieces of the jigsaw began to fit into place. "Are you telling me that Naomi is a *Mossad* agent?"

The general smiled wryly. "No, she is not—and I do not for one moment believe that she has any Soviet connections, either. Naomi stayed in the army for a year or two after her compulsory military service and did some work for the Mossad. I should be proud if she had continued, but we have not seen eye to eye on that and on various other things for some time now. The fact is, Mr. Cable, that I have seen Naomi only once in the last two years."

Once again Cable felt sorry for the old man. "Then how can you be so sure about her—she was acting more than suspiciously in Vienna."

"Quite possibly she was—in your eyes."

"What do you mean?"

"Naomi went to Vienna because she wanted to get away from Israel; she did not say so, but I think she also wanted to get away from me. Even though I am retired, I have maintained an interest in the Gyor case; I daresay my personal desire to find him has been instrumental in keeping the case alive. You could call it a vendetta."

Cable said nothing. The old man was revealing more than he should and Cable did not want to interrupt and give him time to think.

"In the last year my old colleagues needed to check various records in Hungary, to be certain that we had, indeed, pinpointed Gyor. I directed them to one or two former friends of mine, people I had helped Wallenberg to save who are still in Budapest—I hoped they would feel they owed me something. In one or two cases our embassy found them suspicious and frightened to cooperate. That was understandable—I left Hungary nearly forty years ago. I wanted to go and see them myself, but that was forbidden by Melchior." He shrugged. "So Naomi agreed to act as my personal representative and go for me. She went to Budapest three times and collected vital information."

"I thought you hadn't seen her for two years?"

"Just once—I went to Vienna a few months ago to brief her for this mission. She does not *hate* me, Mr. Cable, we simply found it hard to go on living under one roof—and she was willing to do this moonlighting for the Mossad because she knew how much it mattered to me, her father."

Cable fixed him with a hard gaze. "That is an interesting story, General. I am more inclined to believe that Naomi was still a Mossad officer—with me as her target."

Reichmann's face darkened, then he shrugged again. "I have told you too much already, Cable—you can believe it or not as you choose. But you have my word as a soldier that you were not a Mossad target in the last year—you were written out of our calculations long ago—and that what I have told you is true."

"If Naomi was helping your service to identify this man Gyor, I never had any inkling of it."

"Why the hell should you? It was a *secret* operation, Cable—and she would never have known that Gyor had any significance for you or your people." The old man stood up, suddenly looking vulnerable again. "The fact is that Naomi is not a professional Mossad officer, but she is one of the few people who knew about Gyor—and she has vanished. That is why I am so concerned. Desperately concerned."

28 Hungary

ESPIONAGE IS LIKE WAR—long periods of hanging around, waiting for something to happen, interspersed with bursts of action. After leaving the little Arab house in Jaffa, Cable moved fast. He took a taxi back to Maxim's, packed, and settled his bill. By then a car from the consulate in Jerusalem had arrived, carrying a disgruntled local resident.

They drove north along the coast in silence, parking when they were clear of the city. Ryder sent the driver for a walk along the beach and Cable studied an airline timetable. "I'll get the Lufthansa flight to Frankfurt at five," he announced briskly. "There's a good connection to Vienna. Now I must do some telegrams and you must see they go off Flash this afternoon."

"Whatever you say, squire."

Cable contemplated the waves breaking on the shore, then asked curtly, "Could you leave me alone, please?"

Ryder shrugged, with a glance that said "Up yours," got out of the car, and walked off in the opposite direction to the driver. Cable already had the report clear in his mind; he enciphered it quickly, using a block of squared paper balanced on his knee. From time to time he took out the recent photograph of Istvan Gyor, which Reichmann had given him, shaking his head in utter disbelief. When he had finished, he burned the one-time sheets in the car's ashtray; thin spirals of blue smoke wound out of the vehicle's open windows. Seeing them, Ryder came back. "You finished, then?"

Cable handed him three sheets of figures. "Send it personal for Nairn, addressee to decipher."

"Don't I get a copy?"

"No."

"Bloody funny way to run a railway, I must say." Grumbling, Ryder got back into the car. The driver started the engine and headed for the airport on the road to Jerusalem.

*   *   *

Sarah was taken back to Hungary in a military aircraft, with two bluecap guards. They landed at an airfield somewhere out in the *puszta*. She could see nothing but rolling steppe as she looked down from the cabin window—no sign of a town anywhere. Dusk was gathering as she was escorted down the airplane steps. The airfield looked little used, but she noticed six Mig fighters, lined up outside a hangar built of corrugated iron, and a few huts. The red, white, and green Hungarian flag hung limply from a flag pole.

On the tarmac her guards pulled her hands behind her and snapped handcuffs around her wrists again. One of the familiar black prison vans was waiting and she was hustled into it, sitting awkwardly on the metal seat along one side in the back, because of her pinioned arms. There was a long wait and she watched the small round windows in the side of the van growing darker and darker, until it was pitch black outside. She began to need to pee and banged on the locked rear door, but no one came. Eventually the engine started and the van jerked into motion.

Her physical need seemed to recede with the motion of the van, even though she began to be oppressed by fear. If they were going to try her, she would be found guilty and sentenced. To what? Years in a labor camp? Death? She began to cry quietly, feeling hopeless, depressed, and very scared. After a time she slid down to sit on the floor, still weeping, wedging her shoulders into a corner, with her legs stretched out in front of her. They were too thin and straight. In the dim blue glow from the light in the roof, they stuck out like two narrow tubes covered in coarse black cloth—making her look, she thought wryly, like a rag doll thrown away by a child. The thought amused her and she stopped crying. She began to feel drowsy and was smiling to herself when she fell asleep.

*   *   *

Sarah awoke with a start as the van suddenly jerked and stopped. The blue light had gone out and her first thought was that they had crashed. She blinked in the darkness and tried to stand up, pushing her body gingerly up the side of the van. Somewhere outside there was a thunderous explosion and the van rocked, sharply, throwing her to the floor with both her ears singing, warm blood trickling from a cut on her head. She heard several single shots and the rattle of a machine pistol—the sounds metallic and distorted by her temporary deafness—and then shouting. A voice was bellowing and cursing at the door of the van; the buzzing in her ears made it sound like a recording of the Chipmunks. Then she realized that the words were *English*. Her heart leapt and she shouted back, "It's me, Sarah Cable! Get me out! *For God's sake* get me out."

The English Chipmunk voice yelled, "Lie down! Get flat on the floor!" There was a pause followed by the crack of two shots. The door opened with a screech of buckled steel and a man was peering in: young, wearing jeans and a parka, holding a smoking pistol. "Good evening. Are you Miss Cable?" he asked anxiously. Her ears were clearing and his voice sounded almost normal now; even so, she giggled at his incongruously polite tone.

"Yes, I am."

"Then get out quickly." He put out a hand to help her down, then spun her around physically and she could feel him lifting her pinioned wrists up high; she bent forward to help him. "Keep bloody still," he snapped. The explosion of the cartridge took her by surprise and the metal bands scraped her wrists excruciatingly as the bullet split the chain holding them; but her hands were free. She looked around in a daze, trying to rub her numb wrists back into life. They were on an unlit road, with high fir trees to each side, swaying against the dark sky. All the glass in the cab of the van had been shattered by gunfire or an explosion and two figures lay sprawled forward on the dashboard, evidently dead. A rivulet of blood was dripping from one of their bodies, down the metal of the van to a spreading black pool on the road. Another man in jeans and parka was leaning inside, smashing a radio with the butt of his gun. A motorcycle was propped on its stand, a few yards in front of the van, with a red lantern balanced on its petrol tank.

The man who had rescued Sarah seized her and sprinted into the trees, pulling her along behind him. "We've got about ten minutes to get clear of this shitty country," he panted. "For God's sake run like hell."

She ran behind him in the dark, stumbling over exposed tree

roots and slipping on dead leaves. Her prison shoes came off but she kept on running in bare feet, sharp stones cutting into her. Suddenly the trees came to an end and they were in a field. A small aircraft was standing in darkness, its black shape outlined against the deep purple of the sky. As they appeared, the engines spluttered into life and Sarah could hear the gathering beat of the propellers. She reached the plane and felt herself being pushed through an open door; she scrambled into the cabin and lay on the floor, her chest heaving painfully as she panted for breath.

The two men rolled through the door after her and it was slammed shut. Kneeling up, she saw white headlights switched on under the wings, blazing ahead to illuminate the field as the engines roared and the plane bumped forward. It gathered speed and suddenly she realized that they were in the air, the lights out again and the engine noise falling as the aircraft leveled out. The three of them sat upright on the cabin floor and one of the men spoke. "You okay?"

"Yes," she said shakily.

"Fine. S-sorry there are no seats, except the one beside the driver. You c-can have that, if you like. I'm John Peters and he's Elwyn Evans. We're S-SAS."

Sarah found his stammer as incongruous as his politeness, in the circumstances. She sat staring into the darkness. "I suppose I ought to be crying with relief or something . . . but I just can't believe it. I've got used to being locked up. How did you know where I was? How did you stop that van? Where are we going? It's all just too confusing."

"I w-wouldn't know how the f-funny men found out where you were landing and the van's route—we were just told." The man called Peters laughed. "We stopped it by me standing in the m-middle of the road with a m-motorbike and wearing a Hungarian police helmet, waving a red light—anybody who isn't on the run stops for the p-police, it's a natural instinct. Then Elwyn chucked a grenade through the cab window so that your escort w-wouldn't have the chance to use their emergency radio."

"It's incredible—I'd given up hope of anything like this ever happening. How long did it take to plan?"

"About a week," said the other man. "But it all depended on getting you back near to the frontier. We couldn't have sprung you like this from Soviet territory. The timing was difficult too—we knew your route only an hour ago. We were in Austria until then." He paused. "And we were afraid there might be a third guard—in the back of the van, who'd shoot you before we could get you out." He did not add that if the rescue had failed his orders were to kill Sarah and his partner before shooting himself.

Sarah felt cold as she realized how close she had been to death and began to cry with relief. The SAS man put his arms around her shoulders. "Stop that," he said sternly. "Keep calm—we aren't out of the woods yet. We're still in Hungarian airspace, hedge-hopping. You won't be safe until we're over the border—then we'll land at Graz."

She stared out of the window into the blackness. "How much farther to the border?"

"About thirty miles. We should be safe enough till then, so long as no one finds the van and raises the alarm."

The pilot turned his head and shouted back at them, over the drone of the engines. "Twenty-five miles to go."

"T-twenty-five?" stuttered Peters, staring back out of the window. "*S-shit!* Can't you get it any faster? I'm sure there's a f-fighter back there. Could just be one of the frontier patrol, but it seems to be coming after *us* . . ."

The small aircraft started to lose altitude. "I must be below their radar," bawled the pilot. "And if he puts on speed to catch us, he'll end up in Austria—I think we'll make it. We're almost over the frontier."

"Yes, he's turning away."

At that moment a flare burst away to their right, casting a magnesium white light all around them, followed by another to the left. "Eyes down!" yelled Peters. "It's the border and someone's spotted us. Hang on tight!"

Tracer shells started to explode in front of them, like a fireworks display. "I suppose that fighter *did* spot us—and radioed the border," panted Sarah, clinging to a webbing strap as the plane banked sharply, twisting to avoid the barrage from below. Then there seemed to be sparks and smoke all around them as the plane was buffeted by an explosion very close. The floor tipped wildly and Sarah lost her grip, sliding down toward the cockpit. The cabin was full of smoke, orange flames were crackling along one wing and the engines had stopped: there was no noise except the roar of burning and the scream of the wind outside.

The impact was sickening and Sarah lost consciousness for a few minutes. When she came to she was being dragged out of the plane, which was half buried in a plowed field. People were running from some nearby farm buildings and she could hear that they were shouting in German. They were in Austria.

Sarah stood up and kissed the three SAS men in the dark. Their cheeks tasted foul and she realized that they were still covered in black face-paint. They smelled of sweat and exertion. "We made it!" she cried. "Thank you all—*thank you.*"

29 | Vienna

It was nearly midnight and Cable was alone in the house in Himmelstrasse when the doorbell rang. He opened the front door to find Nairn standing there, alone. An embassy car was parked at the curb.

"David?" Cable looked puzzled. "Good lord—I wasn't expecting a reaction this quickly! I only got back from Tel Aviv an hour ago. I thought you were still in London."

"May I come in, Bill?" Nairn hung his coat in the hall and walked through to the drawing room. "Do you have a single malt for an old friend?"

"Glenmorangie?"

"Ay—that would do very nicely."

Cable poured two generous glasses of whiskey and sat down apprehensively in an armchair, for there was something odd about Nairn's manner. "You got my report?"

"Yes I did, thanks, Bill. I've also got some news about Sarah."

Cable started nervously, all the fear he had been suppressing suddenly showing in his face. "What's happened?"

"Sarah is safe. We got her out tonight."

Cable put his glass shakily onto the parquet floor and sank his head into his hands. "Oh thank God, David. *Thank God.* I can't believe it—I thought she must be dead." He began to weep. "You mean she's really *safe?* Where is she?"

Nairn looked away and poured himself another whiskey. "She's here in Austria, at Graz." He went out into the hall and fumbled for his pipe in the folds of his overcoat. When he returned Cable

[212]

had recovered himself. "Sorry about that, David. You say she's at Graz? When was she exchanged—and when can I *see* her?"

"She wasn't exchanged, Bill. The bastards wouldn't play ball. They were going to put her on trial in Budapest—a nasty piece of revenge, directed at you—so I used an SAS team to snatch her out. We were bloody lucky—it worked and they got her out at nine this evening. It wasn't a complete success. I'm going to have to explain away two dead Hungarian militiamen and a light aircraft crashed in a potato field in Burgenland." He sipped his whiskey reflectively. "Who bloody cares."

"But is she okay?"

"Yes—apart from a few burns and cuts. She's in hospital for a check; and I want Skilbeck to spend tomorrow afternoon debriefing her. You can see her in a day or two."

"But I want to see her *now*. I've got my own car here—I'll drive straight down to Graz. Where can I phone her?"

Nairn held out his glass for a refill. "You can't—she's sedated and she'll be asleep for at least twelve hours. She looks okay physically, Bill, but she's been in a Soviet jail, in solitary and threatened with death, for nearly three weeks—it's bound to leave a mark. She could have gone to pieces completely. In fact, I don't think you need worry—I spoke to her tonight and I think it's had the opposite effect. It's toughened her up a lot."

"I'm just incredibly relieved that she's free, David—I've been so bloody terrified. I thought they'd kill her after I deceived them. Oh God—I must *see* her."

"You will, Bill, as soon as it's practical." He lit his pipe and studied Cable. "Now tell me—how did you find it, being back in the stable for a few days?"

"Not so fast, David—*when* can I see her?"

"Soon. I asked you a question."

"The last few days? Oh, if I hadn't been worried sick about Sarah all the time it would have been almost nostalgic—the Firm was always more my scene than being an ambassador."

"Ay, I know. Look, Bill—I've gone to a lot of trouble to get young Sarah back and she'll be here the day after tomorrow. She's okay, I promise you—so now I want something from *you*, before it's generally known that Sarah's out of Hungary."

Cable pulled himself together. "If Sarah's really safe I'll do anything—absolutely anything. What do you want?"

"How do you feel about Laszlo Kardos—Istvan Gyor, now?"

Cable shook his head slowly. "I don't know. I began to wonder about Laszlo when you focused on Naomi's father and the Hungarian Jewish background . . . but I still couldn't believe it when Reichmann told me. We were talking in this little Arab house in Jaffa when suddenly he said, 'Of course Istvan Gyor is the man you know in Vienna as Laszlo Kardos.' I was shattered."

"Why?"

"Well—weren't you? It's not just that he's what he is—a priest and a Vatican diplomat—he seemed such a nice bloke, so genuine. I thought he was a man of integrity, I trusted him—he was as much of a friend as another diplomat can be in a place like this."

"It was brilliant cover."

"More than *cover*, David—he's become his new self, completely. He's a good diplomat—bloody good—and respected in the Church hierarchy. A lot of people trust Laszlo—I almost confided in him myself, when they were trying to blackmail me."

"It took him nearly thirty years to get where he is now. Must take a funny kind of mind to leave your own country and become someone else, living in strange lands, for all that time . . . and he'll go on being a priceless source for them for as long as he's free and making a report every night."

"What are you going to do about him? Don't forget the Mossad are after him as well."

"That's where you come in, Bill. You want to destroy him, don't you?"

Cable hesitated. "Do I? He was a kind of friend—I'm not sure what I want anymore."

"For Christ's sake, Bill—he betrayed you something rotten." Nairn's voice hardened, with a sudden cutting edge. "You've been tormented with fear for nearly three weeks and Sarah's been through a vile experience that could have sent her out of her mind! She's had to go into hospital to recover—and there may be no mental scars but there'll certainly be a few physical ones from the plane crash."

"You didn't tell me that."

"It's nothing too bad. But get one thing clear, Bill." Now he was shouting. "Kardos *knew* what was happening every step of the way! He sat with you in a restaurant while your daughter was locked in a freezing cell designed to turn a human being into a cowed animal—to destroy her will, her health, her dignity, and, in the end, her sanity."

Cable heard his glass shatter as it hit the floor. "You don't mean they *tortured* her, David?" He leapt up. "What the hell are you playing at—is that why she's in hospital, why you won't let me see her?"

"No, no. Calm down—she wasn't tortured, just kept in rather lousy conditions. She'll tell you herself."

Cable ran his hand through his hair. "But what are you asking me, telling me?"

"Kardos was in charge here. He knew everything. He was helping them to manipulate you—he must have helped them to kidnap Sarah in the first place. He may even have been there when they did it."

". . . in that case I think you're right . . . I could take him apart with my bare hands. . . . I've been betrayed too often—too often to forgive anymore."

Nairn thought Cable was about to mention Naomi as well, but instead he lapsed into silence, staring savagely into the darkness outside the french window. "That's my boy," said Nairn almost inaudibly. "Just hate the bastard—I don't want you half on his side." He relit his pipe. "The thing is, Bill, he's a priceless catch—he's been in the West masquerading as a Vatican diplomat for the best part of thirty years. I don't want him skipping off safe to Moscow before we can get at him—and when he hears about Sarah, he just might. He doesn't know that we're onto him, but he must have developed mighty sensitive antennae after all this time living with a false identity."

"Why not simply arrest him?"

"Only Austria could do that and they won't—he has diplomatic immunity and anyway he's committed no crime against *Austria*. I have a solution, Bill, but it won't operate for a few days." He smiled inscrutably, thinking of his long telephone conversation that afternoon with Melchior. The Mossad planned to kidnap Kardos and take him to Israel. That was fair enough—they had uncovered him and he was their game, but God knows what would happen after that. Melchior wanted to pump him dry and then quietly shoot him. Reichmann had some notion of exchanging him for Wallenberg, whom he believed to be still alive somewhere in the Gulag. Nairn wanted the chance to interrogate him, to find out just how much of the British intelligence network he had managed to compromise. The Cousins wanted to "nail him to the fucking wall." No one had bothered to tell the Vatican. He turned to Cable. "So we have to make sure he doesn't take fright and leave before we're ready to move."

"How can I do that?"

"He was feeding Moscow Center everything he knew on PIRANHA, among many other things. So they must know that half the Poles are still here. If they're going to have a second try, Moscow will want to know—with date, time, method, everything, so that they can pick them up or take them out like last time."

"So?"

"So they won't be asking *you* again, Bill. You tried to con them before and they've no hold over you now that they've lost Sarah. . . . The one thing to keep Kardos here is Kirov's need for conclusive information on the Polish operation. She doesn't know what to believe—are our telegrams cancelling it authentic, or are they a blind?"

"Who's this Kirov, David? Some bastard in Moscow?"

"A dangerous lady called Nadia Alexandrovna Kirova, the only woman at the top of their intelligence hierarchy. Adopted the masculine form of her surname, Kirov, some years ago although they say she's rather attractive, in fact. We've crossed swords before. I think she's behind all this—it's got her nasty little fingerprints all over it."

Cable sighed and stood up, walking over to a bookcase to pick up a photograph of Sarah and Lucy as children. "What do you want me to do?"

"Kardos is in Rome for the night. Some sort of meeting of diplomatic representatives of the Holy See. He's acting normally, following routine—but he *must* be scared. He's back tomorrow afternoon. I want you to call on him at his apartment, early tomorrow evening—very casual, drive yourself. Treat him like a friend, tell him the good news about Sarah—don't say *how* she was released—and tell him there's a big meeting about PIRANHA in two days time. Say I'll be there—and Berger of the CIA. Say you'll arrange for him—Kardos—to come."

"You think he'll believe me?"

"Maybe—maybe not—but I think it'll keep him here for forty-eight hours, which is all we need. He's the only source Kirov has who can report on this meeting—and he'll hang on just to be sure."

"Supposing he doesn't?"

Nairn sipped his whiskey thoughtfully and shrugged. "We can't keep him here. The Austrians have been asked to delay him at the frontier if he tries to leave by car or at the airport—they might find some way of holding him for a day or two, though I doubt it. But I think he'll stay of his own accord."

* * *

Next morning Cable rose with a hangover. Nairn had stayed late, reminiscing about old times, and they had drunk a great deal. He could not keep his mind from straying to Naomi while he was shaving; after years of solitude he had become used to her being there when he woke in the morning. He brushed the thought away savagely.

Fritz came with the car, Skilbeck already seated in the back, and they drove north to Klosterneuburg as Nairn had instructed. Cable felt tense. He was irritated at being kept apart from Sarah—and worried that he might not be able to lie his way through the day in accordance with Nairn's script.

At the abbey they drove through the main gates and across the yard to a small archway at the side of the church. Fritz followed an alley between high buildings until they were parked in a cobbled courtyard, well hidden on the opposite side of the monastery, away from the area open to the public. Skilbeck led him into a tower and up a spiral staircase. Tadeusz Rozinski and two other Poles were waiting for them in a dark-paneled room looking down the steep bluff to the town.

Cable shook hands formally and studied the view from the window for a few minutes: to the left was the bus station and the quaint medieval alleyways of the town, ahead the Danube was hidden by trees on which the leaves had turned brown, broken up by the curved glass roof of a modern swimming pool. He sat down and left the talking to Skilbeck.

The younger man explained that his government had consulted with Washington and decided that, after the first failure, Operation PIRANHA must be canceled. It was of course Rozinski's operation, but there was no question of further assistance with transport, communications, or arms. The Poles should stay in hiding for a week or two—then they would be helped to resettle in the United

States or Australia. Not a flicker of an eyelid nor an inflection of his voice suggested that the message was not totally authentic. "I don't like deceiving them," Nairn had said. "But if the opposition has them under observation they must *look* and *act* like men who've been told to give up. We can tell them we've changed our minds later."

Rozinski responded angrily. "This is ridiculous! We have spent more than a year preparing this operation and I am *certain* it will be successful once we can enter Poland undetected. This is the time to press on—while they think they have destroyed us, while their guard is down!"

"It's no good arguing with *us*," snapped Skilbeck. "We are just messengers—the decision is made." Cable relaxed, his elbows on the dark oak table, only half-listening to the hour of emotional Slavic rhetoric that followed. From time to time his eyes strayed to the white ivory crucifix on the wall and he wondered for the hundredth time how Kardos could have masqueraded as both diplomat and priest without detection for thirty years.

After an hour the conclusion dictated by Nairn was reached— there would be a meeting with all parties in a few days. If everyone agreed with Rozinski, London and Washington would be asked to reconsider.

* * *

The car took Skilbeck straight from Klosterneuburg to get the train to Graz, and Cable spent the rest of the day in his office at the embassy. Around five he was driven back to Grinzing, changed into a tweed jacket, and got the Volvo out of the garage.

Kardos had an apartment provided by the Vatican in Theresianumgasse, close to the Belvedere Palace, in the Fourth District. Cable had rehearsed his lines and drove straight there, aiming to arrive at about six-thirty. He weaved through the traffic on the Ring, and turned left at Schwarzenbergplatz. The Soviet war memorial was directly ahead: a bronze soldier—incongruous with shield and banner as well as a submachine gun—standing on a pillar surrounded by fountains. Cable drove to the right of this eyesore, down Prinz Eugen Strasse, then right into the quiet street where Kardos lived.

Outside the apartment block, Kardos' official car was parked at the curbside. It was a Mercedes and Cable noticed, for the first time, that it was not one of the two-liter 220 models favored by many embassies in Vienna, but a luxurious dark blue sedan with a powerful three- or four-liter engine—a curiously fast car for a staid diplomat.

He entered the hallway and took the lift to the second floor. The door of the apartment was opened by a white-coated manservant. Cable remembered that it had always been opened in that way—perhaps Kardos arranged it so that he could get out by a back entrance if the visitors were unwelcome. He wondered whether the manservant knew his master's true identity—was he really a bodyguard?

Then Kardos appeared, eyes smiling above the bushy black beard, as warm and welcoming as ever. "Bill—my dear fellow, how nice to see you! I have just heard your good news. How wonderful for you."

"Good news?"

"About Sarah's dramatic rescue, dear boy—it's all over Vienna. I'm so delighted for you! Come and have a drink."

They went into the elegant drawing room and Kardos produced Campari and soda. Sitting there in his clerical collar and black stock, under the Botticelli *Madonna* from the Vatican collection, he looked every inch the Jesuit, the cunning monsignor from the Holy See. His smooth confidence was picked up by Cable, who told his lies about Piranha and the proposed meeting with Nairn and Berger as if he believed them himself. Kardos nodded seriously. "I *should* certainly appreciate a briefing afterwards, Bill, if you could arrange it. But now, if you'll forgive me, I have to change into a dinner jacket—I have to dine with one of my more old-fashioned clerical colleagues tonight."

Cable shook hands, promising to be in touch in a day or two, and left. In the Volvo he felt a wave of self-disgust. He had been betrayed—by Kardos and by Naomi; now he was trapping Kardos in turn—perhaps into his death, certainly into something which would destroy his freedom and his spirit. Part of him could only admire the man—he was a genius, nothing less, who'd given his whole life to a cause greater than himself . . . and part of Cable could only hate him. He wished to God he could see Sarah.

On an impulse, he drew into an empty space outside a cafe in Favoritenstrasse. He was in no hurry to go back to the empty house in Grinzing, so he went inside and ordered a beer. The cafe was small and smoky, its walls covered with faded travel posters of

Greece. Clouds of steam rose from an espresso machine on the counter and the beer was kept in a range of refrigerated cupboards with wooden doors behind. Four unshaven men in blue overalls were playing cards in a corner and the only other table was occupied by an old man with the black and yellow armband and white stick of the blind.

Cable drank his beer at the counter, trying to avoid conversation with the barman, who wanted to discuss the latest financial scandal in the building of the new city hospital. When it was clear that the quiet, solitary drink he had planned was impossible, he paid for his beer with a twenty-schilling coin, pocketing the change without looking at it, and left.

He drove back to Schwarzenbergplatz and took the road toward the Danube, vaguely thinking that he might cross the river and have a drink at one of the quiet *Heuriger* on the Bisamberg before going home, since he wasn't allowed to see Sarah until tomorrow. At Praterstern there was heavy traffic on the big traffic circle and he was held up at a red light. There was a Fiat van just ahead of him and beyond that a dark blue Mercedes.

The light changed to green and the Mercedes turned right toward the Reichsbrucke. With a jolt Cable saw that its licence plate was WD 1—it was Kardos' car; and, although it was some way ahead, there was no mistaking the head behind the steering wheel. Kardos was driving himself and was alone. Cable kept the Volvo a few cars back and his brow creased with puzzlement. If Kardos was going to dinner with a Church colleague, the bridge across the Danube out of Vienna was a strange direction for him to take. He must be going to a meeting with his controller or to a dead-letter drop. Cable followed, curious.

30 Vienna

THE TWO CARS CROSSED the Reichsbrucke, past the lights of the United Nations building, lying like a dinosaur on the far bank of the Danube. The Mercedes kept on down Wagramerstrasse, stopping carefully at each set of traffic lights, with Cable always keeping three or four cars behind. The traffic was light—so light that when they reached open country, there was no other vehicle between the Volvo and the red taillights of the Mercedes, about two hundred yards in front.

The narrow road stretched ahead, a straight line across the flat plain of the *puszta*, and as the streetlights came to an end the Mercedes began to accelerate fast. At that moment it dawned on Cable that Kardos was not going to any dead-letter box or secret meeting: he was heading straight for the frontier. He was getting out.

The line of shadowy lime trees at the roadside began to flash by with increasing speed in the dark. Cable knew that he should turn around and make for the embassy—couldn't he get the Austrians to stop Kardos at the border? But would they? Kardos was a diplomat, entitled to free passage out of the country—he had committed no crime against Austria. And he would reach the frontier with Czechoslovakia in half an hour—there was no time to arrange anything. Cable accelerated after the twin red lights, already half a mile away, remembering the loaded revolver in the car's glove compartment. He leaned back, hands gripping the steering wheel at the end of straight arms, his mouth set in a harsh line. He was on his own—and he was going to settle this himself.

The Mercedes began to move even faster; Kardos had realized, if he hadn't before, that he was being followed. The power of his car was unbelievable. The Volvo's engine was roaring as it topped a hundred, with Cable willing it to go faster, but the Mercedes vanished from sight as the road curved—then reappeared a few minutes later as Cable steered into a long, straight stretch. The noise fell and the car seemed to be flying along, carrying Cable cocooned in darkness. Outside there was nothing to break up the vast night sky of the plain except the black outline of the tower of a grain dryer and a cluster of cables looping across the road between pylons. Occasionally his headlights glanced across roadside calvaries or the ponderously turning beams of pumping engines on the marshes. There was no moon—just the twin points of red far ahead and the blue glow from his dashboard.

He flashed through a sleeping village, his tires drumming on the cobbles, white headlights raking the long, low shapes of single-story houses, then the road was smooth again, running parallel to a railway. A freight train was rattling by, pulled by a heavy electric locomotive in another, more workaday world. It vanished behind them and Cable slewed around a parked minibus. He drove like an automaton, never falling below a hundred, surprised he still had the skill. After the weeks of fear and tension, it was a relief to have just one, all-consuming objective.

Another village—Ganserndorf—but the road through it was wide and neither of them slowed. An orange light flashed, mournful and alone, at the crossroads in the center. For a moment Cable was dazzled by the lights of a massive truck coming in the opposite direction, before accelerating out into open country again. For five minutes his eyes peered into the emptiness ahead—and then he realized that the red lights had vanished. Somewhere in Ganserndorf Kardos had lost him.

* * *

For the second evening in succession, Nairn had found his way to the basement of the embassy. He was pouring himself a third White Label, adding the bottle to his other empties on the counter, when the security guard came in. "Thought you might be down here, sir. We've got Mr. Skilbeck on the line—from Graz."

"Can I take it here?"

"Of course—there's a phone in the corner, sir."

"Thanks."

"Oh—and your car's outside, to go to the station."

"I'll be right up." Nairn picked up the telephone and listened as Skilbeck was connected.

"Is that you, Sir David?"

"Go ahead, Paul—remember it's an open line." Nairn concentrated for ten minutes as Skilbeck ran through his discussions with Sarah. At the end he grunted. "Fine—you're coming back to-night?"

"Yes. I think I've got everything important—after all, most of the time she was in solitary and didn't see a soul."

"That's what I expected. Good night, Paul—I suppose you and I will pass somewhere in the mountains—I'm getting the night train down to Graz."

"Shouldn't I stay here, then?"

"No, I'd like you back here tomorrow—I want your report typed up before I go back to London. I just feel like having a word with the girl myself."

"Okay. How did Cable get on with our mutual friend?"

"Don't know—I was hoping he'd phone before I had to leave. I tried ringing Grinzing but there was no answer—he must still be out."

"Bit odd, isn't it?"

"I expect they're having a long chat, maybe dinner together. Check it out when you get back tomorrow."

"The Cousins have our friend under observation, don't they?"

"Supposedly."

"I'll check on that, too."

Nairn put the phone down and hurried upstairs to the entrance hall. One of the security guards unlocked the door for him. "We put your bag in the car, sir."

"Thanks a lot, Manley."

The security guard watched the Cortina drive to the end of the street, where it turned left toward the Sudbahnhof. He locked the door, then the inner steel gate, and went back into the guardroom. "A real gent—one of the old school," he said to his companion. "Not like some of the jumped-up pricks you get these days."

"What is he—staff inspection?"

"No—Six. High up—number two, some say. Anyway, he's got more stars than that berk Barron, or Cable, or any of them in this shithouse of an embassy. He was in Moscow after the war, y'know, on visiting terms with Stalin."

"Straight up?"

"Sure. Bit nippy in here, isn't it—has that bloody heating failed again?"

"Think so." The junior guard winked at him. "I've got the kettle on." He pulled a half-bottle of rum and a package of PG Tips out of the wooden cupboard.

* * *

After his first furious curse at the loss of Kardos, Cable pumped wildly on the brakes until the big car slowed down; he was breathing heavily, like a runner at the end of a marathon, when it finally stopped, crunching on the gravel by the roadside. He turned on the light and pulled out a map. "Fuck," he breathed, as he looked at the red lines marking the roads. "Fuck, fuck, *fuck!*"

Kardos was on the wrong road for the official crossing point at Bratislava—or the one at Mikulov to the north. This road would have taken him straight to the frontier—the river Morawa—if he was going to cross illegally. But there had been a fork at Gansendorf and he must have taken the other route, cutting across south to Marchegg—where Cable had once stared across the river frontier into Czechoslovakia with Naomi. It was farther, but maybe Kardos had arranged to cross there; whatever the reason, that was where the bastard was going.

Cable glanced out of the window, reaching across to take out the revolver. The car had stopped by a little stone shrine; it contained a jam jar of wild flowers, standing in front of a crudely painted picture of St. Christopher carrying a child across a river. "Pray for me, Chris," he muttered. "And give that other bastard a puncture." He gunned the car into a tight turn, back into the village.

The road was slower, often built on causeways meandering across marshes as he got closer to the river, but he never encountered another vehicle. Nor did he catch sight of Kardos' red taillights again. It was an eerie drive, his headlights burning a white tunnel into the darkness, the flat beds of reeds silent and black on either side. The speedometer said that he was traveling at ninety, but he had no sense of momentum, except when he cornered sharply with the engine roaring and felt the tires of the big car slide on loose gravel. He was concentrating so hard on speed—willing the Volvo to go faster, shouting aloud "Move, you bugger, *move*"—that it was a shock when, only fifteen minutes later, a stone tower loomed up in the darkness. It was the ruined gateway through the medieval walls of Marchegg. Cable felt a cold calm take over his mind and body as he sped the last half mile through the sleeping town, up the rutted lane to the embankment overlooking the Morawa. There was nothing to think about—just action. He had been betrayed. He was going to kill.

The Volvo stopped with a jerk as he stamped on the brakes. He had been right—the Mercedes was there, parked by the monument to the Austrian customs service, topped by its eagle. He jumped out. The river was flowing by fast, lapping the stones at the edge of the embankment, and there was a strong wind whining through the trees. Behind him the town lay in darkness; across the river, the Czech shore was also dark, a watchtower outlined against the mauve sky—for there was now a little light from the moon through breaks in the swirling black clouds.

Cable gripped the revolver and scrambled out of the car. The wind dropped for a moment, leaving an eerie silence. He could hear no human sounds. There was no sign of Kardos. He swore quietly—the time lost in Ganserndorf could have been enough to let the bastard escape. But how? Czechoslovakia was only a hundred yards away, but now Cable could see the black waters rushing past and feel the chill in his bones. In this temperature the river would be freezing. It would be suicide for a man of sixty to risk the currents and the cold. Kardos could not swim across. He would have to steal a boat.

Cable turned up the collar of his jacket, holding it around him against the bitter wind. The gusts were so strong that he had to lean forward with an effort to move against them; he half-ran toward the trees that came right down to the water's edge a hundred yards away, expecting every minute to see a figure safe on the other shore. The path gave way to rough gravel and Cable stumbled, falling heavily to the ground. The revolver slipped from his grasp and his right wrist cracked as it took the weight of his falling body.

"Shit," he hissed, scrabbling for the gun, waves of pain telling him that his wrist was either sprained or broken. His left hand found the steel barrel of the revolver and he rose to his knees unsteadily.

And then he heard it: a wheezing, rasping sound just audible above the howl of the gale. Peering into the woods, his eyes could distinguish a black shape among the vertical lines of the trees. Kardos was kneeling outside a small hut, working a hand pump— the oval shape beside him was a rubber dinghy, now fully inflated. He must have kept it there for years as a precaution.

Cable lifted the gun, cocking back the hammer with his thumb but knowing that he could never hit anything with his left hand. "Kardos!" he shouted, his voice harsh, rising to a scream as the effort inflamed the pain in his arm. "You're surrounded and covered. Keep still and raise your hands or we'll shoot you down where you stand!"

The figure ignored him, bouncing the boat down to the water's edge. Cable shouted again. "Kardos—stop there!" He fired one round. The noise sounded like a cannon shot, reverberating in the darkness as the bullet whined away. "Now understand that we're serious! Get your hands up or we'll gun you down, you bastard."

The figure turned. "Don't be silly, Bill. I know you're on your own." The familiar voice boomed through the wind with no trace of fear.

"Yes, I'm alone—and I'm armed. If you put that rubber boat in the water I can sink it with one shot! You can't get away, Kardos. I've come to kill you. I've come to kill you for Sarah, but if you surrender I'll have to hand you over. It's your choice." He fired another shot into the trees. This time it passed close to Kardos and the shadowy figure flinched.

The shadow turned and came closer, until Cable could see his face, a pale gray patch half obscured by the black beard, eyes burning white and bright. "I really think you mean it, Bill." The voice sounded less confident but tinged with a sneer. "I always thought you too unstable to be an ambassador. Perhaps we should trade."

"No bargains. Just stand there and put your hands up."

"No bargains, Bill? But I have something that is above price, my friend. Will you trade?"

"Trade what?"

"I have something your masters would give their right hands to know. Just throw that gun into the river and let me cross over quietly. In exchange I'll tell you." His tone was still mocking.

"No."

There was an explosion somewhere near Kardos and Cable felt a fierce, searing pain in his right shoulder. Its force knocked him to the ground and he clutched the wound, plunging his fingers into warm blood. He looked up to see Kardos standing over him, holding a pistol.

His former friend stooped and picked up Cable's revolver, tossing it in a silver arc out into the river. Cable's head was swimming with pain, but he could hear Kardos speaking, a voice echoing far above him. "You bloody fool, Bill. Why do you think Moscow wanted you, when they already had me? Why?" His voice was lost in the wind, then it came back—harsh, tinged with a triumphant sneer. ". . . because Rozinski was their man, because the whole lunatic scheme was dreamed up by Kirov—you've heard of Kirov, haven't you? She's out of your league old friend. She set the whole thing up . . ." For a moment Cable's pain masked everything. ". . . an armed uprising . . . an excuse to crush Poland from outside without the Polish Army resisting. An absolute necessity . . . no buffer state can be allowed to drift to the West. The whole Rozinski thing was so farfetched—she needed you to check that your people really *believed* it, could really believe anything so absurd. Oh, Bill—you bloody, bloody fool."

Cable groaned as he moved his shoulder. "Were the other Poles genuine . . . apart from Rozinski?" He could hardly force the words out.

"Oh yes, patriotic idiots all. You should never have gotten involved, Bill. Particularly as now I'll have to finish it for you." Kardos stopped abruptly and, through a haze, Cable saw him raise his pistol, then lower it again as there was a lull in the wind and the sudden roar of a motorcycle. Kardos hesitated, looking away from Cable toward Marchegg. "God—the gendarmerie!" He turned and ran.

Cable raised himself on one elbow, feeling that his jacket and shirt were soaked in blood. Somewhere below him he could see the lights of two motorcycles, engines popping as they bumped up from the town. On the river, Kardos was already halfway across, paddling swiftly, hunched low in his dinghy, crossing at a sharp angle as the current swept him downstream.

He reached the far shore and a searchlight came on in the watchtower, scanning the riverbank. It settled on Kardos as he scrambled ashore, a portly figure, one arm shielding his eyes from the glare. Something was shouted from the watchtower through a bullhorn. Kardos tried to call back, but his voice was carried away in the scream of the wind. There was a second challenge as he moved toward the tower, still surrounded by the pool of dazzling white light.

The shots came with no further warning: three, crashing out from a carbine with no pause between them. Kardos stumbled at the first, throwing up his arms before he fell to the ground. The second and third rolled his body, jerking convulsively, over and over. Two guards were running from the tower but they were too late to stop him rolling into the river, sliding down the bank in slow motion, a lifeless bag of clothes. The body vanished beneath the swirling waters.

*　　*　　*

Cable stayed staring at the river until the motorcycles stopped and two policemen in helmets and goggles were looking down at him. "We heard shouting, *mein Herr*," said one in thick Burgenland German. "Is something wrong?"

Cable fell back to the freezing ground, still clutching the wound in his shoulder. "You might say that," he muttered. "Do you think you could get me a doctor?"

31 | Vienna

CABLE'S WOUND was not serious—the bullet had passed clean through the flesh of his shoulder—but bad enough to require a day or two in hospital. The embassy arranged for him to be taken into the Josefspital, a small, discreet place run by nuns, on the outskirts of Vienna.

His first visitor was Skilbeck, early on the morning after the chase to the border. He was shown in by a nun in a white habit and raised his eyebrows at the crucifix over Cable's bed. "Seems you can't get away from the Church, Bill, what with Kardos an' all. How's the shoulder?"

"Not bad. Why isn't Sarah with you?"

"I spent all day with her yesterday. She's in hospital too—down in Graz—and I'm afraid she'll be there for a couple of days yet. She's worn out after three weeks in jail and her legs have some burns after the plane crash."

"She's going to be all right, isn't she?"

"Of course, Bill."

Cable sank back on the pillows. "I bloody well hope so. It seems very odd, having her free but not being allowed to see her—I'm wondering what you're all up to."

"We're not 'up to' anything, Bill—a spell in hospital is just a normal precaution."

There was an awkward silence, eventually broken by Skilbeck. "Look—I'm sorry to be official, Bill, but I think you'd better tell me all about last night. I must get a report off today."

*   *   *

Skilbeck listened in silence, taking notes on a small pad. He nodded slowly when Cable described his final exchange with Kardos. "Nairn was suspicious of Rozinski all along. We ran a few checks that came to nothing and decided to go ahead anyway, giving him the benefit of the doubt. Stupid bastards, weren't we?"

"But why on earth should this Kirov *promote* an insurrection in Poland?"

"Lots of reasons. It was going to happen anyway—this way she could control it, guarantee to crush it because there could be no element of surprise. It's an old Cheka ploy—to take over the opposition and run it. They were doing it with Reilly and the Trust back in the twenties. And this way she could stage-manage the whole thing to make it look like gratuitous Western aggression against the Polish people—to discredit Solidarity and the Church as traitors promoting an armed uprising. Above all to discredit the Pope, who's turned into a real pain in the arse for the Kremlin."

Cable shook his head, flinching from the pain in his shoulder as he moved. "And Kardos? Was he a genuine priest? How did he become a Soviet agent? I still can't believe it you know—he was a friend of mine, not just another diplomat."

"The Mossad know more about that than us. A Laszlo Kardos was certainly ordained in Hungary, at Esztergom, in 1947. The Mossad believe he died in prison—that *your* Kardos was an AVO officer called Istvan Gyor who took his place and was infiltrated into the West, then into the Vatican's service, as a refugee in '56. Equally well, Gyor might have been infiltrated into the Church by being ordained, then acted as an AVO informer, but in that case his five years in jail doesn't fit—unless, of course, he wasn't really in jail at all. We don't know yet—maybe we never will."

"I like your second theory best. Laszlo Kardos said he'd spent all his time as a priest in Hungary working with the poor—it would make a kind of twisted sense if he was a Marxist who'd gotten ordained."

"Yes—but it's a long step from that to becoming a diplomat and an agent. The Holy See is bloody embarrassed—to put it mildly."

"Is Rozinski still free?"

"Yes—but under close surveillance. We'll have to confront him and tell the other Poles soon. The survivor of the first wave was a chap called Jozef Gierek, who was smuggled out last week. He may have more conclusive evidence to confirm that Rozinski is phony. I don't know what we'll do with him or with the rest of the Poles—there are fourteen of them still cooped up around Klosterneuburg."

For the rest of the day Cable dozed, for his shoulder became inflamed and the doctor gave him pain-killers. Late in the afternoon the young nun came in again, with downcast eyes. "Are you awake, Mr. Ambassador?"

Cable groaned and raised himself slowly on his pillows. "Then you have telephone call." The nun smiled. "Your daughter telephones from Graz."

"Hello, Daddy—they wouldn't let me phone before, but they got me out! Isn't it terrific?"

"Thank God." Cable felt foolishly emotional and there were tears in his eyes. He wanted to say that he loved her, but instead he heard trite phrases coming out. "How are you, darling? How did they treat you?"

"I'm fine, Daddy. How are *you?*" She sounded remarkably cool and matter-of-fact. "I had lunch with that nice David Nairn today—quite a change, they don't seem to use knives and forks where I've been. I'm going to stay here one more night and fly up tomorrow. I'll be at the airport at two o'clock."

"Wonderful—I'll meet you."

"Only if you're fit enough, Daddy—I think the embassy will look after me. I'll come and see you in hospital."

Cable hesitated. He hadn't imagined it like this. This was a different Sarah: not just matter-of-fact—almost distant. "No, love—I'll be there," he said.

* * *

Nairn appeared unexpectedly next morning. "I've got your car outside, Bill. I'm going back to London on the one o'clock flight, an hour before Sarah arrives—I thought you might give me a lift."

Cable continued to shave awkwardly with his left hand. "Anything you like, David—you seem to have hijacked the car already." He gave a wry grin. "I'm sorry I lost your prize mole for you."

"I'm sorry too—it'll take some time now to work out how much harm he did—but it can't be helped. It's water under the bridge."

Fritz drove out on the autobahn in bright sunlight. Nairn lay back in the leather seat and seemed to doze as they flashed past little groups of summer houses, each set in its tiny, neat garden, and the massive oil refinery just before the airport. As usual the refinery was covered in a gray haze, the only color the flickery orange flames of its two flare towers. Cable thought that Nairn's face looked more like parchment than ever; and he had the crumpled appearance of a man who had been up all night.

They followed Fritz, who was carrying Nairn's suitcase, to the British Airways check-in. Then Nairn went through passport control to the departure lounge and Cable followed him, showing his red diplomatic identity card to be allowed in. Nairn bought two beers and they sat at a blue plastic-topped table.

"You're coming to London in two or three days, aren't you?" Nairn sounded tired and Cable felt certain that he was gravely ill. Cable nodded. "Personnel Department in the FCO wants to see me—I suppose they'll want me to leave Vienna."

"Obviously. They're bound to move you after Sarah's kidnapping. Standard practice. You can hardly go on serving in a post where you have daily contact with the Russians."

"No—I suppose not. Perhaps they'll give me the boot altogether."

"I doubt it." Nairn sipped his beer and seemed to come to a decision. "Look here, Bill. You'll have that plucky daughter of yours safely back in less than an hour, so you can spend a few minutes thinking about yourself for a change." There was a long silence, then Nairn looked at Cable very directly. "Thirty years ago, Bill, when you first came to work in my section at Cheltenham, I picked you out as a flyer. I vaguely thought you might succeed me as I moved up the service, maybe to the top." He smiled ruefully. "Well, you've had a few ups and downs since then, so have I. Just now I'm not too well—"

"Is it cancer, David?"

"No, it's not. It's my heart and I suppose it may kill me in a year or so. I'll certainly have to retire quite soon—the chief would like me to go now, in fact—so the service is coming to an end for me. Look, Bill—you're a good intelligence officer, but a lousy ambassador. If you felt like coming back into the firm from the diplomatic circus, I'm sure I could fix that now."

"After all that's happened? Are you serious, David?"

"Never been more serious in my life. I think the questions that came up after Vietnam are all answered now. There's nothing else the Soviets can do to you. They've tried to blackmail you and failed—and they certainly aren't going to kidnap Sarah again. You wouldn't be at the top table anymore—and you'd have to work from London, of course. No more overseas postings. But I think you'd be useful."

Cable started to laugh. He took a draught of beer and burst into laughter again, his guffaws causing heads to turn all around the departure lounge. Nairn looked irritated: "What did I say that's so funny?"

"Oh David—it's just that you're too late. A couple of years back I'd have been grateful. I hated being chucked out after Vietnam— but now I've had enough, Christ, more than enough. The Queen's had thirty years of my life, God bless her, and now you can bloody well stuff it. All I wanted was to do some kind of useful job, but there were two kinds of people I found I couldn't trust. My enemies and my friends. I've been screwed by some bitch in Moscow and by that shit Stuart in London. I'm sick of half-truths and scheming and betrayal. I could live for another twenty years—and I'd like to spend them in better company."

Nairn made to interrupt, but Cable shook his head. "No, David, let me finish. You've been kind and you're the best intelligence officer I've ever met—but I'm not too keen on being a pawn on your chessboard anymore either."

"I always thought of you more as a knight." Nairn gave his thin ironic smile.

"*Exactly*. So thanks a lot for asking—but no."

"What will you do instead?"

"I haven't a clue yet, but I'm not staying with the diplomatic service, even if they still want me."

"I see," said Nairn gruffly. "Well—don't be too hasty. Think about it."

"There's nothing to think about. But thanks, David anyway."

Nairn lit his pipe, tamping it with a box of Swan Vestas until it was drawing well, as if he needed time to reflect. Eventually he muttered. "There's something else, Bill."

"Yes?"

"News about Naomi."

"Naomi?" Cable felt a sudden flash of anger. "Then why the devil didn't you say so at once? Where is she?"

"I'm sorry, Bill—but I think I may have been wrong about her. I've heard from Ryder in Jerusalem that she turned up in Tel Aviv, shortly after you left."

"And what conclusion do you draw from that—if it's true?" snapped Cable. "I told you what her father told me, about her working for the Mossad, and he asked us to help trace her after she vanished—but you did bugger all about it. Then you told me you thought she'd skipped to Budapest—on her way to Moscow."

"I'm sure a phone call to Reichmann's villa in Tel Aviv will find her." Nairn fumbled in his pocket, looking embarrassed, and pulled out a tattered envelope, which he pushed across the table. "Ryder sent me the phone number." He sank his beer as the loudspeakers crackled and his flight was called: *BA601 Abflug nach London*. "I must go, Bill. Good luck. Keep in touch." He hurried off, leaving Cable looking stunned.

As soon as Nairn had vanished through the security check, Cable walked pensively out to the concourse, making for the post office. There was a row of glass cubicles for international calls: you booked the call and then paid for it afterward, without having to feed coins into a box while you were talking. He showed the clerk the tattered envelope. "I want this number in Tel Aviv, please."

The clerk wrote it down and started to dial. "Box number two, *mein Herr*."

The number was ringing in less than a minute and was answered in Hebrew by a woman who sounded like a housekeeper. "May I speak to Naomi?" asked Cable.

"Who is calling?" She also spoke English.

"My name is Cable—I'm a friend from Vienna."

"Hold on please." There was a long silence before the woman came back. She gave him no lies or evasions about Naomi being out and ringing back. "I regret that Miss Reichmann does not wish to speak to you," she said.

* * *

An hour later Sarah was running toward him with fair hair streaming behind her and coltish legs flying in all directions. "Oh, Daddy! I thought I'd never see you again." He flung his left arm

[*234*]

around her and kissed her. She buried her head in his shoulder, then stepped back and looked at him appraisingly. "What's happened to your other arm?"

"I got a bullet in the shoulder. What about you—Skilbeck said you were hurt in the plane crash?"

"I'm a bit bruised and there's a burn on my leg which still hurts, but I'll be fine." She seemed less distant than she had on the phone.

"How bad is it, darling?"

"Not too bad." She bit her lip. "There'll be a few scars, that's all, and I may not want to wear a bikini for a bit. But it doesn't matter, honestly." She put her arm firmly in his. "It's fabulous to be back—let's go home and celebrate."

32 Klosterneuburg

ROZINSKI was left to the other Poles. He belonged to them, not to the British or the Americans, and he had entered Austria illegally, so to the authorities in Vienna he did not exist. The group of fourteen met that evening in a room at the abbey in Klosterneuburg—the same room, high in a medieval tower where Cable and Skilbeck had sat two days earlier. The meeting was secret and no outsider was ever told what took place. For the first hour, Rozinski was present, then he was taken out and locked in a cellar. At the end they had elected Jozef Gierek, the only survivor of the abortive drop near Krakow, as their new leader.

That night a grave was dug in a wood above Greifenstein, on a bluff overlooking the Danube some miles to the north. It was still dark when a car left the monastery the next morning carrying four men. They drove in silence, down the hill into the town and then north past Kritzendorf. After twenty minutes the car turned off the main road and hairpinned up through dense forest, to park by a pile of cut logs.

The four men walked into the forest. The morning sun was now slanting through the trees and mist rising from the damp path of leaves and pine needles. Rozinski began to tremble when he saw the grave open and waiting for him. Suddenly he broke away from the two men holding him and tried to escape into the trees. The fourth man drew a pistol and took aim in a leisurely fashion. A shot cracked out. Rozinski leapt into the air from the impact, then fell backward, screaming and clutching the gaping exit wound in his belly.

The three men did not increase their pace, walking slowly to their former leader, who was now writing on the ground emitting choked, gurgling, animal cries as he coughed dark blood. The man with the smoking pistol looked down in contempt. Rozinski's face had turned the color of putty, great beads of sweat standing out on his forehead. His forearms were red to the elbow as his hands tried hopelessly to staunch the ragged wound above his groin. The screaming faded to a sobbing whimper of agony. The three men stood in silence, watching curiously, without pity. They finished him with a single bullet in the head.

*   *   *

Cable and Sarah spent a week at the house in Grinzing, talking, laughing, walking high in the forest and going out to their old haunts. Both of them seemed to accept that they would soon be leaving Vienna and would never come back.

The moment he knew that Naomi was in Israel Cable had wanted to get the next plane to Tel Aviv; but then Sarah had returned and he could not leave her. They badly needed to be together. He wrote a long letter to Naomi and sent it off with an air ticket to Vienna, but there had been no response. Even if he was bound to fail, he knew that it was just a matter of time before he returned to Tel Aviv to find her. Meanwhile he tried to telephone her every day, sometimes more than once, but each time the reply from the housekeeper was the same.

On the sixth evening, he took Sarah out to dinner at the Drei Husaren, in the old town of Vienna, near the cathedral. First, they sat on the terrace in Grinzing and she poured two gin and tonics. Although it was now October, the city below was still sunlit. "It's a lovely view," she said dreamily. "I'll miss that. But not much else, I think."

"Have you decided what you want to do?" he asked.

"Before all this happened I thought I might study languages, if I could find a university to take me. Now I'm really not sure— maybe I'll just get a job, if I can find one."

Cable was about to say something when a man dressed in black came around the side of the house—but this time it was a dispatch rider from the embassy, clutching his motorcycle helmet and goggles. He saluted and handed Cable an envelope. "A personal telegram, sir. Shall I wait in case there's a reply?"

"Thank you—yes, please wait." Cable went inside and ripped open the envelope. There was another stamped SECRET inside it. This contained a piece of copy paper: a telegram addressed to Skilbeck that he had deciphered himself. It was from Nairn and copied to Cable:

PRIORITY: ROUTINE
CLASSIFICATION: SECRET

FOLLOWING PERSONAL FOR SKILBECK, COPY TO CABLE, FROM DEPUTY DIRECTOR-GENERAL, SIS:

BEES UNDER QUEEN SWARMED IN EARLY TODAY AND DISPERSED TO HIVES SAFELY. READ AND DESTROY.

Cable smiled to himself as he burned the piece of paper in an ashtray—so this time it had worked. They were a bunch of brave men and he wished them good fortune—they deserved it.

Back on the terrace Sarah looked at him questioningly. He nodded, with a slight smile. "Nothing important," he said, but he could see that she understood. "Let's go and have some dinner."

* * *

Next morning Cable woke early and stepped out onto the balcony overlooking the city. Autumn had settled in: there was no sun and Vienna had a gray, cold appearance. In the summer one tended to forget that this was really part of Eastern Europe, wherever the frontier might have been drawn after the war. He shivered and went inside. Wandering downstairs in his dressing gown, he was surprised to find Sarah in the hall. There was a small suitcase on the floor and she was phoning for a taxi. Cable was puzzled. "Where on earth are you going?" he exclaimed. "We're supposed to be driving back to England tomorrow."

"No, Daddy. *You're* driving back to England tomorrow, unless you have anything else to sort out here?" She raised her eyebrows quizzically. In her sensible, belted raincoat she looked and sounded like a visiting social worker. "I've got some things to sort out too, like getting a job and applying to a university for next year. I'm going to stay with my friend Margaret for a few days. And I must *hurry*—I'm on the eight o'clock flight."

Then the taxi arrived, its diesel engine thudding at the curbside, and she was gone. He stood at the open front door, watching the taxi vanish around the corner into Grinzing, and felt suddenly empty.

On an impulse he went upstairs to his study and dialed the number of the Reichmann villa in Tel Aviv. It was the seventh time he had tried and, after the clicks and silences as the international connection was made, he listened to the number ringing for some time. There was no answer.

*   *   *

Cable spent the rest of the day packing and loading cases into the Volvo. Whatever the Foreign Office decided, he knew that he would be leaving Vienna, so he might as well take his clothes and personal things with him. The house in Teddington had been standing empty since the last tenant left a month before; no doubt he and Sarah would be living there again quite soon.

Or would they? He had spent less than a week with Sarah since her rescue, before she had dashed off to London; but it had left him feeling somewhat flat. Sarah had suddenly become independent, grown up. He did not see her staying with him for much longer; wherever he would be in six months' time, it was likely to be alone.

As darkness fell, the house became more and more gloomy— and Cable more and more depressed. He decided to walk down into the village for a glass of wine and something to eat before going to bed early—he would leave very early the next morning. There was a certain macabre symmetry about it; he had spent his first evening in Vienna like that when he arrived two years ago, alone, before Sarah came from London.

He almost ran into her as he reached the pavement. She was paying off a taxi just outside the gate. She turned around, putting the change into her handbag, and was there, smiling slightly, looking up at him. "Hello, Bill."

"Naomi! What are *you* doing here?"

"Aren't you pleased to see me? You rang up often enough."

"Pleased? I'm bowled over, flabbergasted—but I thought . . . ?"

She looked at him gravely. "What did you think?"

"Shall we go and have a drink?"

"Okay." She shrugged. "Just one—I'm not sure I'm staying yet."

"But you've come all the way from Israel."

"I have a job and a flat here—I was coming anyway. Here—this is yours." She handed him an envelope.

"What is it?"

"The air ticket you sent me. It's unused."

* * *

They sat awkwardly in the corner of the nearest *Heuriger*, close to the warm blue-tiled stove. "You threw me out," she said evenly—but he could feel the passion that she was suppressing. She sipped a *Viertel* of red. "You thought I was spying on you and you threw me out."

"I know. I was wrong—I must have been mad."

She looked at him sharply, pushing the thick black hair back from her eyes with her right hand. "It hurt, Bill—it hurt a lot. I didn't deserve that."

"I'm sorry. Where did you go? *Why* did you go, come to that?"

"I was furious with you and miserable as hell. I knew I was being watched all the time—I didn't know who by. I think my father told you I did a few trips to Budapest for the Mossad?"

"Yes, he did."

"He was wrong to do so—but now you know anyway. I was collecting copies of documents about Kardos—the real Kardos that is—photos of him as a young man, his ordination papers, prison record and so on. They were hard to get hold of, because everything AVO could find when Gyor took his place had been destroyed. Kardos was executed of course, sometime between 1950 and the rising in '56."

"I thought so."

"I didn't like concealing what I was doing from you, Bill. I hated it, but I had no choice." She sighed and met his eyes hesitantly. "After we had our spectacular row in the Cafe Landtmann, I spent the evening alone at my apartment. I cried a lot. I cried until there weren't any more tears left and I felt empty, just wishing I could die—and then I realized that they were patrolling outside on the pavement. Two men. I thought they might be KGB—and suddenly I got bloody scared."

"Scared of what?"

"I don't know—does one ever? Being rubbed out, perhaps, or kidnapped like Sarah—I'm so glad she's come back, Bill."

"So am I."

Naomi nodded. "So there I was—suicidal one minute, afraid of being killed the next. A real mess . . ." She laughed bitterly.

"What did you do?"

"I cleared out. Went down the fire escape and walked out the back way. I had no luggage or anything—I've had some training in how to vanish you know . . . I got a taxi to the Sudbahnhof and took the night sleeper to Rome. No one spotted me. Not your lot, not Kardos' friends, not even the Mossad!"

"I'm sorry you were so scared—and so alone. It was mostly my fault."

"Yes, it was—and I haven't forgiven you yet. Wounds don't heal so quickly . . ." She looked away, down at the empty wine glass, thoughtfully. "So next day I was in Rome, staying in a *pension* near the central station under a false name—I called myself Angela Lambert and said I was British. I wandered about for a couple of days, hating you all—you and Kardos and his friends. I lived all that time on credit cards. You don't need much cash these days— it's amazing. I didn't want to go back to Israel because my father and I don't get on anymore—but I was afraid to come back to Vienna and I couldn't hide in Rome forever." She shrugged. "In the end I thought I'd be safest in Israel so I got a bus to the airport and took the next El Al flight to Tel Aviv." She looked up at him again. "And that's it. Not a very exciting story, really."

He put his hand on top of hers and she did not pull it away. Everything in him wanted to trust her again, but still he hesitated. "Were you planted on me by the Mossad?" he asked quietly.

She looked at him sharply; the deep brown eyes had the same sad, candid look he remembered from their first meeting, the night of the explosion at the Palais Auersperg. "No, Bill. If you ever ask me again I'll walk out—I'll walk out and *never* come back—but I'll answer the question just once. No—I wasn't planted on you. I fell in love with you as me, not as ex-Captain Reichmann of the Mossad." She gave a half-smile tinged with tears. "I was in love with you, you bastard—and I think I still am."

33 Salzburg and London

THEY SET OUT in the green Volvo three days later, speeding down the autobahn toward Salzburg, past the familiar green meadows, the lakes and the mountains. Naomi drove, studying the road with intense concentration and leaving Cable alone with his thoughts. At the end of the journey, or soon after, he would be free—unemployed, more or less bust, but free. Even the slightest doubt seemed a betrayal of the slim Jewish girl beside him; but he was nearly fifty and she not yet thirty, not much older than Sarah. Was he just living out a middle-aged fantasy . . . ?

At one point he switched on the car radio. The Austrian news said that food riots had broken out in several cities in Poland and that the Polish Army had not broken them up as expected. The future of General Jaruzelski was in question. Cable wondered whether it would all have happened anyway, without the arrival of Gierek and his arms.

That evening they stayed in Salzburg, at the Pension Struber on the side of the Hohensalzburg away from the river and the town. The windows of their room looked up at the fortress, its black bulk looming against the sky at dusk. A row of lights wound down the hill toward them, marking the houses in Nonberggasse. Somewhere among them was the safe house where he had first met Rozinski. Cable drew the sensible Austrian curtains and turned to find Naomi facing him, naked.

She raised her arms around his neck and kissed him gently. "I love you, Bill," she whispered. "And I want you *now*. Not after dinner when we've talked and we're sad."

"Why should we be sad? We're together and I haven't felt so happy for a long time."

"Life is full of choices, Bill." Her eyes looked troubled for a moment. "I understand that." Then her face lit up with a smile; she started to unbutton his shirt and kissed his injured shoulder, whispering, "For God's sake, don't let me hurt you, darling." She drew him onto the bed. He was moved by the lines on her forehead, the careworn look that had come back into her face. "I love you, my little Hungarian witch." He folded her in his arms and suddenly she seemed very small and vulnerable.

* * *

The following morning an elderly man was walking slowly along the towpath by the Thames at Chiswick. Although stooped, he was tall—even taller than the leggy blonde who walked beside him a little stiffly, blue trouser suit hugging her slim hips. A cold wind was gusting down from Kew Bridge, clattering halyards against the metal masts of a row of dinghys pulled up on the mud, but neither the man nor the girl seemed to notice.

"So that's settled, then," he said, as they paused to watch a tug with a string of barges chug by. Sarah thought how small they seemed compared with the massive grain carriers on the Danube. "We'll try you out for a year as a temporary, then give you special leave to go to college. If you want to come back afterward, you'll have to pass the tests in the usual way, but I'm sure you'll find that no problem. A month in a Soviet prison is equal to a university degree here, any day of the week."

"It's very kind of you, Sir David—I'm terrifically flattered, you know. You're taking an awful risk—do you think I'll be any good at it?"

"I hope so. Your father was. He was brilliant, until they crucified him in Vietnam—and still not bad even then." She smiled as he lapsed into his soft Scotch accent. It was attractive, like his bushy black eyebrows—he wasn't nearly so awesome as she had thought at first, when he'd come to see her in the hospital in Graz.

"Poor Daddy," she said. "Will he get another embassy, d'you think? I'm not sure he really wants one."

"Nor am I, Sarah—and anyway, I don't know. Now are you ready to go in to Century House? I've done my bit, but you'd better meet Michael Marshall straightaway if you're going to work with him. He's expecting you."

"Do I have to go today? I feel a bit nervous about it and my leg still hurts, you know."

"Don't be ridiculous, girl. You're tough as old boots." Nairn looked her up and down appraisingly. "My God, I wish . . ." He paused and laughed.

"What do you wish?"

"Never mind, lass." They stopped by the black Rover, drawn up where Hartington Road joined the towpath. Nairn opened the rear door. "Take Miss Cable in to the Cut, Len," he said to the driver. "I'm not coming in today—have to see my doctor this afternoon."

"Very good, sir. Shall I pick you up tomorrow morning?"

"Ay—at eight as usual."

The car drove away toward Kew and Nairn turned back in the direction of his flat. From a distance his stooped figure looked very old, but close up he was smiling, impishly.

* * *

Cable's shoulder was still painful, so Naomi drove all day across Germany and France, along the ubiquitous concrete motorways which now crisscross every country in Western Europe: a dreary eight hundred miles in twelve hours. The dusty Volvo drew up on the quay at Le Havre at nine in the evening. The orange funnel of the Townsend Ferry could be seen, lit by arc lights, swaying gently behind a row of sheds.

It had been Naomi's idea. "I've never been to England, Bill. Let's do it slowly, take one of the longer ferry routes where we can cross overnight and have a cabin. I want to steam up Southampton Water in the dawn, as if we'd just arrived from America or somewhere."

There was a cafe in a row of modern shops opposite the quay, unpretentious except for its name—le Restaurant Southampton. They dined on *fruits de mer* and *steak au poivre*, washed down with a red Bordeaux, and the Volvo rattled up the ramp into the hold soon after ten.

* * *

When they woke in the small cabin, the ship was rolling slowly and Cable lay in his bunk watching Naomi dressing. She smiled at him. "I'm going on deck, Bill. We dock at seven and I don't want to miss seeing England."

They stood on deck, arm in arm, quite alone, as the ferry moved slowly into Southampton Water, which was gray and misty in the half-light. In a moment of certainty, Cable knew that he could not imagine a life without this girl.

Soon after seven, the car was waved through the dock gates by a helmeted policeman and Cable switched the radio on. ". . . *in Poland,*" said the familiar BBC voice. "*Food riots have continued in Gdansk, Poznan, and Krakow. It is now clear that many units of the army are supporting Solidarity and the protestors. The army is rumored to be taking up defensive positions along the border with the Soviet Union and the new General Secretary of the Communist Party has announced that any interference by other Warsaw Pact states will be resisted with military force.*"

Naomi reached over and squeezed his arm. "They've done it, Bill, after that first failure. They've *done* it—isn't it fantastic?"

Cable stared ahead out of the windshield. It was starting to rain. "Have they? Let's see how it ends before we celebrate." The radio crackled. "*The Pakistan crisis. On the frontier between Afghanistan and Pakistan, Russian tank divisions and artillery are continuing to mass and there are reports of heavy air bombing of camps in northern Pakistan, occupied by Afghan refugees. The Soviet government claims that these camps are training and supply bases for Afghan rebel guerrillas operating against the communist regime in Kabul, and in an ultimatum threatens to invade Pakistan within twenty-four hours to destroy them if firm action is not taken by the Pakistan Government. The President of Pakistan has flown to Washington and two aircraft carriers of the U.S. Indian Ocean task force are making for Karachi.*"

Cable shook his head. "Thought that would be the response. Let's see how that ends, too." Naomi switched on the windshield wipers and he stared ahead in silence as they whirred from side to side.

"What are you thinking about, Bill?"

"I was remembering a lunch I once had with Laszlo Kardos— something he asked me."

"What was that?"

He shook his head. "It doesn't matter—at least, I hope not."

RAOUL WALLENBERG

RAOUL WALLENBERG is not a fictional character. He joined the Swedish Legation in Budapest in July 1944: a diplomat sent from Stockholm, at the request of the United States and the World Jewish Congress, his was the daunting task of saving Hungarian Jews from extermination. Millions had already died as the Holocaust swept through Europe, but Hungarian Jewry had been spared because their country's fascist government was allied to Nazi Germany. In 1944 this immunity ended when German troops occupied Hungary; under Adolf Eichmann the SS arrived in Budapest, and mass deportations to the gas chambers in Auschwitz began.

Wallenberg's resistance to the deportations included creating a system of special passports giving thousands of Jews the protection of Sweden's neutrality and placing numerous buildings in Budapest under the Swedish flag in which Jews could take refuge until the end of the war. He backed up these tenuous measures by bribery and intimidation of the German and Hungarian authorities. Showing great courage even in the face of violence and threats to his life, he saved at least thirty thousand Jews from death in Auschwitz between July and December 1944.

The Red Army occupied Budapest in January 1945 and immediately arrested Wallenberg. No reason for their action has ever been given. Since his work was supported by American funds, perhaps he was suspected of being an American agent who would present a threat to the Soviet plan to install a communist government. He was taken to Moscow, imprisoned in the Lubyanka—and despite international pressure over nearly forty years, has never been released. He was only thirty-two when he was arrested in 1945—and there is clear evidence that he survived in Russian prison camps, despite harsh treatment, at least into the mid-1960s. He may have died at that time, although there are many who believe that he is still alive in a Soviet prison. Whatever the truth may be, Raoul Wallenberg was one of the most heroic figures of the Second World War—and one of the most mysterious and tragic victims of the cold war that followed.